PRAISE FOR L

'Refreshingly, jo...
Sunday

'Genuinely od...
The Guardian

'This entertaining, light-hearted mystery is told from a refreshingly
novel perspective'
Daily Mail

'A quirky and charming cosy mystery'
Katy Watson, author of *The Three Dahlias*

'Fans of Richard Osman's superannuated detectives,
welcome to your new club'
A. J. Finn, author of *The Woman at the Window*

'A collection of delightfully batty characters, a disdainful tortoise, a
wonderful plot and a guaranteed smile on every page'
Ian Moore, author of *Death and Croissants*

'Quirky, hilarious and darkly twisty, Agnes Sharp and her wonderfully
drawn friends are unforgettable characters'
Sam Blake, author of *The Mystery of Four*

'A surprisingly complex mystery, written with heart and affectionate
humour that conceals a dark undercurrent of murder and mortality'
Antony Johnston, author of *The Dog Sitter Detective*

'Utterly superb. It is as rich and enticing as a perfect cup of cocoa –
sweet at first taste, but with something delightfully, deeply,
deliciously dark within.'
Deanna Raybourn, author of *Killers of a Certain Age*

'Swann's mystery is different, delightful and deep'
Washington Post

'Fans of *The Thursday Murder Club* books will find much to like here'
New York Times

By Leonie Swann

The Sunset Years of Agnes Sharp
Agnes Sharp and the Trip of a Lifetime

THE SUNSET YEARS
OF AGNES SHARP

LEONIE SWANN

Translated from the German by Amy Bojang

Allison & Busby Limited
11 Wardour Mews
London W1F 8AN
allisonandbusby.com

First published in Germany as *Mord in Sunset Hall* in 2020.
First published in Great Britain by Allison & Busby in 2023.
This paperback edition published by Allison & Busby in 2024

Published by arrangement with Soho Press, New York, with the
assistance of Rights People, London.

Copyright © 2020 by Leonie Swann
English translation copyright © 2023 by Amy Bojang

The moral rights of Leonie Swann to be identified as the author of this work and
of Amy Bojang to be identified as the translator of this work have been asserted in
accordance with the Copyright, Designs and Patents Act 1988.

All characters and events in this publication,
other than those clearly in the public domain,
are fictitious and any resemblance to actual persons,
living or dead, is purely coincidental.

All rights reserved. No part of this publication may be reproduced,
stored in a retrieval system, or transmitted, in any form or by
any means without the prior written permission of the publisher,
nor be otherwise circulated in any form of binding or cover
other than that in which it is published and without a similar
condition being imposed on the subsequent buyer.
A CIP catalogue record for this book is available from
the British Library.

10 9 8 7 6 5 4 3 2 1

ISBN 978-0-7490-3053-7

Typeset in 11/16pt Sabon LT Pro by
Allison & Busby Ltd.

By choosing this product, you help take care of the world's forests.
Learn more: www.fsc.org.

FSC
www.fsc.org
MIX
Paper | Supporting
responsible forestry
FSC® C171272

Printed and bound by
CPI Group (UK) Ltd, Croydon, CR0 4YY

For Fyo, who left too soon

PROLOGUE

COLD-BLOODED

Hettie felt hot. She had spent too much time on her sun stone and the afternoon heat had got into her shell and was incessantly buzzing around in her head. Like any responsible cold-blooded creature, she had to do something about restoring the balance, and the right place for that was traditionally the shady ravine of old plant pots behind the sky-high wooden structure where ferns grew unchecked from cracks, and snails felt their way across the damp earth.

Hettie got going, one scaly foot in front of the other. Over the gravel path, underneath and through the hydrangeas, past the big stump.

But there was something different. Where normally the wooden structure loomed, there was nothing – a big, gaping nothing, and shadows behind it. Like all tortoises, Hettie didn't have much time for curiosity, but this unknown realm of shadows attracted her. She crawled up the ramp, hesitated briefly at the sunshade border and glided on into the pleasant coolness. Her shell brushed against old wood, smoothed by time and countless Big Feet. She could smell the Big Feet even now, near and unmistakable, salty and leathery.

In principle, Hettie had nothing against Big Feet, they had always treated her with respect and were sometimes accompanied by Lettuce-holding Hands. Emboldened, she crept on, deeper into the shadows.

Back there. Aha.

She could see straight away that something wasn't right with the Big Feet. Unlike most of their contemporaries, they weren't flat and firmly on the ground, but had their pointy end sticking upwards, up into the ether, where sunlight cut through the half-dark and dust stars danced.

Highly unusual. This little pair was strangely motionless too. Clearly unwell, Hettie had never come across an ill Big Foot before. Now a feeling a bit like curiosity came over her, or if not curiosity, then at least appetite. As an experiment, quite daringly, she bit into one of the Big Feet. The foot did not fight back, and triumphantly Hettie bit down a second time, more out of principle than enthusiasm. Leathery and hard. Not to her taste. But wherever there were Big Feet, Lettuce-holding Hands weren't far away. She decided to go looking for them, and to her amazement, discovered that on the other side of the Big Feet it went on, on and on, a whole realm of hills, valleys and humps.

And indeed back there, deeper in the dark, was a Lettuce-holding Hand. Only it wasn't holding any lettuce, but seemed bent double, not dissimilar to a dead spider. Tortoises are generally impatient folk, but Hettie was an exception. She could wait. Above all for lettuce. She found a comfy place at the foot of the hilly landscape. Not too warm and not too cold. Cosy, but not claustrophobic. She could grow to like this place.

However, after some considerable time had passed and no lettuce had appeared, Hettie had had enough of waiting around. Apart from that, the hills next to her that had started out as pleasantly temperate, had got colder and colder, uncomfortably cold, and the flies were starting to get on her nerves. To start with it was only two or three, and Hettie had ignored them in true tortoise-style, but now there was a whole cloud of them circling overhead. Buzzing, ducking and diving, flitting around the hills and Hettie herself. When one of the flies had the audacity to land on Hettie's head and tried to drink out of her eye, the tortoise shuffled indignantly out of her place and walked through a strangely sticky, metallic-smelling puddle and out into the afternoon sun again.

1

EDWINA'S BISCUITS

The doorbell rang, and Agnes Sharp abandoned the search for her false teeth, simultaneously pleased and annoyed.

Pleased that she had even heard the doorbell – her ears hadn't really been playing along recently, and sometimes all she could hear was a high-pitched, nerve-jangling ringing, accompanied by a rushing sound. So, the doorbell was a welcome change.

On the other hand, it would be quite embarrassing to open the door without the aforementioned false teeth, unclear and toothless. But the caller had to be gotten rid of before he had the idea of going snooping around in the garden – teeth or no teeth.

'I'm coming! Juft a minute!' Agnes bellowed into the hall, then she sallied forth. Out of the room. Mind the threshold. And then the stairs. A step forward, a step down, then bring down the other foot. A vertigo-inducing moment without any sense of balance, a deep breath, then gather courage for the next step down. And so on. Twenty-six times.

A minute, my foot!

The doorbell rang again.

Her hip grumbled.

The doorbell rang once more.

'Juft one moment, for God fake!'

When she reached the first landing, a real rage had built up in her, towards the stairs, the caller, the renegade false teeth, but also her housemates. Why did she always get the difficult jobs? Like scaling the stairs. Or taking out the bins. Or . . . absolutely everything.

Edwina would have made it down the stairs somewhat quicker, but she would of course have been useless at the door. Bernadette was sitting in her room crying her blind eyes out. At this time Marshall was mostly somewhere on the Internet, unreachable, connected to the computer as if by the umbilical cord. And you obviously couldn't expect Winston to attempt the descent without the stairlift.

Why had nobody repaired the stupid stairlift?

Then Agnes remembered that it had been her job to call for it to be repaired, but with her unreliable hearing and her aversion to the telephone she had kept putting it off. It was her own fault then, as so often seemed to be the case these days.

The only scapegoat left was the caller, and her rage towards him was mounting.

She had mastered the last step and was dragging herself to the front door with a calculated slowness accompanied by the doorbell's *staccato* chimes. Did they think she was deaf? What was the buffoon playing at? What did they even want at this time? And what time was it anyway?

Agnes fumbled briefly with the latch, then threw the door open. She would have liked to give the caller a piece of her mind, but nothing came to her.

'Yef?' she snapped. She didn't quite carry it off and got even more annoyed.

'Err . . . Miss Sharp?' The caller peered rudely past her into the house. A bloody whippersnapper with officious glasses and a briefcase under his arm. This couldn't be a good sign. Agnes crossed her thin arms, while the whippersnapper switched on a winning smile, rather too late.

'Miss Sharp, I have wonderful news for you!'

He really shouldn't have said that. Up to now Agnes had simply planned to get rid of the troublemaker, but now she lost it. Wonderful news? Today of all days? It was too much.

Despite her missing teeth she tried a friendly old-lady smile – with moderate success, as she gathered from the puzzled look on the sales rep's face. 'Oh, for me? How lofely! Come frough to the sitting room.'

He only had himself to blame!

'Anofer bifcuit?'

Where on earth were her teeth?

The whippersnapper silently shook his head. He had taken a single bite of his biscuit and since then had been sitting strangely tensely in the battered wingback chair, chewing. Agnes poured piss-yellow herbal tea into his cup and studied the brochure the intruder had pushed into her hand with feigned interest.

The visitor put the half-eaten biscuit back on the plate – a cold clatter like stone on stone. Edwina's biscuits were generally even spurned by the mice, but for occasions like this they were priceless.

'Do you liff on your own?' the whippersnapper asked with a mouth full.

He didn't want to swallow or spit, so he was stuck.

Agnes thought about Winston and sobbing Bernadette, about Edwina, who was probably trying to find her inner balance through yoga, about Marshall, and finally, about Lillith, and sighed deeply.

The visitor nodded sympathetically.

'What we offer if perfect for people like you. We manage your houfe, take care of renting it out. We take care of everyfing, whilft you fpend your golden funfet years at Lime Tree Court . . .' He went quiet and fixed his gaze strangely past Agnes on the floor, where Hettie the tortoise was passing by with her usual elegance.

And on her shell – the false teeth! Presumably they'd been travelling around the house by tortoise for quite a while, a disembodied, mobile grin. Exactly the kind of thing Marshall would find funny.

Agnes leant right forward, fishing for her false teeth and grabbed them. Hurrah! She quickly put the dentures into her mouth and beamed at the whippersnapper with rows of pristine teeth.

'Golden sunset years, you said?'

'Wifout finanfial worrief!' The sales rep gave in and stood up. 'I'd freally luf to ftay and chat, but I . . .'

'You're going already? What a shame. Are you sure you don't want another . . . ?'

Agnes picked up another biscuit threateningly, but the whippersnapper was already on his way to the door, and a good thing that he was too.

Because Lillith was lying out in the woodshed, a bullet in her head and a smile on her lips. It was going to be a tough day.

They held their crisis meeting in the sunroom on the first floor. It was easiest for Winston that way. Agnes had prepared tea and got Edwina to take the teapot and cups upstairs. They had real biscuits out of a packet too.

Agnes took an experimental bite – her dentures held firm – and looked around. Marshall was next to her, upright and sharp-eyed. Next to him Edwina was in one of her impossible yoga poses with a dreamy expression on her face. Winston just looked calm and sad in his wheelchair. Dignified, like Father Christmas. The scoundrel! How did he do it?

Unlike Winston, Bernadette almost never seemed dignified. Instead she came across like a Mafia boss, not least because of her dark glasses. She had calmed down a bit, but it was the calm before the storm – or, better put, between two storms. With a downpour.

To Agnes's right there was a gaping empty chair.

'The engineer for the stairlift is coming tomorrow,' she reported. After she had finally picked up the phone, it had been surprisingly easy to get the appointment. 'Marshall has ordered the groceries for next week online. Loo roll too.' Marshall gave her an encouraging smile. Another crisis averted.

'And as regards the problem in the shed . . .'

'She is not a problem!' interrupted Bernadette. 'She's Lillith!'

'Not any more,' said Agnes softly. 'That is the problem.'
Bernadette made an unhappy sound.

'It is *warm* for the time of year,' Agnes continued. 'We can't just do nothing . . .'

'We can put her on the stairlift!' Edwina beamed. 'On the stairlift, up she goes, upstairs. Into her bed. Peacefully in her sleep. Maybe she'll even recover! And if not . . . peacefully in her sleep!'

'She is *not* going to recover,' said Marshall decisively. 'And as far as peacefully in her sleep goes . . .'

'Indeed!' Bernadette puffed bitterly.

'We could just call the police,' suggested Winston. At heart, he was someone who liked order. 'The police usually deal with such matters.'

'We *could* do that,' said Agnes, 'if we knew where the gun was. Without the gun . . .'

Three pairs of eyes turned to look questioningly at Marshall.

Bernadette's dark glasses reflected the light.

Marshall seemed confused for a moment, then sheepish. 'The gun . . . it was in the shed. I had it . . . and then I was in the thingummy . . . in the sitting room, and . . . I must admit . . .' He attempted a military stance, but didn't pull it off completely.

'We *don't* know where the gun is,' Agnes repeated. 'And now if the police come and find it – shall we say, somewhere in the house – it could look suspicious.'

Edwina's laugh rang out.

Bernadette snorted.

Winston nodded sagely.

Nobody had anything useful to say. Typical.

The high-pitched ringing started up in Agnes's ear. She used the acoustic intermezzo to think. How long could they wait before reporting Lillith's death? On the one hand, it was definitely an advantage to leave her in the shed for a while, especially in this heat. The more time that passed, the more difficult it would be for the police to make sense of it all. On the other hand, it could obviously seem suspicious if they kept Lillith's passing to themselves for too long. Sure, most of the people in the village had them down – completely unjustifiably – as a load of senile hippies, but at some point, even they had to notice that one of their housemates was missing. When exactly? After a day? Two days?

Edwina said something. It wouldn't be anything sensible. Agnes drank a mouthful of tea and waited for the high-pitched ringing to go away.

Bernadette took her sunglasses off her nose, got a tissue ready and waited for her next sobbing fit.

Winston patted her knee to comfort her.

Marshall said something to Agnes, and she acted like she understood him. An attentive look and a short but encouraging nod should do it.

Then the ringing suddenly disappeared, and Agnes heard the word 'umbrella,' as Marshall looked at her expectantly.

'Well, yes,' said Agnes unsure.

'Just an umbrella,' Marshall repeated. 'That's all. But it doesn't make much sense.'

'How could you!' hissed Bernadette. Her blind eyes stared into empty space. It had an unsettling effect. 'Just like that. Without a goodbye, without . . . anything!'

'With a goodbye, it wouldn't exactly have been a surprise,

would it?' Agnes responded more sharply than she'd intended. Typical Bernadette, making a drama out of the whole thing. They had all agreed! It wasn't as if Lillith's sudden death wouldn't haunt her, quite the opposite, but sometimes you had to think practically.

'We're all going to drink our tea,' she said decisively. 'And take our pills. And then we'll have a look.'

'For Lillith?' asked Edwina delightedly.

'For the gun!' said Agnes. 'Winston and Bernadette will look here on the first floor. In Marshall's room, obviously, but in all of the others too. Everywhere. Edwina and I will look on the ground floor, and Marshall will take care of the garden.'

She looked at a row of long faces. 'Just like Easter!' she cried cheerily.

'Work smarter, not harder.' Winston said, and grinned.

First, they looked in the kitchen, then in the sitting room. Agnes let Edwina climb ladders and peer under sofas and tried to keep a cool head. Together they looked in the vases on the cabinet, behind the books on the shelf, in pots and boxes and jars, behind cushions and under blankets and even in plant pots – and brought a whole host of useful things to light. Three of Edwina's biscuits, hard and firm like the day they were made, eight pairs of reading glasses, a hearing aid, a blood pressure monitor (that's where it went!) and pills aplenty, craftily hidden in nooks and crannies. Someone in the house wasn't taking their medication as prescribed. Agnes would follow up on that later. They just had to . . .

For the second time that day, the doorbell rang.

Terrible timing.

Edwina was already at the door and opened it.

'Cooey!' she said.

Agnes rushed after her, as fast as she could. Edwina answering the door was rarely a good idea.

From the other side of the door came a serious male voice. 'The police!' cried Edwina excitedly. 'It's the police, Agnes! Look, how handy!'

Agnes rushed. The police? Already? It was too early, much too early! They didn't have a plan yet! Maybe Bernadette had . . . ? No. As far as she knew Bernadette didn't think much of the police . . .

'Do come in, Inspector,' Edwina blathered excitedly. 'We were just looking for—'

'The tortoise!' gasped Agnes, who had finally made it to the door. 'We've lost our tortoise.'

The policeman made a strange face and stepped inside hesitantly. He was in uniform. So far, so bad. 'Miss Sharp? Agnes Sharp?'

'I'm Edwina,' corrected Edwina, but the policeman didn't allow himself to be distracted and looked Agnes in the eye with, to her mind, a much too critical look. She felt herself getting hot. 'Are you the homeowner? Miss Sharp, I need to talk to you briefly. Regarding a very serious matter.'

Serious! Oh God. What to say? As little as possible! She would have preferred to deal with the policeman straight away in the hall, but Edwina had already taken him by the arm and led him into the sitting room, where following their hunt it was full of vases, pots and jars standing everywhere.

Incredulously, the policeman looked at the pile of pills and the mountain of reading glasses.

'We—' said Edwina, and Agnes hastily interrupted her.

'Just ran away, the cheeky thing. We've looked everywhere!'

'In pots?' asked the policeman.

'She likes to play hide and seek,' Agnes explained, without batting an eyelid.

'Please take a seat,' murmured the policeman in an official tone and motioned to the sofa, where the biscuits were lying. 'What I have to tell you might be quite a shock for you both.'

'We're not made of sugar,' snapped Edwina.

But what the policeman had to tell them really was quite a shock.

'Mildred Puck?' Agnes asked for the third time. She was sitting uncomfortably on the rock-hard biscuits. 'Dead?' Her head was swimming. Mildred? Why was the man talking about Mildred? Something wasn't right!

'Shot dead,' said the policeman. 'On her own terrace. In her deck chair.'

'What a coincidence!' cried Edwina and clapped her hands together.

'It's not really a coincidence,' responded the policeman. 'We suspect that the perpetrator broke in through the garden and Mildred surprised him. I have to ask you if you noticed anything unusual today? Did you see – or hear – anything?'

'But . . .' mumbled Agnes shaking her head. The Mildred she knew hadn't been capable of surprising anyone for years. Total . . . invalid. She felt dizzy. Mildred *too*? It didn't make any sense!

'I don't want to worry you unduly,' murmured the policeman and looked awkwardly at the pills in front of him. 'But, if there really is someone trying to rob vulnerable senior citizens . . . we would ask you all to be cautious, make sure doors and windows are locked. And if you notice anything unusual, please don't hesitate to . . .'

He gave Agnes his card.

Agnes hesitated.

'But Mildred is . . . Mildred *was* an invalid. We, on the other hand . . .'

She fell silent. It was pointless trying to explain the difference between a torpid vegetable like Mildred and her little community of active senior citizens. She took the card, sighing. Of course. The print was far too small. Their chances of correctly reading the number in an emergency and dialling it on the phone were about as good as Hettie the tortoise's.

'Biscuits?' asked Edwina and fished a specimen from under her joggers.

'Not while I'm on duty,' said the policeman with a hint of a smile. Edwina lost interest and slid from the sofa into one of her yoga poses. The cobra if Agnes wasn't mistaken.

The policeman's smile quickly vanished.

'There is no need to panic,' he said. 'But you should be vigilant. And we would be grateful of any information.'

'Of course. That's very thoughtful of you.' Agnes noticed her heart was pounding wildly. Maybe the whole Mildred thing wasn't a catastrophe at all. Maybe it was an *opportunity*! Edwina had finished her cobra and wandered through to the hall.

'Did she . . . die instantly?' asked Agnes.

The policeman looked at the pills again with seeming fascination, and the way he said nothing told Agnes that it hadn't been a quick death. Not at all.

She shuddered.

'Were you close?' The policeman tore his gaze from the pills and looked at Agnes. His eyes were red and tired and somehow *shocked*, and for the first time Agnes felt that he wasn't just a policeman, but a human being too with floppy, sand-coloured hair and a beer belly. He even looked a bit familiar to her. These days, with some people, she felt like she had already met them, as if there were a finite number of faces in the world and at some point, when you'd lived for long enough, you had seen them all.

'We had known each other for a long, long time,' she said quietly.

The policeman opened his mouth, presumably to say something sympathetic, when a little triumphant cry came from the hall.

'Gotcha!' cheered Edwina.

The gun! Agnes's heart leapt about in her chest like a tormented frog.

Edwina! No!

Not now!

The high-pitched ringing was back, and Agnes clung to the arm of the sofa. She watched helplessly as the policeman jumped out of his chair and rushed to the door. She couldn't do anything, say anything, and the wonderful opportunity that had just presented itself was slipping through her fingers. Like sand. Like peas and pastry forks and coffee beans. Like quite a few things these days.

Then Edwina was back again and was blabbering excitedly and inaudibly into her ear, and then the policeman appeared, beaming, with Hettie the tortoise in his big policeman hands.

Agnes woke up, squinted and could see four quite blurry but clearly concerned faces above her. She made sense of the colours and shapes as well as she could and tried to concentrate.

Edwina.

Marshall.

Hettie the tortoise.

And the policeman.

Somebody was holding her hand.

Agnes groaned. The policeman had to go!

She opened her mouth, but no sound came out. She rolled her eyes towards Marshall, then back to the policeman. Once. Twice.

'I think she's having a fit,' said the policeman.

Marshall seemed to have understood what Agnes wanted. 'Pah, fit. The old girl was just a bit hot. These things happen!' Agnes sighed gratefully.

'I think she wants a glass of water,' said Marshall.

The policeman laid Hettie on Agnes's rib cage and rushed out of the room. 'Where's the kitchen?'

'Back left,' called Marshall, being deliberately vague. Agnes could hear the policeman pulling open doors in the hall. She found her voice again.

'He's got to go!' she hiss-whispered. 'Right now. It . . . it's an opportunity!'

Hettie the tortoise tried to eat one of her mother-of-pearl buttons.

'And if I hear the words "old girl" again, there'll be trouble!' Marshall grinned and let go of her hand.

The law enforcement official returned with a red face and a glass of water.

'I really didn't want to shock her like this. At first, she seemed to take the news quite well. I mean . . . we thought it would be best if the neighbours . . . it really is a bit remote here, you must be careful . . . are you sure we shouldn't call the doctor?'

Strange that nobody really spoke to you any more, just because you were lying on your back – or on your stomach in Hettie's case. They all talked over you, literally. Agnes looked up, as words were sailing over her, like she wasn't there at all. She had a drink of water and watched as, in a rare moment of unity, Marshall, Edwina and Hettie tried to get rid of the policeman. It was probably Hettie who made the final call with her impatient snarl.

The policeman distributed a few more of his cards and bits of advice, then Marshall and Edwina manoeuvred him towards the door.

Hettie and Agnes looked at each other. 'That was close!' Agnes exhaled.

Hettie hissed in agreement.

And then . . .

Agnes was a girl with thin, sun-tanned limbs, white socks and pigtails reaching down to her bottom. Agnes didn't like her pigtails. The boys pulled them. The girls teased her.

But her mother wouldn't hear of it.

When she skipped, her pigtails skipped too.

But now they were hanging limply.

Agnes was standing beneath a cloudless summer sky watching someone squash firebugs on a stone. The bugs were running back and forth, but they didn't stand a chance.

'Why are you doing that?' asked Agnes.

The sun was warming her neck. A bird was singing. Agnes wanted to go home.

'Because it's easy,' answered the someone.

Agnes opened her eyes wide and stared into Hettie's wise tortoise face. Hettie was the youngest member of the household, but also the most sensible. That sometimes gave Agnes food for thought.

She was still lying on the sofa with her feet on a cushion. Her pigtails were long gone. Agnes had other problems now. She tried to sit up. Hettie snarled disapprovingly. 'Could someone possibly take the tortoise . . . ?'

Edwina picked up Hettie and gave her a sloppy kiss on her shell. Agnes got hold of the arm of the sofa and heaved. Somebody pushed from behind and then finally she was sitting upright, if a little askew.

She patted her hair (ravaged of course), sighed and looked at everyone. Bernadette had joined them in the meantime and was listening with her head tilted to one side looking in the direction of the sofa. Marshall had pulled up a chair; Edwina was sitting cross-legged on the rug, and Hettie, who finally had solid ground beneath her claws again, made off with dignity.

Agnes gathered herself.

'There's good news and there's bad news,' she said. 'Mildred Puck is dead.'

'Is that the good news?' Bernadette asked drily. She had got herself a plate of fondant creams and was hoovering them up, one after the other, like a confectionary vampire. The question stung Agnes. She and Mildred had been friends, best friends. But obviously that was a long time ago, and since then Mildred had spent a considerable amount of time making herself thoroughly unpopular with everyone.

'The bad news is that some burglar is going around bumping off old people,' Agnes corrected. 'And the good news is that he's using a gun to do it!'

'Ah!' said Marshall.

'Poor Mildred,' said Edwina. 'Why is that good?'

'We can pin Lillith on him!' Agnes explained excitedly. 'Don't you understand? It's ideal! Two old ladies shot in the garden, practically at the same time! Everyone will think that this burglar is responsible for Lillith too. Now we'll go to the shed and find her. We can cause a bit of a ruckus and run about all over the place. And then we'll call the police!'

'The police again,' Edwina said, bored.

'Good plan!' echoed from above where Winston was sitting on the landing listening.

'Why should I be a part of this?' snarled Bernadette not quite as skilfully as Hettie, but venomously nevertheless. 'When nobody ever . . .'

'Because there are no fondant creams in prison,' said Agnes. 'That's why.'

Things turned out to be rather more complicated than she had expected. The police didn't just come and pick Lillith up, but put up yellow and black plastic tape, striped like hornets, took photos, took samples and searched the garden. Agnes was worried about her hydrangeas.

And the flies! All of the flies! Agnes hadn't reckoned on those, that Lillith would attract so many flies in such a short space of time. It had been a shock for them all. Now Agnes was standing befuddled in the hall wanting nothing more than a nap. Police officials hurried past her. Edwina and Hettie had disappeared, Marshall was being questioned in the garden, and Winston was looking down from the landing with curiosity. Bernadette had used up the house supply of tissues and was now sobbing into toilet paper in the sitting room. A policewoman was helping her.

Agnes didn't have anything more to do, other than get in the way. She leant on the doorframe exhausted, when a shadow fell over her.

'Hello there,' said an unfamiliar voice.

Agnes squinted into the light and looked into two sparkling green eyes, the brim of an antiquated feather hat hovering over them.

'I'm Charlie,' said the feather hat. 'The newbie! Fabulous house!'

Agnes groaned. The newbie. In the excitement about Lillith and Mildred she had completely forgotten.

At that very moment two police officers carried a stretcher past. On it a big white plastic bag, still surrounded by hopeful flies.

'Oh,' said Charlie with the feather hat. 'I've come at a bad time.'

Agnes remembered her manners.

'No, not at all. I'm Agnes,' she said and offered her hand. 'And, err, that was Lillith.'

'Ha!' Charlie took her hand and shook it enthusiastically. 'Good timing then, huh? Fabulous!'

Agnes attempted a smile. 'Welcome to Sunset Hall!'

2

CURRY

Once again nobody else seemed to want to take responsibility, so it was left to Agnes, who was tackling the stairs for the third time that day, to show Charlie her new room. It took a while. Lillith and Mildred were whirring around in her head. Mildred and Lillith.

Mildred. Lillith.

Lillith. Mildred.

And a thousand hungry flies.

Agnes's knees felt wobbly.

She had to have a rest on the landing.

'The stairlift is being repaired tomorrow,' she said apologetically.

Charlie waved dismissively, and sat down beside her without waiting for an invitation. It was better that way, and Agnes didn't know whether she should be grateful or annoyed. Charlie smelt unfamiliar, not just like laundered clothes, hand cream and *eau de cologne*, but stranger and more surprising. Real perfume, Agnes assumed. A hint of wood and iris, and beneath that something else, something familiar, but difficult to identify. Maybe just human?

Winston was sitting up on the landing smiling and dignified. 'There's a lot going on today,' he said sympathetically.

Agnes's hand surreptitiously slipped from Charlie's forearm. 'This is Charlie,' she said. 'The newbie. And that's Winston. He's stuck at the moment.'

'Hello there,' said Charlie, and Winston doffed an imaginary hat from his bare head.

'Your room is back there to the left,' Agnes explained as she slowly, but purposefully, pushed past them both. She wanted to finally have her nap.

'Fabulous,' said Charlie.

The door swung open, and Agnes squinted.

It had been her mother's favourite room, and sometimes Agnes thought she could see her standing there at the window, a slim silhouette with a straight back and her hair up. Violets and sunlight, a delicate tea set on the little table in the bay window and sometimes, if she was lucky, the aroma of coconut macaroons.

But this time the stars didn't quite align. Agnes looked through Charlie's eyes and saw the dust on the mantlepiece and the sun-bleached patch on the rug. The bed was freshly made, thank God, but someone really should have gone to the effort of putting out a few fresh flowers . . . Only with no stairlift and all the excitement?

'En suite, desk, sitting area,' she explained superfluously. 'As agreed.'

'Hmmm,' said Charlie and took off her feather hat. The

hair beneath it was white and silky like swan's down. And long. Down to her bum. You would get a couple of decent plaits out of it.

'A splash of colour maybe . . .' she murmured, throwing her hat in the direction of the coat stand and landing it. 'And houseplants of course. We'll get there! Fabulous!'

'It has a lovely view of the garden,' Agnes said defensively and drew the curtains. Dust danced in the sunlight. Together they looked down at a labyrinth of hornet tape and some police officers clambering about in it wearing white bee suits. Agnes spotted a damaged hydrangea.

'Ah,' she murmured. 'Normally . . . it's idyllic.'

'Does this happen very often?' Charlie asked, standing next to her. Her red fingernails tapping the window sill searchingly.

'I hope not,' Agnes mumbled, but deep down she had this uneasy feeling that she would soon be seeing more of the hornet tape, in the garden, in the house, everywhere. And the flies . . . She shuddered, waggled her hands about, and decisively closed the curtains again. 'I'm sure you'll want to freshen up,' she said, nodding cheerfully and making her way towards her nap.

At the door she turned around again. Charlie had sunk down onto the bed and was stretching all four of her limbs revealing a shocking amount of leg in the process.

'I hope you'll feel comfortable here at Sunset Hall,' said Agnes.

'Sunset *Hall*!' Charlie repeated. It sounded mocking, but friendly too. 'More sunset than hall, I would argue. Just like me!'

'It is what it is,' Agnes responded perhaps a little too harshly.

When it came down to it, Charlie was right.

'Tea's at four!' Agnes reminded her.

Obviously, it took a bit longer for them all to gather in the sunroom, around some rather beaten-up-looking, anaemic Chelsea buns. The police had finally left, leaving behind a load of hornet tape and good advice. After his chat with the police officer, Marshall looked pale and grey, deflated like a pre-sucked fondant cream. Bernadette had finally cried herself out and was listening to everyone with an almost perky countenance. Edwina picked away at her bun. Winston poured the tea. Charlie was sitting amongst them chatting in a red kimono like some kind of bird of paradise. About her summers in the South of France.

About her third husband, the rogue. About hospitals, they were the *absolute last-ditch*. Why was she blabbering the whole time? Nerves, Agnes assumed. The move to Sunset Hall was a huge step for every new arrival.

Charlie finally shoved a bit of Chelsea bun in her mouth, chewed and swallowed unenthusiastically, and Agnes took her chance. Someone had to explain the house rules to the newbie after all.

'Mostly we all eat together,' she said quickly. 'Usually in the dining room, unless the stairlift is broken and Winston . . .' She realised she was running the risk of tying herself in knots, and started again. 'Everyone gets his own breakfast from the kitchen depending on when he gets up. Not before. Obviously not.' Frustrated, Agnes stared at her napkin. In her head her thoughts were arranged neatly in rows, one after the other, like beads on a string, but more and more often they seemed to get twisted in her mouth. The outside and the inside. The two were getting further and further apart. She sat in exasperated silence.

'Or she,' Charlie said with her mouth full.

'Mostly she,' Agnes admitted. 'There's a list of smaller chores, but other than that we have a cleaning lady.'

'Sylvie,' Winston said appreciatively.

'She also bakes for us,' Edwina added, pointing towards the shapeless Chelsea buns. 'I bake too!'

Marshall rolled his eyes. Bernadette groaned.

'A physio comes on Wednesdays . . .' Agnes tried to not allow herself to get confused. 'Mainly for Winston, but anyone can . . .'

'Ha!' said Winston.

'Sometimes she cooks . . .' Edwina continued.

'On Fridays we have frozen pizza,' said Bernadette. 'Or we order fish and chips from the pub.'

'We discuss what groceries we buy,' Agnes explained. 'And what we cook. We discuss everything.'

A sudden silence fell over the table like a cheese dome. Recently there had been a raft of things that had not been sufficiently discussed.

A whole raft of things.

A car horn sounded outside followed by a deep, bloodcurdling bark.

'Ha!' said Charlie. 'Thomas and Brexit! Fabulous!'

Thomas turned out to be a young, unashamedly handsome wearer of sunglasses. White shirt, healthy tan, ripped jeans. Normally Agnes didn't think much of jeans, never mind ripped jeans, but in this case . . . While the more mobile factions of her group went to take a closer look in the flesh, Agnes observed from the window as the fairy-tale prince dutifully lined up suitcase after suitcase at the front door, whilst a grey hurricane raged in his van. The van was rocking.

Then Charlie was on the veranda, closely followed by Marshall and Edwina.

'Darling!' Charlie opened her arms and Thomas let go of the suitcases, rushed towards her and gave her a peck on the cheek. A *peck*. More like a full-blown smacker on the cheek. Agnes was glued to the glass.

'Is one of those for me?' Edwina was jumping around on the veranda like a little kid.

Charlie pointed at Edwina. 'Edwina. Marshall.' Then with a sweeping gesture, 'SUNSET HALL!'

From her window, Agnes couldn't see Marshall, but he had to be down there somewhere in the shadow of the front door. She could imagine it. Hands behind his back. Sceptically. Militarily.

'Very nice!' The youngster picked up the first suitcase.

'Looks really good actually! Shall I take them straight to your . . .'

'Would you, darling?'

Their eyes met for a moment and something flashed across their smiling faces. A kind of sadness.

'So, that's it?' Thomas said quietly. 'You're sure . . . ?'

Charlie seemed to nod, then she suddenly threw her hands in the air.

'Fabulous!'

Agnes watched suitcase after suitcase drift through the front door, presumably up the stairs, presumably into Charlie's room. What in the world did Charlie have in all of those suitcases? Agnes could vividly imagine: feather boas, fur coats, lace blouses, diamond brooches, little bottles of perfume, nail varnish.

Her thoughts turned to Lillith, who had also arrived one day with her suitcases, accompanied by her grumpy daughter. Something had to be done with her things. Would they be collected? Someone would have to get in touch with the daughter – or did the police do things like that?

A sudden silence pulled her back to the present.

The stream of suitcases had ceased; the space in front of the house was empty.

Then there were voices on the stairs. In the hall.

Agnes rushed back to the table. She didn't want to be caught spying. Her mother had never liked it, and presumably people nowadays didn't either.

Nobody liked a spy. Apart from Edwina of course. Edwina had once been a kind of spy herself.

As the door flew open, she threw herself into the nearest chair. Charlie of course. And the tireless jeans-wearer.

'The sunroom,' Charlie declared. Thomas had taken off his sunglasses and was nodding dutifully. 'My grandson Thomas.

This is Agnes. She's organised the whole thing. Great project!'
The finger pointed again, and Agnes had to drag herself out of
the hard-won chair to greet Thomas properly. Organised? Ha!
Charlie didn't know her very well.

Apparently, she had gone a bit over the top with the
greeting because Thomas gently removed her hand.

'I'm going to bust a move then, Gran . . .'

Charlie nodded. 'Of course, darling. Thank you so much.

'And don't forget Brexit!' Thomas laughed. 'As if!'

Bust a move? What move? And Brexit? Who could forget
Brexit? The two of them were speaking a language that Agnes
didn't really understand, and she realised she envied them.
Recently it seemed to her that she had to fight for every
shred of understanding, and here everything just seemed to
be babbling along like a brook. Then the helpful grandson
was already halfway out of the door, 'busting a move,' Agnes
assumed, and Charlie was watching him go, her eyes glistening
damply.

At some point Agnes managed to make it to her wingback
chair and close her eyes, but the conditions weren't quite
conducive to a nap. There was something going on out in the
hall; she could hear voices, footsteps, laughter. Edwina let out
a little cry of delight.

Agnes considered checking to make sure everything was
alright. She was tired, too tired to go to the door, let alone
to the stairs. Let the others screech! She was exactly where
she belonged. She would just sit there until . . . what was for
dinner tonight? And whose turn was it to cook? Hopefully

not Edwina. Lillith possibly? They would have to rewrite the rota – not much could be expected of Lillith's culinary skills now . . .

And then all of a sudden Agnes was sitting high up in the apple tree. The cool night air giving her goose bumps on her bare arms. She peered down where the first windfalls grew like pale boils out of the black grass.

Fear was everywhere, in the moonlight that caught in her night dress, much too white; in the rough bark beneath her hands; in the wind, making the leaves riot; in her breath, too quick and too loud; even in the nightingale's song.

Quiet, quiet!

Don't make a move! Not a sound!

Because down below, beneath the apple trees, there was a monster roaming about.

'Agnes, we're going out for a curry!'

Agnes's eyes shot open, she wrestled with a cushion for a moment and looked around in a fit of panic, but it was just Edwina in her blue going-out coat with gleaming eyes and red cheeks.

'Out of the question!' is what she wanted to say, but instead she just huffed, 'Huh!'

A hairy face had appeared behind Edwina, brilliant white teeth, a damp, flexible nose and surprisingly soulful eyes.

Agnes wondered how quickly she would be able to make it to the bathroom door – not quickly enough! The wolfhound swept past Edwina – my goodness, he reached up to her shoulder! – and went about undertaking an extensive sniff-inspection of the carpet.

'She's treating us!' Edwina explained. 'We're taking a taxi!'

'Treating us?' mumbled Agnes. The sniffing nose came closer.

'She said we should celebrate her new start.'

'Celebrate?'

'To be honest, I just don't like cold cuts. Especially on my first night. Are you ready?'

Charlie with her ridiculous feather hat again. Obviously! Something wet touched Agnes's hand, and she recoiled.

Where her cushion had once been there was now a huge grey dog's head, black nose to the front, fur all over the place.

Agnes could hear herself laughing. It sounded mildly hysterical.

Then a pink tongue poked out between sharp teeth and licked her hands. It tickled. It was quite a damp affair. Agnes stopped laughing and caught herself really smiling. It was fun being licked. It made her feel alive . . . somehow.

She carefully reached out her hand and touched the fur. Silky, in a bristly way, and warm.

The back end of the dog was wagging.

'He likes you!' Edwina said enviously. 'Shall we go now?'

Agnes remembered the latest crisis and reluctantly let go of the dog's head. Brown eyes looked up at her reproachfully, then off the wolfhound went again, always following his nose. 'We can't just go out for a curry,' said Agnes. 'Not on the day they picked up Lillith! Have you forgotten again? How does that look?'

'But I've *never* been to an Indian restaurant!' Edwina stamped her feet, and Agnes would have liked to remind her that she had once been married to an Indian man – albeit not always particularly successfully. But why bother?

'Ah! Hmm. That's obviously . . .' At least Charlie seemed to appreciate that the curry thing wasn't such a great idea, and blushed beneath her feather hat. 'I didn't mean to . . . It's just, I didn't even know her . . . We'll wait a while, huh?'

'And cold cuts are . . .' Agnes broke off. She had wanted to inform Charlie that cold cuts were one of their culinary highlights, but the dog had snatched the cushion and was shaking it back and forth growling. Agnes held her breath.

'Brexit!' Charlie's voice suddenly sounded harsh as whiplash, and the dog immediately let go of the cushion, bounded over the coffee table and parked himself in front of Charlie on his furry backside.

'This is Brexit!' Charlie declared proudly. 'He's just a bit playful still.'

'Ah,' mumbled Agnes at a loss. For her Brexit was something going on non-stop on the radio. Hairy, sure, but not *that* hairy.

'But . . .' she hesitated. Who had decided Charlie could just bring her huge dog with her? How in the world were they going to cope with it? Bernadette, who couldn't see? Winston in his wheelchair? Marshall, who had just recently marched out into the garden with a gun and now couldn't remember a thing? And Edwina, whose head was full of nonsense and yoga. Sometimes it was even a challenge to command the necessary respect from Hettie the tortoise, so such a big animal . . .

'Brexit!' Agnes repeated disapprovingly. The dog panted at her cheerfully.

'Brexit is coming!' Charlie explained with utter conviction. 'You have to move with the times. Stay on the ball and the like . . . Brexit loves balls!'

Of course they all had a curry, just not in style at the restaurant, but on the quiet in the sunroom, out of plastic cartons and foil trays. Without further ado, Charlie had ordered something for them all.

'That is not Indian food,' Edwina complained for the hundredth time, chasing chickpeas around her plate with her fork.

Agnes blew a gasket. 'It bloody is!'

Then she felt childish. It wasn't Edwina's fault that she was a sandwich short . . . Why did she let herself be goaded? She should have known better!

'Delicious,' mumbled Winston for the hundredth time, clutching Charlie's hand and miming a kiss. 'What a wonderful cook you are!'

'Charmer!' Charlie pinched Winston's cheek as if he were a schoolboy, and Agnes looked down at her curry with mixed emotions.

'What's the story with the dog?' she whispered to Marshall. 'Who told her that it's okay?'

'Well,' mumbled Marshall, 'we have Hettie, and I thought . . .'

'Hettie is quite a compact thing,' Agnes hissed. 'Brexit however . . .'

'I thought it was a hamster,' Marshall admitted. 'She asked

if she could bring her cute little friend with her . . .'

He looked so embarrassed that for a moment Agnes was tempted to pinch his cheek too. Instead, she shook her head disapprovingly. Charlie had only been there a few hours and had already managed to create chaos, not just out there on the dining table, where there was an unholy pile of plastic rubbish, but also in here, in her head. She exhaled deeply.

'It'll all work itself out somehow,' Marshall said reassuringly.

'Hmm?'

'You know, with Brexit!'

'That's what they say on the radio as well,' mumbled Agnes. 'Personally, I don't believe a word of it.'

Bernadette suddenly leapt up, wobbled a bit and raised her glass of mango lassi. She was too shaky and the mango lassi sloshed over and dripped onto the table.

'To Lillith!'

'To Lillith!' The others raised their glasses too. More lassi sloshed, and the high-pitched ringing started up again in Agnes's ears.

She wondered if anyone was toasting Mildred over there in the big house. Probably not.

Mildred of all people! It made her think. Deep in thought she shovelled more rice and spicy sauce onto her plate. Had it really been a normal burglar that had killed her neighbour? Strictly speaking he could have just marched up to her, and Mildred, who was in a vegetative state in her wheelchair following her stroke, wouldn't have been able to do the slightest thing to stop it. So why the violence? And why had the attacker not broken in properly after the murder? Nobody had said anything about an actual burglary!

Agnes sipped her lassi thoughtfully and listened to the high-pitched ringing.

She had to admit she was looking forward to the funeral.

Later that evening, once the bin was full of plastic cartons and Agnes was unpleasantly burping curry, Marshall ceremoniously fetched the black book from the safe. They sat in silence as Charlie entered her name and filled in the questionnaire. Then they signed one after the other, first Charlie, then Winston with a flamboyant squiggle, Marshall with two jagged letters, Bernadette big, jolly and a bit off the page. Edwina drew a butterfly.

Agnes wrestled with the pen for a moment, but then got hold of it and signed. Her signature looked scrawly and strange. Charlie sat at the table, still and a bit pale, and for once wasn't finding everything fabulous. Bernadette went towards her – celebratorily, but also a bit shadily with her gangster sunglasses – and pulled her into a badly aimed embrace. 'Now you are one of us!'

Agnes and Marshall looked at one another. Marshall was nodding almost imperceptibly.

Only Agnes could tell that his hands were shaking as he crossed Lillith's name out of the register and put the book back in the safe.

3

BETTER BISCUITS

The next morning everything looked a bit rosier. Agnes was woken by a lark singing and lay there for a moment, still swaddled in sleep. Nothing. No ringing, no problems, no dead bodies to worry about. She was just Agnes, and for the moment that was enough. Then she stretched and her hip made its presence felt. Not just Agnes then. *Old* Agnes. Every morning it was a little shock. How could seventy-eight years have sailed by like that? Or was it eighty-seven? Better not to think about it.

With the help of the bedpost, she carefully manoeuvred herself into an upright position. Cool morning air tickled her forearms. It felt good. She could use a little break from the constant heat. Heat attracted flies and Agnes had had enough of flies for now.

The curtains billowed ominously in the wind, and she was suddenly wide awake. Old, half-forgotten things floated up from the bottom of her pool of memories. She couldn't just sit on her painful hip and do nothing. That just wouldn't do! She gave herself a shove. Bare feet touched cool floorboards. It felt exactly as it had during her school days, or later on, when she was engaged and woke up at all hours with her head full of scattered thoughts. Emboldened by familiar floorboards, Agnes stood up and padded to the window to get the wildly flailing curtains under control. Then she jumped. There was a dark shadow in the garden looking up at her: Brexit with a mouth full of hornet tape!

Ha! Fine by her. The sooner that stupid tape was out of her garden, the better. She gave the dog a friendly wave.

Brexit wagged his tail.

Agnes opened the wardrobe, to just get . . . and hesitated. For years she had always just grabbed something from the wardrobe, no matter what it was, as long as it was clean, weather-appropriate and easy to put on. Skirts with an elasticated waist, baggy jumpers and cardigans – but it didn't seem good enough to her any more. Not with Charlie strutting about the house in red kimonos showing a bit of leg. Agnes's fingers brushed a jacket made of fine green velvet – too warm obviously, then a delicate lilac dress that she hadn't worn in . . . but no, she would never be able to get a handle on the zip. And apart from that, it was only yesterday that they had picked up Lillith and the hideous flies from the shed, so Agnes could hardly rock up in pastels. Her hand kept searching and finally found a respectable black skirt with snaps and a blouse with black lace. For a while she struggled with the round and strangely uncooperative buttons on the blouse, then she managed it. She washed her face and hands in the bathroom, combed her now wispy hair and held it in place with a few clips. Her teeth had spent the night in a dip and were grinning at her encouragingly from the edge of the sink. Agnes rinsed them carefully and put them into position. Tried a smile. It was weird how well you could smile with teeth that weren't your own. What else? Perfume? Did she even have any . . . ?

She padded over to her desk and managed to wrench open the top drawer. There we are! Chanel No. 5. But on closer inspection she realised the bottle was empty, dried-up, faded away, vanished, vamoosed. Chanel had slipped away long ago. Instead, Agnes came across a little golden lipstick case and went back into the bathroom with her find. She twisted the red lipstick cone up and painted away. Her heart was racing. She could feel her heavy pigtails again and the disapproving look of her mother, but also the thrill, fizzing like sparkling wine. Once she was finished painting, she pressed her lips together. Then she dabbed a touch of red onto her cheeks and rubbed it in.

There we go! She felt good.

On the way out of her room Agnes ventured a look in the mirror: a skinny, withered lady in black, a bit like dried fish, but also almost elegant, with a nice blouse, weird hairdo and surprisingly red, somewhat uneven lips. Her eyes peeked out from beneath wrinkly eyelids, alert and even a little aggressive, and they were still *her* eyes, the eyes belonging to the girl with the pigtails. Blue and inquisitive. That was good. This time she would hardly make it up an apple tree, but it would help to at least maintain a cool and alert air.

Agnes was pleased with herself.

She managed to get down the stairs without incident and quietly hobbled into the kitchen. She was normally the first person at the breakfast table and that was just how she liked it. Quiet. Undisturbed. She put the kettle on and looked in the fridge without a great deal of optimism. It had been a few days since Sylvie had been shopping and all the interesting groceries had vanished. Fruit. Yoghurt. Ham. All gone.

It would be a boring breakfast. Agnes got herself some butter and jam, poured some tea, put bread in the toaster – and was suddenly eye to eye with Brexit.

He was back from the garden and looked hungry.

'Oh!'

He was so big!

'Go away!' Agnes whispered.

Brexit panted hopefully.

'We haven't got any more ham,' Agnes said truthfully.

Brexit was not discouraged.

Agnes cut a slice of bread and threw it into his mouth.

Snap. Gone.

His tail wagged.

She started to cut another slice, but then she thought better of it. On the radio they were warning of food shortages due to Brexit; she couldn't just feed all of their provisions to the dog. So, she stood up straight to her full height – which was as much as about eight inches taller than the wolfhound – and thought back to what Charlie had done.

'Brexit, down!'

Brexit gave her a look, of surprise or reproach, she couldn't tell, and then really did stretch out on the kitchen floor – a vast, furry, mountainous landscape at her feet.

'Good boy!'

Agnes threw him a second round of toast as a reward and thought to herself that maybe Brexit was actually a good housemate – the only one in the house who did what he was told. She poured milk into her tea and buttered her toast. As she went to sit down to eat, Edwina suddenly appeared in the doorway.

'You look colourful,' she said clapping her hands together. 'Colourful and black!'

Colourful was a shameless exaggeration. It was just a bit of lipstick after all. Agnes wanted to silence her with toast, but she was already back in the hall.

'Agnes is colourful and black!' she shouted. 'Colourful and black!'

She could kiss goodbye to her quiet breakfast now. Marshall rushed through the door in his dressing gown, saw her sitting at the table, coughed. Slowly, but systematically Bernadette felt her way into the kitchen like a snail with invisible feelers. Charlie floated in wearing her red kimono.

'Is that all?' she asked calmly. 'Just a bit of lipstick?'

'Lipstick?' Bernadette repeated disapprovingly. How could she disapprove of something she couldn't even see? Look who's talking, with her fat behind and never-ending fondant creams!

Agnes could feel real red joining the drawn-on rouge. She stood up.

'I'm going out!' she said emphatically. 'Over to the Pucks'. Someone should extend our sympathies to them. Someone who looks a bit presentable.' The idea had only just come to her, but it suddenly seemed brilliant.

'But we never go to the Pucks'!' Edwina exclaimed. '*Nobody* goes to the Pucks'!'

'This is an exception!' With a pang of regret Agnes left her breakfast and made her way to the front door, both cross and emboldened. Maybe she could find out a few things, uncover something that the police had overlooked.

She got her walking stick out of the umbrella stand. Normally her walking stick embarrassed her, but now it felt right. Like a weapon. A sword, a cutlass, a dagger! Agnes stepped out onto the veranda and slammed the front door shut behind her.

Driven by determination and a healthy dose of rage, she made it across the veranda, along the path, past her beloved hydrangeas and up to the front gate. Then she noticed how quickly her heart was racing and how rapid her breathing was. She felt dizzy. Her left foot was unhappy, her hip in uproar. Agnes allowed herself a little rest and looked back at the house.

At her house.

At the house of her life.

Sunset Hall.

The house hadn't begun its life as Sunset Hall. When Agnes was growing up it had been optimistically called Morning Cottage, but a few years ago, when her house share came into existence, someone from the village had painted over the sign in red paint. *Sunset Hall*. Some yob. It was meant as an insult, but for some reason Agnes and her housemates liked it. You had to face your weaknesses, turn them into strengths. Sure – maybe they weren't spring chickens any more, but that didn't mean they couldn't still have a decent sunset!

So, they hadn't scrubbed off the red paint. Instead they had registered the new name with the authorities. It suited the house quite well, Agnes thought. Strong. Warm. Dramatic. She liked the way her home nestled in greenery, a fat, contented duck of a house surrounded by cypress and apple trees, birches and elderflower bushes.

The trees had got so tall – and the shadows beneath them had got so big. An impressive wisteria snuggled around the façade and the sky was reflected in the windows.

All except one.

One of the windows on the first floor seemed darker than the others.

Someone was standing up there.

Someone was watching her.

Agnes spun around – or wanted to spin. What came out was more of a lurch. Why did they have to gaze after her just because she was wearing a bit of lipstick? It wasn't exactly the most free-spirited thing you could do.

Determined, she turned her back on the house and followed her walking stick across the road and cross-country into the park. Hadn't there been a path here before? Nobody seemed to use it any more. Obviously not.

She pushed her way through grass and overgrown bushes, slipped, caught herself thanks to her walking stick, and in doing so noticed she was still wearing her slippers – dusky pink with a red pompom. Not exactly mourning dress, and they weren't much good for cross-country either!

But Agnes had already come too far to give up. She decided to ignore the slippers and pushed on up a gentle slope, then trudged through some pine trees. As a child, had she really run from house to house in five minutes, often five, six, seven times a day?

These days the journey seemed to drag on for an eternity, but in the end, Agnes could see the big house appear between the trees. Not a duck, but a majestic and somewhat discontented swan. She could feel her heart pounding again, not just because of the exertion, but also excitement. Unease? Fear? Maybe even joy? She wasn't sure.

She followed the neat gravel path, and, panting, she dragged herself up a couple of pristinely white swept steps. The door was no longer red and cheerful, as it had been before, but black; the brass lion with the ring in its mouth was still there, seemingly beckoning her today just as it used to back then.

Agnes touched the lion's nose tentatively and gently, like greeting an old friend, then she knocked and listened to the house, a house she hadn't been in for many decades.

Knocked again.

She gulped. Her determination had secretly deserted her. She would have gladly run away, but as things stood, she probably wouldn't have even made it down the marble steps before someone opened the door.

So, she placed her walking stick in front of her and waited. The ghost of Mildred Puck answered the door.

Agnes had been prepared for the sight, but despite that it was a shock: the same face, tired and furrowed, but still with a hint of its former beauty. The same hair, chin-length, jet black and shiny. Not real any more, yet somehow . . . The same dark eyes, like deep, deep wells. But the face didn't have any of Mildred's spite. It was soft, almost dreamy.

And shocked.

A ghost's face.

'Agnes!' Almost imperceptibly.

Mildred's ghost wrung her hands.

'Hello, Isobel,' Agnes said quietly. 'May I come in?'

Isobel looked back into the hall as if to ask someone's permission.

'I . . .'

'Thank you.' Agnes didn't wait for long. She pushed past Isobel, always following her walking stick.

The grand hall. To the left the library, next to it the drawing room, straight ahead led to the hunting room. Just as it had been. Everything, everything, everything. The colours, the light, even the velvet-padded silence. A time machine. Agnes could feel her pigtails again.

She looked back at Isobel, still standing incredulously at the door, and – mightily late – remembered her manners.

'What a shock!' she said. 'I am so sorry. I just wanted to offer my condolences. I . . . I was wondering how you've been getting on?'

A strange expression suddenly crossed Isobel's face, not exactly hostile, but not friendly either, and far, far away. She seemed to be listening for something.

'Are you on your own in the house?' Agnes asked. 'Do you need any help?'

She leant on a little table. The same hall. The same glittering chandeliers. Fragmented sunlight. The same smell of leather, wood and dusty roses. She suddenly regretted having marched off without breakfast. She felt weak and a bit flustered. Stars flashed in front of her eyes. The hall seemed to be spinning.

Perhaps not such a good idea to hand oneself over to a murderer in such a dizzy state. Or at least half a murderer. If you believed the rumours. Obviously, Agnes didn't have much time for rumours. And yet . . .

'Help? Oh, I have help.' Isobel gasped. She rang a little silver bell, and a maid appeared, complete with white apron and bonnet. Who knew that things like that still even existed!

'Tea in the drawing room?' she asked, still with a strangely distant expression on her face, and opened the corresponding door.

Agnes wobbled gratefully through it. She was suddenly happy not to be alone in the big house with Isobel. Did she really still know her, even a little bit? Isobel had always been the more approachable of the twin sisters. Softer, more warm-hearted, but sadly also a bit fragile. A sandwich short, most thought. And then she and Mildred had locked themselves away in this house for decades. Because of the rumours going around. The years could really change a person. Especially from the inside. Just because she looked partway like Isobel from the outside, it wasn't guaranteed that the same Isobel was still in there.

'Tea would be wonderful.' Agnes admitted.

Isobel showed her to a suite of chairs. It was only now Agnes noticed how difficult Isobel was finding walking. Wasn't there something, a story about a hip operation, where something went wrong? Although hardly anybody dared to set foot in the big house, the rumour mill in the village was astonishingly well informed. The servants, Agnes presumed.

'How lovely that you came . . .' Isobel sunk into a chair and sighed with relief.

Agnes sat down too. 'A bit late . . .' she mumbled.

'A bit late,' Isobel agreed. 'But still . . .'

The maid brought tea, and she fell silent.

Agnes watched hungrily as milk and golden tea danced in wafer-thin porcelain cups. The accompanying biscuits looked good too. Moist and chocolatey. A million miles from Edwina's rock-hard creations.

Isobel laid a napkin across her lap and smoothed it with her fingers. Wrinkled fingers. Immaculately manicured. Smoothed and smoothed.

Agnes took a biscuit, dunked it in her tea until it was soft enough for her false teeth, bit into it and chewed. Isobel wouldn't poison her! Not straight away anyway.

Isobel seemed to relax too. She let go of her napkin and even had a sip of tea.

Agnes had been ready for many things, but not for the familiarity that joined them at the table after a few silent moments, like a third, long-awaited guest.

'Delicious!' Agnes said after a while of peaceful chewing and sipping.

Isobel smiled. 'Better than anything your Sylvie manages, I assume?'

Agnes was surprised. Isobel knew an astonishing amount about Sunset Hall.

'About back then . . .' Agnes had decided to take the bull by the horns, but Isobel put her off with a wave of her hand.

'Yesterday's news. The day before yesterday's. I can understand why you . . . You wanted a *life*. And we were stuck here.' She broke off. 'Let's talk about something more cheerful: Mildred!'

'Mildred?' Agnes was shocked.

Isobel bent right over the table towards her.

'She's not even dead!' she whispered, her eyes sparkling.

Agnes blinked. Blinked back memories, maybe tears too.

'Oh, no, Isobel!' She gasped. 'This time she really is!'

Edwina rushed along beneath the trees barefoot. Firs perhaps. Or spruce. Once she would have known exactly. Once she had been on first name terms with all of the trees. She touched one of the trunks. 'Ernesto,' she mumbled and carried on along the row of trees. 'Fred. Tasha. Martin McCaw. Frankie the Knife.' She attempted a curtsey, then went back to her mission.

Lillith had instructed her to keep an eye on Agnes. But which eye? Edwina closed the left, then the right. Not an easy decision.

Finally, she chose the right eye and carried on.

She had gone to the Pucks'. The Pucks' of all places! With one eye, Edwina looked over to the big white house sceptically. Nobody went to the Pucks' voluntarily. A woman with two heads. Two women, who looked like one. And one of them had apparently done away with the uncle. With poison. Or a dagger. Or both. It was a long time ago, and the reports contradicted one another, and without doubt they had been royally embellished over sherry and tea and canapés and lemon drizzle cake. But they all agreed on one point: the two of them only got away with the dark deed because it couldn't be established which one of them had committed the murder.

Edwina ducked to get through ferns and bushes. Rhodo-thingys. She crept closer, circled the house, cautiously peeped through the windows. Lots of windows. They had beautiful things, the Puck sisters, you had to give them that. Vases with blue dragons on them. Velvet-covered sofas in spice tones. Naked women in marble and bronze.

And then she finally discovered Agnes, small and somehow helpless-looking between two printed cushions, a biscuit in her hand, her lipstick a bit smudged. Edwina was jealous. She wanted lipstick too. Tomorrow she would creep into Agnes's room and try out the lipstick. Tomorrow or maybe even today.

She watched Agnes dunk the biscuit into her cup and then bite off a fair chunk of it. That was strange. At home she always claimed not to like biscuits, but here, where they might be laced with poison . . .

Poison and dagger.

Edwina shuddered. Both methods were amateurish in her opinion.

Only now did she notice the thin dark figure sitting opposite Agnes, back to the window. Black hair to her chin.

That must be the remaining Puck sister.

She couldn't see her facial expression, but she could see Agnes suddenly stop chewing, leave her biscuit and her eyes getting wider and wider.

Edwina sailed happily past the window, back to the trees.

Agnes at the Pucks'.

Biscuits with poisoners.

Wide eyes.

It was just the sort of thing Lillith would have been interested in.

She had set off with slippers and walking stick, and with slippers, walking stick and a limousine Agnes returned. After the tea Isobel had rung her little bell again and after a quick, bony hug, had her bundled into a car, gently but decisively, by a maid and a sturdy-looking chauffeur.

Agnes didn't know whether she should be offended or relieved. Of course, she would have made it back on her own. Of course she would.

No question.

However, the limousine was comfortable.

As the car purred along the narrow road, for a second Agnes thought she saw Edwina amongst the trees.

Edwina, with one eye shut.

Agnes had expected a big entrance. Her in slippers and lipstick.

In a limousine.

In the Pucks' limousine.

They should all have been looking out of the windows, wide-eyed and a bit envious, Winston on the first floor, the rest in the sitting room. Someone, maybe Marshall, could have taken a few steps towards her out of curiosity, someone else could have explained to Bernadette what a spectacle was to be seen on their drive.

But nobody was there, not even Hettie the tortoise.

A few scraps of hornet tape drifted lost in the wind, and the first withered leaves crinkled on the veranda.

Agnes looked up at the house, then down at her slippers, which looked wet and misshapen. Something wasn't right.

With the help of walking stick and chauffeur, she made it to the front door, and then the car had already purred off again, like a particularly vivid hallucination.

In a bad mood, Agnes opened the door and slipped out of her beaten-up slippers.

Everything hurt, and the high-pitched ringing was back.

56

She wanted to call out, but what was the point if she couldn't hear the response?

She looked into the sitting room: empty.

In the hall she came across a young man in overalls, getting to work on the stairlift. He said something and Agnes nodded favourably.

'Very good!' she mumbled.

It didn't seem to be the right response as the overalls-wearer quizzically scratched his chin, where some sparse stubble was fighting through, and went back to his work shrugging his shoulders.

Agnes padded on to the kitchen. Like a morgue. Half-eaten toast on plates and three coffee cups in various stages of being drunk. Half-drunk. Whatever. In any case it was strictly against the house rules to just leave the dishes like that. Charlie had to be behind it. She had probably used Agnes's absence to take the whole crew out for breakfast. To the Indian or the French place, or wherever it is you have breakfast these days. But that couldn't be right either. At least Edwina hadn't gone with them, she was in the woods with one eye shut.

Without much hope, Agnes dragged herself to the dining room. The dining room, when it was used, was only for mealtimes, and definitely not before midday. Agnes pushed down the door handle, and the high-pitched ringing played its own merry tune.

There they all were sitting in front of her, silent as a painting, Bernadette to the left, Charlie and Marshall to the right. Brexit was asleep under the table, Hettie the tortoise had manoeuvred herself into a corner and was fruitlessly scratching at the skirting board.

A podgy middle-aged woman was sitting in the middle cleaning her glasses.

'Oh!' Agnes said, in a not particularly ladylike way. She felt like an intruder – in her own house!

The woman in the middle let go of her glasses, stood up and offered Agnes her hand. Her lips were mouthing inaudible words. For a moment, Agnes stared cluelessly at her hand, then she shook it. Her walking stick fell to the floor without a sound, and the crash woke Brexit. Charlie pulled up a chair for her. Agnes sat down gratefully and watched the woman with the glasses and her housemates talking.

It seemed to be somewhat emotional. Bernadette was wringing her hands. Marshall stayed very still, always a bad sign, and Charlie had her arms folded. The podgy woman was speaking emphatically and even accusingly stuck her finger in the air every now and again.

For the time being Agnes couldn't make rhyme nor reason of the whole thing. Was she a plain-clothed policewoman asking awkward questions? Or was it because someone had tipped the general rubbish into the recycling bin again? But the woman . . .

Agnes recognised her and didn't recognise her at the same time. There was something familiar about her, maybe the way she sometimes put her hand to her temple when she was talking, maybe the way her nostrils flared. She had lively nostrils that didn't really seem to match the rest of her face.

And then it came to her: Lillith! Lillith had had the same lively nostrils, the day before yesterday. That could mean only one thing: Lillith's daughter had turned up – and she was asking some very awkward questions.

This time Agnes was almost happy about the high-pitched ringing. At least she didn't have to hear all the accusations that were presumably raining down on her housemates. Shot in the garden shed! Something like that would never have happened in a proper home. Next to nothing happens in proper homes, and if this crazy idea hadn't . . .

Agnes followed the pattern of the tablecloth with her finger, diamonds and crosses, crosses and diamonds.

It was almost entertaining.

'I'm sorry that my mother's death is boring you.'

Agnes started. The high-pitched ringing was gone, and she – had she fallen asleep? At the dining table? With Lillith's daughter there? Impossible! And yet her head felt woozy and like cotton wool, and she couldn't really remember what had just happened.

She pulled herself together. She was the lady of the house after all.

'Lillith's death has affected us all very deeply,' she said, emphatically she hoped. 'The house won't be the same any more.' Only as she was saying it did she realise it was true. Something had changed. Something decisive. Forever. 'If you have the impression that we don't care, then you're wrong.'

She wanted to get up from the table with gravitas, but something went wrong, she lost her balance and plopped back on her chair. 'Maybe now you'd like to get your mother's—'

Lillith's plump daughter cut her off with a wave of her hand and suddenly didn't look so clumsy and middle-aged; she almost looked a bit dangerous.

'I don't want to collect anything,' she said quietly. 'I want to leave something here. A promise.'

Agnes watched as her housemates cast surprised glances at one another. Brexit, who seemed to have an antenna sensitive to changes in mood, stuck his head under Charlie's chair.

Silence.

The daughter waited. And waited.

'What's that?' Agnes finally asked, although she actually didn't want to hear the promise in the slightest. She had an uneasy feeling.

The daughter folded her hands and looked at the table, as if there were an invisible script she could read.

'As a child I always told everyone my mother was a mermaid. One of those selkies. She falls in love with a fisherman, and when the man steals her fish skin, she has to stay with him, on two legs. Then she has to do his laundry and bring up his children. But she never stops yearning for the sea. And that's how it was. Mum never stopped yearning for something. She was never truly present. Always away with her thoughts. At work, perhaps, although apparently, she was only a fertiliser rep. I never believed that. I still don't. It doesn't even matter now.'

Agnes and Marshall exchanged looks. Lillith hadn't sold fertiliser – her daughter was quite right.

'Then she was pensioned off, and I thought, now all the secrecy is over. And suddenly she wanted to come *here*. Supposedly so as not to be a burden to me, but I don't buy that.'

A tear struggled over the daughter's cheek. What was she called again? Agnes could vaguely remember a name . . . Pippa? Lillith had had a great deal to say about her – and definitely not all good. Pippa started to maul her glasses again. Without her glasses her eyes looked younger, watery and pale, as if she really were the child of a mermaid. And hurt. And absolutely furious.

'There's a reason Mum wanted to come here,' she said, putting her glasses back on. 'A reason she obviously didn't tell me, yet again. A kind of secret. And it wouldn't surprise me if that's the reason she was shot in that shed!'

Silence lay over the table, like a depression. Pippa had hit the nail on the head. But she wasn't finished yet.

'And this time I will get to the bottom of it! I'm so fed up with all the secrecy. Either somebody tells me what's going on here, right now . . .'

Nobody said anything. Obviously. What could they say?

'I thought as much!' The daughter laughed mirthlessly, but also somehow triumphantly. 'It doesn't matter! I will find out what's going on here, even if I have to turn over every stone in this bloody house.'

With that she got up, much more dramatically and successfully than Agnes, and swept to the door. On the way she came across Hettie, who had abandoned the skirting board and was crawling towards new adventures. For a minute it looked as though Lillith's daughter wanted to stand on the tortoise, but then she just picked her up, turned her over and placed her in front of Agnes on the table shell down, feet up.

The door slammed shut, and Hettie's gnarled legs flailed helplessly in the air. How someone as splendid as Lillith came to have a daughter like that, was a mystery to them all.

4

LETTUCE

'I don't know why she's so het up,' said Charlie. 'In the shed, surrounded by her seedlings. Bish-bash-bosh. I know people who would give their eye teeth for a lovely death like that!'

'She knows nothing,' Bernadette said. 'What could she know?' Bernadette was maybe sometimes a little emotional and too fixated on fondant creams, but amidst all the drama had a razor-sharp mind ready to spring into action.

'Nobody knows nothing at all!' Edwina had returned with leaves and burrs in her hair, and both eyes were in use again.

'We can put Lillith's things in the loft.' Marshall interjected. To his mind, there was hardly any problem that couldn't be solved with the help of the loft. The suggestion met with general agreement. Even Hettie hissed approvingly. She'd had her feet firmly back on solid ground for a while now, and Edwina and Charlie were spoiling her with lettuce.

Then it was quiet for a while, they were all lost in their own thoughts, up in the loft, back in a home, where people yearned for a nice death, or over at the Pucks' house, where Mildred's ghost might be getting served a light lunch.

All that could be heard was the tortoise's leathery chomping and chewing.

'We should plant Lillith's seedlings,' Edwina said at some point.

They looked at one another, all except Bernadette, and she nodded in approval.

That was it! Planting seedlings was just what they needed right now.

The garden shed looked exactly as they remembered – and then again it didn't. The garden tools were resting against the wall as usual, and in the meantime the tape had by and large disappeared thanks to Brexit. On the big table at the window, rows of young plants stretched hopefully towards the light. It smelt like earth – but not just that. On the floor planks you could still make out a white chalk outline – and an unpleasant brown stain. But the biggest difference was what *wasn't* there: Lillith, with dirt on her hands and in her hair, her rattling asthmatic breaths and her lively nostrils. The shed had been her domain, and now, overnight, it had transformed into a no man's land.

Marshall sighed. 'She's not coming back, is she?'

They all knew what he meant. Finding Lillith shot dead in the garden shed was one thing, the silence afterwards something else – and it was harder to bear.

They silently busied themselves watering the seedlings and allocating them good positions in the garden. Lillith would have done it better, but they were trying. Marshall dug, Bernadette carefully loosened the seedlings from their pots, Agnes watered, Charlie planted, Winston looked on favourably, and Edwina sang the plants a sun song.

Then it was done. The sun shone cheerfully on the band of ambitious young plants – anemone, buddleia, toad lily, black elderberry – and they felt better. Lighter. As if Lillith had sent them a postcard from the other side. 'Arrived safely. Wonderful weather. The food is fantastic!'

As they made their way back to the house in high spirits, singing and chattering, dirt on their hands and spades over their shoulders, a policeman was suddenly standing in front of them. 'Whoa there!' It was the same kind policeman that had warned them about the burglar yesterday. But now he didn't look so kind, more stressed. He was holding one of the scraps of hornet tape in his hand.

They fell silent and stood there, caught red-handed. Marshall put down the spade, Edwina folded her dirty hands behind her back. Was digging in the garden suspicious? If the radio and papers were to be believed, criminals spent an inordinate amount of their time gardening, in order to make body parts, drugs or murder victims disappear – or murder weapons . . .

'Hello,' said the policeman eyeing the spade. 'Sorry to disturb you.'

'Not at all,' Agnes responded. 'We've just finished.' She offered the policeman her hand and noticed too late that it was dirty and muddy, with black lines under her fingernails and a damp, earthy smell.

'Err.' The policeman looked down at her hand doubtingly, then back at the spade. 'As I said yesterday, we have to interview each of you individually, to gather as much information as possible. Obviously, we can do it at the station, but since some of you aren't very mobile, we thought it would be better . . .'

'Why would we want to be mobiles?' Edwina protested. The policeman wasn't deterred.

'I'm Sergeant Tom Wink, my colleague Inspector Locke is waiting at the front door, and it would really help us if we could start straight away. I am sure you all want to help us get to the bottom of your friend's murder as quickly as possible. And one more thing: we don't use this stuff just for a laugh.' He held the scrap of hornet tape towards Edwina. 'If we tape off an area, we don't do it for decoration.'

'Clearly,' Marshall mumbled.

'If we tape something off, we expect it to remain taped off.'

'It's Brexit's fault!' Agnes explained nervously.

The policeman groaned.

'Could we have red tape next time?' Edwina asked, willing to compromise. 'Or maybe pink? It would go better with the hydrangeas.'

'No!' snorted Sergeant Wink and led them towards the front door.

Inspector Locke was waiting at the door, as threatened, smiling beneath her surprisingly short cropped hair, and shook each of their hands. Her eyes were not smiling.

Then everything went bish-bash-bosh, as Charlie would have said.

The door swung open and Hettie hissed towards them grumpily, but was forcibly removed to the sitting room by the police. Charlie claimed she had to take her pills, and was brought a glass of water. Then they sat in the sitting room like a bunch of chickens and acted like them too. All aflutter. A bit headless. Even Bernadette, who actually should have had the most experience with situations like this, was on tenterhooks.

Edwina was playing I-spy-with-my-little-eye.

Agnes wanted her knitting stuff, but couldn't summon the energy to drag herself to the stairlift. And wouldn't it look suspicious if she made off upstairs? She thought about all of the places they had looked for the gun yesterday, and – with a dull feeling in her stomach – the places they hadn't looked. Dozens of hiding spots suddenly came to her, all as if they were made to house a gun.

Charlie drummed her fingers on the back of the chair. Agnes noticed with a certain feeling of satisfaction that her well-groomed exterior didn't appear quite as glamorous as it had that morning. A bit rumpled, more like. A bit frazzled.

Bernadette was the first to be led off to the dining room for questioning and appeared back in the hall again surprisingly quickly. Hadn't seen anything. How could she have? Bernadette knew exactly how to deflect awkward questions quickly and convincingly. Instead of sitting back with them, she briefly straightened her sunglasses, then floated upstairs on the stairlift.

Charlie was next up, then Marshall.

Marshall's interview took a small eternity, and Agnes got hungry again.

'I spy with my little eye,' said Edwina, 'something that is green!'

'Hettie,' said Agnes, bored. If Edwina said something green, it was *always* Hettie, although to Agnes the tortoise actually looked more brown and yellow-ish.

'Correct!' Edwina looked at her with respect. 'I spy with my little eye something that is . . .'

Little wonder that Bernadette had disappeared straight after the interview. I-spy wasn't exactly her favourite game. Or had she been forbidden from going back into the sitting room? So they couldn't get their stories straight? *Should* they have got their stories straight? Agnes tried to imagine what was unfolding over in the dining room, and didn't manage it.

'Red!' said Edwina, presumably not for the first time. 'Red, red, red!'

Agnes opened her eyes wide. 'The lamp? Winston's blanket? The vase?'

Had they looked in that vase yesterday?

'No,' Edwina cried triumphantly. 'No, no, no!'

'Not fair,' Winston mumbled, and suddenly Agnes knew what it was.

'My lipstick!' she said proudly.

Edwina pouted, then she was ushered through to the interview room by Inspector Locke. Interview room. It had barely been an hour, and in Agnes's imagination, her cosy dining room had already transformed into a sort of torture chamber, the curtains shut and a single lamp standing on the table, dazzling them and turning the police officers into silhouettes.

Agnes shuddered.

'Awkward situation, huh?' Winston said next to her. 'At least the stairlift's working again!'

As Agnes sighed, Winston reached out to pat her hand. She sighed for a second time. Patting was not going to help either. She wanted to pull her hand away, but then she saw Winston's face. He looked somehow unfamiliar, sad and for the first time, not dignified. Just old and exhausted.

Agnes closed her eyes and let Winston do as he liked. Maybe these things also worked the other way round, and Winston could pat himself better. Maybe anything could be patted better, even Brexit. Maybe . . .

'Asleep!' said a voice over her. A short-haired voice. Agnes recognised the inspector, but didn't open her eyes. If she just pretended to still be asleep, maybe they would leave her in peace. 'My God, is it tough,' groaned another voice. Sergeant Wink.

'You'd get better witness statements in a kindergarten.' Agnes felt a hand being carefully placed on her shoulder.

'Mrs Sharp. Mrs Sharp, are you ready?' Agnes held firm. She felt like Hettie the tortoise. Sleep was her shell, and as long as it was over her, nobody could touch her. And the hand really did let go of her.

'I mean, it's not a no man's land here,' Wink moaned. 'Someone marches into two gardens in broad daylight and shoots two old ladies – and nobody sees or hears a thing?'

'Half of the folks here can probably see and hear next to nothing anyway,' Locke mumbled. 'I had expected more from the staff over there. Or from the weird sister.'

'She's one of these dinosaurs as well,' Wink said disparagingly.

'Under different circumstances she would be one of the first we would be interested in, but in this case . . . the poor old thing can barely walk. I can hardly imagine her running through the woods with a gun! The recoil alone . . .' He laughed, somewhere between sympathy and scorn.

'Apart from that, she's in pieces,' his colleague added. 'The last living relative, Poor thing! And the staff aren't much help either. Very tight-lipped. Probably worried about their jobs. Can't blame them. But Sunset Hall takes the biscuit. None of them remembers even the most basic of things. Where they were. What they were doing. When they last saw the victim. And when you ask again, they go on about garden plants and tortoises.'

'They're just old folks,' said Wink. 'They can't see straight. Helpless. It's a miracle nothing happened sooner.'

Agnes screwed up her eyes, depressed. They were approaching it the wrong way round. The mystery wasn't Lillith! The mystery was Mildred Puck!

Suddenly a mobile rang above her head, and the inspector picked up.

She said 'yes' and 'okay' a few times, and then once 'oh!' and 'good grief' and 'that really helps us,' thanked the person and hung up.

Silence.

Agnes's ears pricked up. Something was happening in the silence above her. Something that couldn't be heard.

'We have new information about the weapon,' the inspector finally said. 'A pistol from the Second World War. Real collectors' piece apparently.'

'What?' shouted Wink. 'But that . . .'

His boss interrupted him. 'Gives the whole thing a different slant, doesn't it? I mean, what sort of burglar runs about the place with an antique pistol? Seems personal to me. And local. Maybe it wasn't a random attack – maybe it was something completely different!'

'Are we sure the same murder weapon was used in both crimes?'

'According to Paul there is absolutely no doubt about it,' Locke said contentedly.

Agnes felt as though the chair had suddenly been pulled out from beneath her – not just the chair, but also the rug, the floorboards, and even the ground. The same murder weapon? That was completely impossible! It couldn't . . . or could it? What did it mean if it really was the same gun? The police seemed pretty certain. Agnes tried to think logically, but no thoughts came. Who would . . . ? Was it possible that Marshall . . . ?

She must have made a noise, as the police hand suddenly appeared on her shoulder again.

'Ah, Miss Sharp. You're awake! Very good!'

Agnes squinted and looked up at two very happy police officers. Two police officers, who were suddenly onto something.

The dining room appeared far less scary than Agnes had pictured it. The police really had closed the curtains and switched on a few lamps, but it made the room snug rather than sombre. She was proud of Sunset Hall.

Locke pointed to a chair, and Agnes sat down with a groan. Her body had had enough of all the backwards and forwards, and wasn't playing ball any more. Her head was spinning. *The same murder weapon. The same murder weapon.* It couldn't be!

There was a suspicious little box on the table.

'A recording device,' Wink explained and pressed a button. 'With your permission we would like to record our conversation.'

Of course! It just surprised Agnes how small the device was. In her day . . .

'How long had you known Mrs Lillith Wright?' Locke asked.

Agnes squinted. Thought about it. 'Four years,' she said unsure. Was it really only four? It seemed like more.

'And how did you meet?'

'Femoral neck fracture,' Agnes explained. That didn't seem to satisfy Wink and Locke as an explanation, so Agnes extrapolated.

'We were both in rehabilitation after fracturing our femurs, we were bored, and we started talking. Mainly about plants and gardening – but also about . . . well, life. It turned out we had a few things in common. Or things we didn't have. Far too little company. Far too big houses. Lillith had a daughter, but she got on her nerves. Just because a few things don't work any more doesn't mean you want to be treated like a small child, you know?'

The police officers looked at her sceptically, so Agnes carried on.

'And, well, we decided to move in together. To help one another. To have a bit of fun!' Obviously, it wasn't the whole truth, but Agnes had decided that the whole truth was none of the police's business.

'And then you both moved in here?'

'Not just us two,' said Agnes. 'We looked for other housemates as well. First was Marshall. Then Edwina. A bit

71

later, Winston. Then Bernadette. And now Charlie. It's a big house. But it was our idea, mine and Lillith's!'

'And did Winston and err . . . Marshall fracture their femurs as well?'

'Oh, no,' cried Agnes. 'It was Marshall's hip, as far as I know, and Winston was recovering from a stroke. But we were all fed up with being looked after, patronised and pushed around. So, we just went for it.' She smiled. 'Sparks flew to start with!'

'Really?' Wink leant forward curiously.

'Well, someone buys tinned sausages, and everyone else hates tinned sausages. Someone dries their socks on the sofa. Or keeps their dentures in a glass on the kitchen table. Or walks straight through the house in muddy shoes . . .'

Wink signalled for her to stop.

'The thing with the muddy shoes was Lillith,' Agnes admitted. 'But we got her out of it. It's not a reason to kill someone.'

'Of course not,' Locke reassured her.

Agnes held her tongue. Had she said too much?

'How do things stand financially?'

Agnes looked at them blankly.

'Well, Mildred Puck was obviously very well-off, so we did wonder if there was a connection there?'

'To Mildred?' Agnes frowned. 'We all have our pensions. And most of us had our own house or a flat before. But what happened to it . . . We have a pot for housekeeping and one for emergencies, and then everyone has their own . . .' She realised she was flailing her arms about unnecessarily.

'Did Lillith ever mention arguments over her house? With her daughter perhaps?'

Agnes almost smirked. Podgy Pippa was under suspicion! She caught herself just in time and just shrugged her shoulders.

'Would you say that Lillith had any enemies? In the village maybe? Or from her past?'

Agnes shook her head, but that didn't seem enough for the police.

'Obviously everyone in Duck End thinks there's something wrong with us, just because we've given human company another shot . . . They'd rather rot away on their own. Petty-minded. So, we're not very popular, but enemies . . . ?'

'Could that perhaps be because you threaten visitors with a shotgun?' Locke asked softly.

They already knew about that then! 'It wasn't even loaded,' Agnes said wearily. 'And I didn't make a threat. I just . . . pointed. For them to take a running jump.'

The social worker's face! Agnes had to stifle a smile.

'And Mildred? Did she have enemies?'

'Oh, Mildred had lots of enemies. Mildred *collected* enemies. Like . . . like stamps. Before, I mean, when she was still . . . with it. But now . . .'

'Did you know each other well?'

'More like for a long time. We went to school together, and then we . . . lost sight of one another.' Not really out of sight. More like out of mind.

'Did you never visit when she had the stroke? And what about her sister, Isobel?'

Agnes shook her head again, part defiance, part shame. 'Nobody visited.'

'Why?'

73

Agnes thought about it. Did the police know about the thing with the uncle? It was the kind of story nobody forgot, the kind that was told from one generation to the next, accompanied by a crackling fire and languorous horror. But it was also a long, long time ago. And she didn't want to unnecessarily denigrate Isobel. 'Mildred was a very argumentative person. Clever, subversive, dogmatic. A true snob. And Isobel is very . . . eccentric. Why would you put yourself through that?'

'Is there a connection between your friend Lillith and Mildred Puck? Did they know each other perhaps?'

The questions were coming thick and fast now and Agnes's head was spinning. Had they known each other? Lillith could easily have trudged over to the grounds of the Pucks' in her dirty shoes any time, to have a look at the impressive rhododendron collection. But this wasn't about that. *The mystery is Mildred, not Lillith. And the murder weapon. The same murder weapon.*

That is the mystery.

Locke asked something else again, but Agnes wasn't listening any more.

'I'm hungry,' she said. All she had eaten that day was Isobel's exquisite biscuits. And then all the thinking and listening and planting and walking about . . .

Wink stood up. 'I'll get you something.'

Good cop, bad cop. Classic!

Whilst Wink strolled into the kitchen, Locke suddenly leant forward and looked at her intensely. 'Do you know anybody who is in possession of a revolver from the Second World War?'

Agnes shook her head truthfully. She had no idea where the revolver was right now.

Then Wink was back and, with a smile on his face, he placed a plate of Edwina's biscuits in front of her on the table. More like *bad cop, bad cop*, then!

Agnes clenched her false teeth. It was about time she got out of there. She wobbled back and forth on her chair a little and fell head-first onto the table.

'I really don't know what you were thinking!'

Marshall's face hovered over her, his bushy grey eyebrows frowning morosely. Father Christmas eyebrows. Agnes grinned.

'What are you grinning about?' Marshall spat.

Agnes stopped grinning and turned her head to get her bearings, first to the left, then the right. She was lying on a sofa again, this time in her own room. With the help of the newly repaired stairlift, they had managed to get her upstairs, and although Agnes had only pretended to faint this time, she couldn't remember a single thing about the journey. Who was there? Marshall . . . and who else?

'Have they gone?' she asked. Marshall nodded.

'There we go. I just wanted . . .'

Agnes was fed up of lying on her back like a beetle. She tried to pull herself up, but slid on the upholstery and sank back into the cushions. Where were the others? Something was unsettling her. Something had gone through her whole body like an electric shock. She felt it deep inside: a shaking. A trembling. Something had changed. Something crucial.

Lillith. Mildred. The gun. Marshall. Marshall. Lillith. The gun. Mildred?

Agnes tried to get the words in the right order: Lillith. The gun. Marshall. Mildred.

That was it! *The same murder weapon!* That was what the police had said. And Agnes knew where she had last seen that gun: after Lillith's death, as they had all stood there as if struck by lightning and Marshall, the gun in his hands, had disappeared unsteadily between the hydrangeas.

He could easily have just walked out of the garden, over to the Pucks', the same way Agnes had gone that morning in her slippers. Marshall was good on his feet after his hip op. Nothing for him to tear through amongst the pines and rhododendrons. Nothing to put the gun to Mildred's sleeping head and . . . But no, not to her head. It wasn't a quick death, the police had as good as admitted that yesterday.

Where to, then? Agnes couldn't imagine. And anyway, the rest of the scenario wasn't right either. Marshall a murderer? What did he have against Mildred? He hadn't even met Mildred! Had he mistaken her for somebody else? For who? Nothing made sense.

Agnes realised her hand was still searching for a hold in the upholstery and that someone was calling her name.

'Agnes, Agnes, calm down. This is exactly what I mean! You're there and then you're not there again. It's one thing to put the wind up the police, but we're – we're worried, Agnes.'

Marshall didn't seem annoyed any more, but genuinely concerned.

And that was exactly what didn't make sense about the

whole thing, Marshall was her housemate, her ally in respect of online shopping and loo roll, maybe even her friend. She didn't want to suspect him. She *couldn't*.

What now? Agnes reached out her hand towards Marshall and let him help her up. Should she let him in on it – should she let all of her housemates in on it and tell them what the police had said on the topic of the murder weapon? Perhaps someone else would have a brainwave for a change? Unlikely, but not impossible.

But something stopped her. Like an instinct. Many years ago, high up in an apple tree, Agnes had learnt to trust her instincts, so now she plumped for a middle ground.

She patted the space next to her on the sofa, and after some hesitation, Marshall sat down, so warily that Agnes nearly laughed out loud.

'Relax, Marsh. I'm fine.' Apart from my hip, feet and shins, fingers, momentary dizziness and obviously the high-pitched ringing in my ears. 'I'm fine,' she repeated. 'It's *you* I'm worried about!'

'Me?' From the look on his face Agnes could tell Marshall was worried too. She went on.

'It's one thing to forget things from time to time. We all forget things. Of course. But the thing with the gun is important. We have got to find out what's happened to it. You *must* remember something!'

Marshall looked as if he was scared, and suddenly Agnes was frightened too. Marshall was never scared – that was so irrefutably certain, it could have been written into the house rules:

20. *Please do not put half-eaten items of food back into the fridge!*
21. *Used cups belong in the dishwasher!*
22. *Marshall never gets scared!*

But now he was scared, and Agnes suddenly had an awful empty feeling in the pit of her stomach. She stuck to her guns regardless, looking at Marshall questioningly, until he grabbed her hand, then let go again and finally said something.

'I'm sorry, Agnes. I *want* to remember, really, I do. It's just . . . things disappear. Words, faces. One moment they're there and the next . . .' His hand clutched at thin air. 'But I know they're missing and that drives me mad. Lillith was lying here' – he pointed at the floor – 'and the gun was in my hand, like a lead weight, although it's actually quite a lightweight gun. I remember very clearly. I could *draw* it. And then: nothing. Fog. Terrible, thick white fog. And then I'm sitting in the sitting room as if nothing had happened. Feeling good. Buoyed. Even allowed myself a little practical joke . . .' He grinned.

'Aha,' said Agnes. She should have known! Hettie as teeth transport was something that only Marshall could have dreamt up.

'And then I heard Bernadette snivelling and it came back to me. But not everything. You're asking what I remember, and the only word that I can think of is 'umbrella.' But at the same time, I know it's not really about the umbrella. It's driving me mad!' He stood up and ran his fingers through his hair. 'Perhaps . . . perhaps it's my time soon too.'

Agnes wanted to say 'of course not,' but Marshall had already stormed out of the room, and she was alone with the image looking back at her from the mirror on the wardrobe: pale, a bit rumpled, but on the whole still elegant. Her lipstick had disappeared, obviously. Instead, resplendent in the middle of her forehead was the imprint of one of Edwina's biscuits, round, red and unmistakable.

5

PEACHES AND SHERRY

Over the next few days Lillith's belongings moved up to the loft shoebox by shoebox, a little caravan of things that were no longer needed. Books (mainly about gardening); folders of papers; small, twee porcelain figures; a photo of her daughter, not yet as podgy; a surprising number of shoes, knickers and lace hankies. Agnes and Charlie gathered the things, Winston packed them masterfully, Edwina hauled them triumphantly along the hall, and Marshall carried them up the ladder into the loft.

Outside, autumn was moving in like a tempestuous and not particularly polite guest. Leaves bade adieu to their trees, chased through the garden by Brexit in wild pursuit. Birds ruffled their feathers, squirrels planned their hiding places, fat bumblebees harvested the final nectar of the fading summer in their little fur coats. Every day a rustling, crackling grave of colourful leaves gathered at the front door asking to be swept away. In the mornings the windows were fogged up, and you could see frost on the hydrangeas and, if you ventured outside too early, your own breath. In the evenings lots of gangly insects strayed into the house in search of light and warmth, and floated through the rooms gesticulating wildly.

They discussed whether they should put the heating on. As usual Bernadette and Winston were in favour, Agnes and Marshall against. Charlie was on the fence.

Three pot plants died, and they discovered that it wasn't only the plants that missed Lillith. The house missed her too. The post that came in the morning remained in an untidy heap, nobody plumped the cushions in the sitting room or organised the cutlery in the dishwasher. The fruit yoghurt in the fridge went off because nobody other than Lillith dared eat it. Conversations turned to squabbles more quickly than usual, Hettie scratched at closed doors more often than normal.

It was as if they were getting to know Lillith again, a different, quiet, industrious, harmonious Lillith. A Lillith they really could do with right now.

It was quiet outside.

They didn't hear anything from the police for days and nothing from the podgy daughter either. For someone who intended to leave no stone unturned, she wasn't particularly active.

That should have reassured them, but it didn't. They were hearing *too* little.

Sylvie came and cooked and cleaned, much more efficiently than usual, and hardly said a word to them. You could tell she didn't want to be there, that she wanted to go home as quickly as possible, to the village, back to the herd, to safety. Her Chelsea buns turned out even more misshapen than normal.

The physiotherapist cancelled the Wednesday appointment until further notice.

Charlie ordered brushes and paint pots and went about painting Agnes's mother's favourite room a rosy coral colour. The rest of the time she mooched about the house in her red kimono moaning about feeling cooped up.

Edwina did headstands and still wanted to go to the Indian restaurant.

Bernadette demolished legions of fondant creams and listened to the world from her window.

The household was hell-bent on keeping the garden in good shape, just as Lillith would have wanted, and spent a lot of time collecting leaves, pruning hedges and cutting back shrubs. Marshall was clearing out the shed, but Agnes knew he was really trying to clear out his memory. He was often still out and about on the garden paths at dusk, looking for the elusive umbrella, the umbrella that it wasn't really about at all.

Agnes watched him from darkened windows, silently gnawing away in vain at the mystery of the common murder weapon like a captive dormouse.

One afternoon they were busy shoving the leaves they had collected into a huge plastic sack – Winston and Charlie were raking the leaves; Agnes, Bernadette and Marshall were scooping; they had stuck Edwina in the sack to stamp the leaves down; the sun was shining; the leaves smelt good; and Edwina was squeaking with pleasure – when Bernadette suddenly stopped feeling for leaves and raised her head. Her dark sunglasses reflected the cloudless sky.

'Someone's coming.'

Now they all listened. Nothing. Or almost nothing.

Bernadette did not mishear things, and Brexit, who up until then had been watching them collect leaves like a gracious lord of the manor, jumped up and ran towards the garden fence.

Panic broke out. They hadn't seen anybody for days, and now that somebody was finally coming, they were busy with a suspicious gardening activity again. Winston let go of the rake and rolled off, Charlie tucked a few strands of hair behind her ears, pinched her cheeks and rushed after Winston. Agnes grabbed Bernadette's hand, and Marshall helped a protesting Edwina out of the sack.

They instinctively gathered at the front door, to head off the visitor. Agnes clasped her hands. Edwina did cartwheels.

Humming.

Purring.

Brexit barked his deepest bark. Something rolled up the drive. Agnes tried to imagine what it would be like to be bundled into a big police car and arrested.

Then a familiar limousine floated over the white gravel, politely cleared its throat and stopped. A chauffeur got out and opened the door. Mildred's ghost glided out of the car, patted Brexit's head and elegantly limped towards them.

It's a shame there's not a photographer here, Agnes thought. Normally they had difficulty getting a decent group picture. Someone was always blurry, mostly Edwina. But right now, they were all staying wonderfully still.

'Hello,' said Isobel in her melodic, always slightly amused tone. 'I hope I've not come at a bad time?'

'Not at all,' said Charlie. 'We were just tidying up.'

Agnes thought the creepy thing about Isobel was how *normal* she seemed. They shook hands, then Agnes tried to get the whole party into the house away from the prying eyes of the chauffeur. Winston led the way to the dining room, but then he suddenly slammed the dining room door shut and made a bold three-point turn.

'Too cold,' he moaned. 'We'd be better off sitting in the sitting room.' Agnes wanted to protest, but Winston seemed pretty sure of himself, so they sat down in the sitting room like a really polite murder of crows.

'So, this is where you all live,' Isobel said and looked around with curiosity and a kind of longing. Charlie complimented her hair, Marshall twirled his moustache, Edwina introduced Hettie to Isobel. Hettie allowed herself to be tickled under the chin. Then nothing else came to any of them.

'Tea?' asked Agnes. She knew what was proper.

'No tea!' Winston said quickly, went pale, red and then pale again. It was really out of character.

'But . . .' Agnes protested, but Isobel gestured for her not to worry.

'Oh, I spend all day drinking tea. To be honest I'm sick of the stuff.'

'Coffee?' Agnes asked and observed Winston go red again. Isobel shook her head.

'What I would like to say is quickly said. As it is, poor Mildred will have to be buried. This Thursday. I have made all of the arrangements, but I thought it would be nice if a few people came. Real people, not just, you know, staff.

'I know it was a long time ago, but I thought . . .'

Agnes cut in. '*Of course* we'll come, Isobel. No question at all. We'll gladly come.'

She liked funerals, the seriousness and solemnity of the ceremony, but also the fact that at funerals people crept out of their emotional shells, were vulnerable, gave things away about themselves. And if you were lucky the sun shone on the flowers and afterwards there was something interesting to eat. There was nowhere you could feel more alive than at a good funeral.

Isobel sighed. 'That's . . . a relief. On Thursday morning Mildred will be laid out in the chapel, in case anybody would like to say goodbye. I don't really think many people will want to say goodbye, but it was included in the package . . .' She shrugged her shoulders. 'It's obviously all a bit tight, because of Lillith.'

Lillith! Nobody had said anything to them about her funeral, but it made sense, after all their former housemate couldn't be kept in a plastic bag forever. And of course, the bitter, podgy daughter hadn't thought it necessary to invite the household. 'We should say goodbye to Lillith too,' Edwina declared.

They made it their business to squeeze all of the funeral details out of Isobel. Cremated. Close family ceremony. Thursday morning. Lillith wouldn't have liked it because human ashes are really bad for plants, but what could you do?

They promised to fit in both Lillith and Mildred, then they ran out of conversation topics again.

Agnes offered tea again and observed Winston going white and red once more, then she accompanied her former friend to the door.

'Thank you,' said Isobel, and Agnes nodded.

'Poor Mildred!'

'She wasn't easy,' Isobel said, and seemed to be watching Agnes keenly.

Agnes shrugged her shoulders. 'Who is? Was it you that found her? I mean, afterwards . . .'

'Mildred? Oh no, I was having a lie down. Thank God. Maria was hysterical.' Isobel shuddered.

'And did you *see* her? I mean . . .' she said, unsuccessfully searching for delicate words.

Isobel knew exactly what she meant.

'No,' she said quickly. Too quickly. It seemed strange to Agnes. If Maria had come to *her* in hysterics, with the news that *her* sister . . . On the other hand, Isobel had always been a bit squeamish. In fact she had spent nearly her whole life avoiding unpleasant things. Head-in-the-sand tactic.

When Agnes went back into the sitting room, they all looked like they had seen a ghost too. A whole host of ghosts.

'She's not *that* bad,' Agnes said defensively, but Winston didn't seem to hear her at all.

'It's back,' he whispered.

'What is?'

'The gun!'

Obviously with her rebellious hip, Agnes was the last person to set eyes on the gun. As she trudged along the hall, she thought about the strange formulation Winston had used. 'It's back.' Not 'it's been found.'

'The gun's back' – as if it had walked back into the house after a little outing and sat down at the dining table.

And once Agnes had finally made it through the dining room door, she saw, that that's exactly how it was. The gun really was sitting at the table, or rather, *on* the table, resting neatly on a red napkin and looking as innocent as it was possible for a gun to look. A real collectors' piece.

Agnes's heart was racing. Something wasn't right. 'Where did you find it?' she asked.

'Right here!' Winston gesticulated impatiently towards the table. He was sweating. 'That was close. If Isobel had seen it . . .'

'I'd imagined it to be bigger,' said Charlie. By now they had learnt that Charlie imagined most things to be bigger.

'It's big enough,' Marshall responded.

After the initial shock, a certain relief spread through Agnes. After eating she had gone outside with Marshall to tackle the leaves, and hadn't let him out of her sight since. Marshall *could not* have put the gun on the table. And that meant . . .

After the relief came a bigger shock. They had all gone into the garden together. None of them had stayed behind or disappeared in the meantime. *Someone else* had walked into their house and put the gun on the table. It was clever. Cold-blooded.

'Oh,' Agnes said, and then again, 'Oh!'

'Exactly!' Winston had had the longest amount of time to get used to the idea of a gun on the dining table, and seemed collected and dignified again. 'Someone borrowed it and brought it back!'

'Most considerate!' Marshall smiled grimly.

'Are none of you pleased at all?' asked Edwina. 'We've been looking for it for such a long time, even on top of the wardrobe!'

'The question is: Why is it here?' Bernadette said conspiratorially. Her mafia glasses glinted.

Agnes gulped. Bernadette was right. Someone had taken the risk, despite Brexit, to creep into the house and plant the gun theatrically on the dining table. He must have meant something by it – he or she.

'Well, anyway, he got rid of the murder weapon,' said Winston. 'And we're stuck with it now. Maybe he just wanted to pin Mildred on us.'

'But then it would have been better to hide the gun a bit,' responded Agnes. 'Well enough for us not to find it, but not so well that the police . . .' She broke off. 'Apart from that, it's a bit *late*.'

'I wonder . . .' Bernadette's fat hands patted across the table towards the gun.

'Fingerprints!' Agnes warned, but Bernadette laughed. 'The only fingerprints on this thing will belong to Marshall. If that. After all, whoever this is, they're clever. I'm interested in something completely different . . .'

Bernadette's fingers closed around the gun, turned, patted, delved. They all watched her, spellbound.

'Three empty chambers,' she said finally.

Agnes wanted to say 'oh' again, but just about managed to stop herself. Lillith had been killed by a single, very clean shot to the head. Either the murderer had used more than one bullet on Mildred, or . . . The gun had been on its travels for nearly a week, plenty of time to . . .

'Do you think somebody else has been shot?' she asked quietly.

Nobody answered. It was possible. But who? And *why*? 'That's quite unsettling, isn't it?' Charlie whispered. She was green around the gills and wasn't finding everything fabulous for a change.

Agnes nodded. This wasn't someone who just wanted to get rid of a murder weapon.

Someone had gone to the effort of smuggling the gun into the heart of the house, right in the middle of the table, where day after day they made their way through their Chelsea buns and stews. It was spiteful.

Personal.

Intelligent.

I'm watching you! was what the gun was saying.

I know what you're up to!

Maybe it was even saying, *You're next!*

Agnes could read it on her housemates' faces as one by one they all came to the same conclusion.

Bernadette placed the gun back on the table. Marshall started to systematically search the room, for clues presumably, maybe also for wiretaps, booby traps and who-knows-what. Whatever it is military people look for.

'Are we going to hide it again?' Edwina asked.

'Yes,' said Winston. 'I think that's a very good idea. And it had better be a bloody good hiding place!'

An hour later, as dusk was already glowing blue through the windows, they were back at the dining table, still pretty shaken up. The gun was already in its hiding place now, and would stay there, they hoped.

It was a crisis meeting and Agnes served tinned peaches with whipped cream. To her surprise she realised she felt good. Keyed up, but good. She didn't feel any fear, more like a tingle of expectation. The high-pitched ringing had shut up, her hip was forgotten for the time being. Since her childhood Agnes had understood that bad things could happen, and now and again they did just that. Full stop.

No need to panic.

Looking at her housemates told her that they felt the same. They had all been in professions that required a high level of resilience, and now, in a crisis situation, a bit of this old work ethic returned.

For a change, instead of looking dignified, Winston looked determined and not a bit harmless.

Marshall was sitting even more upright at the table than usual.

Bernadette was saying nothing, in a threatening way.

Edwina was playing with the peaches.

Even Charlie had composed herself a bit and was letting Brexit lick cream off her fingers.

Agnes got up without any balance issues and tapped three times on her teacup with her peach spoon. Expectant faces turned towards her.

'First, the most important thing,' she said, 'whoever had the audacity to put that thing on the table' (beforehand, as a precaution, they had agreed to use the word *gun* as little as possible), 'will soon find out that they're messing with the wrong people!'

'Hear! Hear!' cried Winston.

Agnes continued, emboldened. 'We're not going to be

silenced that easily! We will find out who it was and what he's up to, and stop him in his tracks!'

'Or her!' said Charlie, who valued equality in all things.

'Or her.' Agnes confirmed.

'Will we also be putting something on their table?' asked Edwina.

'Maybe.' Agnes liked the idea. 'What then?'

'One of Edwina's biscuits!' shouted Winston. They all laughed.

'A dead frog!' countered Edwina. 'A Chelsea bun!'

'A walking stick!'

The discussion was getting out of hand, and Agnes banged repeatedly on her cup to get order. Without success.

Then it suddenly occurred to her: 'False teeth! Then he'll know exactly who he's dealing with!'

'Hear! Hear!' cried Edwina now. The idea found common assent and soon they were all busy imagining what the intruder's face would look like when he discovered their teeth on his table.

But they weren't there yet.

Agnes tapped on the cup again, and this time quiet ensued. 'We have to find him first,' she said. 'And for that we've got to go out.'

'Into the garden?' asked Edwina.

'Even farther. To Duck End. Out into the world!' Agnes made a dramatic gesture and momentarily lost her balance. 'We have to talk to people, ask questions, observe things. We've got to be clever about it. And' – she looked at the group – 'ideally, we should write down what we have found out before we forget it again.'

'Hear! Hear!' Marshall raised his teacup to toast Agnes. Then, they hungrily tucked into the peaches.

Afterwards, Bernadette presented a bottle of sherry from her personal stash. They decided to cancel dinner and spent the rest of the evening drinking sherry and eating peaches, recalling old times.

Bernadette told the story of the drug baron who was terrified of poodles.

Marshall shared edifying anecdotes about his anti-terror work in the desert, teeming with scorpions, sunburn in unusual places and cultural misunderstandings.

Winston told stories about a secret code he had developed and that consisted entirely of chocolate bars.

Edwina explained 'cow face pose' and the 'warrior' and how best to hide a knife in your underwear.

Charlie was incredibly quiet and indulged in the sherry. It was a wonderful evening.

In the end, Charlie, Bernadette and Marshall had to make use of the stairlift, as well as Agnes and Winston, because they weren't so steady on their feet any more.

Back in her room, Agnes didn't bother with her nightie for long – even on good days and in full possession of her motor functions it was a lengthy process peeling herself out of her clothes and squirming into her nightie. Now with the swaying floor and the uncontrollable giggling fits, such an undertaking didn't seem advisable. Hic!

She threw herself onto the bed in full regalia, wiggled her slippers from her toes and switched the light off. The bed seemed to be swaying, the darkness slowly sucked the warmth of the alcohol out of her body. Dizziness and slight nausea remained. Like being at sea.

What had seemed hilarious to her, now took on a much darker tone. Someone was watching them. Mocking them. Knew their habits. Was playing with them. Was damn sure of himself. Agnes thought about whether she knew anyone who was that arrogant. Nobody came to mind. Mildred perhaps, back then, a long time ago, but Mildred was being prepared for a very expensive funeral and for once seemed to be above all suspicion. Who else?

Sure, they all had a past and in their time, they had trodden on the toes of some dangerous and sinister people, but that was a lifetime ago. Was that what it was about? Or was it maybe about something completely different?

She realised she was shivering. Just as she went to crawl under the covers, a noise made her stop. Something gliding, followed by a muffled *click*. Agnes knew the sounds her house made at night, from the dormice scuttling in the roof, to the groaning water pump, and the spontaneous sighs of the old floorboards.

This noise wasn't one of them.

This noise was strange.

The longer Agnes lay there motionless, holding her breath and listening to the silence, the more certain she was: someone was there. They were not alone in the house any more. She fought the temptation to crawl under her bedcovers, attribute it all to the alcohol and her strained nerves, and hope for the best. She knew that wouldn't help. The best didn't just happen, and it didn't help at all to hide under real or imagined bedcovers.

With an inaudible groan, she slid out of bed. Her hip

protested. Her slippers were lost in the darkness somewhere, so she padded towards the door barefoot and carefully pushed down the handle.

A wide, shadowy figure was waiting out in the hall. A fat hand covered her mouth. Agnes could smell sherry and fondant creams. A second hand found hers, felt up to the shoulder and then Bernadette's mouth was at her ear.

'One person. In the sitting room,' she whispered almost inaudibly. 'He's back!'

Agnes thought for a moment. The shotgun was down in the broom cupboard, and contrary to what she had told the police, it was definitely loaded. If she could somehow make it to the cleaning cupboard, she had a chance.

'Wake the others,' she whispered. 'I'm going down-stairs.'

Bernadette nodded quickly and disappeared astonishingly soundlessly into the darkness.

Agnes limped towards the landing and after a few painful steps realised that there could be no talk of walking. If she really wanted to get downstairs, she would have to take the stairlift. Not exactly textbook, but at least the stairlift was running like a charm after the repair.

She slid onto the seat, took a deep breath and pushed the red button. Just as the stairlift started to move, the high-pitched ringing returned, and Agnes floated down into the dark, deaf and defenceless.

6

CHICKEN SOUP

The stairlift came to a halt at the foot of the stairs, and Agnes stared into the darkness, trying to ignore the high-pitched ringing. She could make out the outlines of the grey stone floor below her, a shimmering path into the unknown. Obviously, she could have just pressed the button a second time and beat a not-so-hasty retreat back upstairs, but that would have been embarrassing, in front of Bernadette and the others, and on top of that she would have had to tell them about the sound in her ears, and what did it have to do with them, anyway?

So, she slid as soundlessly as possible off the stairlift chair, suppressing a groan, located the wall and felt her way towards the kitchen. Obviously, she could forget about tracking down the intruder in the dark now, but with a bit of luck she would make it to the kitchen and grab the shotgun . . . after that she would have to improvise.

Something brushed against her foot. Agnes wanted to scream. Instead, she breathed out slowly and felt around with her toes.

Small. Round. Not particularly soft.

The next minute a short sharp pain confirmed her suspicion:

Hettie had made herself comfortable on one of the warm tiles next to the radiator and felt she had been rudely awoken.

Agnes gently pushed the tortoise to one side with her foot and groped her way farther along the hall. First door on the left: lounge.

Opposite the dining room.

The third door, leading to the kitchen, was open.

Usually, the kitchen door was *not* open, because Hettie could get stuck in between the fridge and the shelves and then only with a whole lot of bother and laborious moving of furniture could she be coaxed out into the cold light of day. Obviously, it was possible that somebody had just forgotten to shut the kitchen door, but . . . Agnes felt a draught. Moving air.

Someone *was* there.

She tried to recall the layout of the kitchen. It was surprisingly easy. Remembering yesterday's meal was usually a hopeless task, but the kitchen hadn't changed for years, and Agnes could see it clearly in her mind's eye, a big square room. Stone floor that wouldn't creak. The table in the middle. Two routes led past it towards the broom cupboard: left and right. To the right, the fridge, the plate rack and a dresser; to the left, the sink, the hob, the worktop. The worktop with the *knife block*.

Left was quite clearly the right choice. Even if she didn't make it to the broom cupboard, she would have the opportunity to arm herself on the way. She set off and got hold of the cool, smooth sink top at hip-level. So far, so good. A small gap, then the hob. Agnes's hands wandered cautiously over the hotplates. Finally, the worktop, and there . . .

Agnes froze. There was something there. A flicker in

the darkness. A draught. Something kind of warm. Barely perceptible, but suddenly she knew instinctively, through decades of training, that someone was standing in front of her.

Skin and bones. She had never liked that expression, it seemed trite to her, and imprecise somehow, but at that moment she understood exactly what it meant. Skin and bones. Nothing in-between. Nothing protective. Never before had she felt so much like a collection of fragile bones.

Skin, bones and a plan.

Agnes threw herself across the worktop, got hold of a knife and stabbed into the darkness. Then the high-pitched ringing disappeared and suddenly all hell broke loose. Someone was screaming, maybe it was her. Something crashed into her, but through some kind of miracle she managed to hold onto the worktop at the last minute. Banging and another scream. Someone shouting her name.

Someone was shouting: 'Hear! Hear!'

Agnes tightened her grip on the knife and stumbled against the kitchen table in the dark.

Then suddenly the light went on.

Dazzled, Agnes lost her bearings briefly. The world was spinning. Stars were flashing in front of her eyes.

A moment later she had composed herself and finally saw what was going on.

She was still standing next to the kitchen table, wielding a ladle. On the other side of the table was Marshall with his fruit knife, in the doorway Edwina in a vividly floral nightie. Between the three of them stood the intruder wearing jeans, a black sweat-shirt and a ski mask, his blue eyes wide with shock, his hand to his temple. They were all a bit bewildered.

The burglar recovered first and fled past Agnes and the ladle to the kitchen door. Edwina looked at him quizzically for a moment, then stepped aside. But, as the burglar pushed past her, something happened, quickly and almost casually. The intruder lurched, crashed into the hall wall, stumbled and fell. Agnes lowered the ladle.

A scream.

He tried to pick himself up.

'Shit!'

Edwina stepped closer. 'Hear! Hear!' she said, but the burglar was back on his feet, escaping. He shoved her aside and ran along the hall towards the front door.

'Stop him!' cried Agnes. Fear and confusion were forgotten. She could suddenly only feel rage towards this person, who was roving about their house uninvited and putting guns on their table.

But none of them were agile enough to stop the intruder, and the next minute he had disappeared from Agnes's sight.

She heard footsteps, then a crash and another scream. Marshall and Edwina had long since disappeared into the hallway, and even Agnes made it to the kitchen door with astonishing speed. From there she had an overview of the situation, Bernadette was standing at the other end of the hall, arms crossed like a bouncer in a flowing nightgown, she was wearing her sunglasses even now. Did she sleep with them on? In any case, it was a good effect. Winston, a cap on his head and a poker in his hand, was coming down on the stairlift. Charlie and Brexit were standing on the top landing, both with unkempt hair. Edwina and Marshall were looking at the floor, where the intruder was cowering, a bit perplexed. He had tripped over Hettie, fallen over and was surrounded. Now he was just sitting on his backside looking from one of them to the other, open-mouthed. His ski mask had slipped to the side a bit, and Agnes spotted a trembling chin with sparse stubble.

For a minute they all just looked at each other blankly, then Brexit made the first move. He glided down the stairs and licked the burglar's masked nose. The burglar whimpered.

Agnes couldn't take it any longer. That chin looked familiar. She padded along the hall, pushed Brexit aside and pulled the mask off the intruder's face in one fell swoop. The burglar buried his head in his hands, but only once Agnes had been able to cop a look at his horrified face. Blue eyes, sand-coloured hair, cheekbones and a fresh bump on his temple.

For a minute Agnes was disappointed – she had imagined her shadowy adversary differently. Then her memory returned, she knew this whippersnapper. Had only recently . . .

But whilst she was mulling it over, the man started to speak with an unsteady voice.

'I didn't mean to . . . I just wanted to . . . It's all a big misunderstanding!'

Hettie hissed and attacked the whippersnapper's knuckles with a targeted bite.

'Ow!'

'She doesn't like lies.' Agnes warned. Above all she didn't like it when you pushed her off her warm sleep stone in the middle of the night, switched on the light or tripped over her, but they didn't have to let the intruder in on that now, did they?

The burglar pulled away from Hettie towards the wall. The next minute Marshall had stepped next to him, and the whippersnapper found himself handcuffed to the radiator.

The stubbly chin started trembling again.

Charlie came down the steps with a flowing mane of hair. 'Goodness gracious!' she said over and over, running her fingers through her hair, making it stand on end even more. 'Goodness gracious!'

'Who is it?' Bernadette asked excitedly. 'Who is it?'

'Just a man,' said Edwina somewhat disappointedly. 'But we've got him!' She thought for a minute. 'I'll get some biscuits.'

Whilst Edwina was looking for biscuits in the kitchen, Agnes was wrestling with her own body. Her hip hurt. She suddenly felt dizzy and a bit ropey, and to cap it all she had cold feet too. She had to think. Think where she had seen that whippersnapper's face before. And a bit of a sit-down after all the excitement couldn't hurt.

'What now?' she asked to hurry things along. 'We can't call the police again!'

'No police!' Bernadette declared.

The others nodded. They had had enough of the police and their bumbling investigative methods. You had to do everything yourself.

The burglar got a little paler, if that was possible.

Winston had transferred himself from the stairlift to his wheelchair and eyed the burglar, then the poker.

'Who sent you?' grumbled Marshall. 'Are you working alone? What's the thing with the gun all about? Is anyone else dead?'

'Dead?' squeaked the man and started whimpering away again, in a new, more high-pitched tone. 'Who's dead? I just wanted to . . .'

'We ask the questions,' snorted Marshall.

Agnes tugged at his sleeve and rolled her eyes. Ten minutes alone with Hettie, Brexit and Edwina's biscuits should be enough to put the intruder in a cooperative mood.

Marshall understood. He dropped the knife into his dressing gown pocket and offered Agnes his arm. Agnes doddered with him into the sitting room and gratefully sunk into the first available chair. The others hesitantly followed.

Charlie headed straight for the drinks cabinet and started pouring golden liquid into little glasses. Agnes declined. There was a whippersnapper chained to their radiator out there, not exactly an everyday situation; a clear head was required. Not all problems could be solved with alcohol. She noticed she was still holding the ladle in her hand, and laid it discreetly on the side table.

'There we go.' said Winston. 'We've got him! Now we just have to make him talk.' He looked down at the poker thoughtfully.

Charlie emptied her glass and gave herself a refill. 'I imagined him bigger!' she declared.

'Older,' mumbled Winston.

'And somehow . . . smarter.' Marshall sighed.

Agnes had to silently agree with them. Why on earth would this clumsy oaf have killed Mildred and put the gun on their table like a gauntlet? Maybe he was just a skilled actor. But what if he had nothing to do with the gun? Maybe Lillith's daughter had sent him to have a nose around?

'We've got to listen to what he has to say,' she declared. 'And he seems familiar to me somehow.'

'Me too.' Marshall nodded.

'Me too,' Charlie agreed.

For a minute Winston looked like he was going to follow the general trend, but then seemed to reluctantly decide against it.

The door opened and Edwina came in, a big plate of biscuits in her hand, a hissing Hettie under her arm.

'He doesn't like biscuits,' she said sulkily. 'And he doesn't like Hettie either.'

They all listened to what was happening in the hall. Apart from Brexit's tail wagging, not a sound could be heard from out there.

Since the Edwina method obviously hadn't borne any fruit, they couldn't put it off any longer.

'I'll give it a go.'

Winston made an elegant about-turn and rolled out. Brexit's tail wagged more quickly, then Agnes heard whimpering again, accompanied by Winston's soft voice. Finally, a muffled impact, and then Winston was back in the sitting room.

'He's passed out.' Winston looked sheepish.

'Goodness gracious!' Charlie knocked back the golden contents of her glass and rushed out into the hallway.

'Really, Winston!' Agnes was reluctant to leave her comfy chair. She had never taken Winston to be the brutal type, but if she was honest, she didn't know exactly what he used to do back then in the Secret Service. Something secret, no doubt.

'I didn't do a thing!' Winston pulled his nightcap off his

head. 'I asked him if he was sitting comfortably, and then I showed him the poker . . .'

Bernadette sighed deeply.

'And next I wanted to tell him that I'm sure we wouldn't need to resort to such methods, but then he just . . . I didn't touch him!' Agnes had finally made it out of her chair and was hobbling to the door, miffed. Marshall offered his arm again, but she brushed him off. You had to do everything yourself.

The burglar was lying on the floor unconscious, getting his face licked by Brexit. Agnes suddenly felt sorry for him.

'Brexit, down!'

Edwina prodded the burglar with her foot. 'Is he dead?'

Marshall shook his head. 'Everything's alright, I'd say. A bit pale maybe.'

The intruder's head was bent back, his sparsely covered chin pointing straight up in the air.

And suddenly Agnes knew where she had seen that chin before.

'The stairlift engineer!' She felt betrayed. The stairlift engineer was definitely not the one going around bumping off old ladies – that would have been too bad for business. Whatever was in front of them, it was not the solution to the mystery.

'Indeed!' said Charlie.

'Indeed,' mumbled Marshall, but in the way he said it, Agnes knew he couldn't remember a thing.

'Can we keep him?' asked Edwina.

'I don't think so,' Agnes answered regretfully. The thought of having a stairlift engineer at their beck and call did appeal to her. 'First, we need to get him back on his feet. And then we'll find out why he's here.'

They decided to get the burglar back into the kitchen and revive him there. Marshall released the handcuffs, Winston provided his travel wheelchair, Edwina and Marshall manoeuvred the unconscious man into the chair, Charlie pushed him into the kitchen, and Marshall bolted the door.

Bernadette made tea, Charlie got a portion of frozen chicken soup out of the freezer and heated it in a saucepan. Edwina patted the stairlift engineer's cheeks.

Then they waited for him to come round.

For a while nothing happened, but then the whippersnapper's eyelids began to twitch. He moved his head. Opened his eyes. Looked from one of them to the other.

And quickly shut his eyes again.

'We know you're awake!' Marshall said in a not unfriendly tone.

The burglar blinked, looked at them all and exhaled deeply. 'Give the boy something to eat first,' said Agnes. 'And hot tea. Hot tea's good for shock.'

They went about pepping up the burglar with tea and chicken soup. Afterwards he confessed to everything. It wasn't much. The whippersnapper was called Sparrow. At least that's what his friends called him. Regrettably most of those friends were on the internet. All of them, to be exact. And the internet was expensive. Sparrow was doing an apprenticeship to become an electrician in the neighbouring village and had recently started specialising in stairlifts – and paying his clients nocturnal visits to lighten their housekeeping budgets.

'Not by much. A twenty, maybe a fifty. Anyone living in a

house like this doesn't have to worry about money. I bet you wouldn't have even noticed.'

'Of course we would have noticed,' Bernadette said indignantly.

Agnes wasn't so sure. It wasn't a bad business model.

'Do you know Mildred Puck?' she asked softly.

Sparrow shook his head. Agnes believed him – after all she hadn't seen a stairlift over at the Pucks'.

'And Lillith Wright? Or her daughter? Pippa? Podgy woman with watery eyes?'

'Never heard of them.' He was acting a bit more confidently. 'I just break in. I didn't mean anything by it. It's just . . . My wages are a joke!'

Marshall smirked. 'No offence, but you're not a very good burglar! You're loud. You can't see very well in that ridiculous ski mask. And you're not even wearing gloves. Fingerprints everywhere!'

Sparrow stuck his bottom lip out sulkily.

'But he is excellent at repairing stairlifts,' Agnes said conciliatorily. 'And he's here now. With a few tips and the right training . . .' The idea came to her and Winston at the same time. Their eyes met. Winston smiled quietly in anticipation. Agnes bowed her head to an almost imperceptible nod, then she poured Sparrow the amateur-burglar a second cup of tea.

'Breaking in isn't as hard as it first seems,' she said softly. 'You just have to be mindful of a few simple rules.'

They explained a few basic principles of undercover work to Sparrow and then told him what they wanted from him.

Saying goodbye to their burglar was almost a bit emotional. Sparrow gushed with thanks for the tea and chicken soup, and insisted on shaking each of them by the hand.

Winston ceremoniously pressed a chocolate bar into his hand. 'If things go wrong, just eat it and throw the wrapper over our garden fence. Then we'll know something's not right and we'll be in touch.'

'Or just call us,' said Agnes. 'If it rings for long enough, somebody usually picks up.'

Sparrow looked at the chocolate bar in his hand with reverence.

'Is there something in it?' he asked. 'A stimulant or something?'

'No,' Winston explained. 'But in my experience, it's good to eat something sweet in a crisis. And drink tea. Tea and chocolate are part of a successful agent's basic kit.'

'Above all chocolate,' Bernadette mumbled.

Sparrow, who refused to use the door like a regular visitor, left the house burglar-style the way he had come in, through the toilet window on the ground floor. Agnes, Edwina, Winston, Charlie, Brexit and Marshall watched over the toilet seat as he leapt outside with youthful vigour and carefully wiped the window handle with a tissue afterwards, just like they had discussed.

Marshall nodded appreciatively, Edwina and Charlie waved, and then their new friend had disappeared into the dark garden. Cold air blew in through the window. Agnes shivered and scrunched up her toes to provide the bare stone floor with as little surface area as possible.

'What a nice young man,' said Edwina. 'Polite.' Bernadette nodded.

'And nobody's fool,' added Winston. 'At least not all the time.'

Agnes didn't say anything. She squished up her toes even more and thought about the future. It had been a long while since she had thought about anything like a future, and not just about today, yesterday, and above all, the day before the day before the day before yesterday. The day before the day before the day before yesterday was a double-edged sword. Sometimes rosy, sometimes terrifying, but always immutable. Known. Sucked dry by too many trips down memory lane.

The future, however, looked different. In reality, there were lots of possible futures: one where they got caught, another where they didn't. A future where the murderer out there left them scared and frightened, another where they got wise to him. Agnes's cheeks were burning. She had got wise to a lot of things in her life – why not this too? A late, but strangely personal story. In this clumsy, but enthusiastic whippersnapper, they had found a kind of ally, someone they could send out into the future on his strong young legs, to carry out the most uncomfortable parts of the investigative work. Someone whose inconspicuous stubbly face nobody would connect to them. Suddenly the future looked unusually rosy.

Agnes laid her icy hands on her hot cheeks and grinned. 'Isn't it unethical?' Charlie asked, her voice wobbling. 'To give him all those tips? And where did . . . ?'

'His wages are a joke!' Edwina declared.

'And he only steals from senile people, who are guaranteed not to notice,' Bernadette added disparagingly. 'If nobody notices, it's not a real crime.'

'If you all think so.' Charlie yawned loudly. 'In any case, Brexit and I need our beauty sleep now.'

7

CREAM SLICES

Only for Brexit had the beauty sleep gone off without a hitch. He was sitting at breakfast bright-eyed, with silky fur and a wet nose, while the rest of the household woozily stirred cups of tea and coffee, plagued by doubt, aches and pains, and pronounced hangovers.

Had they really caught, concussed, revived, and trained a burglar in the night? It seemed too fantastical to be true.

Hettie was treating them all with disdain, Charlie was dishing out headache pills, Bernadette was groaning at regular intervals, Winston spurned his toast, and Agnes was making plans. It wasn't enough to befriend an eager-to-learn whippersnapper – they had to go out into the world themselves, to Duck End to be precise, to conduct their own enquiries, and Agnes knew exactly where – on the slippery, treacherous parquet of the weekly coffee morning. It promised to be an eventful day.

She slammed her teacup on the table and felt herself and her housemates flinch.

'Put something decent on,' she said. Her voice cracked. 'We're going to Duck End!'

Obviously, they didn't walk, at least not into the village. And the only one who looked even halfway decent standing at the bus stop was Brexit. Charlie had put a red leather collar with matching lead on him, and he cut a fine figure with his silky grey fur. It went downhill from there. Agnes was wearing a black blouse and lipstick again, but in her haste had massively overshot and looked something like you might imagine an evil stepmother to look. Step-grandmother. Winston had interpreted 'decent' mainly as 'warm' and paired his knitted nightcap with a psychedelic patterned wheelchair blanket from the seventies. Charlie was wearing her coat and feather hat again, and to top it all, a fox stole, complete with fox's head. The fox's resin eyes stared at them with disdain. Bernadette was a cloud of conflicting shades of red, Marshall was wearing at least three uniforms at once, and Edwina had Hettie under her arm instead of a handbag.

Agnes sighed. 'We really could have done without Hettie,' she murmured.

'Hettie has never been to Duck End,' Edwina retorted.

'With good reason. She's a tortoise. She doesn't *need* to go into the village.'

'But she *wants* to! She said so.' Edwina held a stoic Hettie up to Agnes's face.

Agnes tried to push her away. 'It's not a fun day out!'

'Now it is!'

They were squabbling so loudly they almost missed the bus that passed Sunset Hall once an hour and ambled sedately into the village. Winston put his hand out just in time. The bus driver braked, eyed them incredulously through the windscreen and eventually grudgingly opened the door.

They clambered onto the bus and looked around.

Two fat teenagers were sitting on the first row chewing gum and blowing bubbles, but Hettie's stern look made them stop the bubble blowing.

'We should sit down,' Agnes said and eyed the narrow rows sceptically. This wasn't how she remembered buses to be. The windows were so dirty you could hardly see out. And it stank.

None of them wanted to sit on the designated disabled seats, and they squeezed to the back of the bus as best they could. Winston and Brexit blocked the aisle.

The bus driver looked as though he wanted to say something but decided against it and sped off towards the village.

Agnes hadn't been to Duck End for an eternity. Since Marshall had set up the internet and groceries, and doctors and stairlift engineers came to them direct, the village seemed surplus to requirements. But it was still there. At least partially.

She clambered off the bus with the help of Charlie and Bernadette and surveyed the scene, the high street. The crossroads. The village green and pond.

So far, so familiar.

One of the three village shops had closed down. Faded posters were stuck to the shop windows. Agnes tried to remember what you used to be able to buy there. Women's clothes? Or was that in the sixties? She could remember an orange dress that had really tempted her back then. Later a hardware shop had moved in and most recently a funeral director. Even that didn't last. But now there seemed to be somebody trying to drum up business, with the help of a gun. Agnes remembered her mission, grabbed Marshall's arm, got caught on one of his many medals and pointed down the street.

'Down there!'

They passed a corner shop that seemed to specialise in alcohol, and almost lost Edwina in the second-hand shop next door, then they finally got to the crossroads. The pavement was slippery, and Agnes, who was too proud to take her walking stick, had to cling to the bemedalled Marshall more than she would have liked.

The village hall had new windows, but apart from that it was sitting in the landscape just as prosaically as Agnes remembered.

On the door was a sign.

Coffee Morning!
Cake, company and good conversation.
EVERYONE WELCOME!

'Golly!' said Charlie, straightening her feather hat. 'They'll have anyone!'

Edwina lifted Hettie into the air like a trophy.

Marshall pushed Winston up the wheelchair ramp.

Bernadette felt her way along at the rear like a gangster snail.

Agnes took a deep breath. Her last visit to the village hall hadn't gone well. She couldn't remember the exact cause of the argument, but she remembered the carrot cake flying through the air, shrill voices and the vicar stonily calling her a taxi afterwards.

'Well then,' she murmured to bolster herself, and pushed down the handle.

'Well then,' murmured a chorus behind her.

The only one who could muster even a hint of enthusiasm for the coffee morning was Brexit, who entered the village hall politely wagging his tail. Nobody greeted him back.

Once they had all struggled through the door, the hubbub of muted conversations stopped. Coffee cups were put down, glasses pushed up noses, hearing aids turned up in anticipation.

A woman in support stockings and a bun approached them, her arms bent in front of her like a praying mantis.

'No dogs!' she announced.

'But it says . . .' Charlie pointed outside and saw that a man with thick glasses was folding up the sign and putting it away.

'He's a guide dog,' Bernadette said quickly. '*My* guide dog!' She grabbed the lead, but got hold of Charlie's fox stole and patted its head. Charlie caught on and pressed the lead into Bernadette's hand.

'And a very good one too,' she said proudly.

The woman made an unfriendly noise, somewhere between a buzz and a growl.

'Fabulous!' Charlie pushed past the praying mantis grinning manically, and Bernadette was dragged into the room by Brexit, past dumbstruck senior citizens, heading straight for the cakes.

The others rushed after them and surveyed the offering.

A lemon drizzle cake. A dry-looking madeira. Biscuits. The

biscuits looked much better than Edwina's – you had to give the coffee morning that.

And then strawberry cream slices. There were only two cream slices left.

'Hmmm,' grumbled Charlie. 'Where's the coffee then?'

Agnes pointed to two big Thermos flasks standing a bit lost on a side table.

The praying mantis appeared beside them again. 'The sugar's over there.' she said begrudgingly. 'There's no milk left.'

'Golly.' Charlie gasped for the second time.

'Don't you have any lettuce for Hettie?' Edwina looked down accusatorily at the meagre spread of cakes.

'Tortoises aren't allowed either,' admonished the praying mantis.

'She's a guide tortoise,' Edwina responded and shut her eyes. 'And a very good one too!'

The woman gave up and retreated to her corner, where a posse of senior citizens quickly gathered, whispering venomously. Agnes sighed. Obviously, everyone knew who they were – the hippies from Sunset Hall – and everyone had heard the crazy rumours about them. Those rumours annoyed her. What did people expect? Orgies? The chance would be a fine thing! They were just happy if they had their own false teeth in their mouths and there was enough loo roll in the house.

Edwina took a biscuit to try.

Brexit lost interest in the cake buffet and dragged Bernadette towards the kitchen.

'And what now?' Marshall murmured next to Agnes.

'Act normal,' Agnes whispered back. 'Drink coffee. Sit down. Not all together. Sit with someone else. Be approachable!'

She led by example, poured herself a drink, took a cream slice and threw a coin into the collection pot. Then she made her way towards a little group of horrified-looking coffee morning attendees.

'Is that free?'

'Err . . .' A man with tufts of white hair behind his ears searched for an excuse, but couldn't find one. He looked down and nervously stirred his coffee.

'Excellent.' Agnes sat on the chair with relief. At last. Everything hurt again. Or was that still? Either way, her hip had had enough of all the clambering about and was making its presence felt.

She had a sip of coffee – not bad at all – and exhaled. 'That's the ticket!' she said and smiled over at her petrified table companions. Two women in mouse-grey were sitting next to the unimaginative man with the tufts. Identical hairstyles. Sisters, Agnes guessed, or related somehow. Nobody seemed familiar to her.

She had been a bit afraid of seeing all the long-known and not particularly well-meaning faces again, but what frightened her much more was how few of the coffee-slurping senior citizens seemed familiar to her. Was her memory deserting her, or was it her contemporaries who had absconded on the quiet? It didn't matter. Even the new generation of coffee morning attendees didn't give a very open-minded impression.

To tempt her table companions out of their reserve, she tried a forkful of cream slice. Out of the corner of her eye, she watched Winston wheeling over to three knitting ladies and Edwina introducing Hettie to a man with a beard.

'Delicious,' she said. The cream slice was really good. 'Did one of you make it?'

The two mouse-grey ladies went red, and the man with the tufts shook his head emphatically.

'Olive did,' murmured one of the mouse-grey ladies.

'Olive *always* makes the best cakes,' added the other mouse-grey lady with a certain envy.

'Olive.' Of course. The name rang a bell with Agnes. A belligerent woman with a sly look and aggressive, somewhat jerky movements. If she remembered rightly, Olive had been involved in the incident with the carrot cake. Maybe she had even *baked* the carrot cake in question. Agnes looked around.

'Olive isn't here today,' said the first mouse-grey lady.

'Olive's always here,' the other responded.

They both stared at one another.

'Awful news about Lilly,' lamented the tufted man who had finally remembered his manners. 'What sort of world are we living in? My condolences.'

'Lillith,' Agnes corrected and took a second bite of cream slice. The mishap at Sunset Hall had got around then. 'It was obviously a huge shock for us.'

'Obviously,' the man murmured like an echo.

One of the mouse-grey ladies leant forward. 'Is it true that . . . I mean, we heard . . .' She broke off and stared sheepishly at her madeira cake.

The second mouse-grey lady was braver. 'She means the thing about . . . well, that she was disembowelled . . .'

Hettie had always feared that there had to be a great deal of Big Feet in the world, but what she saw after the Lettuce-holding Hands finally put her on the floor, was beyond her wildest expectations.

Big Feet as far as the eye could see.

Big Feet in white, cloud-like leather covers.

Big Feet in thin black leather covers.

Big Feet in red and brown and blue, fabric, leather, or stinky plastic, with stripes and spots and stains, dirty or clean or somewhere in-between.

Big Feet that in turn seemed to have another single pointy foot.

A whole forest of foot creatures, all terribly busy swaying and turning and tapping and making short, flat jumps forward.

And no lettuce anywhere to be seen.

Hettie quickly observed the scene, then she'd had enough.

She stalked off, straight ahead, towards a familiar-looking radiator. Radiators were normally warm and pleasant, and it felt a bit cool in Hettie's shell. She made surprisingly bad progress on the smooth, shiny ground.

When she was finally near enough to feel the warmth of the iron structure in front of her, she suddenly felt herself being lifted up. The Lettuce-holding Hands had interfered again! Hettie flailed her legs in frustration and hissed indignantly.

The next minute it became clear to her that something wasn't right. The hands were holding her wrong, the wrong way up, head down, plastron up. It was outrageous, disrespectful, and it wasn't at all like the Lettuce-holding Hands.

No, something else had grabbed her!

Hettie hissed in a new, higher-pitched tone and thrashed about even more violently, but before she could really fly into a fury, the strange hands had let go of her and she was falling.

Falling and falling, managing to just about tuck her head in and land with a rustle and not too hard somewhere in partial darkness. She stopped hissing in order to better assess the new situation.

A dark, warm fluid trickled down her neck.

'Disembowelled?' The cream slice lodged in Agnes's throat. She coughed. 'No. Of course not. What nonsense!'

'I wouldn't want to talk about it either,' said the second mouse-grey lady with a sly look.

'So awful,' warbled the first mouse-grey lady sympathetically.

Agnes searched for the words. 'That's really . . . Who comes up with these things? Lillith was not . . . I saw her with my own eyes. It was a completely clean gunshot to the head.'

That didn't seem to reassure her table companion.

'We just wanted to say how sorry we are,' reassured the man with the tufts.

'But we obviously wondered if it had anything to do with the gentleman callers,' the second mouse-grey lady remarked pointedly.

Gentleman callers! Agnes clutched the cake fork and grappled with her self-control. She suddenly remembered what had triggered the carrot cake incident. She had told the coffee ladies about her plans for the house share, and Olive and a few of her cream slice admirers had played vice squad.

'It's a house share, not a brothel!' she wanted to shout, when a hand touched her shoulder from behind.

Agnes looked up. Two resin fox-eyes peered at her sympathetically.

'Everything alright, Agnes?' Charlie asked.

'Depends.' Agnes got up, without deigning to give tufty and the mouse-grey ladies a second glance. 'How about you?'

'Well, you know. I've got madeira cake in my teeth and that chap over there just made me a none-too-ambiguous proposition. Good conversation – my foot! Bernadette has disappeared into the kitchen, and Edwina has misplaced Hettie. But Winston and Marshall are a hit!'

Agnes looked around and saw that Charlie was right. Winston was sitting amongst a circle of cackling ladies patting hands left and right, and a posse of admiring sixty-year-olds had formed around Marshall, fluttering their thin eyelashes and fingering his medals. 'Oh, my goodness!' Agnes suddenly felt the urge to grab her housemates by the arm and drag them home, away from the coffee morning's permed temptresses. On the other hand, they did seem to be having a wonderful time, and they had come out to make conversation after all. Agnes's stomach felt ropey and she blamed the cream slice. Perhaps the cream was a bit past it, or perhaps Olive had chosen today of all days to poison her coffee morning companions. That seemed like something she would do.

How could it be that Olive's cream slices were there, but she wasn't?

And where the hell was Hettie?

Agnes scouted round for Edwina and spotted her disappear on all fours under the table with the praying mantis. One of the ladies at the table squawked, the others pulled away indignantly. Agnes got the feeling the 'everyone welcome' sign would live in the junk room from now on.

'Oh, my goodness!' She gasped a second time. 'Best we see to Hettie first.'

She enticed Edwina out from under the table with a few empty promises and went to look for the rogue tortoise.

She wasn't on the buffet, the floor seemed tortoise-free and the man Edwina had last introduced Hettie to apparently couldn't remember anything.

'I knew it wasn't a very good idea.' Agnes was worried. Hettie was a fighter, but she was only a tortoise. Anything could happen.

Edwina leapt onto a chair and shouted loudly for Hettie.

Conversations died down and the ladies with the perms let go of Marshall's medals to see what was going on – half outraged, half envious because there was someone who could still climb on a chair so easily.

Winston looked over at them and raised his eyebrows quizzically.

'Hettie's missing,' Agnes hiss-whispered into the sudden silence.

Everyone could hear it.

For a moment, everything seemed to freeze, and Agnes thought she could hear scratching somewhere in the silence, but then senior-citizen-pandemonium broke out.

'The murderer!' whispered a lady with a double chin.

'He's struck again!' cried one of the mouse-grey ladies, her eyes sparkling.

'Nowhere's safe . . . !' wailed someone behind Agnes, and then they were suddenly all on the move. Crutches and sticks were drawn, wheelchairs set in motion, coats torn from chairbacks. They were all speaking at once, and Agnes thought she heard the words 'gentleman callers' on more than one occasion. She grabbed for a biscuit, maybe to throw it. But at who?

'Hettie is a tortoise!' Charlie tried to calm them. 'And she hasn't been murdered either!' Nobody listened to her.

Soon the village hall was deserted. Only the members of Sunset Hall were left.

'Gosh!' Charlie poured herself a cup of jet-black coffee and sank onto a chair.

Marshall started to quietly laugh amongst his circle of abandoned cups.

Agnes was suddenly hopping mad and threw the biscuit. It flew past Marshall's ear and landed in a coffee cup with a plop.

Marshall laughed even more loudly. 'Wonderful idea, this coffee morning, Agnes! Great!'

He hiccupped, coughed a few times, then it went quiet.

And in the silence, scratching.

'Hettie!' Edwina jumped down from her chair and ran to the cakes. Nothing – but the noise was definitely coming from this corner. She looked under tables and behind furniture, then Charlie pointed mutely at the bin.

The paper cups and plastic forks in the bin were trembling.

'Golly!' Charlie said for the third time that day and valiantly reached into the rubbish with her manicured fingers. A moment later she unearthed Hettie. The tortoise was grumpy and drenched in coffee, but completely unharmed and was immediately patted dry with Edwina's skirt.

Now Agnes felt really sick, and not just because of the cream cake. Someone had thrown an innocent tortoise into the bin, just to get one over on them. Just because they were a bit unconventional with their supposed gentleman callers and didn't seamlessly fit in at the coffee morning. Everyone welcome – my foot!

'What the devil?' said Winston, but the devil was biding his time.

Edwina was holding Hettie to her ear like a phone. 'Hettie wants to go home,' she declared.

'She's not the only one,' murmured Marshall.

They were heading to the door *en masse* when Agnes suddenly stopped.

'What about Bernadette?'

Bernadette had disappeared into the kitchen with Brexit some time ago, and they hadn't seen her since.

Agnes suddenly went cold. It was out of character for Bernadette to not be at the centre of things. Had something happened? Sure, Brexit was there, at first glance a formidable wolfhound with soft fur and a soft heart, but a dog couldn't do much about a bullet. Was it possible they hadn't heard a gunshot? Or two? How good were these silencers nowadays? Or had they just allowed themselves to be sucked in by the senior citizen panic?

She looked over at Marshall and realised that he suddenly looked worried too. He pointed at the kitchen door and put a finger to his lips. It was quiet behind the door and from her vantage point through the little window, she could only make out a section of kitchen ceiling and shelves. The shelves seemed harmless.

Marshall cautiously stepped closer and peered for his part through the window. He shook his head and Agnes relaxed a little.

The next minute the window was filled with grey fur and white teeth. A pink tongue shot across the glass leaving a wet trail not dissimilar to a snail's.

'Brexit!' Charlie cheered.

The door swung open and Brexit skidded into the room unharmed and in high spirits. His red lead dragging loosely behind him. Where was Bernadette?

Agnes plucked up the courage to go into the kitchen.

Empty.

But a second door led out to the deserted carpark, and there was Bernadette with another woman, leaning against the wall like two teenagers. They were both wearing sunglasses, both smoking cigarettes.

'You lot again,' said Bernadette in a not unfriendly way when she heard Agnes, Charlie and Edwina's footsteps, and furtively stubbed out her cigarette. Smoking was against the house rules, but they weren't at home after all.

'Bernadette, we were . . .' What? Worried? Just because a pack of pensioners just panicked? Agnes suddenly felt foolish.

'Just leaving,' she said finally. 'The coffee morning's over.'

'Already?' The other woman blew smoke into the cold autumn air. 'All the better.'

'This is Rosie. She helps in the kitchen.'

'*Scrounges* in the kitchen,' Rosie corrected with dignity. 'Otherwise, wild horses couldn't drag me here!' She was quite possibly the least rosy person Agnes had seen for a long time, pale as a Sunset Hall Chelsea bun, with wrinkly yellowish cheeks, hair dyed a fiery red and incongruous bright red lipstick. Huge sunglasses perched on her nose although it wasn't sunny at all. Rosie didn't seem like someone who would get het up about gentleman callers. Agnes liked her instantly.

'Well then!' Rosie slipped Bernadette another cigarette, then got a headscarf out of her coat pocket, tied it carefully under her chin and walked across the car park towards the high street.

'Bye, you mole!'

Agnes was shocked. Until now nobody would have dared call Bernadette a mole, but the cigarette smoke seemed to have put her housemate in an unusually affable mood.

Bernadette linked arms with Charlie. 'Nice get-together,' she said. 'But your guide dog's rubbish.'

'What a washout!' Charlie moaned, once they had crammed into the draughty bus shelter, hoping against their better judgement for a punctual bus. 'Never again!'

'Well, I thought it was fun!' Winston grinned. 'Two girls gave me their number.'

'Four.' Marshall grinned back. 'And I've got a lovely stuffed cabbage recipe too.'

'Five,' said Edwina, but nobody believed her.

'The crucial thing is to lightly braise the cabbage first,' Marshall declared.

'What else?' asked Agnes.

'Obviously it also depends on the quality of the mincemeat,' Marshall said thoughtfully. 'And someone asked me . . .' He broke off. A blank expression crossed his face. Agnes didn't ask any more.

They were silent. The bus was taking a while.

'At least we've got Hettie back,' Agnes said after a while. The coffee morning had been her plan, and it was a *good* plan. Investigate in the field. Ears to the ground. Engage in conversation. Good plan, bad results. It happened. It wasn't her fault that in this case the field was full of bigoted tortoise-haters. But she had to silently admit that Charlie was right. What had they learnt apart from there wasn't good cake to be had with the coffee morning attendees? Or good anything for that matter. Only once the bus was trundling along the road again, horrendously late, and she was belching cream cake with every pothole, did it occur to Agnes that actually they had learnt something.

Something important.

Olive wasn't there.

Olive was always there.

Olive, the self-appointed queen of the coffee morning.

Olive, who stuck her nose in everything.

Olive, who was a sour old prune and sure to live alone.

Olive, who would never ever have brought cream slices without having some herself.

Olive, whom nobody would really miss.

At least not very quickly.

As soon as the bus had dropped them at Sunset Hall, Agnes limped into the house, got the telephone and dialled.

Marshall was searching. He had forgotten what it was he was searching for, but that didn't stop him from systematically pulling books off the shelf, opening them and closing them again. Was he looking for a word? A picture? Something that would fall out of a book, or something hiding behind a book? He didn't know, but he knew it was *important*. Vitally important.

One book after another slid into his hands, opening like butterfly wings, revealing nothing and closing again. He made an impatient gesture as if to clear the fog. But the fog was in his head, constantly moving vapours that could hold him captive from one second to the next. It was enough to drive him mad. Or rather he had already gone mad, disappeared, MIA, *poof*! The others just didn't know it yet. They didn't know what kind of levels the fog had now reached – thank God! And now only his improvisation skills and well-trained habits, that were more deeply ingrained than thought or memory, stopped him from constantly giving himself away. Just now, he had suddenly found himself standing in his room in full dress uniform like a stranger. *What business do you have here? Name? Papers?* In his jacket pocket four telephone numbers, scrawled on scraps of paper, one on a napkin. Who did these numbers belong to? What did they mean? And why did he suddenly feel like laughing? He didn't like it. The person in the fog was suspicious, someone who should be viewed with mistrust and caution. Someone who was capable of anything.

Marshall realised that he was suddenly holding an old photo album in his hands. Agnes's album. He should have put it back on the shelf like a gentleman, but instead he looked on as his hands flicked through the pages, from the back to the front.

Agnes on a deckchair on the veranda, squinting into the light. A bit smoother, a bit fuller than he knew her, more hair, but unmistakably Agnes. He flicked back and watched her getting younger, less familiar, more beautiful. Agnes in the garden. Agnes in the sitting room. Agnes at the seaside with windswept hair. Mostly alone, mostly a bit wary. Who had taken the photos?

Then a leap in time.

Agnes amongst men in uniform. Police. No smile, but no wariness either. A cooler, more direct and determined look straight at the camera.

And even earlier.

Agnes in a light dress, with lipstick and a radiant but forced-looking smile.

He thought about the lipstick that she'd started wearing recently, and how this small change had unsettled him. Small things suddenly worried him; subtle differences made him unsure. What if it had always been like that? What if he just couldn't remember?

The fact he had shot Lillith was having surprisingly little effect on him. He had given his word. A man, his word. That's just how life was. But something else was troubling him. Something that he had encountered in the fog, short and sharp like lightning. Something that flashed now and then, for maddening seconds at a time and then disappeared into thin air.

An umbrella. The umbrella was the only tangible thing, but obviously it wasn't enough. The umbrella was only half the truth. Umbrellas didn't move by themselves, and this one had been moving. And beneath it . . . Umbrellas were there to cover things. What was hidden beneath the umbrella? Or who?

Marshall looked reproachfully at the young, smiling Agnes in the picture. *Why didn't I meet you back then? Why only now? What's the point?* Agnes didn't respond, and suddenly Marshall was miffed. He wanted to keep flicking, deeper into the past, watch Agnes becoming a teenager, a girl, a child, but his hands had other plans. They snapped the book shut, stroked the worn leather spine once more and pushed it gently, but decisively back onto the shelf.

He sighed. Maybe it was slowly getting to the point of saying goodbye as planned. He was ready. At least felt ready. Better than constantly seeing a stranger in his clothes. Better than wandering through the fog alone.

But somebody out there had other plans. Someone had put a gun on their table, *his* gun. Someone was playing a cold-hearted game – with all of them presumably, but above all with Agnes. An old game. So, there was nothing left for him to do, but persevere, hold his ground, a lone guard in the void.

Marshall was searching.

8

CANAPÉS

Suddenly, Agnes was awake. Sunlight was streaming rosily through her closed eyelids. She blinked, carefully stretched and smiled. It was going to be a good day; she could tell straight away. Something was flitting around at the edge of her consciousness, a kind of thrill of anticipation. Like Christmas when you are twelve and have lain awake all night and then actually fall asleep and wake up, still a bit woozy, but certain that something special awaits.

Like your birthday.

Like Easter.

Like . . . a funeral!

Agnes got herself out of bed with an unusual amount of vigour. Her hip didn't like it, of course not, but that didn't matter to Agnes today. She had always liked funerals, right down to her first, which had been a revelation, a rush, a triumph. Other funerals had been more difficult, sadder, but never without giving her the feeling that everything somehow had its place. Apart from that, funerals were an invaluable source of information for anyone wanting to find out something about both the dead and the living.

Black coat. Black hat. Black dress.

She dragged the clothes out of the wardrobe and threw them onto the bed. The hat looked a bit like it had been forcibly removed from a crow. She tenderly brushed the dust from the shiny black feathers. The hat was a real favourite of hers.

Agnes padded into the bathroom humming, turned on the shower, waited until the water ran warm through her fingers, and struggled out of her nightie and onto the plastic chair that the physio had put under the shower for her. To be on the safe side. She stared down at her wrinkly and strangely crooked toes as the hot water ran over her back. Her hip liked that.

After a few languorous minutes she remembered what day it was, soaped herself and thoroughly rinsed. Getting dry was always like a wrestling match with a somewhat ungainly, but fluffy boa constrictor. At least her false teeth practically cleaned themselves.

The dress was a challenge, the black silk tights a nightmare, but somehow, she managed both without any major incidents. Her hair looked weird again – when had it got so thin and limp? But that's what the hat was for. Agnes pinned it on with a hat pin – hopefully it would hold – and felt better straight away. What else? Lipstick! This time the application went more smoothly. A bit of rouge on the cheeks – nothing was more important than looking healthy at a funeral, so that nobody got any silly ideas. And then, sunglasses. Nobody could see exactly what was going on behind a pair of sunglasses. Whether you were crying (unlikely), whether you had briefly shut your eyes for a nap (possible) or whether you were watching your fellow human beings with a keen, unerring gaze (definitely).

Agnes checked in the mirror and was satisfied. She could have been in a Mafia film. Or a political drama. Or perhaps . . . a murder mystery.

'I want a hat too!' Edwina crossed her arms over her dark-blue coat and refused to get into the waiting taxi. Agnes had just searched Edwina's bag for Hettie – the tortoise had had enough adventure over the last few days and should stay at home. But now it had occurred to Edwina that she was the only one standing in front of the house without a head-covering – and she didn't like it one bit.

Marshall was wearing his uniform again – enviable that you could just show up anywhere in uniform – and a matching military hat. Winston valued warmth as always and had pulled a dark woolly hat over his ears, Bernadette had an ill-fitting men's fedora on her head, and Charlie wasn't wearing the ostrich feather hat, but a snug elegant pillbox hat with a little lace veil falling dramatically over her face. Agnes nodded in approval. Here was someone else who understood funerals.

It was only Edwina, whom nobody had said anything to about a hat, and now she was in a huff.

'The hat isn't important,' Agnes said impatiently. 'You can go without a hat as well.'

'Then take your hat off!' Edwina threw her head back stubbornly. 'If one of you takes your hat off, I'll come with you.'

Nobody wanted to give up their hat, so they continued to

stand around the taxi at a loss.

'What is it now?' the driver shouted impatiently. 'Any time today is fine . . .' He didn't have a hat himself and was obviously freezing.

Agnes groaned. They were running late. If they didn't leave soon, they could forget about saying goodbye to Lillith. Personally, Agnes didn't mind – Lillith was with them there in the garden far more than she ever would be in a box or little tin at the cemetery, but it would cause bad blood. Gentleman callers were one thing – not turning up to a friend's funeral quite another. It wouldn't just mean tutting and head-shaking but would arouse suspicion too.

And the last thing they needed was suspicion.

Agnes stamped impatiently and immediately regretted it. Ouch! 'Fine! I'll get you your stupid hat!'

She struggled up the veranda steps again, closed the door and looked around in the hall in the hope of finding something usable on one of the coat pegs, but there was only an old scarf and a shopping bag hanging up. Not even Edwina could pull off a scarf as a hat. Up the stairs to her wardrobe? That would take too long! The stairlift was comfy, but agonisingly slow, even for someone like Agnes who really had no excessive need for speed. What then? She peeked in the sitting room, discovered nothing resembling a hat and limped towards the dining room. Then it suddenly came to her.

Kitchen!

Wall cabinet!

Third shelf.

There a dusty tea cosy was holding court over sugar

bowls and cake forks. The tea cosy, a stitched bell made of aubergine-coloured velvet, wasn't particularly popular in the house, above all because it didn't really keep the tea warm. But as a hat, it was heaven-sent.

Agnes clamped the newly anointed hat under her arm and had just dragged herself to the door when the phone started ringing in the hall.

Ringringring.

Ringringring.

She ignored the sound out of habit and opened the front door.

Her housemates looked at her expectantly. The taxi driver had lit a cigarette and was disrespectfully puffing smoke into the cold autumn air. Outrageous!

Ringringring.

The phone sounded agitated, and somehow . . .

Agnes sighed, closed the door again and made her way to the phone, her heart pounding.

Ringringring.

Just as she was about to pick up, it stopped ringing. Typical! But then, before she could head towards the door, it started up again, more agitated than before.

Agnes picked up and listened into the receiver.

'Hello?'

At first, she thought there was something not right with her hearing again, because there was nothing there, just a rattling.

Rattly breathing.

'Hello?' Agnes asked again.

'Ssshee,' it rattled into the phone. 'Ssshee's . . . Oh my God!'

132

Finally, Agnes thought she recognised the voice.

'*Sparrow?*'

'I-I-I w-went . . . A-and ssshee's . . .'

Definitely Sparrow, their stairlift engineer and amateur burglar. But you couldn't get any sense out of him.

'Have you still got the chocolate bar?' Agnes asked gently.

'Have I got the . . . what?'

'Eat it,' said Agnes. 'Get it out of your bag and eat it. Now!'

'I can't,' Sparrow groaned. 'I'm standing here right next to . . . to . . . *her*! I can't even *think* about chocolate bars!'

'Okay' Agnes said and thought for a moment. 'Maybe you should get a bit farther away? Take . . . Have you got one of those phones that takes photos?'

'Of course.' Sparrow said, indignant even in his panic.

'Then take a few photos. And then *go*. And when you're back at home, eat the chocolate bar and make a cup of tea. That's an order!'

She hadn't said that sentence for a long time. It warmed Agnes's heart.

Someone was knocking on the front door. Damn, the funeral! She'd completely forgotten!

'I have to go!' she said and heard Sparrow whimpering on the other end of the phone.

'Be brave, young man! Good work! Eat your chocolate bar. I'll be in touch!'

She put the phone down before Sparrow could protest, padded off and swung the door open.

The taxi driver! He had finished his cigarette.

'Any time today?' he asked.

'Of course!' Agnes said and pushed past the man with dignity. She pulled the tea cosy over Edwina's head and smoothed down her black coat.

'Shall we go?'

'That really is a stupid hat!' Edwina cried in delight.

The tea cosy suited her brilliantly.

Agnes hadn't been to the cemetery for a long time. Weird actually. She liked it there. Soft earth clung to her plump, round heels. Ferns waved their elegantly curved arms. Headstones greeted her like old friends.

Most of them *were* old friends.

Leonora Miller.

Aldwin Puck.

Titus Coldwell. The most important headstone of all.

Agnes was tempted to quickly reach out her hand and touch the mossy weathered stone, to make sure that it was still there, that it was real. But she didn't dare. At a cemetery, everyone was on the look-out for gossip, and there was no sense in giving herself away now, after all these years.

'Which way?'

Agnes squinted. The others looked at her impatiently.

'Which way, Agnes?'

She remembered she was the only one who knew where to go, and pointed between the trees along a narrow gravel path. 'The chapel is behind there.'

'Chapel' was an exaggeration. Previously, the light little building had served as the vicar's greenhouse, but a few velvet curtains and a somewhat melodramatic blood-red carpet had transformed it into a place where you could say goodbye to the departed in a more or less solemn fashion.

Agnes smiled to herself. A greenhouse. Lillith would have appreciated that.

'I think we're too late.' Charlie mumbled.

'Nonsense,' Bernadette said rattling the door handle. 'We can't be too late.'

In her haste not to miss Lillith, she practically fell into the room.

The door clanked.

Gravel crunched.

Winston's wheelchair rattled.

All eyes were on the new arrivals. It wasn't many eyes.

There stood the podgy daughter, Pippa, and a bald-headed, nervous-looking glasses-wearer, a bored curly- haired teenager and a girl with purple hair, in front of them a flower arrangement and a metal vase with a lid.

'What the . . . ?' started the daughter. 'I said, close family only!'

'We are a close family!' Edwina declared and stood up to her full height beneath her tea cosy.

Lillith's daughter didn't seem to appreciate that and spat back, 'Am I not even allowed to say goodbye to my own mother in peace?'

'No!' Agnes was even a bit surprised at herself, but she was always on top form at cemeteries. She sensed Marshall quietly, but militarily, position himself next to her.

'Hear! Hear!' cried Winston.

'Hello, Lillith.' Bernadette said softly.

The daughter looked as though she wanted to say something scathing, but she just made a chortling sound, a bit like a guinea fowl with trouble laying, and stared at the metal vase again.

Agnes followed her eyes. That was it then. A bit of ash in a tin with a lid. All that was left of Lillith and her green fingers. Somehow . . . unsatisfying.

Edwina tugged her sleeve. 'Lillith isn't here.' Her aubergine-coloured tea cosy hat trembled with disappointment.

'She's in the tin,' Agnes whispered back.

Edwina looked at her in disbelief.

A cemetery official, identifiable by his proper dress and professionally composed expression, opened the door, walked to Lillith's daughter and whispered something in her ear.

The daughter glanced at the clock in annoyance.

'Already? But it's . . .'

The man murmured something apologetic, then he motioned for them to go outside.

The daughter pulled out a tissue and was led outside by the nervous glasses-wearer. The others followed. Only the girl with purple hair looked truly sad.

'I'm sorry,' the cemetery attendant said cheerfully. 'There's a lot on at the moment.'

'How long is it going to be?' Agnes asked looking round for somewhere to sit. 'We're waiting for Mildred as well.'

The man shrugged his shoulders. 'Half an hour or so. We've got to rearrange to make space for the coffin. And then all the flowers . . .' He waved his hand to make clear what an imposition all the flowers were.

Agnes saw Edwina was the last to leave the chapel and noticed with relief that she had finally taken the tea cosy off.

'And are there any refreshments . . . ?' Even as she was saying it, she knew it was nonsense. They weren't at the theatre after all, and presumably nobody had accounted for people who wanted to go to more than one funeral in a day.

The cemetery attendant looked doubtful. 'You can sit on the benches over there, and if you'd like I'll fetch you a glass of water.'

Agnes shook her head. 'No water, thank you.' She had no desire to spend valuable time at the cemetery looking for the nearest toilet.

So, they plopped themselves on two stone benches in the shade of the cemetery trees, Bernadette, Charlie and Edwina on the left; Agnes and Marshall on the right, Winston in his wheelchair between the benches. They silently watched the removals. Their position was out of the wind and almost cosy. Agnes regretted not having a bag of sherbet lemons to pass round.

And as they watched bouquet after bouquet of flowers drift into the chapel, it became clear to Agnes that this was theatre. Pure theatre. But why? And for whom? This kind of showing off wasn't really Isobel's style. She had always been the quieter of the two, more shy and subtle. More devious, some said, but they didn't know Isobel very well. She probably just wanted the best for her sister. Or was there more to it? Something like a guilty conscience, maybe? After all, for some years Mildred had lain in the house helplessly whilst her sister shouldered everything. In the space of a few years a lot of guilt could build up, Agnes knew that from experience.

One thing was certain, Mildred would have loved all the expense!

When it seemed like it was impossible to stuff any more bouquets into the modest chapel, the stream of flowers dried up. Next the coffin arrived, on a type of barrow, not particularly dignified. But what a coffin, as big as a ship, black and shiny like raven's feathers. Music started up, a dark, solemn funeral march, and suddenly the cemetery was full of people.

There was Isobel, limping, leaning on her chauffeur, an unused hankie in her hand. There was the girl who had served the biscuits to Agnes, there were the gardeners, doctors and nurses.

Obviously, the people from the village hadn't wanted to miss out on seeing this spectacle. Isobel had been worrying about nothing.

Agnes saw some people from the coffee morning and regretted not having a few of Edwina's biscuits with her to throw. She recognised the praying mantis, the mouse-grey ladies, the man that had put the sign away, and one of the brazen permed ladies who had given Marshall her number. At least one. The mood was festive in a subdued way. For most of the mourners it was probably less about saying goodbye, and much more about making sure Mildred really was dead.

No sign of Olive, the cream slice maker. Of course not. Agnes knew exactly where Olive was right now.

'Not bad,' Winston said next to her. 'If only half as many people turn up at my funeral . . .'

'The question is why they turn up,' Bernadette mumbled.

'I think it's starting,' Charlie said to nobody in particular. 'Fabulous!'

Marshall got up and helped Agnes up too. Winston rolled off, and Bernadette grabbed Edwina's arm. Edwina didn't say anything. That unsettled Agnes. It was rarely a good sign when Edwina held her tongue.

Agnes would have preferred to have mixed inconspicuously with the other mourners, but Isobel saw her, waved her over and pulled her into a vice-like embrace.

'Thank you for coming,' she whispered into Agnes's ear. 'It means a lot to me.'

'Naturally . . .' Agnes whispered, although *naturally* wasn't the right word.

Isobel squeezed her hand.

From then on, Agnes was right at the front. Carried away from her housemates as if she were riding a wave, she went into the chapel with Isobel and was next to her as she came to a stop in front of the open casket.

Agnes wanted Marshall and his medals to hold on to. Instead, she leant on her umbrella. There Mildred lay, immaculate as she had been in life, at least before the unpleasant story with the stroke. Carefully made up. Shiny black hair like a cap. Hands folded. Wrinkles smoothed. Elegant white dress. Innocent, strangely virginal. Weird choice of colour.

And there stood Isobel, carefully made up, shiny black hair like a cap, hands folded, in an elegant black dress.

They looked so similar, even now. How difficult and strange it must be for Isobel to practically bury herself. No wonder she wanted to have a familiar figure like Agnes next to her.

Agnes didn't look down at the dead woman. Instead, out of the corner of her eye, she observed the emotions playing in quiet waves around Isobel's narrow lips. Wonder. Disbelief. Sadness, obviously, but also tenderness – and for a fraction of a second, a smile.

Agnes sank into her memories as if into a deep dark pond.

She knew what it was like to lose a twin.

Isobel and Mildred.

Agnes and *Alice* . . .

Someone coughed behind her and Agnes jumped. She had no idea how much time had passed, but she was still standing there leaning on her umbrella staring at the dead but still kind of worried-looking Mildred. Her hip was hurting. She felt a bit dizzy.

Isobel leant over and whispered something into dead Mildred's ear. Then she was suddenly hanging round Agnes's neck howling.

Agnes murmured, 'Isobel, Isobel,' and struggled to balance. Where was Marshall when you needed him? Where was the snotty chauffeur?

Then suddenly the vicar was there and, not a moment too soon, he relieved her of the howling Isobel. Agnes reeled and found an arm. Marshall, thankfully. Somehow, she managed to hobble behind the coffin to the grave with the rest of the mourners and, leaning on a headstone, follow the proceedings quite comfortably. The vicar was balder than Agnes remembered, but still full of enthusiasm for God and the ever-after. Mildred transformed from a widely disliked, myth-enshrouded poisoner to a high-profile citizen, to a philanthropist, a pillar of the community, and the chance of eternal life seemed rosy too. *The Lord is my shepherd* and so on . . . Agnes could well imagine what the *lord* thought of little sheep that only got in touch when the worst happened: not much!

Really, Mildred would have laughed.

'Ashes to ashes,' droned the vicar. 'Dust to dust.'

It was the dramatic pinnacle of the funeral, and Agnes peered through her sunglasses at the group. Most of the mourners looked calm to some extent, some even contented. The standing would be over soon, and drinking and gossiping could begin. With an expression of deep concentration, Isobel stared down at the coffin. For someone who hadn't known Mildred at all, Charlie looked surprisingly upset – or was it *because* she hadn't known Mildred? Edwina looked shocked too and was holding her tea cosy to her chest.

As usual the vicar didn't know when enough was enough and droned on: about Mildred's youth and background, her actions and deeds, all far-fetched.

Luckily the high-pitched ringing started up for Agnes again, just at the right moment, and she used the sudden acoustic break to have a think.

'Disembowelled,' the mouse-grey lady had said. That was obviously nonsense, just like the story about the gentleman callers. But perhaps not completely. After all it was a pretty absurd idea. Too absurd to just be plucked out of thin air. There was *something* in it. Nobody had disembowelled Lillith, Agnes had seen it with her own eyes. But Mildred? Maybe it was just a bit of a mix-up? And maybe not disembowelled . . . but something *similar*. Agnes remembered the policeman's fixed, shocked stare. Undoubtedly, he had set eyes on something unpleasant – more unpleasant than a simple, clean shot to the head.

The idea unsettled Agnes. It meant that maybe the murder wasn't a *practicality*, but something personal, deep and dark and twisted. Unpractical murderers were the most dangerous. Just like the vicar, unpractical murderers mostly didn't know when enough was enough . . .

A big raindrop landed on Agnes's nose, a second streaked her sunglasses, a third, fourth, fifth hit the crow hat. Within seconds it was tipping it down. Agnes moved away from the headstone, struggled with her umbrella for a moment and finally got it open. She waved to Marshall to join her under the umbrella, but he was just standing there with a horrified look on his face staring into space.

For a panic-filled moment Marshall didn't know who they had just put into the grave. Agnes maybe? Geraldine? His mother?

But no, Agnes was standing next to him, one eyebrow quizzically raised, his mother and Geraldine were long gone. Umbrellas opened around him, black and grey, brown and red. A sea of umbrellas – and amongst them the one he had seen in the fog; of that he was suddenly sure. But which one? And where? Who was hiding beneath it?

Someone tugged his sleeve gingerly. Agnes. She gestured him over, waving him under her umbrella, and Marshall realised his face was wet. His face, his ears, his shoulders. Strange, that. He was suddenly sure that back in the fog he hadn't been wet. An umbrella, but no rain! What did it mean?

Agnes pulled him towards her into the dry with gentle force. She looked worried. He hated it when she looked worried. He hated being under the umbrella too. He couldn't stand the sight of umbrellas.

The vicar had finally come to the end of his sermon, presumably motivated by the rain. He blessed, nodded and shook hands. Then Marshall remembered again who was in the coffin. The second dead woman. The one he hadn't really known. Mildred. The neighbour. Shot with his revolver. Shot in the fog.

The surviving sister took a final look at the coffin, turned to them expecting Agnes, but saw him first and retreated. Good job too! Weird twin! He found Isobel creepy. He didn't like how she was suddenly hanging all over Agnes. Not a word all these years, and all of a sudden . . . What did she want? What sort of a friend wasn't to be seen in a single one of the photos in Agnes's album?

Right now, she looked harmless though. Exhausted, hurt, and yet relieved, virtually euphoric. The difficult task had been completed; life could go on. Or was it something else making her eyes glisten? Something like triumph?

She blinked and the moment was gone.

'Thank you,' she said with moist eyes looking past him. 'Thank you, Agnes! Please do come for drinks at the vicarage.

There's champagne and canapés – Mildred would have liked that, don't you think?'

Agnes nodded, her hands being squeezed again. Marshall would have simply loved to forgo the procession of umbrellas and the canapés, but Agnes needed something to hold onto.

Then Marshall stared mistrustfully at the row of dripping umbrellas leaning against the wall of the vicarage. What were they doing here – and what was he doing? Someone was pulling his arm – Agnes, and the next minute he had a glass of champagne in his hand and was watching plates of canapés with salmon, prawns, roast beef and caviar float past him. Agnes tried a salmon canapé; Winston had a whole plate full on his lap and was explaining the selection to Bernadette. An unfamiliar woman with a perm smiled at him expectantly and even winked. Charlie came over to them with her glass of champagne wanting to clink glasses. Glasses clinked. What was it all about?

'Why aren't you eating anything, Edwina?' Agnes asked suddenly.

Edwina was holding the tea cosy in both hands shaking her head. 'No free hand.'

'Then put the thing down!' Charlie said and reached out her hand towards the purple monstrosity. The next minute she recoiled. 'What's all that dirt?'

'It's not dirt,' Edwina said indignantly. 'It's Lillith.'

9

GIN AND TONIC

At home they poured Lillith out of the tea cosy into a much-loved coffee tin and found a good position for her: amongst spider plants and begonias in the flower window.

Agnes threw the velvet tea cosy away and thoroughly washed her hands.

'What were you thinking?' she scolded, but true to form Edwina hadn't really been thinking at all, except that it would be good to have Lillith back home, in whatever form that may be.

And somehow, she was right.

'Once a member of Sunset Hall, always a member of Sunset Hall, huh?' Charlie asked. 'Fabulous!'

Mission accomplished, Charlie and Agnes sat on the sofa and put their feet up. Agnes drank some tea and Charlie had a little glass of gin and tonic with ice and lemon. It was quiet in the sitting room. Edwina had disappeared after the handwashing, to sulk presumably, Winston and Bernadette had gone for a nap, and Marshall had wandered upstairs mumbling something about the internet. Agnes was beginning to have doubts. Was he really always on the internet, or was he roaming about elsewhere, in the past perhaps, or in his own head? What was he spending the whole day doing?

Agnes didn't like it. She was tired too, downright dog-tired – in any case more tired than Brexit, who was lying on a rug gnawing on a bone, scratching behind his ear with great dedication every now and again.

But for some reason she didn't want to lie down. Something was troubling her. Something was gnawing away at her, stubbornly and enthusiastically like Brexit on his bone. The funeral ran through her mind over and over, but there was nothing unusual. Apart from the fact that Edwina had pilfered Lillith's ashes, and the resulting, somewhat hasty departure from the vicarage. Agnes would have stayed longer, despite her hip doing red-hot somersaults. She would have liked to have observed the mourners for longer, later, when, relaxed by champagne and canapés, the masks they wore everyday would slip a little. That always happened, and it would have happened this time too, if it weren't for Edwina with her stupid ideas and that idiotic tea cosy . . .

Agnes made a disgruntled sound.

Charlie nodded next to her and knocked back the gin and tonic. Then she shuddered, 'Murder funeral, huh? Better than the television!'

'Much better!' Agnes said with utter conviction. Since the Brexit story, there wasn't much point in the television any more. Recently it had got so bad that they had decided to banish the television to the cellar. And there it stood, without a socket. Served it right!

'It's a shame you can't go to your own funeral.' Charlie sighed and looked reproachfully at her empty glass.

Agnes groaned. If only you could go to any funeral in peace, without tea cosies and crackpot ideas, that would be something! Had the murderer been amongst them – maybe close enough that she only had to reach out her hand to touch him? The murderer – the murderess? He or she?

It didn't take much to fire a gun like that. A child could do it . . .

Suddenly Agnes was sitting up in the apple tree again. The wind tugged at her shirt, leaves whispered, the cold crept up her toes. But this time she wasn't alone. Her twin sister, Alice, was sitting next to her. And Alice was smiling.

Agnes suppressed a shudder. The monster was close, so close she could smell his body, clean and strange, lemon and leather.

Don't look, don't look, don't look, Agnes begged. *Don't look up! Anywhere but up!* The children at school told anybody that would listen she was a witch. Now she would have liked to be a witch.

'Agnes, darling, come out! Come, little mouse! I can see you! I'm coming to get you!'

Alice squeezed Agnes's hand and put her finger to her lips.

The monster hadn't seen them yet. He was standing right underneath their tree turning his head back and forth. Then he leant against the trunk and laughed, delighted that Agnes hadn't come out. Delighted that there would be a real chase this time.

It was this laugh that banished Agnes's last doubt.

Please, she thought. *Please, Alice.*

Alice nodded, seriously and somehow wisely, as if she had heard Agnes. Her delicate rib cage rose. A single deep breath. She took aim slowly and carefully. Her fingers closed around the handle of the heavy sledge hammer again; it had taken the two of them untold effort to drag it into the apple tree.

Then Alice let the hammer fall.

Plonk.

A shockingly mundane sound, low and dull. Chopping damp wood made sounds like that, buckets filled with water or sacks full of flour.

Beneath them something like a sack full of flour slumped onto the grass.

Plonk.

'Shit!' cried a voice. Something clattered. The whispering of the apple tree leaves fell silent. Agnes struggled through many decades back to the present day. The hammer had fallen long ago, the sack of flour cleaned up. Buried – but perhaps not forgotten? And there was another noise from the past, a wet noise.

Dripping.

Agnes opened her eyes wide.

Charlie on all fours, a stain on the carpet, a glass rolling. Charlie chasing it.

Brexit trotted over to them to see what all the fuss was about. He sniffed the stain, found an ice cube and crunched it noisily. Then he stood between Agnes and Charlie politely wagging his tail, his quizzical dog eyes looking from one of them to the other.

'I've got it!' Charlie had recovered her glass and stood up a little unsteadily. She lurched into the kitchen and came back shortly after with a fresh drink.

'Didn't sleep well?' she asked throwing herself next to Agnes on the sofa with exaggerated vigour. Was she drunk? Again? Maybe Charlie was an alcoholic? That was strictly against the principles of the household. Agnes would have to have a serious word with Marshall.

'I wasn't asleep,' she said stroppily. But then the coffee table cast a long, accusing shadow, daylight was fading a bit, and the old grandfather clock in the corner was ticking ominously. How long had they just been sitting there for? Where had the time gone?

'Ha!' said Charlie winking at her. 'Gin and tonic?'

Agnes had her principles. No platitudes, no chewy baked goods that could ruin your false teeth, and no alcohol before it got dark. But it was never too late to jettison long-kept principles. She nodded. A gin and tonic seemed like exactly what she needed.

'Fabulous!' Charlie went into the kitchen again and soon came back with an appealing-looking glass. Little bubbles danced around ice cubes. They clinked glasses silently and somehow celebratorily, and Agnes sipped. There! She felt better already.

'Who's Alice?' Charlie asked suddenly. The relaxed, comfy feeling that had just come over her abruptly vanished again. She wasn't just sleeping without realising – she was talking in her sleep as well! For a minute Agnes was tempted to pretend she hadn't heard Charlie's question. Where was the high-pitched ringing when you needed it?

But it was too late. She had heard the question and sloshed a bit of her gin and tonic in shock. Now Charlie was sitting next to her looking at her expectantly and not drunk in the least. Brexit nudged her knee.

'Alice is . . .' Agnes began – not so much because of Charlie, but because a polite dog deserved an answer. 'Alice *was* my sister. My twin sister. She was like me. We were inseparable.'

Inseparable until one day . . . Suddenly, Agnes knew exactly when she had last seen Alice: at the cemetery, surrounded by fresh flower wreaths, next to the brand new, highly polished headstone of Titus Coldwell. Scratched knees, wild unruly hair all over the place and a broad grin. Alice had winked at her, but Agnes, paralysed by guilt and a kind of numbness, had hardly looked up. And when she had finally dared to look over at her, the only thing next to the headstone was an over-hanging, vaguely Alice-shaped branch.

Agnes reached out her hand and scratched Brexit behind the ear. Brexit's eyes rolled back blissfully.

Charlie raised her eyebrow, more out of curiosity than sympathy. 'Dead?'

'Disappeared,' Agnes said curtly.

Was Alice dead? Strangely she had never really dared to think about it, not back then or later either. What and where was Alice if she wasn't dead? Agnes tried to imagine how she would look today: petite, almost elegant, but also a bit like dried fish.

Like me, thought Agnes. *Just like me.*

Charlie nodded thoughtfully. 'Makes you think, a funeral like that, doesn't it? Even with this project here . . . I mean, to imagine it rationally is one thing, but when you see a bit of dust or a coffin like that . . . really upset me, if I'm honest.' Her glass was empty again.

Brexit was panting.

'Mildred has nothing to do with us!' Agnes said sharply. Too sharply.

Charlie raised her eyebrow again. 'Unlikely. Unlike you lot, I'm no expert, but to be honest . . . I haven't been here long, but as far as I can see everyone here is carrying a whole load of baggage around with them. Figuratively speaking. You really don't know each other that well.'

She broke off and stretched, unladylike, but still graceful somehow.

'We know each other well enough,' Agnes responded as decisively as she could.

'Nonsense,' said Charlie. 'One knows next to nobody well enough. Take me for example. What do you know? I mean, we corresponded, but in all honesty . . .'

'Marshall checked everything,' Agnes explained half-heartedly.

'Maybe he checked what I told him. But what I *didn't* tell him . . .'

'Marshall checked *everything*,' Agnes said with more emphasis.

'From what I've heard Marshall recently mislaid a gun at quite a decisive moment. So he claims, anyway. I don't want to say it's not true, but it doesn't exactly fill you with confidence, does it?'

Agnes would have liked to defend Marshall, but she didn't know how. Charlie was right in some ways. She clutched her gin and tonic hoping that the high-pitched ringing or some other form of higher power would bring the conversation to an end soon.

But Charlie was only getting started. 'The question is: Who trusts who? Personally, I trust Brexit, and that's it. Please don't get me wrong, I think this is a wonderful project. Fabulous initiative! I'm happy I'm here. But one mustn't be naïve.'

Naïve? Her? That got to Agnes. 'We have been living here for years. There has never been . . .'

'Sure, sure, but it's the first time something has *happened*, isn't it? Theory and practice. Something like that inflames passions!'

Agnes wondered if her hip would co-operate with a sudden departure from the sofa. She had had enough of this conversation. What did Charlie want from her? Had she come to cause trouble? It seemed like it.

'Marshall is an interesting man, but is he all there? And Bernadette – quite honestly: Was she in the Mafia or what?'

'She was undercover for a long time,' Agnes said apologetically.

Charlie snorted. 'Undercover. Ha! Winston is obsessed with chocolate bars, and Edwina . . .' She waved dismissively and exhaled pointedly.

Agnes was suddenly wide awake.

Chocolate bars? Winston? Chocolate bars! There was something . . .

'Fuck! Shit! Fuck!'

Charlie looked at her in surprise.

Agnes had a secret weakness for obscenities, but she wouldn't have let Charlie catch her at it so easily, if it weren't for . . . chocolate bars! The telephone ringing and ringing and ringing. Sparrow on the other end of the line, Sparrow, who had carried out their mission and was so worked up he could hardly speak. She had sent him home with nothing more than advice to eat a chocolate bar and then she had just forgotten him! Maybe he was still sitting there, high on chocolate and sugar, close to a nervous breakdown while she was slurping gin and tonic. It was unforgivable.

She struggled off the sofa despite her hip's protests.

'Wake the others! Dining room! Right now! It's important!'

When, a short while later, Sparrow was standing at their front door in a boiler suit with his tool bag, he didn't look as if he had eaten many chocolate bars. To Agnes he seemed thinner than before, paler, more jittery. She led him to the dining room, where the others were already sitting around the table, eagerly, but also a bit annoyed to have been rudely awoken from their afternoon nap. To calm their nerves, Agnes poured them tea.

'Is the stairlift broken again?' Edwina asked cheerfully.

'No,' said Agnes putting a cup down for Sparrow. 'Not the stairlift. I had an idea and asked Sparrow to find the missing bullet for us, you know, the third one that was shot from the murder weapon. And . . .' she paused dramatically, 'I think he found it.'

Sparrow stared at the steam twisting out of his teacup, and shuddered.

'I . . . I knocked on the door first, but nobody . . . And I heard noises. Not . . . human sounds, but something. So, I went through the garden. I had gloves on, like you said. No footprints, I checked. The back door was open, and I went into the house. I called out. I had thought of an excuse, but nobody was there, there were just these weird noises and a . . . smell, so I carried on. She was in the kitchen . . .' He fell silent.

'Did you take a few photos, like I said?' Agnes asked softly.

The amateur burglar swallowed and nodded. He rummaged through his pockets and finally unearthed his phone. His hands were shaking so much that it slid out of his hand and skidded across the oak table. He finally got a hold of it and got a picture up.

Agnes squinted. Damn, without her reading glasses she could hardly make out a thing!

Edwina, who didn't just have supple joints, but also damn good eyes, sneaked a peek at the screen.

'Amateurish!' she said. 'What a mess!'

Agnes took the phone from her and sent her to look for her reading glasses. And Winston's reading glasses. Charlie's reading glasses and Marshall's too. None of them could make out much on the screen without their glasses. Only that it was red and, as Edwina had said, a mess.

While they waited, Agnes explained how she had tracked down the third bullet.

'It was the cream slice!' Agnes sipped her tea, relishing the moment. She had noticed a detail that hadn't occurred to anybody else. Her brain was still working, even now, after all this time. 'Olive's cream slices were there, but not Olive herself. And Olive doesn't bake to make other people happy. She bakes to be admired. Give away a few cream slices just like that without being there herself? No chance! Not Olive. So, I asked myself what was going on with her. Obviously, anything could have happened, but then presumably the whole of Duck End would have known about it. She's the biggest tattletale imaginable. But nobody knew anything. So, I rang Sparrow, gave him her address and asked him to pop round. And he found her!'

Agnes tapped Sparrow's phone. 'Good work, Sparrow!'

The stairlift engineer smiled weakly.

Agnes continued. 'Olive is exactly the sort of person to stick her nose in things that don't concern her. And it seems like this time she stuck her nose in the wrong thing. Now we have to find out what it was!'

'Hear! Hear!' Bernadette chimed.

Charlie whistled through her teeth in recognition.

Winston grinned and Marshall clapped his hands to give Agnes a little round of applause.

She felt herself going red and quickly had a slurp of tea.

Maybe it was her age, or she really was naïve like Charlie had said, but in that moment, Agnes made the decision to trust her housemates come what may. She had made a lot of mistakes in her life, trusted people who hadn't deserved it and mistrusted the wrong people. Now, from a distance, it seemed plain and simple: to be taken in by someone was embarrassing and painful, undoubtedly, but not to have trusted someone when it would have been advisable – that was the deeper pain. No question. It was the kind of regret that wore you down year after year, from the inside out. Agnes was too old to battle with a guilty conscience in her final years.

Winston, Bernadette, Marshall, Charlie and Edwina were by

no means perfect, but they were a team. Her team. Together they had embarked on a dangerous journey, probably their last. It was a matter of life and death, dignity, freedom and honesty. It was about not just mindlessly sticking your spoon in the wall because you were old. And now to cap it all a murderer was making their lives difficult. Somebody who had tasted blood and developed a thirst for it. Someone, who had put a gun on their table! The least they could do was depend on one another!

Edwina returned with a fistful of reading glasses, and it took a while for everyone to find the right ones. Then they passed Sparrow's phone round.

'Goodness gracious!' said Charlie looking around, presumably for another gin and tonic. But there was only tea.

Winston winced. 'Subtle, it isn't!' he said.

'Not nice!' Marshall agreed.

Bernadette was banging impatiently on the table, so Agnes took the phone out of Marshall's hand and described the contents of the picture as well as she could.

'A kitchen. Flour on the floor. A baking tray. She's lying on her back, with her head leaning on the fridge. A blood smear where she's slid down the fridge. More blood on the floor. Her face . . .' Agnes hesitated for a moment. 'There's really not much left of her face. And – there are cats . . .'

Sparrow wretched and rushed out of the room.

Nobody said anything, while Agnes searched for the words.

'As far as I can see, she was shot straight in the face. At close range. Not nice.'

'Are you certain it's Olive?' Bernadette asked.

Agnes thought about it. 'The hair fits and the clothes.

Olive had this weakness for lilac, as far as I know, that's right, and she's wearing an apron. In theory, it could be someone else, but that's not likely. There's flour, and you can possibly make out some footsteps, but the cats have been running around all over the place and . . . well, you'd have to look more closely.'

'Let's go there!' Edwina said clapping her hands together. 'I like cats!'

Agnes had no marked sympathy for the cats that had so thoughtlessly tucked into their owner like that. She shook her head.

'It's a crime scene! If we turn up at a crime scene again, even the most stupid police officer will get suspicious. No, we've got to be clever . . .' She thought about it. 'Someone else had to find her. And soon! That . . .' she pointed to the phone, 'is really no fit state.'

Sparrow appeared at the dining room door. 'Can I . . . can I maybe go?'

Winston nodded. 'Of course, my boy. We'll just copy the photos, if that's alright with you.' Winston passed the phone to Marshall. 'And then you should delete them, yeah? And forget about it. You've really helped us out.'

Sparrow laughed drily. 'Forget about it? No chance! Are you going to find him?' he asked. 'Whoever did it?'

'We're definitely going to try,' Agnes said softly.

'Or he'll find us,' Bernadette murmured gravely. 'And then God help him!'

'Or both,' Edwina said optimistically.

Marshall grabbed the phone and peered through his reading

glasses. 'She was baking,' he said. 'Probably for the coffee morning. The murderer came through the back door, just like Sparrow, Olive turned around and . . .' He pondered. 'The oven door is closed, yet the baking tray is . . . why did she have the baking tray in her hand?'

Agnes understood what he was getting at straight away. 'The murderer!' she cried. 'Olive knew him! She offered him something!'

'And *he* shot her,' Bernadette said drily. 'Obviously not a fan of home baking.'

'What was she making?' Edwina asked.

Marshall enlarged the photo with two fingers. 'Muffins,' he said. 'That really is a bloody good camera!'

Sparrow, who was slowly getting a bit of colour back, smiled proudly.

'No cream slices,' said Agnes. 'If Olive didn't bake the cream slices, then who did?'

'And who took them to that godawful coffee morning?' Charlie asked.

The answer was obvious. The murderer! Agnes swallowed. She had scoffed one of his cream slices – a pastry baked by a murderer! No wonder the thing had sat so heavily in her stomach. At the same time, she was excited, almost euphoric. They were so close – only a cream slice away from the killer!

Marshall disappeared upstairs with Sparrow's phone, presumably to copy the photos to his computer. The others sat there sipping their cold tea.

Winston gave Sparrow a few new chocolate bars and patted his hand.

'You were a really great help, Sparrow. Great work – but I completely understand if you want nothing more to do with the matter.'

Sparrow exhaled. 'It's alright, I think. At least I had someone to call . . . I never want to *ever* stumble across something like that again. He . . . he's got to be found! You've got to find him!'

'Or she,' pointed out the ever politically correct Charlie.

'We're doing our best,' said Agnes.

Marshall brought Sparrow his phone back and the up-and-coming burglar toddled off, through the front door this time, with a thoughtful, but strangely determined look in his eye.

Agnes got Edwina to bring her the house phone, dialled a number and disguised her voice.

'Helloo? Vicaar? It's Mary!' In their day there were Marys everywhere, and the vicar had never been particularly good at telling his flock apart. 'I have a big favour to ask of you! I was at the coffee morning yesterday – yes, wonderful, wonderful – and there were these excellent cream slices. Olive made them, of course, Olive. And I would reeally like the recipe. But Olive's not answering the phone, and I'm not as mobile as I used to be, and well, I'm getting a bit worried. Maybe . . . she's had a fall, or something? Would you perhaps pop by, vicar? Just to be sure that everything's alright?'

She put the phone down before the vicar could protest.

'So, now they'll find her, hopefully!' she said. 'And we should start to make our own enquiries!'

'I think we should discuss the timeline,' said Winston.

Winston was a systematic thinker.

Marshall went over to the cupboard, opened a drawer and got a pencil and paper out. He laid the paper on the table and drew a cross.

'That's Lillith,' he said.

'That doesn't really look like Lillith,' Edwina carped. Marshall didn't allow himself to be riled.

'Here.' He drew a small circle. 'The gun disappears that same day. Here' – another cross – 'Mildred is shot, also on the same day. Then there's a gap. Seven days. And then' – a rectangle – 'the gun turns up on our table again. Olive is shot somewhere in between. The question is: When?'

Agnes tried to call the gruesome picture to mind. The blood brownish and rusty, the skin on Olive's neck purple. Not fresh, but also not decaying. And she was baking – probably for the coffee morning!

'Before the coffee morning!' she said. 'The day before the coffee morning.'

Bernadette took off her sunglasses and directed her unseeing eyes into the distance. It was a good effect.

'Whilst we were raking leaves in the garden, someone shot Olive and then hotfooted it straight over here and put the gun on the table! It's so . . . brazen – almost playful. Like . . . like something a child would do.'

10

FROZEN PIZZA

Edwina had retreated to her yoga mat and was going through asanas. Cow face, crow, dove, warrior, sphinx, swan and butterfly, and then just to be sure, the crow again, but the warm feeling of calm in her head that usually accompanied her practice didn't really show up this time.

There had been too many changes recently, and Edwina felt a bit lost. Everyone was dreadfully busy with the hunt for the murderer, as if it were the most important thing in the world. She could have told them a thing or two, but what was the point? Nobody took any notice of her. Why was it alright to shoot Lillith, but make such a song and dance about Mildred and Olive? Plus, they'd hardly known Mildred, and Olive not at all. What difference did it make if they were there or not? And she, Edwina, had to carry the can again. Not fair! Agnes was impatient with her, Bernadette boring, and more and more, Marshall had this distant look in his eye. Not all there. That was what people sometimes said about her, but they were mistaken. She, Edwina, was completely there, every finger, every toe. She could feel it. People were weird. Everyone was weird. Charlie had forbidden her from helping to paint the bedroom, and Edwina loved coral-red. Winston was planning something and spending far too much time scribbling symbols on little scraps of paper. How boring! Even Hettie seemed to have her own worries at the moment and was endlessly scrabbling around in the autumn leaves.

In times past, Lillith would have helped her in moments like this. She had shown her how to transplant a seedling, prune roses or make compost, and afterwards the world had always felt a little bit better and more solid.

Edwina got up from the yoga mat with a feeling akin to hope and padded downstairs barefoot, into the sitting room and over to the flower window. She got Lillith's tin and ambled to the sofa. Then she carefully unscrewed the lid.

'Hey, Lillith,' she whispered into the tin. 'Lillith? I don't want to disturb you, but I have one or two questions?'

She listened. No answer came, of course it didn't. Edwina wasn't stupid, even if everyone treated her like a five-year-old. She knew that ashes couldn't speak – but that didn't mean she couldn't speak to the ashes by a long shot!

'I'm bored,' she admitted. 'You're gone, and Hettie's digging, and Marshall's spending too long staring at the computer. They've hidden the gun, and I don't know where it is. Nobody likes my biscuits, not even the burglar, despite being chained to the radiator.'

It occurred to her that, in her tin, Lillith might not be up to date, so she summarised the happenings of recent weeks as best she could.

'You're dead, Lillith, unfortunately. Now you live in a hard shell, like Hettie. Someone shot Mildred. Mildred from over there. The rich vegetable. She had a much better funeral than you, but that doesn't matter because now she's in the ground and you're here with us, in the flower window. The police came, and Charlie moved in. Not into your room,' she explained quickly. Lillith could be possessive of her room. 'Into the room with the bay window. Charlie and Brexit. Brexit is very hairy, but everyone likes him. We didn't go out for a curry, but we went to the coffee morning, and someone threw Hettie in the bin, and the burglar repaired the stairlift. Now Olive is dead, but it wasn't us. We planted the seedlings outside and raked the leaves. And we miss you.'

There. That actually summarised it all quite well.

Lillith remained silent, as expected, but Edwina liked her silence. Understanding, calm, not annoyed, as was sometimes the case with her other housemates.

'I'm worried about Agnes,' Edwina confessed. 'She's so impatient, not at all like her, and sometimes I think she can't hear what I'm saying. Or anything at all. She thinks about the past too much, and now this Isobel is there hugging her . . . I think she's dragging her into something. I don't think she's good for Agnes.'

Edwina sighed deeply, put Lillith on the coffee table and screwed the lid back on the tin. There. It was good to get things off her chest.

Before putting Lillith back in the flower window, she put her lips right against the lid of the tin and whispered something so quietly that surely only her friend in the tin could hear.

'Hey, Lillith?' Edwina hesitated for a moment. 'I don't think Agnes is taking her pills any more.'

Lillith had always stressed how important it was for Agnes to take her pills.

That evening they had frozen pizza, a favourite meal, masterfully warmed up in the microwave by Winston, but nobody expressed the usual enthusiasm. Marshall and Charlie chewed mechanically, Edwina left the crusts, and Agnes pushed the pizza slices around her plate like a puzzle. She thought about faceless Olive, who had so quickly ended up as cat food.

Had they already found her? Agnes hoped so. She would have liked to be at the crime scene to make sure everything ran smoothly, but obviously that was out of the question.

If she was caught hanging around at Olive's house, it would look suspicious, hip problems and false teeth, or not.

The matter of the cream slices on the other hand . . .

It would take a while for the police to suss out the cream slices, if at all. In the meantime, it couldn't hurt for Agnes to surreptitiously make a few enquiries. How did the cream slices get to the coffee morning? Who brought them? It was too late for today, but tomorrow she would take the blasted telephone to task and ask around.

Her thoughts were interrupted by a little plastic pot of pills, suddenly appearing in front of her. Winston, the logistical talent, and responsible for the distribution of medication in the house, patted her hand briefly, pushed a glass of water towards her and then rolled on to Bernadette with the next ration of pills. And then Charlie. Marshall. Edwina. Colourful pills for everyone. Blood pressure and eyes and joints and God-knows-what. A likely story!

Agnes sighed.

Normally they sat together for a while after dinner chatting about this and that, but that evening the dining room emptied quickly, and soon Agnes was the last one, still sitting at the table with her pills.

One red. One blue. One green.

One blue. One green. One red.

Green. Red. Blue.

Blue. Red. Green.

Agnes played around with the pills on the table for a while, then she drank the water, stood up, went over to the kitchen and slid the pills down the gap behind the sink.

Blue.

Green.

Red.

Later on in bed, Agnes tossed and turned, and couldn't fall asleep.

Had Olive been a victim of opportunity? Had she just been in the wrong place at the wrong time and offered the wrong person one of her muffins? Had she been a witness that had to be eliminated? Or was it about something completely different? What did Olive and Mildred have in common? Did they have anything in common?

Olive was a bit younger than Mildred, a downright spritely woman in her mid-sixties, she had been healthy and active – too active for a lot of people's liking. Olive had meddled, exactly like Mildred before the stroke had put an end to her meddling. Was that it? Had they both chosen the wrong person to meddle with this time? Had the murder been revenge – or a pre-emptive strike?

Agnes thought again about the pictures Sparrow had taken for them, and pulled the blanket up to her nose. It took a lot to just shoot someone in the face at close range like that. So, not a purely pre-emptive strike then.

A murder with feeling.

And whoever had committed it, sauntered straight over to theirs afterwards and put the murder weapon on their table. Concerning. What was it supposed to mean? It was a message, undoubtedly. But one Agnes wasn't able to decipher.

Suddenly the bedcovers seemed heavy and oppressive. The pizza was sitting heavily in her stomach. Her hip joint hadn't yet forgiven the day's escapades and was glowing like a piece of coal. Her head felt as if too many people were speaking at once, in hushed tones, so that Agnes couldn't understand a single word. It was driving her mad.

She shook the covers off and switched on the light. Things couldn't go on like this. She could either fruitlessly toss and turn for hours on end, or she could do something.

She slid her feet into her slippers and went to look for her dressing gown. Then she stepped out into the hallway, hobbled three doors along, took a deep breath and knocked.

Once. Twi . . .

Marshall flung the door open, as if he'd been standing there ready with his hand on the handle. He was wearing a dressing gown as well, a non-military stripe, Agnes realised, and his reading glasses. She definitely hadn't woken him up.

'I just wanted to . . .' Agnes said and hesitated.

'The photos!' Marshall nodded and gestured towards his computer, Olive's kitchen already glimmering glaringly and cold, and in far too much detail, with muffins, cats and a lot of red.

Agnes gulped and stepped closer. Marshall gallantly pushed the desk chair towards her, and Agnes sank onto it gratefully.

'We've got five pictures in total,' Marshall explained clicking the mouse. Blurry shapes danced across the computer.

'That's from the front, I think, that's from the side, that's from above. And another one from farther away. Very blurry unfortunately, the rest, but despite that it might help us some more.'

Agnes nodded. She could imagine how much Sparrow's hands must have been shaking as he took the photographs.

Marshall clicked back to the first photo. 'This one's the best. I wish we could make out something in the flour, tracks, prints, anything. I enlarged everything, but the cats . . .' He shrugged his shoulders in frustration.

Agnes looked at the picture trying not to get distracted by red, dead Olive. She must have been missing some sort of detail up to now. There was always some sort of detail.

It struck her how organised Olive's kitchen was – apart from the mess on the floor. Flour, sugar, baking powder, rice, pasta, lentils, coffee and tea were tidily arranged in big, neatly labelled Kilner jars. Even the notes and magnets on the fridge above the blood smear were arranged in rank and file, and the cutlery . . .

Agnes hesitated. Her eyes wandered back to the fridge. The row of notes wasn't perfect!

She pointed to the photo. 'There's something missing!'

Marshall nodded. 'Maybe just a shopping list. Something she didn't need any more.'

Agnes shook her head. 'Then she would have taken the magnet off or filled the space with that note.' She pointed to a small square of paper right at the bottom that looked a bit lost hanging beneath the others and even had a few blood spatters on it.

Someone like Olive, who had a jar clearly and visibly containing coffee beans and labelled it *coffee* for good measure, would not have tolerated a gap like that. Agnes was certain. Olive was a neat freak – that's why she'd got so het up about her house share.

'But she didn't! Why?'

'Because she didn't have time,' said Marshall quickly. 'Or because . . .'

'It wasn't her at all!' Agnes finished. 'Maybe it wasn't Olive at all who removed that note. Maybe the *murderer* took it.'

Agnes grinned and was happy that in all the excitement she hadn't left her false teeth on the bedside table as usual. Marshall grinned back, then he grabbed Agnes's hand and planted a tender little kiss on the back of it, right where blue veins shimmered through the papery white skin.

It was over before Agnes could blink, think, or go red. Did it even happen? She closed her mouth and swallowed.

'Shall we see what else Olive had on her fridge?' Marshall cried with vigour, grabbed the computer mouse and conjured a new rectangle onto the screen. Olive's fridge appeared enlarged, but grainy and not easy to see. Agnes squinted and stared. They largely seemed to be handwritten notes. Recipes probably – or lists. That seemed like Olive. The image was too blurry to be able to decipher too much, but Agnes could well imagine.

1. *Roast.*
2. *Bake.*
3. *Put the fear of God into the clowns at the coffee morning!*

But it hadn't come to that. Agnes looked again. She could make out some photos, two self-satisfied looking cats and one of a chubby-cheeked child with chocolate round his mouth.

'Could it have been a photo?' she asked. 'The missing thing?'

'Possibly,' Marshall murmured. 'Only, most photos these days are digital. On phones. If it's incriminating material – it's hardly something you'd pin to the fridge now.'

Agnes shrugged her shoulders. What did Marshall know about fridges? Or about Olive? She tapped with her finger.

'What about the bottom row?'

Marshall clicked, and Agnes saw something that looked

like a bill, business cards, brochures. All unreadable.

She made a frustrated, unladylike loud noise. But wait. That brochure there – she had seen it before. The same unpleasant combination of yellow and green. The same childish yellow font.

'That's the Lime Tree Court brochure!' she said. 'The guy was here last week. A real slimeball! He didn't like Edwina's biscuits!'

She had to grin again. What was wrong with her? Murder photos shouldn't cause so much amusement! Or was it nerves?

'Could that mean something?'

Marshall shook his head. 'The whole neighbourhood probably got one.'

Agnes nodded. 'Got it and threw it away. Like me. Only Olive stuck it on the fridge. Why? Besides' – a new thought – 'I don't think Olive could have afforded it!'

Marshall laughed a chortling laugh. 'You would be surprised what these old dears manage to put by in the course of their lives!'

All of a sudden, Agnes was furious with him. What did Marshall know about old dears? Why was he thinking about what they put by? He sounded like a legacy hunter, and he was well taken care of and had an important job in their household! It was time to put a little dampener on things.

'Do you think Charlie's an alcoholic?' she asked abruptly.

Marshall stopped chortling and looked baffled.

'Charlie? Why? No.'

'And did you screen her?'

By nature, a household like theirs would experience losses now and then, and if their project was to survive, they had to find new recruits, take in new housemates. Fresh blood. But they had to be the right housemates. One false move and the whole household was in danger. Agnes, Lillith, Bernadette and Marshall had discussed the matter at length. Edwina hadn't taken part in the discussions – as a rule it was better to present things to Edwina as a fait accompli.

Fresh blood was Marshall's job, for one because he had done something similar in the military, but also because he was the only one who knew what he was doing on the internet and didn't just know how to switch a computer off and on, but also all the things you could drag up from databases, discussion forums and chats. And he had *contacts*.

Up to now, Agnes had blindly trusted Marshall, and their first new member really had been a stroke of luck, but she still wasn't sure about Charlie. She *liked* her, a lot, that wasn't it. But, was Charlie the right person? What about her nerves? Would she cope with the strains of an unusual household like theirs in the long-term?

'Of course I screened her. She's serious, no doubt about it. Couldn't have been easy to arrive on the day Lillith . . . And since then, there's been a lot going on . . .' Marshall waved dismissively. 'I think that considering the circumstances, she's doing fabulous!'

Fabulous! Exactly what Charlie always said. Agnes felt a little twinge and then a bigger one, because she felt mean and selfish.

'Brexit's really alright,' she admitted reluctantly, 'and I

like Charlie. It's just – she's not like us. She doesn't have the same background, and you know . . . It's probably just a bit much for her. As long as you're sure you checked everything?'

Marshall looked hurt. 'I'm as sure as I can be!'

'But?' Agnes delved. She didn't like the look on his face.

Marshall sighed. 'I don't know how sure that is. I . . . There are gaps, Agnes.'

'Gaps?' Agnes asked in horror. 'In the checks?'

'In everything!' Marshall ruffled his thin grey hair with both hands. 'Gaps in *me*! Until now it hasn't been so bad, but since the thing with Lillith . . . I sometimes don't know how I ended up in a room or what day it is, or . . .' He made a dismissive hand gesture. 'I really don't want to burden you with this, Agnes. We've got other things to worry about at the moment. It's just – one day there's only going to be gaps left, and . . . it's terrifying.'

'Oh!' said Agnes, and the next moment she attempted a seriously meant, but extremely awkward hug, sideways on from the chair, somewhere around rib level. 'It won't come to that,' she whispered. 'That's what we're here for!'

Marshall nodded and took her hand. And then they were eye to eye.

The high-pitched ringing started up, and although Marshall suddenly seemed to have a lot to say, Agnes didn't hear a word of it. She nodded now and then trying to give the impression she understood, but it suddenly became difficult to keep her eyes open. Beneath half-closed eyes she saw Alice standing beside the gravestone again, only this time it was an older Alice with opaque tights and a crow hat.

An Alice like her . . .

Agnes didn't know exactly how it happened, but she woke up in her own bed.

The high-pitched ringing was gone and her mood was rosy.

Someone was ringing the doorbell like mad.

Agnes smiled thinking about yesterday evening. It hadn't exactly been a gentleman caller, but still. And they were a bit closer to tracking down the murderer!

Murderer.

Oh yeah.

Not many nice memories followed.

The thing with Alice.

The thing with Olive.

The thing with the gaps.

And someone should really do something about that diabolical ringing downstairs!

'I'll get it!' a voice from the hallway piped up. Charlie, who despite all the gin and tonics yesterday seemed to be up and about already. Agnes could imagine her wafting down the stairs in her red kimono with her flowing hair. The early morning caller should brace themselves.

'Are you coming, kids? It's the police!'

Agnes was shocked, although she probably should have guessed. They'd found Olive and now the police wanted to check whether there was a connection between her and the other victims. That was all – or maybe not? She manoeuvred herself carefully out of bed, realised she was still wearing her dressing gown, and slid her feet into her slippers.

Out in the hallway she had to wait a while because the stairlift was already being used by Winston. She impatiently hopped from one foot to the other, whilst Winston hovered downstairs interminably slowly, and the stairlift crept back up towards her empty, and if it was possible, even more slowly. She could hear voices downstairs. Charlie. Edwina. Hopefully nobody was saying anything wrong.

Then they all sat in the sitting room squinting, and Agnes had a certain sense of satisfaction. Finally, they hadn't been busy suspiciously digging, instead they looked as dozy and clueless as people in their third – or fourth? fifth? – half of life should early in the morning. Rumpled dressing gowns, hair all over the place, puffy little eyes and befuddled expressions.

The policeman himself didn't look much better. Pale and bleary-eyed, with dark circles under his eyes and unattractive stubble, he droned out his supposedly routine questions.

Had Lillith been active in the church? Agnes almost exploded with laughter, but caught herself in time and shook her head, tight-lipped.

Had Lillith had friends in the village? Did any of them know Olive? When had they last seen her?

Agnes said truthfully that she hadn't seen Olive for years, that they hadn't been particularly close, that her baking skills were renowned throughout Duck End. Edwina was playing I-spy with Hettie, Marshall yawned, and Charlie was trying to get her hair under control with the help of the mirror on the wall. Now and then she looked around imploringly, probably for a gin and tonic.

Finally, it was Hettie who freed them from the pesky policeman again. Edwina had let the tortoise win the game and put her down on the floor. Hettie had made a beeline for the policeman's feet and was eyeing his ankle mischievously.

The policeman, worn down by what was now the third murder in an area normally practically devoid of violent crime, quickly gave up. He said goodbye, promising to keep them updated, and rushed to the door, Hettie in pursuit. Finally!

Agnes couldn't take it any longer. She sent her housemates off to have breakfast and got Edwina to bring her the phone.

The good thing about a village like Duck End was that things mostly stayed as they were. As long as you kept abreast of deaths and other drastic developments, you had a good chance of keeping track of things.

Two young women had once moved into the new terraced houses behind the church: Olive and Theresa. They had become friends and remained friends, probably because they both had a weakness for constant and preferably malicious gossip. Both of them had been married, brought up children, swapped recipes. Both were widowed.

And if Agnes wasn't mistaken, they still lived in neighbouring terraced houses. At least that had been the case until recently. If anybody knew what had gone on with Olive and the cream slices, it was Theresa!

Agnes looked for the number in a yellowed telephone directory, dialled and waited. Hettie, who had missed the exodus to the kitchen was scratching indignantly at the sitting room door.

'Patience,' Agnes mumbled, more to herself than to Hettie.

'Ah, yes, hello, it's Mary here.' Good old Mary in action again! 'Could I possibly speak with Theresa, please?'

'Is that the police again?'

Damn, the police had beaten her to it! But maybe they had asked the wrong questions.

'No, it's just, err . . . Mary!'

'My mother isn't here. She had this funny turn a few days ago and we decided to have her admitted.'

'Oh.' Admitted. The hairs on Agnes's neck stood on end. 'Damn!'

'Pardon me?'

'Errr!' Agnes nearly said *damn* for the second time. What was wrong with her? She stammered. 'Errr, I see, poor Theresa. Could I . . . is she allowed visitors, the poor thing?'

The daughter made an impatient sound. 'Sorry, they strongly advise against visitors in the first few weeks. Lime Tree Court is very strict about that. That goes for the police, and for you too!'

'Oh,' Agnes said a second time and hung up. Lime Tree Court! Again! It was high time someone checked out this Lime Tree Court and its fixed idea of golden sunset years a bit more closely.

'It's like Fort Knox!' Marshall said, lowering the binoculars.

She had fished the Lime Tree Court brochure out of the recycling, noted down the address and bundled them all in a taxi. Now they were standing under the cover of three chestnuts looking down at Lime Tree Court, which was lurking surreptitiously in a dip. A stately property, undoubtedly, the main building with its pretty white façade and tall windows, with well-tended gardens. Contented-looking senior citizens were basking on benches in the sunshine. Carers dressed in white rushed back and forth between them.

A whole host of carers.

So far, so golden. But there was also a high barbed-wire fence, an electric-powered entrance gate and a porter's lodge, that was more reminiscent of a soviet spy film than a wellness oasis.

Apart from that there wasn't a single lime tree in sight! No doubt about it, Lime Tree Court was a big con!

'Poor Theresa!' said Charlie. 'It's a real prison!'

'How are we going to get her out of there?' Marshall murmured.

'We're not getting her out,' Agnes said quietly. 'We're going *in*.'

A cloud covered the sun and it suddenly went cold.

11

ICE CREAM

'It's far too risky,' Marshall said, outraged.

He ignored the ice-cream cone in his hand. Vanilla ice cream was melting, running down and dripping onto the bistro table.

They hadn't gone straight home after their reconnaissance at Lime Tree Court. Instead, at Charlie's suggestion, they had gone out in the nearest bigger town. The nearest bigger town wasn't particularly big, and 'going out' had proven to be a real challenge at eleven o'clock in the morning. Eventually, they had managed to find a deserted ice-cream parlour, which for inexplicable reasons, wasn't closed. They sat at a round table licking their ice creams, some enthusiastically, like Edwina and Bernadette, others hesitantly, and Marshall not at all. Italian music was blaring out of a loudspeaker.

Agnes sighed and licked her scoop of chocolate ice cream discontentedly. Her plan to sneak into Lime Tree Court as a mole had not been well received up to now.

'I don't mean like a real mole,' she explained. 'Not with a

shovel through a tunnel. Just . . . undercover.'

Bernadette huffed derisively.

'Too risky,' Marshall repeated, still making no attempt to prevent his vanilla ice cream from dripping. 'And too much of a long shot. And ultimately, what would we get out of it? Who knows if this Theresa actually knows anything?'

Agnes had explained the whole thing twice already, but it had fallen on deaf ears up to now, not least because of the loud music.

'It can't be a coincidence . . .' she started.

'*Azzurro!*' the loudspeaker boomed.

'Olive is shot, and at the same time Theresa has her "funny turn"?' Agnes shouted over it. 'A long shot? If it's a coincidence, I'll eat my . . . I'll chew my . . .' She couldn't think of anything dramatic that she could chew on, so she licked her ice cream instead. 'Think about it! She lives right next to Olive. She *must* have seen something!'

'*O sole mio!*' resounded from above.

'The murderer!' Agnes screamed in exasperation. 'The murderer, splattered from head to toe with blood, *that* is what she saw! And then she had her funny turn! We've just got to get in there and ask her!'

A young mother and a little tot with a tub of ice cream, who were just about to sit down at the neighbouring table, beat a hasty retreat.

Agnes took a deep breath. 'I've got everything planned. As soon as I'm in there, I find Theresa. I ask her. Done. It's worth a try,' she explained. 'If I'm right . . .'

'And if you're not right, from then on we'll only see you

through binoculars on a park bench,' Marshall said. 'No way!'

Agnes was so furious she almost threw her ice cream at him, even though chocolate was her favourite flavour, but just then a manicured hand touched her arm.

Charlie.

'I think we should go,' she said quietly, but emphatically.

At the other end of the room, behind the counter, the young mother and the ice-cream seller were standing together whispering. Casting worried glances in Agnes's direction every now and then.

'*Bella ciao!*' the loudspeaker blared triumphantly.

It had started to rain and they took cover under the awning of an electrical shop. Nobody said anything. Agnes licked away furiously. She was angry: at the young mother for getting involved, at her housemates for repeatedly giving in and at Marshall for trying to tell her what to do. But above all, she was furious with herself. Deep down inside, deeper than the chocolate ice cream, deeper than the indignation and even deeper than the ubiquitous, quietly humming hip pain, she felt relief. She was secretly happy that she didn't have to carry out her own foolhardy plan. She was *scared* of Lime Tree Court. That was the truth and Agnes didn't like it one bit.

Lime Tree Court was everything that she and her housemates *didn't* want: stick their spoons in the wall, and sit on benches surrounded by carers. Helpless, useless, senseless. Dribbling. Not them! They had decided to keep hold of their spoons to the bitter end, come what may. That's why they lived together, despite all their differences. And if it just wasn't working any more . . . Well, they had made a promise to each other for if that happened.

The alternative . . . Agnes shuddered.

She could remember all too well the room where she and Lillith had come across Chief Superintendent Franklin back then. Her former colleague. Her friend. The old warhorse. During their time in rehab after the femur fractures they had discovered that they both knew him, had both worked with him before, and decided to visit him in his care home.

The room had been cheerfully furnished with armchairs, reading lamps and a small crocheted tablecloth on the side table. But it had smelt. Of canteen food, strong cleaning chemicals, and worse. Of fear and forgetting. The commander had had no idea who they were. As they threw the windows open, he had followed them with his eyes. Astounded. Shocked. Saliva had dribbled out of his mouth. It wasn't his fault, of course it wasn't. It was nobody's fault. Everyone had wanted the best for him, and now this was what the best looked like.

It was nothing like what he would have chosen for himself, that much was obvious.

Agnes and Lillith had said goodbye to him, and Lillith had wiped the dribble from his face with a tissue.

Out in the hall they had looked at one another with tears in their eyes. 'We once had a thing,' Lillith whispered. 'An affair. Short, sweet and painless. Seeing him like that . . .'

'He's not suffering,' Agnes had said. 'At least not too much.'

'It's not that.' It had been Lillith who had said it out loud. 'Not like that. Not for me! Better a bullet to the head!'

'It's not that easy,' Agnes had pointed out.

'Then you have to make it easy!'

They had spent the rest of the day forging plans, with burning cheeks and eyes lit up with excitement. How? Where? Who? A tricky project. A final, daring adventure.

And Lillith had done it! Agnes missed her. What would she have made of her plan to smuggle herself into Lime Tree Court – and of her fear, deep down, that she might like sinking down onto a park bench like that and just letting go?

'I want a toaster!'

Edwina's voice ripped Agnes from her musings. Edwina had long since finished her ice cream and was glued to the electrical shop's window.

'We've already got a toaster,' Bernadette pointed out.

'But this one's red!' Edwina declared.

'Yes, and . . . ?' Obviously, Bernadette wasn't impressed by it.

Agnes was sucking the remaining melted chocolate ice cream out of the waffle cone and staring at the rain. Were they all on the wrong track – with the investigation, just like in life?

Charlie crumbled the rest of her waffle onto the ground and cleaned her hands with a wet wipe from her bag. 'We should go, kids!' The ice cream was finished, and the rain was showing no sign of stopping. Charlie was typing something on her phone, and, sure enough, a few minutes later a taxi appeared. Genius.

The taxi driver helped each of them into the car and insisted on checking whether they were buckled in properly.

'To Lime Tree Court,' he said then. It was barely a question.

'No,' Marshall responded sharply.

'Absolutely not,' Charlie added and gave the man the right address.

The taxi driver whistled. 'Wait, wasn't there a murder there recently?'

'More than one!' Edwina said loftily.

Then it fell silent in the taxi. Edwina was sulking because she hadn't got a toaster, Bernadette too, because Edwina had tactlessly wanted a red toaster. Winston was a bit green around the gills – too much ice cream early in the day, Agnes imagined. Charlie had her hand to her temple as if she had a headache, and Marshall was chewing his bottom lip.

Agnes was contemplating. Assumptions. Other people's, and her own too. That was half the problem with getting old. Not just with getting old, but with murder cases too. Strictly speaking, with life in general. Just because they didn't look fresh as daisies any more, the taxi driver had automatically assumed they belonged in Lime Tree Court. Just because the same gun had been used, the police assumed that Lillith's death was connected to Mildred's murder. Just because Olive had habitually stuck her nose into everything, they assumed that she, as a witness, had had to be silenced. But what if that wasn't the case? What if there was something completely different connecting Mildred and Olive?

'Do you pick up a lot of people from Lime Tree Court?' she asked the taxi driver after a while.

'Now and then. Sometimes a few of the oldies get out and walk around the town, and then usually someone calls a taxi at some point to drive them back.'

'I see. So that does happen.' Agnes looks over at the driver furtively. 'Do you happen to know *how* they get out?'

Marshall gave a warning cough, but Agnes probed deeper.

'I mean, the grounds seem to be quite secure, don't they?'

'I'd say so!' The taxi driver grinned. 'Nuclear bunkers have got nothing on them. But sometimes relatives take someone to a café or to the doctor or something, and then they run off. Not bad business for me, as long as they don't do anything on the seats. That's happened as well.' He cast a warning glance back at Charlie, Edwina and Marshall, who had no intention of messing up his seats.

'Do you think it's nice there?' Agnes asked. 'I mean, are the errr . . . oldies happy?'

'Most of them don't say much.' The taxi driver shrugged. 'Some are relieved. Some cry a bit. Personally, it's not for me. But I couldn't afford the place anyway.'

A good point. Agnes could vaguely remember the price list in the brochure. Steep. That's why the Lime Tree Court management were interested in taking over houses and renting them out. Nobody could afford that on their pension alone. So, how had Theresa, who shared a terraced house with her daughter-in-law and family, ended up in Lime Tree Court so quickly? There was more to it than met the eye, Agnes was sure of it.

As they turned into their driveway, a police car was waiting there.

The friendly policeman got out while his short-haired colleague remained seated behind the wheel.

'Miss Sharp? Would you perhaps quickly accompany us to

the station? We have a few questions to ask you.'

What was his name again? No idea! In fact, he didn't look particularly friendly any more. More mistrusting. He knew that something didn't add up with them.

He just didn't know what.

The police bundled Agnes into the car and made their way to the station with her. Once there, she was led through the reception and ended up in a small, rectangular room.

'Interview Suite,' was written on the door.

The short-haired policewoman helped her onto a chair. What was her name again? Agnes had forgotten. She seemed to notice Agnes's confusion and bent down towards her.

'Are you sitting comfortably, Miss Sharp? Don't worry, it won't take long. Would you like something to drink?'

Agnes nodded. She couldn't remember when she had last had something to drink. Her tongue felt like a prune in her mouth.

'And biscuits? You like biscuits, don't you?'

That depended entirely on who had made the biscuits. Agnes tried to set the prune in motion, to tell the policewoman precisely that, but she had already disappeared.

Sitting opposite her was the ex-friendly policeman sharpening a pencil. Sharpening and sharpening.

Attrition tactic.

Then finally a glass of water and a dubious-looking biscuit was placed in front of her and the questioning could begin.

Agnes almost giggled. Instead, she took a sip of water.

The policeman cleared his throat.

'Miss Sharp, we heard about an incident during the coffee

morning and would like to learn more about it.'

Agnes's ears pricked up. Were they onto the cream slices?

The policeman flicked through his files and cleared his throat again. 'It seems that about four years ago, there was an argument between you and Mrs Olive Spurman?'

Agnes looked at him baffled. Argument? Olive and her?

'At the coffee morning?' the policeman asked again. 'It seems you threw something?'

'Ah,' Agnes said with relief. She remembered it well. 'Carrot cake!'

'Yes, first it was a piece of carrot cake. But then . . .' The policeman looked down at his file again. 'A fork? And a *knife*.'

Agnes went cold. The police were onto something. They were onto her. She had known Mildred and obviously Lillith too, and she had previously attacked Olive. *With a knife*. If that was the only thing the police had dug up, the investigation was in bad shape!

'I didn't get her,' she said quietly.

'Yes, yes. Luckily. But we would like to know, in a bit more detail, what the background to this story was. Why did you attack Olive Spurman?'

'I didn't attack her. At least I didn't want to . . .' Agnes could feel her cheeks getting warm. 'It wasn't about Olive at all. She just happened to be in the front row.' Typical Olive!

'And what was it about?' the policeman asked in a teacherly voice that annoyed Agnes.

'It was about my project. I had decided to start this house share project for pensioners. To help and support one another. At my house. And the snipes at the coffee morning . . . rubbished it.'

'So, you threw a knife at her?'

'I didn't want to throw a . . . I just wanted to throw *something*. It was pure chance that a knife was to hand. I . . . I could have thrown anything. Apart from that, it was a butter knife, one of those blunt ones you spread butter on scones with. Completely harmless!'

'Hmm.' The policeman looked at her doubtfully. 'And did you and Mrs Spurman . . .'

He broke off, because suddenly all hell was let loose in the hallway. A crash. Someone was screaming. Something fell over.

The policeman jumped up and ran to the door. 'Just a moment, please!'

And then suddenly Agnes was alone in the interview room.

A fly buzzed helplessly through the air, in search of a window to throw itself against.

In front of Agnes was the open file.

If that wasn't an invitation! She stood up and stepped curiously closer. The murder files with everything the police knew! It wasn't very thick.

Agnes got even closer and started to flick through.

Page after page of text, and a photo now and then, all blurred, as if she were looking through a steamed-up glass panel. Dammit! Where were her reading glasses? A moment later it came to her: at home, on the kitchen table, where she had put them down after studying the Lime Tree Court brochure. Agnes was angry with herself. Charlie had wet wipes, and God knows what else, in her handbag, and she couldn't even manage to keep essential items like her dentures and reading glasses under control!

But it was too good an opportunity to just let it slip through her fingers. If the mountain wouldn't come to Mohammed, Mohammed would have to go to the mountain. Or at least onto a chair. Like most old people, she was long-sighted. If she managed to get enough distance between her and the file, she should be able to decipher something!

She eyed the seat of her chair. One small step for man, but a completely and utterly impossible leap for her. For Edwina, it would have been no problem, but as far as Agnes was concerned, the wooden seat might as well have been on mars. Unless . . .

She looked around the room. Her eyes landed on the bin. Small, but solid. One of those plastic things that seemed like it would even hold an elephant. And Agnes was no elephant.

She tipped the rubbish out and turned the bin over. If she just stood on the plastic bottom and from there . . .

Agnes didn't give it much more thought. She leant on the wall to steady herself and climbed onto the plastic base of the bin. She nearly fell. But only nearly. Her hip was screaming, but it didn't matter – there was no going back for Agnes. With both hands on the wall, she felt with her foot for the seat of the chair, found it somehow, pushed off and . . .

It hurt so much Agnes needed a minute to gather herself.

She was standing. On two feet. On the chair. Her hands on the wall like someone waiting to be searched. Far below her was the file and even farther down, deep and gaping, the floor. Agnes had no idea how she would ever manage to get back down. But that didn't matter now.

From her lofty height, she could actually make something out in the file!

Mildred Puck was written there. The text beneath it was so small Agnes couldn't decipher it. But farther down: crime scene photos. Agnes needed a minute to get her bearings in the picture.

Then she felt sick.

Unlike Lillith, Mildred didn't look peaceful at all. She was wearing white pyjamas, and, on the photo, it looked like she had been crossed out with a red felt tip. Right through the middle.

A shot in the stomach. Mildred had pressed her hand to the wound and despite that everything was welling out of the opening. That's what the snipes at the coffee morning had meant by 'disembowelled'! Blood everywhere! On the deckchair. On the floor. It took a few minutes for Agnes to realise what that meant: Mildred hadn't died straight away. She had crawled away from her murderer! A blood-red creeping snail trail led right across the terrace.

Just then, the door opened and the young not-at-all-friendly-any more policeman and his short-haired colleague entered the room.

'I've always said, we should screw it . . .' The policeman fell silent, and they both looked up at Agnes on her chair.

Looked down at the upturned rubbish bin and the pile of scrap paper.

Looked up at Agnes again, who was standing there red-handed, supporting herself on the wall.

The older you got, the harder it was to keep the inside and the outside in harmony. In her head everything was normally still clear and nice and orderly, but as soon as she tried to express what was in her head, wires got crossed, and what then actually came out of her mouth, often missed the mark by a country mile. But this time, it was exactly the opposite. Whilst blind panic reigned in Agnes's head, her mouth opened and uttered one word, the only possible word that could get her out of this precarious situation more or less unscathed.

'Mouse!'

It took three police officers to get Agnes down from the chair. One grabbed her under her arms, and a second put his hands round her waist and supported her hip, whilst the short-haired policewoman reassured her. To her great dismay, Agnes noticed tears running down her cheeks, not just because of the hip pain, but also because of the shock and the terribly embarrassing situation. And maybe some of her tears were also meant for Mildred, who after years of severe illness had suffered this terrible, violent death. If there had still been any doubt, it had disappeared now: the murderer was a monster.

Then she was finally sitting with her backside on the chair again, as it should be. She noticed she had the hiccups. Somebody was stroking her shoulder. Somebody passed her a tissue.

Agnes blew her nose noisily and listened to the policewoman explaining that mice were undesirable, but actually quite harmless pests.

'No need to get so upset, Miss Sharp!'

Hic!

'We're getting a car and then we're going to take you home, alright?'

Hic!

Here was a glass of water. And a pill to calm her down.

Agnes sipped some water, but refused to take the pill.

Hic. Hic. Hic.

As she sat on the back seat of the police car, in a haze and plagued by hiccups, something else occurred to her: Mildred's bloody snail trail had led away from the house. She had tried to escape into the garden – as if the danger had come from the house . . .

At home a little reception committee was waiting on the veranda. Edwina, Charlie, Brexit and Bernadette were standing in front of the door, and Winston was waving kindly from a window on the first floor. Where was Marshall? Not that Agnes would have wanted to talk to him. She didn't want to talk to anybody. Not now.

Hic.

The policewoman led her up the steps and deposited her on a chair in the kitchen. Charlie started to make her a cup of tea, Brexit laid his head in her lap.

Out in the hall the policewoman was talking to Bernadette. 'Mortal fear of mice . . .' Agnes heard. 'But it was just a shock. With a bit of peace and quiet . . . Probably imagined it all.'

Hic. Hic.

As soon as the police had said goodbye, Marshall rushed into the room. He was unusually red in the face. 'Agnes, what's all this about mice? What did they do to you?'

Hic.

Agnes waved her hand dismissively. 'I just stood on a chair,' she said, casually, she hoped.

She didn't want to explain anything and definitely not to him.

Hic.

And these damn hiccups were really starting to get on her nerves.

What she needed was a little shock.

She got up unsteadily and headed past Bernadette, Marshall and a teapot-wielding Charlie towards the sitting room.

'Agnes, you really shouldn't . . .'

Agnes ignored their calls and flung the sitting room door open. Sunset Hall was *her* house! She wasn't going to let anybody tell her what to do any more.

Hic.

Then she was suddenly confronted by a little fat person with dishevelled hair, chocolate around his mouth and deep black cherry eyes, who was in the process of putting a plastic figurine into one of her vases.

Hic . . . !

What the hell? What was going on now?

'What's going on?' Agnes snorted.

Marshall appeared next to her, red-faced. 'Agnes. This is my grandson, Nathan,' he confessed sheepishly.

Agnes was so shocked she had to sit down.

Grandchildren, and especially non-adult grandchildren, were strictly prohibited in the house rules.

12

BANGERS AND MASH

'*But, he's so small!*' *Agnes said in disbelief. She waited for a hiccup, but none came. At least the shock had finally done away with the hiccups. But apart from that, the whole thing was a catastrophe.*

'That's just what children are like,' said Bernadette.

'He's still growing,' Marshall reassured her.

'But not at mine!' Agnes sank back into the sofa cushions, exhausted. Winston was busy keeping Nathan at bay in the kitchen, presumably with chocolate bars. The rest of the household had gathered around Agnes in the sitting room and were trying to pep her up a bit. Some tea and a digestive just wouldn't cut it though. A Grandson! Ridiculous!

'The whole thing is strange for me too,' Marshall admitted. 'But what am I supposed to do? Sabrina was standing at the door completely distraught. They haven't gone on holiday. They're getting divorced. And then there's the school holidays . . .' He ran his fingers through his thin hair. His daughter's divorce didn't seem to bother him very much. The holidays, on the other hand . . .

'To be honest, I'm glad she'll be shot of the guy. Total good-for-nothing. Never liked him. But right now, sparks are apparently flying, and she needs . . . *space*, she said.' Marshall looked around the group helplessly. 'What am I supposed to do?' he repeated. 'She just dropped him off here. It's only for a few days.'

'A few days.' Agnes groaned. It just gets better and better!

'Until the end of the holidays. He's . . . got toys with him.'

'Well, that's alright then,' Agnes said with cutting sarcasm. Why did nobody understand how serious the situation was?

It wasn't that she had anything against children – it wasn't about that. It was about the *project*. She and Lillith had realised early on in their planning that their somewhat different house share wasn't very family-friendly. Relatives wanted to help, obviously, they wanted to *care*, but mostly they didn't really know how. They had their own ideas and stuck their noses in things that had nothing to do with them. Mostly they were a bit helpless, a bit annoyed, and had a bit of a guilty conscience. Not a good mix.

And if someone – like Lillith – ended up with a bullet in their head, they could start to ask awkward questions. No doubt about it: the less they knew and the less contact the members of the house had with their families, the better it was for everybody. Obviously, it was alright for someone to pop by now and then – until now they could hardly complain about being overrun with visitors. But if grandchildren were just going to make themselves at home, it was a recipe for disaster!

Agnes became aware they were all looking at her expectantly. Expectantly, and kind of hopefully. They wanted her to give her blessing for the Grandson's stay – after all, it was her house. And they obviously could hardly just chuck him out. But, did that mean Agnes had to approve everything straight away?

'And what does he eat?' she finally asked.

'From the look of him, everything,' Charlie said drily.

'Salad and bananas!' Edwina added expertly. 'Just like Hettie!'

Agnes had her doubts about that. 'You do know, we're right in the middle of a murder case? Someone's going around shooting people! Someone put a gun on our table. This is *personal*! There's a murderer roaming about out there, and we're going to have to look after a child in here! He's . . . He'll . . . mess everything up!' She had to silently admit to herself that it wouldn't be easy for Nathan to find something that hadn't already been well and truly messed up by Edwina, Brexit, Charlie, Hettie and Marshall.

'Well, I think he's darling!' Charlie said. 'A bit podgy. But darling!'

Marshall gave her a grateful look.

'We're managing with Brexit,' said Bernadette. 'So, a child shouldn't really be such a big problem.'

Agnes was just about to remark that Brexit was a well-trained and sensitive wolfhound, this grandson, on the other hand, was a completely unknown entity, but just then the high-pitched ringing started up again. Agnes gave up. She waved dismissively and made it abundantly clear to her housemates that, above all else, she wanted to go to bed. They could talk later. If they must.

Then she flounced gracefully (or, so she hoped) upstairs, limped to her room, slipped off her shoes, and sunk into the pillows just as she was.

Her hip hurt.

The ringing droned on.

There was a murderer running around out there scot-free.

The day had started so well, with a firm lead to Olive's neighbour Theresa and the cream slices, and now, suddenly all there seemed to be was problems. Theresa had been absorbed by Lime Tree Court, Agnes herself was presumably currently the main suspect in a triple-murder enquiry, everyone thought she was afraid of mice, and now to top it all off, a grandson had rocked up. How were they supposed to track down the murderer if they were stuck with that little squirt?

Whilst Agnes stared at the ceiling in frustration, at two long-legged spiders who were busy perfecting their webs, the subject of her misgivings strolled into her room just like that and looked at her with his black cherry eyes. Scarpered already! Aha! The high-pitched ringing disappeared, presumably because of the shock. Agnes stared back. She tried to see Marshall in him, but she couldn't. Why was he so fat? And who did he get those dark eyes from? Presumably from his father, the good-for-nothing.

'I'm Nathan,' Nathan said after a while.

'I know,' Agnes said glumly.

'You're Agnes,' Nathan continued seriously and systematically. That wasn't recent news either. 'You don't want me here.'

Agnes wanted to say something placatory, but nothing came to her. She stared helplessly from out of the pillows.

'It's okay,' Nathan said after a while. 'I don't want to be here, either.'

The inside and the outside. Suddenly Agnes got the feeling she wasn't just dealing with a random grandson, but with *someone*, a whole person. There was someone inside the dark mop head, just like there was someone inside her white-haired head. So different from the outside, but on the inside . . . Agnes couldn't remember when she had stopped being a child. As far as she was concerned, she had always been herself. Obviously, she'd learnt a lot, gained experience. Some of her attitudes had changed, but beneath it all, deep down, she was still Agnes with the pigtails. The Agnes, who used to climb the apple tree late at night. The Agnes, who at a decisive moment, had turned her back and decided to ignore Alice.

These thoughts made the thing with Nathan better, because they made him seem less other. Not catastrophe personified, just a person in a small and overweight shell. But it also made her situation more complicated. A new person had infiltrated the house, disguised as a grandson. Undercover, as it were. A spy! They would have to be extra cautious, so as not to reveal *how* special their household really was.

Nathan seemed to have said what he wanted to say. He nodded briefly and knowingly, as if he had heard Agnes's thoughts, and marched out of the room as purposefully as he had entered. He left behind the feeling that the situation, like so often in life, was a lot more complicated than she had initially thought.

Agnes glanced over at the door to make sure Nathan really had gone, then she looked up at the spiders again, who had obviously finished their renovations and were sitting smugly in their webs.

For some reason, the sight spurred her on. It's not over until the fat lady sings! Just because she couldn't ask Theresa directly, it didn't mean the lead had gone cold. After all, there was still the family. Sure, the stepdaughter hadn't exactly been helpful on the phone, but maybe she thawed when you were face to face. Agnes would think up an excuse, book a taxi, go there and ring the doorbell! She was an old lady, after all. It had a lot of disadvantages, but also one or two advantages: as an old lady you could ring any doorbell you liked without arousing suspicion.

Agnes could feel her optimism returning and with optimism came hunger. She hadn't had anything since the chocolate ice cream. She almost regretted not eating the police biscuit. Now she would have to hang on until dinner. Whose turn was it to cook? Hopefully not Edwina!

As she went through the meal options in her head – pea soup? Bangers and mash? Pasta and sauce? Some kind of stew? – it occurred to her that maybe Theresa wasn't the only one who could help her with the matter of the cream slices: there was Bernadette's new acquaintance Rosie, who helped and scrounged at the coffee morning. Maybe she could tell her how the cakes normally made their way to the coffee morning – and if she was really lucky, Rosie could even say who had dropped off the cream slices. Why had the murderer even bothered with the slices? That was taking a certain amount of risk. There could only be one explanation: he had wanted to prevent Olive's murder being discovered too soon. As long as the cream slices were there, Olive wouldn't be greatly missed by anybody. But Agnes and Sparrow had thrown a spanner in the works! Would he be angry? Would he feel backed into a corner? The thought made Agnes feel uneasy. When a murderer feels backed into a corner, anything can happen . . .

198

She had had enough of the self-satisfied spiders and closed her eyes for a minute. When she opened her eyes again, there was a canopy of leaves above her. The leaves rippled cheerfully in the wind, and now and then a little sun flashed between them, rich and golden. Beneath her, grass, cool and damp. Agnes could smell it.

Then suddenly two faces were floating over her. Identical faces. Black eyes. Dark eyelashes. Black hair.

Two girls. One girl twice.

Agnes blinked.

'Leave her alone!' the first girl said. Not to Agnes, but to herself, just like into a mirror.

But the second girl didn't listen to her mirror-image and moved closer. Agnes saw that she didn't have pigtails, but a modern haircut, chin-length and straight like a cap. She was immediately envious.

The other, sceptical girl, bent down towards her too now, almost reluctantly, as if Agnes were an insect or a worm.

'I know who you are!' said Agnes. Everyone knew who they both were: the twins from the big house. The poor girls. The orphans.

When she wanted to get up, she realised they were standing on her pigtails. One on the left, one on the right.

'Nobody knows who we are,' said the girl on the left haughtily.

That wasn't true. The whole of Duck End had been talking about nothing but the tragic car accident that had made orphans of the girls. Father dead. Mother dead. Now they had come to live with their uncle in the big house. And Agnes was the first person to set eyes on them!

She tried to remember their names.

'Mildred and Isabella,' she said forcing a smile despite the matter of the pigtails.

'Isobel,' said one of the girls.

'Mildred,' said the other. 'Or the other way round.'

They both smiled at one another. It was a very secretive smile. Just once in her life, Agnes wanted to be smiled at like that. So conspiratorially. So completely familiar.

'I've got a twin sister too,' she said. 'She's called Alice.'

That seemed to pique the girls' interest. Mildred and Isobel. Isobel and Mildred. Agnes had forgotten who was who again, but maybe that didn't really matter.

'And where is she?'

Agnes shrugged her shoulders. Alice was never there when you needed her. She hid in hedges and crawled through the undergrowth. Her hair was wild, and she had holes in her stockings.

The first girl released Agnes's pigtail. Isobel?

'Come on,' she said. 'Play with us!'

But Agnes couldn't play because Mildred was still standing on her pigtail.

It was the beginning of a long and complicated friendship.

Agnes woke up and tried to pull herself up, but it was as if somebody was still standing on her pigtail. But no, the pigtails were gone, and it was age preventing her from just getting up. Her lower back. Her neck. And above all, her hip.

It was dusky in her room. She stared up at the ceiling again, which in the meantime the two spiders had vacated.

Screams were coming from the garden.

If she remembered correctly, her first encounter with the twins hadn't just been a beginning, but a double ending. It was the moment Mildred and Isobel had started to be separate – and it was the moment she, with a certain sense of shame, had decided to abandon Alice.

Agnes felt the shame to this day. But she also felt relief.

Her stomach was rumbling.

With a few artful manoeuvres, she managed to get herself up straight. It was cold. Her blouse was rumpled. She fished for her slippers with her toes and lurched off the bed, still in a bit of a daze, towards the window to see what was going on out there now.

There was movement in the garden. Shadowy figures were scurrying through the twilight. Agnes could see flowing, snow-white hair. Charlie? What was she doing outside at this hour? And she could make out Edwina with Hettie under her arm. She opened the window to shout something down, but Charlie beat her to it.

'Nathan?' she shouted into the garden. 'Naaathaaaan!'

Aha, the Grandson. Scarpered already. Nothing but trouble. She had said so from the start! Agnes leant against the window frame and watched her housemates searching. Edwina had climbed onto a bench and was holding Hettie up high so that she could see better, Charlie had got her hair caught up in a hazel bush, and Winston was rolling up and down the gravel path at high-speed telling anyone who would listen that he'd only been in the loo for a minute.

For a second, Agnes wasn't sure if she really wanted Nathan

to be found, but then she caught sight of Marshall standing next to the shed with an ashen, strangely frozen face, and she started to worry. Nathan had said he didn't want to be there. What if he'd just packed his stuff and run away, through the half-dark garden out into the woods? Normally Agnes would have approved of his initiative, but now, since there was a murderer on the loose, she didn't like it. Apart from that, it occurred to her that it was Charlie's turn to cook. And as long as she was hung up in a hazel bush, nobody was going to get anything on their plate. Agnes grabbed a cardigan and headed off to help the others in the search.

She made it to the stairs fairly swiftly, but then she had to wait for the stairlift to reluctantly make its way upstairs at its usual snail's pace. While she waited, she felt like she could sense something moving behind her. She turned around, but it was just the landing full of silhouettes and shadows that, based on experience in better light, turned out to be chairs, a chest of drawers, a lamp and a wheelchair.

But then: something again. A kind of glimmer.

There was something there.

Someone.

This time, Agnes didn't turn around, but observed out of the corner of her eye as a dark figure crept closer. A small figure.

Small and fat.

A stubby finger pointed to the yellow flashing stairlift button.

'What's that?'

'The stairlift.'

'What's the use of that?'

'It's useful if you don't want to climb the stairs.' Agnes pointed to the control panel.

'The yellow light means the stairlift is in motion. Green is go. Red is stop.'

Extremely simple. *Suitable for senior citizens.*

'Can I try it out?' As soon as the stairlift had made it upstairs, Nathan scrambled onto the seat without waiting for an answer. Agnes thought about it. If the Grandson got to the ground floor first, she had no chance of stopping him from doing a runner. On the other hand: maybe he really just wanted a ride on the stairlift, and if they were going to have to endure a few days together, maybe it was time to build up a bit of trust between them.

'Alright then,' she finally said. 'But you have to sit still until the stairlift stops downstairs, agreed?'

Nathan made a hand signal that hopefully meant he agreed, and Agnes pushed the button. The lift set into motion and the Grandson let out a jubilant little cry, a bit like an ecstatic whoop. Agnes watched on nervously as he floated downstairs at a snail's pace, but Nathan kept to the agreement and stayed on his seat until he got to the bottom.

Then he turned to Agnes, with a triumphant grin on his face.

Her heart started to race. Now he was going to make a run for it! The rascal had tricked her!

'Again!'

Agnes was surprised at how relieved she was. She pushed the yellow button, and Nathan and the stairlift made their way back upstairs again.

A quarter of an hour later, Nathan was still on the stairlift. Up and down. Up and down. On the side of the seat, he'd discovered another control panel and had managed to considerably increase the speed. Now, the stairlift zoomed up the stairs at a very respectable pace. Agnes was itching to try it out herself. And apart from that, she had to tell the others that the miscreant Grandson had been found and encourage Charlie to cook something.

When Nathan reached her the next time, she pressed the red button.

'That's enough!'

Nathan pulled a face. 'Once more! You promised!'

'I did not!'

Tactics like that might work with his mum Sabrina or Marshall when he was having one of his memory gaps, but not with Agnes. She kept her finger on the button until Nathan had got off moaning, then she got onto the seat herself.

Green.

The stairlift zoomed off.

It was . . . perhaps nothing to make a song and dance about, but at least a little bit exhilarating. Agnes hadn't gone down the stairs this quickly in years.

At the bottom, she immediately made her way to the front door and onto the veranda.

'Dinnertime!' she shouted. 'And Nathan's inside on the stairs!'

Marshall whirled around and flung his arms around her neck. Agnes was within a hair's breadth of losing her balance. The next thing she knew he was already in the house and up the stairs. Agnes heard a clear 'yuck!' and assumed that Marshall had just unsuccessfully tried to kiss his grandson.

Winston rolled up the ramp, sweaty but relieved, Charlie came along the path unkempt with twigs in her hair.

'The little toad!' she said and glided gracefully past Agnes, hopefully in the direction of the kitchen.

Charlie was no culinary genius but she followed the instructions on the packet, so soon they were sitting in front of a respectable meal of sausages, packet mashed potato, peas and salad.

Agnes dug in. She liked mashed potato, and, even better, her false teeth liked it too.

Nathan, on the other hand, was squashing peas with his fork and chasing sausages around his plate.

'Don't you like it?' Marshall asked with concern.

'I don't like peas,' said Nathan. 'And the sausages are stupid!'

'Then eat the mashed potato!'

'That's stupid too!'

How had he got so fat if he didn't like so many foods?

Agnes looked around the group pointedly. The Grandson was causing problems again. If he even rebelled against sausages, one of the culinary highlights of their week, what would he say about tinned cream of mushroom soup? Or bean hotpot?

Edwina stood up and took Nathan's plate away. She pointed to the salad bowl.

'There's some salad. And I'll get you a banana.'

To everyone's surprise, Nathan actually dug into the salad and then scoffed two bananas straight after.

Edwina looked triumphant, but nobody else shared her good mood. The general euphoria about the Grandson's return had been short-lived.

He was back, good. But what were they supposed to do with him now?

Marshall tried asking Nathan about school, but it was like pulling teeth. Bernadette wanted to know if he was good at sport, and Charlie asked if he liked animals.

Nathan remained monosyllabic, and the conversation quickly fizzled out.

Agnes, who had finished her sausages, was fidgeting about on her chair to relieve her hip, but mainly because she wanted to talk about the case. That was obviously completely out of the question with the little mop head at the table. Up to now she hadn't told anyone about her latest intelligence and her adventures at the police station – and worse than that: nobody was interested.

It was about time they got rid of the Grandson!

'Bedtime!' she announced, as soon as Nathan had the last piece of banana in his mouth.

The idea fell on fertile ground. Her housemates immediately started to enthusiastically encourage their houseguest into bed.

They decided he should sleep on the sofa in Marshall's room. Edwina fetched pillows and blankets, Charlie made the bed, Marshall looked in his grandson's bag for some pyjamas while Bernadette, Winston and Agnes kept Nathan in check.

'I *never* go to bed straight after dinner. After dinner, I watch TV!'

Nathan slid off his chair, kicked the dining room door open

and trotted off. Brexit in pursuit. Winston wanted to follow him, but Agnes stopped him.

And indeed. Five minutes later the Grandson was back, somewhat confused.

'Where's the TV?'

Agnes smirked. She knew exactly where the TV was: in the cellar, where they had taken great pains to move it, because they were all fed up with Brexit (the old Brexit). Apart from that, the TV caused too many arguments: about programmes and the volume, but above all about the remote.

'Got rid of it!' she said full of satisfaction.

It took a while for Nathan to process the information. He went green around the gills and all of a sudden, he looked small, sweet and pitiful.

Edwina, who felt she was the newly appointed expert in all things grandson, piped up. 'Don't worry, I've got something for you!' She rummaged around in the broom cupboard a bit and returned beaming with joy, holding the remote. It was a grand gesture – the remote was one of Edwina's favourite things, but Nathan didn't seem impressed.

'I want . . .' he started in a shrill voice, but Bernadette interrupted him.

'You can just go to sleep now,' she said in her best gangster voice 'or you'll be sleeping with the fishes. I would recommend without the fishes!'

Nathan still seemed undecided, so Agnes got the big guns out.

'And you can ride the stairlift upstairs,' she tempted him.

It worked. Nathan zoomed upstairs on the stairlift; Marshall hot on his heels. The rest of the household breathed a sigh of relief, and Agnes was just about to tell them about the day's hard-earned investigation results, when an exhausted-looking Marshall appeared in the doorway.

'He wants a bedtime story!' he said. 'And he wants Agnes to tell it!'

13

WARM MILK

*Once upon a time there was a little girl. She lived in
a house near the woods. She liked ice cream and
skipping. She liked plums and summer, marbles and hide-
and-seek. She liked white handkerchiefs and red lollipops
and even the taste of cough syrup. She liked books and the
grasshoppers' evening song, and she liked telling tales on
other children in school.*

The girl's name was Clara.

Agnes paused. Was it really a good idea to tell Nathan the
story about her school friend Clara? What for? The whole thing
was an eternity ago, almost forgotten, and now of all times it
came back to the surface. Agnes realised too late that a story
that had children in it wasn't necessarily a children's story. Far
from it.

But the ship had sailed. Nathan was sitting up in his bed,
wide awake and wide-eyed.

'More!'

Agnes seized the forward momentum and aimed to present

everything in as child-friendly a way as possible. If she was clever about it, maybe Nathan would fall asleep before she got to the unpleasant bits.

Obviously, Clara wasn't particularly popular with the other children, and so she sat on her own during most of the playtimes, mostly under a tree, mostly with a book. Sometimes the children threw acorns or stones or rose hips at her, but she always acted like she didn't notice, and so the other children soon got bored.

You might think she lived a lonely life, but she did have one friend. Maybe not a real friend – but a companion.

Me, thought Agnes. Me.

Their houses were a little way out of the village, near the edge of the woods, so they walked to school together every day.

It was a long way they had to go, because there was no school bus back then.

'No school bus?' Nathan cried in disbelief.
'No school bus,' Agnes confirmed with a sigh. If there had been a school bus, then maybe the course of her whole life would have been different!

You might think that two little girls on their way to school would have lots to talk about, but that wasn't the case. Mostly they walked in silence, not really side by side, but just a few steps apart. If one of them tripped or had to tie their laces, the other waited, casually, almost as if by coincidence. If one of them ran, the other ran too. Sometimes they talked about the weather, homework, their toys or their plans for the weekend, but Clara was a show-off and a tattletale, and so as a rule there was no great pleasure in talking to her.

It went on like that for a while, and it would have carried on like that, if one day a new teacher hadn't come to the school. He was different to all the other teachers the children knew. He wore fine wool jackets like a gentleman and small gold-rimmed glasses, and he always smelt good, not just of soap, but of leather and lemons.

His name was Titus Coldwell. His voice was smooth and melodic, but it was sometimes difficult to understand exactly what he wanted of them. His sentences were brimming with words nobody knew. It was clear to see that the other adults admired him, and soon the children admired him too.

But Clara admired him the most.

She tried to suck up to him by bad-mouthing the other children and telling him fantastical tales, but it wasn't received well by him. Instead of rewarding her, Titus Coldwell gave her lines. It was the first time Clara had a detention, and the first time the other girl had to walk home alone, but that didn't bother her much, because Clara deserved it.

From that moment on, Clara's life in school changed. And Clara herself changed too. She suddenly became clumsy and

dropped her books, spilt ink or forgot her homework. She got
another detention. And another. She didn't read any books in
playtime any more, and if anybody threw anything at her or
even just tapped her shoulder, she recoiled like a frightened deer.

It wasn't Titus Coldwell's fault, surely not, he was
nice to Clara, gentle, affectionate almost. Sometimes he
called her sweetie or darling. But the friendlier he was,
the clumsier she became, and he had to give her detentions
over and over again. Twice a week. Three times.

The two girls still went the same way to school, but they
didn't go together any more. Clara was slow, dawdled on
the wayside. Sometimes she just stood there staring into
space, until the other girl ran out of patience and didn't
want to wait for her any more.

'Is this a true story?'

Agnes recoiled. Damn! Nathan still wasn't asleep, and her story was gradually getting down to the nitty-gritty. What had she been thinking?

'Err,' she said. But was it really her fault? Making things up was not her strong suit and the stories from her time on the murder squad weren't exactly appropriate for children either. At least there wasn't a murder in this one.

At least not directly.

At least not straight away.

Agnes gathered herself and tried to change tack. 'All stories are true. But there's a dragon in this one.'

'Aah!' Nathan seemed relieved. He was obviously well-versed in dragons.

One morning the two girls were on their way to school on the country lane again, Clara wasn't dawdling as she usually did, but walking ahead purposefully, when suddenly a red dragon thundered down on her. The dragon was big and loud and scary. It was breathing fire and raining ash down onto the ground. You could hear its terrible loud voice for miles around: toot, tooot! Toot, Tooot!

'Dragons don't go *toot, tooot*!'
Bloody rascal! What did he know about dragons anyway? Agnes glared at him in annoyance. 'This one does!'

Clara should have run, got to safety, into the bushes on the verge, but she didn't. She stepped forward and looked calmly at the dragon. And the dragon grabbed her with his claws, threw her high up into the air and disappeared with her.

And she was never seen again.

Agnes fell silent, a bit upset by her own story and the memory of her friend Clara, up in the air, with floppy limbs like a ragdoll in a blue dress. There was clearly no happily ever after; it was a story that would make it hard for her to get any peace that day at all.

'What happened to the other girl?' Nathan asked after a little while. 'Did she get eaten by the dragon too?'

'No,' said Agnes. 'The second girl made it out of the road in time. She didn't go to school that day. Instead, she went home sick and had to spend a whole week in bed.'

'And the moral of the story?' Nathan asked in a singsong voice, revealing that he was usually dished up a moral after his bedtime story, presumably by the good-for-nothing, or the hysterical Sabrina.

Agnes shrugged her shoulders. 'No idea!' she said honestly.

Nobody had really been able to make rhyme or reason of the situation, not her parents, not the school and not even the police, but definitely not Agnes. Because she was the only one who had seen that Clara hadn't tripped or stumbled, but had taken a single calm, decisive step forward, straight into the path of the red lorry.

'That's a weird story!'

'Maybe,' said Agnes, who didn't want to discuss it any further. 'But, it's definitely a story!'

Before Nathan could ask any awkward questions, she stood up and switched off Marshall's desk lamp, but before she could get to the door, Nathan screamed in the dark for his transformer.

Agnes groaned. She had no idea what a transformer was, but she switched the light back on and tried to look for it in his holdall following Nathan's instructions. The transformer turned out to be a terrifyingly ugly plastic figure. Nathan put it under his pillow with a contented sigh, and Agnes switched the light out for the second time and made her way to her room. She had been planning to tell her housemates all about her latest adventure with the police, but now she just wanted to be alone, preferably under a thick duvet.

Time and memory were strange things. If she was honest, she could hardly remember her mother's facial features, but

Clara's expression floated in front of her eyes as if it were yesterday, as if all she had to do was reach out her hand to touch her pretty, pale forehead.

In the last seconds of her life, Clara's face hadn't been marked with fear and horror, but with a kind of longing.

A kind of hope.

Agnes hadn't understood it straightaway, but in the week after Clara's death that she spent feverish, shaking and wailing in her bed, bit by bit she had realised a few things:

Clara's death was no accident. Clara had *wanted* it.

She had wanted it because something else was *even worse*.

What was worse than a lorry?

The longer she thought about it, the more certain Agnes was that it had to have been Titus Coldwell.

The mumbling and dawdling, the clumsiness, the hundreds of little mishaps . . . With hindsight it was clear as day that Clara had been scared of the teacher. Scared to death. Why had nobody else seen it?

Because Titus Coldwell was a gentle person, with a soft voice and impeccable manners, that's why. Someone people admired. Someone who smelt of leather and lemons. Not terrifying in the slightest. But Clara had seen something nobody else had seen. Seen – or *experienced*.

And anybody who could be so calm and collected whilst letting Clara step in front of that honking, droning, terrifying dragon of a lorry, was not gentle.

He was a monster.

So, many decades later, Agnes was lying in her bed again, her thoughts muddled and jittery like a stirred-up ants' nest, and she didn't dare to switch the bedside lamp off. She had to admit that despite the reassuring gravestone out in the cemetery and despite the long time that lay between them like a thick, protective blanket, Titus Coldwell still made her skin crawl even now.

What made her skin crawl was his empty smile, his grey ogling beady eyes, but above all his hands, that sometimes rested on her shoulders during lessons and gradually, stole their way quietly and stealthily around her mother's waist, around her wrist and her heart. Agnes wasn't sure if she would have found the courage, like Clara, to escape, with the help of a lorry. If it hadn't been for Alice . . .

And after all that, she had just turned her back at the funeral and not given her sister the time of day. If anybody had the right to be angry with her, it was Alice!

Agnes stared up at the ceiling, where the two spiders were active again, casting long shadows. Sleep was out of the question. What did her mother used to do when she couldn't sleep? Warm milk! Had it worked? Probably not, but it was worth a try. Better than tossing and turning, watching the spiders' shadows.

She manoeuvred herself out of bed, found one slipper, but not the second, gave up on the slipper search, made her way to the hall barefoot, and went downstairs at lightning speed on the accelerated stairlift.

It was still warm in the kitchen. A spurned television remote lay abandoned on the kitchen table, and somebody hadn't put their plate in the dishwasher as they were supposed to. Edwina? Charlie? Nathan? Agnes almost got worked up about it but stopped herself in time. After all, she had other things to worry about right now. She got the milk out of the fridge and poured some of it into a small pan and put the gas ring on. You used to have to light the flame with a match, now you just had to press a little button. Now that was progress!

As the gas flames licked the copper bottom of the milk pan, Agnes tried to banish Titus Coldwell from her head. In the end, she had seen through him, and more than that, she had learnt from his example, how to recognise a monster, even the gentle, clever, beady-eyed ones, who smelt pleasantly of leather and lemons. Agnes had spent the majority of her life hunting monsters, and this ability had always earned her good results.

Until now. This time she was fumbling around in the dark.

Everything was pointing towards it being a monster in this case, someone who got a kick out of killing people at close range in a brutal and personal way, but this time Agnes's instincts were silent. The tingling neck, the hollow, uneasy feeling in the pit of her stomach, which always used to show her the way, didn't seem to want to make an appearance. Maybe she was just too old? Or on the wrong track? Was the murderer hiding too well? Agnes had the feeling he wasn't far away, as if all she had to do was reach out her hand, open her eyes and . . .

An unpleasant smell reached her nose.

Burning.

She rushed to the hob, to save the milk, just in time, then she sat in front of her steaming mug of milk at the kitchen table. Too hot! How were you supposed to sleep with a burnt tongue? Agnes blew on it and noticed that a thin skin had already formed on the milk. Yuck!

The feeling of being hot on the heels of the murderer was long-gone, but that was probably a good thing. After all, you didn't catch monsters with feelings, but with thousands of little observations, with persistence and attention to detail. There was something somewhere that would help her. At some point, she would notice a small, decisive detail. There were still a few leads she could follow up, and she would follow Hettie's example and just stubbornly put one foot in front of the other. You didn't always need a grand plan, just the next step.

And suddenly Agnes knew exactly what that step could look like.

'I'd like to borrow Nathan this morning,' Agnes said the next day at breakfast. They were all sitting at the kitchen table unusually early, because Nathan got up before the lark and even before Hettie and had managed to get them all out of bed in the shortest possible time.

There was toast, tea and coffee. The mood was subdued. They already had two tantrums under their belts because Nathan had realised that neither Frosties nor Nutella were on the menu. Agnes didn't even really know what Nutella was, but Marshall had promised to find out on the internet.

Now he raised his eyebrows and made a welcoming gesture

towards his moodily-toast-munching grandson.

Please! the hand said. *Be my guest. Go right ahead.*

Out loud, he said: 'Of course. If Nathan wants to come.'

Agnes nodded. She had long since understood how Nathan worked: carrot and stick. Above all, carrot. It should be easy to convince him to come by promising him some sweet or another or, at a pinch, a transformer.

'What do you want him for?' Charlie asked, not mistrustingly, just astonished, as if Agnes had announced she wanted to go for a walk with a millstone around her neck.

'A collection,' Agnes said. 'For a good cause. It came to me at the funeral. You should do things for society now and then, do your bit. Especially at our age.' It wasn't even a lie. If Agnes really did manage to track down the murderer, then society would have definitely been done a great service!

'Pfff!' Charlie didn't show great enthusiasm for the project. Fine by her. Agnes didn't want anybody sticking their oar in today.

The more she thought about it, the more certain she was that Olive's neighbour Theresa was the key to this case. Mildred's murder was one thing, isolated, air-tight, presumably well thought-out. Olive's on the other hand, seemed improvised to Agnes. The entry through the back door. The chaos in the kitchen. The missing note on the fridge. Somebody had acted quickly, and hopefully made one or two mistakes in the process. And if she wasn't mistaken, one of those mistakes was Theresa. Olive's neighbour had seen something, had got worked up and quickly disappeared into Lime Tree Court. It couldn't be a coincidence! It was high time someone inconspicuously asked a few questions.

And what could be more inconspicuous than an old lady? An old lady with a child! A *granny*! Nathan could clown around and do what he did best – draw all the attention to himself – and Agnes would stand next to him smiling indulgently and quite casually ask a few pertinent investigative questions.

'What sort of good cause is it?' Bernadette asked scornfully.

'Err.' People used to collect for war veterans. Still did, or had the veterans all since gone to kingdom come? The poor? Who was that supposed to be? Children? Poor children? Now Agnes wished she hadn't just slammed the door in the face of the charity collectors. If she had at least let them get a quick word in, she would definitely have had more ideas.

'Is it for tortoises?' Edwina asked hopefully.

'Exactly,' Agnes said with relief. 'Tortoises and other animals. It's for the animal shelter!'

Even Charlie couldn't say anything against that, and Agnes, now finished with her toast, couldn't suppress her thirst for action any longer.

She hurtled upstairs on the stairlift to get her coat. What else did you need for good deeds? A collection tin! A sign! And very importantly: chocolate bars!

As far as the collection tin was concerned, they would have to improvise, but Agnes found a bit of cardboard that had come with one of the grocery deliveries from the internet, and convinced Nathan to scrawl *Save the animals!* on it. Then she borrowed a considerable number of chocolate bars from Winston and tied a scarf around her neck.

Ready!

They would take the bus again because philanthropic grannies didn't normally arrive in taxis, and Agnes already had to start feeding chocolate bars to the rebellious Nathan at the bus stop.

'Boring!' he moaned, as soon as he had scoffed the first chocolate bar.

'It is not boring,' Agnes countered. 'We're knocking on strangers' doors, waiting until they come to the door, and then . . . It's like – knock down ginger!'

'Just without the running away!' Nathan mumbled gloomily.

'It's better without the running away,' Agnes explained. 'We can look into their living rooms. Anyone can run away!' Almost anyone. Anyone except her.

Nathan thought about what had been said for about two seconds.

'Boring!' he then moaned.

'I could tell you another story,' Agnes threatened. She didn't want to blow her whole chocolate stash at the bus stop.

The prospect of a second Agnes story maintained the peace for now. Nathan was silent as they waited for the bus, and he was still silent as they sat respectably on the back seats. Only when they got off in the village did he pipe up again.

'Where's the café?' he asked.

'What café?' Agnes mumbled in irritation. She had grabbed his hand and was rushing as quickly as possible towards the church. Not particularly quickly.

'Well, we're not really doing a collection, are we? You just said that so that Grandad wouldn't find out about it.'

Agnes stood still and looked at Nathan in surprise. 'Find out about what?'

'About the *aifair*,' Nathan explained confidently. '*Aifair*. A . . . fair. *Afair*. *Aifair*. It's connected.'

'It's not connected!' Nathan's theory was at such sixes and sevens that Agnes didn't know where to begin. She realised she had gone red. 'We . . . I . . . Err . . . I'm sorry to disappoint you. But we're really doing a collection, young man!'

Agnes borrowed a collection tin from the church, and Nathan stuck an elephant sticker over the cross. It wasn't ideal because there likely wasn't an elephant in the local animal shelter, but it was better than nothing.

Agnes had decided to start collecting two doors down from Theresa's, so that everything looked completely normal and coincidental. She opened the garden gate, trudged to the front door past a few pitiful anemones, and rang the bell. Her hand, which was holding Nathan's, was sweating. Now she was nervous, after all she knew exactly how collections normally went: somebody opened the door, looked angry and slammed the door in your face. Not nice when you were on the collecting side.

Barking started up on the other side of the door, and Agnes prepared for the worst, but nobody opened the door. She waited mutely.

'Again!' Nathan said, who had already developed a certain ambition, and Agnes obediently pressed the doorbell a second time. The barking continued, but nothing else happened. It was a shame because the dog would surely have donated to the animal shelter.

Finally, they tried the next door. This time nobody barked,

but Agnes was sure she had seen movement behind a curtain on the first floor. Nothing happened, not after the first ring, not after the second, and not even after the third.

Nathan angrily kicked a dachshund-shaped boot scraper, and Agnes was disappointed too. The possibility that they simply wouldn't open the door hadn't even crossed Agnes's mind. She had always assumed that, in terms of getting rid of charity collectors and cold-callers, she had reached the pinnacle of mean-spiritedness, but not even opening the door to someone – that really was brazen!

'I don't want to do the collection any more!' said Nathan. 'The collection's stupid!'

Agnes had to silently admit he was right, but she dragged him onwards, over to Theresa's house. Now was her chance.

She placed her thumb on the doorbell and let it rip. She would just keep ringing until something happened – after all, she couldn't allow Nathan to lose all faith in the goodness of people!

The next minute the door was open, and a dishevelled woman with horsy teeth and eyes red from crying stuck her head out, ready for a fight.

'For the last time! No interviews! And if anybody else rings the bell again, I'll call the—'

'Save the animals!' Agnes interrupted her, pointing to Nathan's sign.

Nathan was holding the sign the wrong way round.

Agnes took her thumb off the doorbell, a little late.

'Huh, animals what?' the woman mumbled in confusion. 'I haven't got any animals! I thought you were from the press . . .'

'Press? No, no,' Agnes said following a hunch. 'But there's a weird guy with glasses loitering around the corner. Best we go inside before he turns up here.'

Without a second thought, she marched past the woman into an untidy living room.

'Save the animals!' Nathan cawed triumphantly.

'I don't know if . . .' the woman said doubtfully. 'It's not really convenient at all!'

But Agnes had already sat down on the first available chair to give her hip a rest, and was gesticulating to try to get Nathan to hold the sign the right way round.

'Oh,' she said. 'It'll only take a minute. There should always be a bit of time for the animals!'

'Save the animals!' Nathan backed her up.

'Well . . .' said the woman, wiping her hands on the seat of her trousers.

'Besides, on our questionnaire you expressed an interest,' Agnes continued cleverly. 'You are Theresa, aren't you?'

'Good God, me, Theresa? God, no!' The woman smiled nervously. 'I'm Annie, the cleaner.'

'Ah!' Agnes feigned surprise. 'And could we perhaps speak to Theresa . . . ?'

'No chance!' said Annie the cleaner. 'Theresa isn't here. Some kind of breakdown, so I'm told. At her age, something like that really knocks you for six . . .'

'Oh my!' Agnes gasped and observed Nathan out of the corner of her eye as he worked his way through a decorative bowl of fruit, bananas first. 'The poor thing!'

'Well, not so poor after all. They took her to Lime Tree

224

Court, I heard. A real stroke of luck.'

Stroke of luck, thought Agnes. *But, for whom?*

Annie dabbed her eyes with a tissue and then noisily blew her nose.

'I can see the whole thing is affecting you deeply?'

'Good God, affecting me?' Annie stuffed the tissue back in her trouser pocket. 'No, no, it's just my hay fever. Everyone else gets it in the spring; I get it in the autumn, and it's particularly bad in a pigsty like this. No, I don't know the lady at all. Today is my first day!'

Nathan was finished with the bananas and now had to decide between apples and plums.

Plums.

Annie put her hands on her hips accusatorily. 'Three reporters have been round already and now you! I really don't know when I'm supposed to get the cleaning done!'

'Errr, well yes, we'd better go then,' said Agnes, rustling a chocolate bar in her pocket to lure Nathan away from the fruit.

They moved towards the door together.

'Save the animals!' Nathan shouted, holding the sign in front of the cleaning lady's face.

She searched her jeans pockets and finally found ten pence, presumably underneath her tissue. Then she stood in the doorway to make sure that Nathan and Agnes really did leave.

Nathan stomped purposefully towards Olive's front door. At first, Agnes wanted to call him back, but then she thought better of it. Olive would definitely not open the door, but if they just left her out it could look suspicious.

Nathan yelled: 'Save the animals!' and banged on the front door with the cardboard sign.

Agnes used the door-knocker.

For a minute she considered what it would be like if Olive really did open the door, a hole in her head and half-eaten by cats.

Not nice.

'You'll be knocking a long time!'

Agnes turned around and found that to the right, on the other side of the terraced houses, a bespectacled little man was clinging to the fence. Almost a whippersnapper still. Only just retired, Agnes guessed. What did he know about life?

'Sorry?'

'Well, the woman's dead as a dodo!' the little man said cheerily. 'I should know – we were engaged!'

14

VICTORIA SPONGE

Agnes almost dropped the collection tin in shock. The lonely coin clinked. It sounded like a laugh. Engaged? Olive? Impossible! Nobody would have got engaged to Olive, not even this little owl of a man.

'I'm sorry,' she said. It didn't really seem appropriate.

'Olive was a wonderful woman,' the man lamented. Only now did it seem to occur to him that he should look upset. 'Too good for this world. What a shock! But' – he leant right over the garden fence and his grin returned – 'they don't get away from me that easily! I saw them! I know who it was!'

The collection tin, complete with coin clattered to the ground.

'Save the animals!' Nathan screamed triumphantly.

Shortly after, they were sitting in a stuffy living room in front of a few prehistoric peanuts that even Nathan was struggling to get excited about. The Queen and three corgis stared down at them from the wall. And then the Queen again. Prince Phillip. Diana. Charles. William and Kate. Other royal faces, whose names escaped Agnes. Even more corgis and in the middle, enlarged to the point of merciful blurriness, Olive, at her front door, with a shopping bag in her hand and a scowl on her face. Black threads were stretched between all the pictures, a bit like the police did in murder cases – at least that's how it was often shown on the television.

The alleged fiancé noticed Agnes's nervous expression. 'It's all connected to Olive!' he murmured. 'She lived such a humble life here, you know, but in reality, she was old aristocracy! Blue-blooded! I saw it with my own eyes!'

Agnes fidgeted about on her chair. From Sparrow's photos she knew that Olive's blood had been just as red as anybody else's, and she started to wonder what this man had seen.

Had she led Nathan straight into a trap? The guy was mad, no doubt about it, obsessed with corgis and Olive. A fantasist. Nobody, not even Olive, who didn't exactly have her pick, would have got engaged to him. A nutcase – and maybe even a murderer?

Nathan hesitantly tried a peanut, chewed and swallowed. He didn't take another.

Agnes was just thinking about how they could best get back outside (throw some peanuts, push over the chair, shove Nathan into the hall, hobble to the door, if need be, hit the fiancé with the 'Save the animals' sign), when the man suddenly grabbed her hand.

'It was *them*!' he mumbled conspiratorially and rolled his eyes towards the corgis. 'I know how they operate! I've documented everything. It's all about the line of succession!'

He rushed over to a cupboard, and Agnes came within a

228

whisker of using the opportunity to escape with Nathan, but the next minute the fiancé was already back, a shoebox in his hands.

Resigned to her fate, Agnes put on her reading glasses and braced herself for more corgis, but they were photos of cars, hundreds of them, black and white. They were all of the same sad little section of road. Black strips at the top and bottom. Taken through the letterbox – the bloke really did have a screw loose!

'I warned Olive!' the man blathered. 'Told her they'd never leave her in peace. That she's too valuable for that. She just didn't want to listen to me. Too good for this world! But I'm not so easily fooled. Here! And here!' He pushed two stacks of photos towards Agnes. 'All taken before Olive's death!'

Agnes looked carefully. A post van. A delivery truck. A mini. A limousine. A fish seller. The man obviously spent a lot of time looking through his letterbox.

The fiancé stabbed with his finger at the fish truck. 'There! She was being shadowed round the clock. I documented everything! And one of them . . .' He ran his finger across his throat.

It wasn't him, Agnes thought. *If it had been him, he would have made a shooting gesture.* Apart from that, she was beginning to doubt whether this fiancé was even capable of instigating a murder like that. She sighed. Nathan flicked a peanut off the table in frustration.

'Save the animals!' he said flatly. 'Save the *hungry* animals!'

The boy was right. The fiancé obviously had nothing sensible to contribute to the hunt for the murderer. Enough of this nonsense – it was time to beat a hasty retreat!

Carefully, so as not to shock the madman, she stood up.

'Really fascinating,' she said. 'But I'm afraid we'll have to be on our way. This animal shelter's not going to save itself, you know?'

'Save the animals!' Nathan cried in relief and shook the collection tin like mad.

And while the fiancé was looking for his wallet and then putting a banknote through the slit on the collection box, in an unobserved moment Agnes managed to slide one of the pictures from the table and salt it away in her handbag. This photo was different to the others. You could clearly make out a terraced-house garden on it, taken diagonally from above, and right in the middle, a bit like a UFO, there floated a big dark umbrella.

'Twenty quid!' Nathan said, impressed, once they had solid pavement beneath their feet again.

'Not bad, huh?' Agnes winked. 'And do you know what? Now we're going to the café!'

She hadn't been in the little village café for years – more of a tearoom actually – and it hadn't changed for the better in the meantime. The chairs were still uncomfortable, the tables wobbled exactly like they used to, and the net curtains at the window were possibly even greyer than before. But there was a cake counter and there, behind a pane of glass, a small, but appetising selection of cakes.

'Choose one for yourself,' said Agnes.

'One?' Nathan asked in outrage.

'One!' Agnes said sternly.

'Save the hungry animals!' Nathan protested, but Agnes didn't allow herself to be swayed. It was about time the boy's

eating habits were directed into slightly more normal channels –
he already looked like a balloon. It couldn't be healthy!

She ordered tea and a scone for herself and then a fruit juice.
After a long and painful selection process, Nathan decided on the
biggest piece of cake behind the glass, a moist Victoria sponge.

Agnes paid with the twenty from the tin, the young café
lady put it all on a tray for them, and they looked for a cosy
little table at the window. Whilst Nathan scoffed the Victoria
sponge and told her all about his transformer with his mouth
full, Agnes turned the stolen photo back and forth in her hand.
It had been taken with a Polaroid camera and was a bit blurry
– the fiancé's surveillance equipment obviously left a lot to be
desired. Despite that, you could clearly make out the garden of
a terraced house, a small patio and a back door left ajar, next to
it five cats were peacefully gathered around a food bowl. It was
the cats that had motivated Agnes to take the photo with her –
she was as good as certain that this was Olive's garden. On the
day of the murder.

And someone with a big umbrella was heading towards the
house!

Agnes kept putting on her reading glasses and taking them
off again, in the hope of seeing more details, but there wasn't
much, just . . .

'He's like a car, only he's not a car. He's a robot disguised as a
car! He's one, but he looks like two!' Nathan babbled.

It didn't make much sense, and – even more disconcertingly
– Nathan had almost finished his Victoria sponge. Agnes tried to
concentrate. There, on the edge of the umbrella, something black
and pointy was poking out. A shoe, better put, the point of a shoe!

'Are you going to eat that?' Nathan asked eyeing her scone hungrily.

'Of course I am,' said Agnes. She buttered the scone and poured herself some more tea. What now?

Really, she should give the picture to the police. No question. But how would that look? A stolen photo, a fraudulent charity collection, stolen money for a Victoria sponge, and all of that from Agnes, who was already connected to the victim by carrot cake, a knife and other missiles?

Not good.

Apart from that, the stupid thing was that the police didn't have a chance. Not really. Their leading assumptions were false.

Three victims.

Three murders.

One murder weapon.

One killer with a secret motive who really had it in for old ladies.

At first glance, that's what it looked like, and you couldn't really blame the police.

But Agnes knew that wasn't the case.

Lillith's death looked like part of the sequence, but in reality, was something completely different, strictly speaking not even a proper murder. More a . . . pact.

You couldn't just go telling the police that though.

The murdering had started later, with Mildred, then Olive. Someone had got hold of the gun after Lillith's death and . . . really it had to have happened spontaneously, after all nobody could have known in advance what would happen to Lillith that day, but somehow it didn't seem particularly spontaneous to

Agnes. More like something someone had been thinking about for years.

Olive's murder, on the other hand . . . What if Agnes was making false assumptions too?

What if . . . Agnes tried to think outside the box. What if Olive wasn't a victim at all? What if she was the *murderer*? First Mildred's murderer and then, because Theresa had seen something important . . .

The thought came from nowhere, and it shocked Agnes. Impossible! But if you looked at things more closely . . . what exactly did they know already? Olive and Theresa, two old ladies, one dead, the other disappeared. A dead body, with its face gnawed beyond recognition, was found in Olive's house, with Olive's clothes and Olive's muffins.

But what if that dead body wasn't Olive at all, but Theresa?

In that case it could have been Olive herself who dropped off the cream slices at the coffee morning, to draw out the discovery of the body, post-mortem so to speak. And then she could have settled in at Lime Tree Court under Theresa's name, where new arrivals were conveniently isolated for a while. It would have been the perfect opportunity to get herself to safety following Mildred's murder.

But what did Olive have against Mildred? Agnes didn't know exactly, but it was easy to imagine *that* she had something against Mildred. After all, in the end, as good as everyone had something against Mildred – and Olive was the grudge-bearing sort who could carry resentments around with her for years and go straight to the police over trifles like a knife being thrown!

Obviously, Theresa's relatives would have had to play along, at least one of them anyway. The daughter-in-law? Far-fetched, but not impossible. Maybe cantankerous old Theresa had been a thorn in her side for a long time? And maybe Olive offered them money, a lot of money, all of the savings she'd squirreled away?

Agnes thought back to the neglected little terraced house. And now suddenly there was enough money for a cleaner? And for Lime Tree Court? There was something fishy going on there!

It was a bold theory with a lot of question marks, but it was a theory. Better than nothing. The longer Agnes thought about it, the more certain she was: it was about time to infiltrate Lime Tree Court and take a closer look at the old lady holed up there under Theresa's name!

'Can I get you anything else?'

Agnes looked down at two pointy black shoes, then up into the café lady's friendly face.

Nathan opened his mouth, but Agnes quickly declined with a wave. 'No, thank you. That will be all.'

The café lady cleared away the empty plates. Agnes stood up, struggled to balance for a moment and dragged a protesting Nathan from his seat and out of the café, past two gossiping women with pointy black shoes.

They stood at the bus stop with three pairs of pointy black shoes and sat opposite two more pointy black shoes on the bus.

Nearly every other person seemed to have pointy black shoes on – or better put: every other woman. The shoe underneath the umbrella was probably a lady's shoe! If she was honest, she had been assuming that the murderer was a woman for a long time. Something about the way the murders were carried out, somehow temperamental and audacious and . . . furious?

When the bus finally spat them out at their stop, Agnes was seized by a strange lethargy. All that effort and the only outcome was the blurry and not particularly conclusive Polaroid photo taken by a madman. What use was that? None at all! Her theory about Olive and Theresa was absurd!

She was imagining things again, that was it! Just like back then!

Agnes realised she was still holding the collection tin with the elephant sticker in her hand, and threw it angrily into the bushes. Investigating! With a walking stick and false teeth! What had she been thinking?

She was tired. She wanted to sit and sleep and knit. Age appropriately. Why couldn't she just be left in peace to have a nap? And then a second nap! And if a murderer in pointy black shoes really did show up, maybe she'd even be doing Agnes a favour!

Frustrated, she stared down at her own pointy black shoes, whilst Nathan tugged impatiently at her sleeve. The rascal was probably hungry again.

Then Agnes noticed that a limousine had appeared beside them almost silently.

A tinted window rolled down.

Isobel's pale face peered out. Quiet, wailing music was playing inside the car. A requiem or something. Agnes gulped.

Isobel looked over the top of her dark sunglasses. 'Agnes. Good to see you. Do you perhaps fancy a light lunch? Salad? Soup? A piece of cake for afters?'

'Yeah!' Nathan celebrated.

Then the chauffeur was standing next to them holding the door open.

Agnes didn't have the energy to protest – or maybe it was her guilty conscience that persuaded her to get into the limousine with Nathan. Since the funeral she hadn't spared a single thought for Isobel – what she was going through didn't bear thinking about!

Funerals were one thing, but the real horror came afterwards. Agnes remembered it well, how her mother had cried over Titus Coldwell, for days on end, at breakfast, at lunch, while hoovering and washing up and even in bed at night, when she thought nobody could hear. Over Titus Coldwell, who really didn't deserve it! Oh, how Agnes used to hate him then, with his beady eyes and fish lips, more than she ever had when he was alive!

The limousine purred past Sunset Hall and Agnes could make out Charlie and Edwina in the garden, performing some kind of dance in white clothes. For a moment she had an almost painful pang of homesickness, but then the car swished on, and Isobel grabbed her hand.

'It's terribly kind of you to come, Agnes! If I'm honest, I can't manage a single bite on my own!'

'Oh, Isobel!' Agnes breathed. Something moved in the pit of her stomach. It felt like a tadpole – or a frog. Losing a sibling was hard enough, but your twin – it was as if someone had cut you down the middle.

Never to be whole again.

Isobel's eyes sparkled behind her dark glasses, presumably with tears.

Agnes squeezed her hand back. 'I know it's hard,' she said. 'It's terrible. But it was also a release!'

Isobel forced a smile behind her sunglasses. 'I know,' she said quietly. 'I know, Agnes!'

Maybe at that moment, they would have hugged and cried together and officially reconciled, then got squiffy on sherry and both felt a bit better – if at that moment a transformer hadn't appeared between them.

'Save the hungry animals!' the transformer demanded in the Grandson's clear, high voice.

'Who's this, then?' Isobel asked, as if she'd only just noticed Nathan.

Agnes swallowed the frog that had climbed up into her throat, and shrugged her shoulders.

'Just the Grandson. He's called Nathan. It's just for the holidays!'

Isobel nodded absently and already seemed to have forgotten Nathan. 'Here we are!'

The car stopped, the car door opened and the chauffeur waited for Agnes to get out. Agnes grabbed his hand and pulled herself out with it. For the first time she noticed how tall the chauffeur actually was. In the limousine he was neatly folded up, but now, where he was standing, she had to tilt her head right back to be able to see his face.

It was a smooth, young chauffeur face with a trendy beard, and despite that, the man didn't look particularly good. He had dark circles around his eyes, as if he hadn't slept much recently. There was nothing wrong with his manners though. He waited until she, Nathan and the transformer had got out of the car, and rushed round to the other side to help Isobel out.

Isobel hesitated for a moment, then she linked arms with the chauffer and limped off. It seemed strangely resolute.

Agnes observed with regret how bad Isobel was on her feet. Was she in pain? Presumably. Poor Isobel!

This time Isobel didn't lead her into the drawing room, but deeper into the house, along a corridor, to the library. She switched on a lamp, and golden light streamed through the silk lampshade. Book spines stood mute and upright. Somewhere an expensive grandfather clock was ticking. Isobel let the chauffeur lower her down into an armchair by the fireplace and gestured for Agnes and Nathan to sit next to her on a sofa.

Agnes sank into cushions and memories.

'Feed the hungry animals,' demanded Nathan.

Isobel smiled and rang a bell, then she said something over Agnes's shoulder, presumably to a maid: 'A light lunch, please, and maybe some white wine.'

'And cake!' Nathan insisted.

'And cake,' Isobel said, winking at him.

Agnes was hardly listening. The library was a time machine. She was suddenly wearing a school blazer again, and a skirt that her mother thought was too short. The pigtails were finally gone, instead last week at the hairdressers she had insisted on a fashionable shoulder-length bob. Stupidly, her hair didn't lie flat like the sisters', but puffed up behind her ears.

Skin, still warm from the sunshine.

Sticky fingers.

Peanut butter on toast, and lemonade.

'Lemonade,' Agnes mumbled.

'And lemonade,' Isobel smiled over her shoulder.

A maid brought a tray with plates, napkins and cutlery and disappeared again.

Expectantly, Nathan stuck a napkin into the collar of his sweatshirt and suddenly looked like a trained pug.

Agnes tried to concentrate.

The library.

Twin headquarters.

Why had Isobel brought her there? Did it mean she'd forgiven her?

They'd spent many lemonade-slurping evenings there in front of the fire, spun dreams and made plans. Outings. Shopping trips. Adventures. The deaths of other pupils at school who were making their lives difficult. The death of Miss Inholm, the needlework teacher, and – more and more regularly – the death of their uncle, who was really starting to get on their nerves with his old-fashioned ideas. All purely theoretical, of course – and yet: Hadn't the uncle actually met his maker shortly afterwards?

They had done homework there, sworn oaths, demolished boxes of chocolates, drunk stolen champagne and tickled each other silly.

Agnes blinked away a few tears. This is where she and Isobel had sobbed in each other's arms after Mildred had run away from home. Just like that. Without saying anything to them beforehand.

Together they had decided to cover up Mildred's flight. Together they had discovered how easy it would be for Isobel to play two in front of their preoccupied uncle. Mildred and Isobel.

Isobel and Mildred.

It was one of those crackpot ideas, that was easy to implement to start with – a prank, a trick, a game – but then developed a life of its own.

Mildred and Isobel.

In the end they hadn't been able to bear it any more and decided that the made-up Mildred had to die.

Drowned.

In the river.

Agnes and Isobel had seen it with their own eyes.

The police looked for the body for weeks, but eventually gave up, and Isobel had been able to concentrate on just being Isobel again. And when the real Mildred had turned up a few weeks later, because she had run out of money, it was obviously a huge surprise.

The food came. Salad with grapes and goat's cheese. Banana bread. Wine.

Agnes suddenly burst out laughing. 'Tell me, do you still remember Mildred's funeral?'

Isobel gave her a strange look. 'Of course. It wasn't even a week ago. I'm not that gaga yet!'

'No, no.' Agnes grinned. 'I mean her *first* funeral!'

Edwina had just dug Hettie out of the earth by the little rose bushes, when suddenly the policeman was standing in front of her.

She only just managed to hide a muddy Hettie behind her back. Damn. Agnes had said that it wasn't good for the police to always catch them digging!

'Good morning, Constable!'

The policeman gave her a funny look. Was it not morning?

Edwina awkwardly wiped her Hettie-free hand on her white sweatshirt. White sweatshirt. White jogging bottoms. Charlie had shown her a new dance. Tai chi. You were supposed to wear white to do it. She had liked the dance, but now it occurred to her that the white clothes weren't particularly practical.

'I . . .' the policeman said hesitantly. 'Err. A few more questions have popped up. For the . . . err . . . for the files.'

Edwina nodded sympathetically. Files were mostly a nuisance.

The policeman looked around furtively. 'If we could have a quick word in private . . .'

Edwina thought about it. 'Okay,' she said finally.

Hettie thrashed about in frustration behind her back. She probably wanted to go back into the soil, but Edwina couldn't allow that. If she wasn't careful, one day Hettie would bury herself so deep, that Edwina wouldn't find her again. Ever.

'Should we perhaps take a seat somewhere?' the policeman asked, and Edwina obediently sunk down cross-legged onto the gravel path. In doing so, she had to take Hettie out from behind her back.

The policeman looked annoyed.

'Hettie stays!' Edwina said decisively. 'She can keep a secret!'

The tortoise looked like a grave robber, covered in earth and suspicious, but luckily the policeman didn't seem interested in Hettie and Edwina's digging.

To start with, he was interested in finding somewhere to sit on the gravel path. He was very ungainly and didn't know what to do with his legs.

Then he started to develop an interest in Agnes.

How long had Edwina known Agnes for?

It was one of those questions Edwina didn't even know where to begin with. She pretended to think about it, whispered to Hettie and then stretched out three fingers from her clean hand towards the policeman.

'About three weeks.'

The policeman didn't seem to particularly like that answer. He tried to cross his legs, but he didn't succeed.

Whether it was easy to live with Agnes?

'Not always,' Edwina admitted. For a moment she considered whether she should tell him about the thing with Lillith in the hat, but decided against it. So trivial! And how worked up Agnes had got! It was a good thing that at least Hettie had stuck by her!

'Why not?' the policeman wanted to know.

'She's moody. And she's got all these rules,' Edwina explained. 'And if someone doesn't keep to the rules . . .'

She paused and shuddered. Last week she really hadn't got any afters, just because she . . . she couldn't remember what she had done, but it really couldn't have been that bad.

And how did Agnes get on with Lillith? Had the two of them perhaps argued sometimes?

Edwina started to rid Hettie of dirt with the edge of her white sweatshirt.

'Constantly.' Mostly it was about Lillith bringing too much mud into the house, just like Hettie, but she didn't want to go telling the policeman that.

He looked really interested now.

Did Agnes know how to fire a gun?

'Definitely,' said Edwina with utter conviction, putting a

freshly cleaned Hettie down on the gravel path. Everyone there knew how to fire a gun. She herself could have done it in her sleep, safety catch off, position, aim, fire. There really wasn't much to it. Did they teach young police officers nothing these days?

As Hettie busily strode down the path, Edwina could see a kind of conviction forming on the policeman's face. Not certainty – not yet – but a firm suspicion nonetheless.

Edwina had led countless interrogations in her time – mostly in back rooms, with dazzling desk lamps and very real threats – and could recognise the signs.

The policeman suspected Agnes! Absurd! Agnes of all people, who herself was trying to hunt down the murderer. Edwina had really tried to answer the policeman's questions as succinctly and neutrally as possible, but she must have said something wrong somewhere. Now he had Agnes in his sights, and it was all her fault. She had to put it right.

And she already knew how.

She jumped up and waited until the policeman had clumsily struggled to his feet, then she tugged at his sleeve.

'I've got something to show you!'

'Is it to do with Agnes?' he asked hopefully.

She nodded and pulled him down the gravel path. They overtook Hettie, got to the veranda and climbed up the three steps to the house together.

The policeman followed Edwina like a lamb.

15

JAM ON TOAST

Agnes was in bed. Wide awake.

Outside the moon was shining, and a company of little tawny owls had gathered for a competitive hooting contest.

There was a lot going on in Agnes's head too. The lunch with Isobel had stirred up old memories, sleeping dragons, that were now circling in her head with iridescent wings, their tails lashing.

She was happy that she and Isobel had got together once more in this lifetime, and she felt a sense of regret that Mildred couldn't be part of it too. Sure, she had got more and more bitter, and difficult with age, but the three of them had once been best friends.

Sisters.

More than sisters even: three twins.

What would Alice have said about that?

Agnes rolled onto her left side to take the pressure off her hip and stared at the moonlit shadows on the wall. The visit to Isobel's had given her renewed self-confidence. Her body may well have become a wobbly and unpredictable thing, but deep down she was still Agnes. Finding monsters was her calling! And her old friend Mildred deserved for her, Agnes, to track down her murderer!

She continued to stare into the night for a while, her eyes glistening, then pulled herself upright on the bedpost.

Agnes slid out of bed and padded to the bathroom. She looked at herself in the mirror for a while. An old woman in a white nightdress, with tangled hair and dazzled squinting eyes, stared back at her. Perfect!

She put her teeth in position, pulled a warm coat on straight over her nightie and started to pack her bag: money for the taxi. Reading glasses. Fondant creams. Chocolate bars. Binoculars. Passport. A small, but sharp knife, just to be on the safe side. Then she slipped on the most comfortable of her many comfortable shoes – not black and pointy, but beige and wide. She would have to cover quite a distance.

As quietly as possible, Agnes opened her bedroom door and tiptoed into the hallway. Nothing stirred. She decided to avoid the stairlift. It was quick but had recently started making strange beeping noises, and she didn't want to risk waking her housemates. Bernadette in particular had the hearing of a bat.

The descent was tedious, but went off surprisingly quietly.

Having arrived downstairs, Agnes rested a bit, had a glass of water, ate a slice of cold toast and called a taxi in whispered tones. She was just on her way to the front door when she suddenly felt warm breath behind her.

A wet nose nuzzled her hand.

Then a warm tongue.

Someone had heard her after all and had come to the door to see her off.

Agnes ruffled Brexit's silky fur. She was strangely touched.

'It's not for long,' she explained in a whisper. 'I've just got to find something out. I'll be back soon!'

Brexit panted trustingly, and Agnes really hoped she wouldn't disappoint him.

As she stepped onto the veranda, there was already a rosy strip in the sky, and a taxi's headlights were glowing on the other side of the garden fence.

Hettie woke up, turned her head still a bit woozily and attempted a few digging motions with her crooked front legs. She hit stone. Typical! In her dreams she had dug a deep, dark hole, that smelt of earth and was wonderful, but in reality, something always held her back.

The tortoise craned her neck determinedly and saw that she hadn't been woken as usual by one of the moving sunspots on the stone floor. No, the responsible sunspot was quite a way away. Hettie crept off pensively, towards the dozy spot.

Something had woken her up, no doubt about it.

Something had been bothering her half the night.

As she plunged into the sunspot and began to soak up the blissful, warm light, she heard it again, quiet and pervasive, more a vibration than a noise.

Dull thudding.

From below.

Coming from the cellar.

246

The sun was already hanging roundly, and a bit garishly, in the sky as Agnes finally lowered the binoculars and struggled to get up from the bench she'd spent the early morning hours on. Her limbs were stiff, as if they didn't belong to her at all; as if they were something that some puppet master had rivetted onto her body. But at least she now had a better understanding of how Lime Tree Court functioned.

It functioned like clockwork.

As soon as the first rays of sunlight had crept above the horizon, carers and nurses had begun to systematically transport patient after patient outside. Then they had gathered on the big terrace, smoked cigarettes and drunk coffee out of paper cups, whilst the old people sat around apathetically on benches or in wheelchairs or roamed aimlessly through the parkland. Agnes was after one of the mobile, but aimless ones.

She waited until an old lady with a muddled expression walked towards the fence. Agnes had already tied the bag with her kit around her waist under her nightie, now she slipped her shoes off, let her coat slide off her shoulders, carefully folded it up and laid it on the bench. Goose bumps spread up her arms, as she padded towards Lime Tree Court, barefoot and determined. The muddled lady on the other side of the fence looked up and saw her.

Agnes waved.

The lady waved back and stepped closer, curious.

So far, so good.

Then they were both standing right next to the fence looking at each other through the bars.

'Hello,' said Agnes.

'Hello,' said the lady and let out a loud fart. 'They've all got a screw loose in here!'

Agnes nodded knowingly. 'Is the food good at least?' she asked.

The lady pulled a face. 'Not always.'

'Not enough sweet treats, huh?' Agnes sympathetically pulled a fondant cream out of her bag. It was in a shiny blue wrapper. Now she had the lady's full attention.

'I'd like to suggest a trade,' she said, and to her consternation, the old lady immediately started taking off her dressing gown.

'No, no.' Agnes gestured for her to stop. 'I just want that thing . . .' She reached her hand out and pointed towards the plastic band on the woman's wrist. Through the field binoculars she had realised that every Lime Tree Court resident was wearing a plastic band like that, and if she wanted to blend in amongst them seamlessly, she would need one too!

'This?' The muddled old lady held out her hand towards her scornfully. 'They've all got a screw loose in here, you know?'

Agnes already had a knife in her hand, grabbed her wrist and cut through the band in one quick motion. It was a sharp knife – Agnes had borrowed it from Marshall.

The woman looked a bit shocked, but also seemed relieved that the band was off.

Agnes quickly gave her the fondant cream, slipped the somewhat stiff band over her hand like a plastic bangle and limped off, through the dew, out from under the shade of the trees.

Out to where she would be seen.

Edwina woke up earlier than usual. Normally she wasn't a morning person, but the sun was shining. It was promising to be a marvellous day. She leapt out of bed, stretched and started her yoga routine.

Sun salutation.

Mountain.

Cobra.

Downward dog.

Locust.

Child's pose.

And Corpse pose.

She put on her blue jogging suit – the white clothes from yesterday were completely ruined after the thing with the policeman. She had shoved them under the bed for now and was planning to smuggle them into the bin later on. Well, that was the end of the tai chi. Shame, but she had other things to worry about now: Hettie loved sun and it was about time somebody let her into the garden, so she could thoroughly warm herself up on one of her sun stones.

As usual Edwina found the tortoise near the heating, in a bit of a bad mood and quite dirty again. This digging really was getting to be a bad habit! Edwina knew what Hettie needed now: a talking-to and a bath. As she slewed Hettie back and forth in lukewarm water and read her the riot act, she remembered the policeman asking all of those awkward questions yesterday.

That's right.

She'd almost forgotten about him.

There was something she had to do!

She meticulously dried the tortoise, carried her outside and put her down on the gravel path with a few final words of warning. Then, after she had made sure the rest of the house was still asleep, she quietly made her way.

Down into the cellar.

The security man was leaning his back on the fence speaking animatedly into a mobile phone. Mostly, it was about a darling, that he 'couldn't,' that 'the boss would kick up a fuss,' and a load of other things that to Agnes sounded very much like lame excuses.

She listened to it all for a while, then she ran out of patience. Decisively, she reached her hand between two bars and tapped the man on the shoulder. He nearly dropped his phone in fright, spun round, saw Agnes and groaned.

'Shit, shit, shit. Not you, sweetie. One of the coffin dodgers has got out.'

Now Agnes strived to get away from the fence towards the road at her lousy top speed, seemingly on the run.

The security guy ran along the fence and spoke into his phone again, not to sweetie this time. Agnes didn't take any notice of him, she just scurried through the dew barefoot. Her neck was tingling, goose bumps spread up her arms. Her heart was pounding, she was out of breath. The high-pitched ringing started up. Suddenly she really was on the run. Suddenly the thought of Lime Tree Court filled her with horror. If she had been able to, now she would have climbed a tree and disappeared, but it was obviously too late for that. At least fifty years too late.

It was difficult to say how long her panicked, deaf flight lasted. Seconds. A small eternity. But suddenly two hands grabbed her by the shoulders. Two more hands clasped her hips and pushed her backwards, into a chair, a wheelchair. Somebody threw a blanket over her and strapped her in. It all happened in a flash.

Agnes didn't put up any resistance. What could she have done? Nobody was ungentle with her, but she still felt liked she'd been manhandled. Without respect. Worse than a dangerous criminal – like a sack of potatoes! A carer in a white blouse bent down towards her and spoke inaudibly into the high-pitched ringing. Agnes tried to nod, but the blanket came up to her neck and limited her freedom of movement.

She was already in motion, flanked by two carers and the blue-uniformed security man.

The gates to Lime Tree Court opened.

Agnes didn't hear them close behind her again with an efficient hum.

Agnes was sleeping for longer than usual. Her housemates had gathered in front of their various cups of tea and coffee and were using the opportunity to speak openly about Agnes.

Because one thing was clear, something was off with her lately.

Yesterday she had come home half-cut in a limousine, and Nathan had told them that they had gone door to door with a stolen collection box and spent the money on cake.

And then there was her sudden fear of mice and the obsession with all things Lime Tree Court.

Murder case, or no murder case – that didn't sound like Agnes at all.

Bernadette shook her head regretfully.

Charlie sighed.

Winston comfortingly patted hands left, right and centre.

Nathan had finished his toast and started to eat Nutella out of the jar with a spoon.

'She's probably just a bit stressed,' said Charlie. 'No wonder. Maybe she should try a joint!' She rummaged in her handbag, but Bernadette shook her head.

'Better not,' she said. 'She had some issues before. Psychosis. Had to give up her job. But that was years ago, Lillith said. As long as she takes her pills, there shouldn't be any problems any more.'

'But there are problems,' Marshall said and took the Nutella jar away from Nathan. He let out a shrill scream in protest and threw the transformer at him, but Marshall didn't even look up. 'We've got to find out what's wrong. And we've got to help her!'

That was the trouble with their household. With some things you couldn't just go to the doctor or the psychologist or anywhere else, like other people, otherwise, hey presto, you were out of the game, straight into the loony bin, hospital or a home. With some things you just had to help yourself.

'We'll cook her something nice!' Winston suggested. 'Some wine. In moderation. A nice dessert! And then we'll just speak openly with her!'

The others nodded. Nobody could resist the magic of a nice dessert, not even Agnes.

'Whose turn is it to cook today?' Marshall asked.

Winston glanced at the rota. 'Edwina!'

Charlie groaned.

'Where even is Edwina?' Winston asked.

Good question! Up to now their conversation had been running far too harmoniously.

Bernadette exhaled. 'In the cellar probably. With the policeman.'

'The policeman?' Marshall asked in horror.

Bernadette shrugged her shoulders. 'Edwina's locked a policeman in the cellar. He's been banging about in there all night.'

Agnes woke up because someone rammed their elbow in her ribs. Probably Edwina. Agnes had already told her a hundred times that that was no way to wake someone up. But this time she was happy. What a nightmare! Had she really . . .

Just a minute!

She opened her eyes wide and looked at a charming park landscape. A pond, ducks, white park benches and colourful autumnal maple trees. The only thing ruining the harmonious image was the vast number of old people roaming about the place. But before she could marvel at it any longer, the bothersome elbow returned. In exactly the same spot. Agnes groaned and looked reproachfully to the side.

Next to her, turned towards the sun, was a row of stoic-looking wheelchairs with predominately just as stoic occupants. Only the guy next to her was grinning and clicking his tongue.

The elbow owner.

Agnes had never seen the man before.

Suddenly she was wide awake. That's right. The binoculars. The farting old lady. The knife. The band. The wild, but lame chase. The wheelchair. Had she really fallen asleep afterwards, or had they . . . ? She wiggled her toes. Still barefoot, but mobile. She stretched her hands. Her hands complied. She felt under the blanket for the bag. Still there, where it belonged. Thank God!

The elbow owner eyed her curiously. 'You're new, aren't you? Fresh from the Whispering Wing, huh? Don't worry, doll, I'll look after you. Pretty girl like you . . .'

The bloke waggled his bushy eyebrows and winked. *Flirting*. Agnes looked the other way in horror. More wheelchairs. The woman next to her was snoring.

'I'll show you how the wind blows!' elbow bloke murmured. But for now, no wind was blowing. Instead, a hairy hand was wandering over the armrest of her wheelchair towards her knee.

Agnes watched it with a certain fascination and considered whether she should reach for Marshall's sharp knife. Her knee was well protected under the thick blanket, but it was the principle of the matter. His hand had no business there!

'Hands off!' she said and gave the adventurous hand a slap.

The bloke just laughed. The hand continued on its journey.

Agnes had had enough. She found the buckle of the wheelchair belt and undid it. Then she cast off the blanket and stood up, a bit wobbly.

There you go. Better already!

'I wouldn't do that if I were you!' the man next to her threatened, but Agnes ignored him. She had better things

254

to do than sit around being pawed by a bloke with bushy eyebrows. Time was of the essence. Sooner or later, somebody would notice that she didn't really belong there, and the farting old lady had to be out and about somewhere too. It was only a matter of time before her cover was blown. Every minute mattered. First, she had to hide her bag so well that nobody would find it, and then . . .

She stepped into the house from the terrace, into a pretty, bright breakfast room, where nobody was currently having breakfast, and then carried on, along a corridor. Only once she had hidden her bag behind the cistern in a toilet did it occur to her that the pawer had actually said something useful.

The Whispering Wing.

That's where the newbies were, and where she must go!

Edwina was crouching down on a wooden box next to the coal hatch, her legs tucked up, listening to the policeman begging.

At first, he had admonished, then warned, then threatened, but after the night in the coal cellar he seemed to have calmed down a bit. Now you could finally talk to him. She had already brought him a little bit of breakfast; a bottle of water and half a slice of jam on toast. If he wanted to earn the other half of the toast, he would have to put a bit of effort in.

Plastic bottles were bad for the environment, but Edwina had been too wary to just put her hand through the hatch with a glass of water. It was an exceptional situation. Hettie and all of the other animals would forgive her.

'Let me out, Edwina,' the policeman cajoled. They were now on first name terms. 'I won't say anything to anyone. I just want to go home to my family. I've got kids. Two pretty little girls. Cleo and Cindy. They'll be missing me already. I just want to go home.'

Edwina was too experienced to fall for a heart-string-pulling tactic like that. Who had names like Cleo and Cindy anyway? And if the two girls really did exist, they would manage without the policeman for a while. She didn't want to keep him down there forever. Of course not. Just for as long as it took for him to realise how absurd it was to suspect Agnes.

The policeman claimed to have already realised that, but Edwina knew that there could be a huge difference between what someone spouted in the coal cellar, and what he really thought.

It was her job to do a lot of persuading.

'Agnes would never kill someone so lightly,' she explained patiently and flicked a bit of jam on toast through the hatch. 'Not even Mildred and Olive. It's really not her style.'

'But she was seen!' the policeman said in desperation. 'There are witnesses. I wouldn't just suspect her like that, Edwina.'

Edwina got up, a bit disappointed, and ate the rest of the jam on toast herself. The policeman hadn't learnt very much so far. But she was patient.

'I have to go now,' she said. 'Hettie needs me. I'll pop by again this afternoon. With a bottle of water. Even though it's bad for the environment.'

A dull thud could be heard in the coal cellar, like a fist hitting the cellar wall, followed by a suppressed scream of pain as well as a torrent of abuse and threats. It was a regrettable relapse. Edwina listened calmly. She didn't believe a word the policeman said. If his phone really had signal, he would have called for help a long time ago. Sunset Hall was an old house with thick walls, and the only room with a halfway reliable mobile signal was Marshall's corner room. Definitely not the coal cellar.

Apart from that, Edwina doubted that the policeman's colleagues knew where he had gone. If they did, they would have turned up by now asking after him. No. He'd gone off his own bat with his absurd suspicion and had tried to bait Edwina with his sanctimonious questions.

Now he was in the coal cellar.

More fool him.

'Lift the red thread. Make a loop. Pull the red thread through the loop with the needle!'

The woman in the white tunic had already explained the process a hundred times, but most of Agnes's fellow knitters had long since lost the thread. One woman was poking away in her ear with a knitting needle, and a man was trying to bite through the thread with his teeth.

Agnes didn't want to stand out by being too competent, so she poked her needle randomly into the ball of wool, and looked around warily. She had aimlessly wandered through Lime Tree Court and, after a few embarrassing encounters, had joined this craft group.

The benefit of the craft group was that the lady in the white tunic was engrossed in a novel and hadn't even noticed that she was now supervising nine, not just eight, 'busy bees.' Another benefit was that you had needles in your hand, albeit woefully blunt ones. And her fellow crafters seemed at least partially responsive.

'Hey,' Agnes whispered to the woman next to her, once tunic lady had disappeared into her book again. 'Nice day today, isn't it?'

The woman next to her smiled and wrangled with the red thread.

Agnes scooted closer, emboldened.

'Weird, this knitting malarkey, isn't it?'

This time she got a nod and a snigger.

Agnes decided that was enough of the small talk, and scooted even closer to the woman.

'I'm looking for something,' she whispered.

The woman next to her helpfully passed her a ball of wool.

'Thank you,' said Agnes. 'Not that. I'm looking for the *Whispering Wing*.'

Now the woman looked a bit shocked, but she clearly understood what Agnes meant.

'My friend's in there,' Agnes explained. 'I'd just like to know how she is.'

'That's not looked upon kindly,' the woman next to her said thoughtfully.

'I don't intend to be looked upon,' Agnes explained. 'And definitely not kindly.'

The woman nodded as if that was a good decision. 'On the other side of the kitchen,' she said. 'Keep following the food smells, then go through the dining room, and on the other side . . . Could I possibly have your wool, please?'

Agnes passed her the ball of wool, which one of her knitting needles was stuck in, and set off slowly and quietly, just as she had come.

She kept the other knitting needle in her fist.

'We can't just leave him in the cellar!' Charlie said agitatedly. She had smoked two joints in quick succession, but the calm she was hoping for hadn't really materialised.

'We can't let him go either!' Bernadette responded pragmatically. 'He'll arrest Edwina. And Agnes. He'll arrest us all if we're not careful!'

To begin with Edwina had denied point-blank that she had anything to do with the furious policeman in the cellar, but after Brexit had pulled her coal-blackened sweatshirt out from under her bed, the evidence was overwhelming.

Now she was sitting there with her arms and legs crossed with Hettie on her lap, in a huff. 'He suspected Agnes. I couldn't just let him go. We'll wait until we can talk some sense into him. Then we'll persuade him. Job's a good'un!'

The others doubted it would be so simple. Sure, during her time in the secret service Edwina had probably learnt one or two useful interrogation and brainwashing techniques, but that was a small eternity ago, and her methodology seemed to have got a bit rusty in the meantime. Apart from that, things like this required time, patience and a considerable budget. She wasn't going to get very far with some jam on toast and gentle lectures in the coal cellar.

'Even if he stops suspecting Agnes,' Winston said, 'he's

not going to like the fact that you've locked him in the cellar.'

'He'll like it even less if I don't let him out again!' Edwina mumbled sulkily.

'We should see what Agnes thinks about it all,' Marshall said. 'Agnes normally has very sensible ideas when it comes to things like this.' Not that they'd had big problems with law enforcement officials in the cellar before – rats at most – but Agnes's judgement could be relied upon in most cases.

She still didn't seem to be out of bed – highly unusual – so they all went upstairs, to gently but firmly wake her. It was an emergency after all.

Marshall had brought her a cup of tea to soften her up. They called and knocked for quite a while.

Nothing.

Finally, Charlie carefully opened the door, stuck her head in, turned to her housemates and shook her head.

The bed was empty and unmade.

Her teeth were not in their glass.

No doubt. Agnes had done a runner. But when? Why? And where to?

'Where's Agnes?' Marshall was in disbelief. He looked behind the curtains twice and then in the wardrobe three times.

'Agnes is having an *aifair*!' Nathan declared, who had followed them with Nutella smeared all around his mouth.

The cup of tea slipped out of Marshall's hands.

It fell to the ground and smashed.

Agnes had managed to get through the dining room and kitchen unnoticed, and even got hold of an exceptionally good sandwich in the process. More luck than judgement. She didn't really like it. Lucky streaks were prone to ending abruptly, and the most important part of her mission was yet to come.

On the other side of the kitchen there was a little lobby area, then a double door with a sign showing a diagram of a nurse with her finger to her lips. The Whispering Wing! No doubt about it. It was cleverly done. The new arrivals could easily be provided for at mealtimes without ever crossing the path of the other Lime Tree Court residents.

Agnes tried the door.

Locked.

She rattled the door, but it didn't budge.

Then she spotted a metal button on the wall, just beyond her reach. She used the knitting needle to push it. What did she have to lose?

For a moment, nothing happened, then Agnes heard a buzz and all of a sudden, the door could just be pushed open. Agnes stepped through hesitantly.

There was a long corridor waiting on the other side of the door. Fresh and white and friendly, with green-painted doors and a tasteful art print on the wall every now and then. It smelt clean. A bit too clean for Agnes's liking – the kind of clean that was covering up something unpleasant. It was predictably quiet. Then something clicked behind Agnes and she spun round. The door had shut. Just the door. Agnes registered that on this side there was no metal button to press. So, it was more about keeping the new arrivals in the Whispering Wing, rather than preventing intruders. Interesting.

She carefully made her way along the corridor. There was a name plate on every door. Agnes, who had stupidly left her reading glasses in the bag, had difficulty deciphering the signs, but with a bit of squinting and back and forth, she managed it.

Emma Leffer.

Marcus Swartz.

Linda Smith.

Amanda List.

Theresa Taylor.

There! The moment of truth. Perhaps even the key to solving the whole case.

If Olive really was hiding behind this door, then it came down to getting away as quickly as possible and going to the police with the information. But Olive was significantly younger and faster than Agnes, who was happy about her knitting needle.

She pressed her ear to the door. Nothing. Then she took a deep breath and put her knitting-needle-free hand on the handle.

16

SLOP

The door slid silently open, and for a moment Agnes was dazzled by light. She had expected a darkened cell, but on the other side of the door was sunshine. Soft piano music trickled through the room, sheer curtains wafted, almost in time. Someone had put a bunch of flowers on a little table. Real flowers, Agnes noted with a certain sense of satisfaction, nasturtiums and anemones, thistles and asters. Picked, not bought.

Paradisial green shone through the window. It smelt of leaves and grass.

Heaven.

Agnes stepped cautiously inside and closed the door behind her.

It took a few moments for her to spot the patient in the light plainness of the room, white on white on white.

White walls. White bed. White pillows.

And somewhere amongst it all, a small white face.

The woman had her eyes closed and was taking slow, regular breaths.

Agnes didn't recognise her.

Panic gripped her. All that effort, all that risk – just for her to be standing by a stranger's bedside?

She took a deep breath and stepped closer. And closer. Bent down towards the sleeping face.

At first glance, it could have been anyone. Any old lady in any old bed, facial characteristics and personality washed away by sleep, sunshine and piano tinkling. But then Agnes spotted lines, patterns, familiar structures. The nose, a bit too short and too round, the eyes close together, the mouth wide, with a tendency for the corners of the mouth to droop.

She did know the face – she had just never seen it so relaxed, so free of worry and prickliness, curiosity and envy.

Not Olive.

Theresa.

She had to sit down. Luckily there was a chair.

Just a few moments before, she had been as good as certain that she would find Olive there, solve the case, expose everything. Now she had to admit to herself that the thought had been absurd.

Role reversal? Identity theft? Here in Duck End?

Olive hadn't possessed the audacity or the imagination for such a daring plan. Nor the time to concoct it. Olive was completely and utterly wrapped up in her little church schemes and biscuit triumphs, and Agnes had just been too invested in her theory to realise that. What was the matter with her? She was seeing ghosts. She should probably start taking her pills again. *Of course* she should be taking her pills! It's just they made her tired and unclear and somehow less herself, and she had thought it would be good to be herself, one last time, at least for as long as it took for the case to be solved . . .

Theresa's eyelids fluttered, and Agnes pulled herself together. All was not lost! Here was Theresa with her mysterious funny turn on the day of the murder. She knew something! She *must* know something!

Agnes carefully laid her hand on the bed, on the place where she could see an arm under the covers.

'Hello, Theresa. Theresa, wake up! It's me, Agnes!'

Nothing stirred. Theresa's eyes continued to flutter, but her eyelids remained shut. Agnes shook her arm, but Theresa still didn't seem to notice anything. This wasn't normal! Agnes looked around imploringly and spotted the stand with the drip on it.

You couldn't hear it because of the piano music, but it was still dripping.

Drip.

Drip.

Drip.

With every drip a little bubble rose in the bottle. With every drip some fluid made its way along the tube towards Theresa's arm.

Some kind of sedative. There was no other explanation for Theresa's deep sleep.

Agnes had come too far to give in to a dripping bottle. She stood up, went around the bed to the drip and, without hesitation, twisted the valve shut.

Then she sat back down on the chair and waited.

'Some more sleeping pills, perhaps?' Charlie asked uncertainly. 'We don't want him to suddenly wake up now, do we?'

Edwina leapt up, put Hettie on the kitchen table and ran off. More sleeping pills was no problem. Everyone in the house had a box on their bedside table. Or two.

'What we've got here would be enough for a cow,' Winston objected.

Marshall promised to look up the correct dose on the internet. Nobody wanted to waste sleeping pills, after all.

Then they stood around the kitchen table watching Hettie mooch past an unusual collection of objects with her normal indifference: a mound of sleeping pills; Charlie's small, but beautifully packaged hash stash; one of Winston's Hawaiian shirts; Bernadette's misshapen red hat; and finally, with a pant of disdain, a pot of coral-red paint complete with brush.

It hadn't been easy to come up with a decent plan without Agnes, but they had got there in the end.

The policeman's hours in the coal cellar were numbered.

'I really don't want to be in here!'

Agnes nearly fell off her chair. The warmth, the quiet, the soft piano music, all like a blanket she first – almost a bit reluctantly – had to shake off.

Theresa's eyes were open and very blue.

'I really don't want to be in here!' she repeated.

'Olive did. Not me.'

Exactly. Olive. Agnes blinked the tiredness away.

They'd already got to the point.

'It's Agnes,' she said. 'From Duck End.'

Theresa looked past her and nodded vaguely.

'I'd like to ask you something,' Agnes continued.

Theresa eyed her with sudden mistrust. 'They said no visitors. That's fine by me! And now you, of all people!'

'It's about Olive,' Agnes explained.

Theresa huffed and tried to sit up. 'It's always all about Olive! I've had enough of her! In the future she can plot her stupid plans on her own! I'll settle in here, like they've all advised me, and then . . . Did you know they do aqua aerobics here? I've always wanted to try that!'

Agnes wasn't interested in aqua aerobics and was starting to lose patience.

'I've got to know what happened to Olive!'

Something moved beneath the bedcovers. Perhaps it was just a shoulder shrug. 'How am I supposed to know?' Theresa looked around; a bit bewildered. 'It's really beautiful here! Olive had been saving for so long, and now I'm . . .' she giggled. 'She'll be hopping mad!'

Agnes suddenly had a sinking feeling in the pit of her stomach.

Theresa didn't know anything. She didn't have a clue!

'Olive's dead!'

Not even that.

Theresa stopped giggling. 'Huh, dead? Have I been here that long?'

'She was murdered!'

'No, really? Was it that nutcase from next door? Olive always said he was harmless, but I was never so sure.'

Agnes stood up, a bit dizzy, clutching at words and straws. Theresa was at Lime Tree Court, even though she couldn't

267

afford it. There had to be a reason for it. Someone had *paid* for it. Someone had an interest in Theresa's being there! She *must* know something – even if she didn't know she knew!

Agnes tried another tack. 'What happened? On the day you . . . you had the funny turn?'

Theresa coughed drily. 'It wasn't a funny turn,' she said. 'A fall. I was in the garden. And then . . . I wasn't in the garden any more. I was on the sofa. With *such* a headache! And I felt dizzy. And nothing worked. Head injury, they said. It's a miracle I'm still alive.'

Agnes was thinking as quickly as she could. A miracle for Theresa – and presumably a big nuisance for the murderer. Head injury. Something like that could obviously be caused by a trip. Or by a heavy object. From behind. From above. Or from the side.

'And before the fall?' she asked in desperation.

Theresa had managed to free one of her hands from the bedcovers, and was making a dismissive gesture. The drip tube was shaking.

'I wanted to go . . . to Olive's? Where else? I wanted to talk her out of it! Eyes bigger than her stomach, that's always been Olive's problem. I wanted to tell her it was a crazy idea, but no . . . she needed the money, she said.'

'Talk her out of *what*?' Agnes had to stop herself from grabbing Theresa by the collar and shaking her.

Theresa looked a bit reproachfully. 'She saw her, you know. She saw her *standing*! Opportunities like that don't come along every day, that's what Olive said. I just wanted to tell her that she'd be better off not messing with *her*. Yes. That's what I wanted to say to her. Strange.' Theresa shook her head, bewildered. 'It's really beautiful here!'

'Who?' Agnes asked in desperation. 'Who did she see?'

Theresa had already opened her mouth to say something, when Agnes suddenly felt like she was being grabbed – by the shoulders, by the hips – and pulled backwards.

'Mil . . .' Theresa stopped and looked in surprise at whatever was going on behind Agnes. Agnes fought off a whole host of hands, but knew she had no chance. Theresa and her bed rapidly receded from Agnes.

'Mildred's murderer?' she bawled. 'Was that what Olive saw? Who, Theresa? *Who was it?*'

Then the ground beneath her feet shifted away, and a stern nurse's face bent down towards her, looked at her bracelet and put her finger to her lips.

'Shhhh. That's enough now. Don't get so het up, Mrs Scott!'

He looked so peaceful with his eyes closed. Like a big, exhausted and very dirty baby. Edwina had punched him in the ribs a few times, and now they were certain: the policeman was out of action.

With great difficulty, Charlie, Edwina and Marshall hauled him out of the coal cellar. Winston attempted to clean him up with a sponge, whilst Edwina and Marshall started to empty the cellar of coal. Luckily there wasn't much left because the house had had modern oil heating for several years. Nonetheless, it was unpleasant and dirty work. After they had finally managed to get the last piece of coal into the garden, they hoovered up the coal dust from the floor and washed the walls with soapy water. Then Edwina, assisted by Hettie, got cracking with a big brush and lots of coral paint, just like she'd wanted to for ages.

It was a good day for Edwina.

'Come on, Mrs Scott, open wide. Just one more spoonful.'

Agnes opened her mouth mechanically. Something mushy was spooned in.

She opened one eye, then the other, and looked into the stern face of a carer.

'Come on, Mrs Scott. You can do it! One more.'

Something turned in the pit of Agnes's stomach, and it wasn't just the slop she'd just been spoon-fed. It was doubt, followed by full-blown panic. For a moment she feared she had finally lost the plot, that she really was some unfamiliar Mrs Scott who was just imagining she was Agnes. A terrible thought.

The world was spinning.

Then Agnes remembered the bracelet. Of course. The carer didn't know her – she had read the name on her bracelet, the name of the old lady in the park! For now, Agnes was just happy she really was Agnes!

Then she looked around.

She was lying in a bed. White bedcovers. White walls. The room was small and square. A small window up high. No flowers. No music.

Not the Whispering Wing.

Just as well. She would take great pleasure in breaking out of this grotty little room. She tried to sit up, but her hands didn't comply. She tried again and realised her arms were strapped to the sides of the bed.

Not good at all.

The nurse noticed her looking.

'Unfortunately, we had to sedate you, Mrs Scott. After everything you've been up to recently.'

Been up to?

A vague memory rose to the surface like an air bubble. A carer kneeling on Agnes, and a nurse clutching her injured hand in pain; blood on the sleeve of her white nurse's uniform. Blood on the floor in the beautiful white Whispering Wing room. It had been a reflex. The nurse should have known better than to just grab someone from behind. Someone with a knitting needle in their hand . . .

Agnes hadn't meant it. She wanted to explain that to the nurse, but her tongue lolled in her mouth in a strangely useless way, and next to nothing came out.

The nurse seemed to notice her unease and comfortingly, but strangely indifferently, stroked the bedcovers. Then she quickly stood up and looked on the clipboard at the foot of Agnes's bed. 'Don't worry, Mrs Scott. As soon as we've sorted out your medication, we'll go on a lovely walk together. To see the ducks. You like the ducks, don't you Mrs Scott?'

Agnes didn't give a shit about the ducks. She jiggled her arm restraints. In vain.

'And until then, let's just try and relax a bit, shall we?'

The nurse put the spoon on a tray and left Agnes feeling completely and utterly unrelaxed.

It was almost evening already, and the heat of the fire thronged towards the residents of Sunset Hall like a cat in heat. They were standing in a circle, and the warm light made their faces soft and innocent, and somehow alike.

There was a light breeze, and sparks were flying. Winston was holding a fire extinguisher on his lap just in case.

Brexit's eyes were glowing like a wolf's.

Hettie was thrashing around in Edwina's grip. Normally she liked the warmth, but the fire didn't seem to suit her.

Charlie moaned for the hundredth time that she didn't have any weed left over for a joint.

Nathan had found some marshmallows from somewhere and held one after another on a stick over the embers.

Bernadette had her hands stretched out in front of her like a sleepwalker, and Marshall was staring silently into the flames as they diligently lapped up the coal, the police shirt and hopefully any other evidence.

Once the fire had burnt down to embers and ash, Bernadette felt her way towards the house to make the call.

The drip was dripping.

Drip.

Drip.

Drip.

And because there was no music playing in this room, Agnes heard every single drop.

Drip. Drip.

She was alone. That was something.

She turned her head to the left, towards the door, then to the right, to the wall. She could still do that, but it wasn't easy. Her head seemed heavier than usual, and it felt hollow.

That was the drip's fault.

With every drop, medication found its way into her body, medication that made her limbs heavy and transformed her tongue into a useless, limp slug.

She didn't have much time left, so she started to think, with all her might, about what she had just learnt from Theresa.

So, Olive had seen something, presumably Mildred's murder. She knew who had done it and instead of going to the police with this information, she had decided to blackmail the murderer. Or the murder*ess* – Agnes was fairly certain Theresa had said *her*. But the killer hadn't played along with Olive's game, instead she'd come by with pointy black shoes and an umbrella, to get rid of the only witness. Why the umbrella? As far as Agnes could remember it hadn't rained properly for weeks. In any case, on the way back through the garden, the murderer had bumped into Theresa and had unceremoniously clobbered her one, presumably with a heavy object. A plant pot? One of Olive's perverse garden gnomes? It would be best if she could discreetly go back to the garden to look for clues. Unlucky for the murderer that Theresa had recovered again, but also lucky that she couldn't remember anything and everyone assumed it was an accident. And to be certain that it stayed that way, the murderer had arranged for Theresa to go to Lime Tree Court where, with the help of piano music and medication, your memory melted away.

With each drop, a kind of numbness spread through Agnes's body.

With each air bubble in the drip bottle, a little bit of Agnes made its way up into the ether.

'Under the hydrangeas,' said Bernadette and pointed vaguely in the relevant direction with her stick. 'I just tripped over him. He's not moving, but he is breathing.'

The short-haired policewoman nodded and made her way over to the hydrangeas, where Edwina, Marshall and Charlie were standing around the unconscious policeman looking innocent. Especially Edwina.

When the short-haired woman spotted her colleague beneath the leaves, she let out a short, surprised sound, it sounded a bit like *umph*.

'Tom? Tom, is that you?'

The policeman, who had been systematically plied with a cocktail of hash, sleeping pills and alcohol didn't make a sound.

'He's dressed a bit strangely, isn't he?' Charlie said, to start the stunned policewoman off. 'We thought: Maybe a stag party that got a bit out of hand? Something like that?'

'In any case, it's not good for the hydrangeas,' Marshall declared sternly. 'You should take him away.'

The policewoman nodded mutely and, after nothing budged with repeated shaking, she called an ambulance.

As the paramedics lifted him onto the stretcher, the red hat fell off his head. Edwina eagerly leapt forward and put it back on the policeman's Hawaiian-shirt-covered chest, where he would see it straight away.

'Perhaps you could ensure that nothing like this happens again,' she said. 'He really upset Hettie!'

Hettie, who didn't like it when strangers got too close to her sun stone, hissed in agreement.

They all sighed with relief once they were rid of the policeman. Now they could finally focus on the real problem:

Where was Agnes?

Agnes wandered through the entwined and only seldom visited halls, chambers and corridors of her memory. Faces appeared in front of her that seemed unfamiliar to her for a moment, then filled with meaning.

Edwina.

Marshall.

Lillith at the kitchen table. Her friend smiled, then pushed her pills towards her. But Agnes didn't look. It was too late for the pills. Far too late. The solution to the puzzle was somewhere here, in the dark, hidden corners of her consciousness, right where the pills wouldn't allow her to go.

A few of her colleagues from the murder squad appeared, shook her hand, said a few words of appreciation. Then Agnes strode along a narrow corridor, past barred windows with murderers and child molesters staring out of them at her. Agnes had put them all behind bars, so nobody had a good word to say about her. Was that it? Was there someone in her past who wanted revenge? But what sort of revenge was that: Getting rid of Mildred? It definitely wasn't just about Mildred, was it? It was about *her* too. Agnes had secretly known that all along.

She stumbled on, into the void. She had gone down the wrong path. Lost. Confused.

But just as she was about to give up, she spotted Hettie the tortoise, with her usual dignity and somehow golden in the darkness. Hettie clearly had a plan, and Agnes started following her.

It was easy because they both went at about the same speed, but after a while Agnes noticed Hettie was getting quicker and quicker, like a greyhound, like a hare, and now she was running too, with flailing pigtails.

Past her mother, who looked disappointed because Agnes had broken off her engagement; past Mildred and Isobel too, smoking contraband cigarettes leaning indistinguishably against a stone pillar.

Only in front of the gravestone did Hettie stop, pluck a daisy and look meaningfully at Agnes. This is where it all started, isn't it? Agnes knew this gravestone all too well. Her heart beat more quickly and not just because of the wild tortoise chase. Titus Coldwell? The man who had been dead for so long, but still sent a shudder down her spine? What did he have . . . ? Only then did Agnes realise what Hettie had really meant. Behind the gravestone stood Alice, her eyes grey, her hair tangled, just like it used to be back then. But unlike back then, she wasn't smiling. Instead she was looking with a distant, hostile look.

She reached out her hand towards her, and Agnes saw she was still clutching the hammer.

Then the white hospital wall was suddenly there again, and Agnes blinked in confusion, awake, but not too awake. Alice? Was that what Hettie had wanted to tell her? Alice had every reason to be angry at Agnes, who had betrayed and forgotten her back then, and at Isobel and Mildred, her new friends, who had taken Alice's place in her heart. And Alice had reached for a weapon once before to solve a problem! Then she had disappeared without a trace, but who could say that she hadn't returned after all of these years, to take revenge on Agnes, Mildred and Isobel for the betrayal? Had she heard about Agnes's house share project – another community she was excluded from? Had she secretly watched her house? Alice liked crouching in bushes and under hedges and was a spying genius. Had she seen Marshall misplace the gun, and decided to finally take revenge on them all – play them at their own game, so to speak?

That meant that Alice had to be somewhere in Duck End now, unnoticed, unrecognised, hidden. Was that really possible? Agnes thought. It wouldn't have been so easy before, but now people were moving in and out all the time. Nobody would really notice one old lady more or less nowadays.

And it meant something else: Isobel and her housemates were in mortal danger! Agnes turned her head away from the wall, towards the door. She had to warn them! She had to get out of there as quickly as possible!

How difficult could it be? All she had to do was find the toilet where she'd hidden the bag, get her passport, and get it across to one of the carers that she wasn't Mrs Scott at all, and that she didn't really belong there. It would be embarrassing to explain how she came to be wandering around the place like a ghost in her nightie with a stolen bracelet, but that didn't matter to her any more. The main thing was to get out of Lime Tree Court.

She tugged at the arm restraints. She had to get to the toilet! Surely, they'd let her go to the loo?

Nothing moved. She tried to call out, but what she produced didn't really sound like her voice, and it didn't make much sense either. Nobody came. After she had thrashed around in vain for a while, she stopped. This wasn't getting her anywhere. The outside and the inside – they had never been further away from one another than now, and if the outside wasn't currently working, she would just have to concentrate on the inside for now.

Even her thoughts seemed soft and shapeless, just like the slop she had been spoon-fed earlier, but with a bit of effort, thinking finally did work.

Agnes tried to remember what Alice had really been like. Astonishingly little came to her. Like her, obviously. Her twin. But completely different too. Wild, dishevelled and bold. Someone who didn't let them plait pigtails; someone who didn't come home for dinner; someone who didn't cry under the bedcovers because her father had left them. Strictly speaking, Alice hadn't been like Agnes at all. She had been like Agnes wanted to be!

From where she stood, Agnes had to admit Alice hadn't been normal even back then. The constant lurking and hiding. The silence. The weird little melodies she sometimes hummed.

Had she even gone to school? Had she had friends? Agnes couldn't remember a single occasion when Alice had had anything to do with other people. She had always just spoken to her. She had only played with her. That's what twins did, isn't it? Twins were one. Twins were complete. They didn't need anybody else.

The drip carried on dripping, *dripdripdrip*, and suddenly finding Alice and saving Isobel and her housemates didn't seem so important at all any more.

Suddenly, all she was interested in was sleep.

17

CHOCOLATE BAR

All along the backwater, through the rushes tall . . .

Agnes was watching the ducks.

She had been medicated now, and a carer had pushed her to the little pond in a wheelchair, so that she could see the ducks. Unsurprisingly, the ducks were white and clean and cute, with sweet yellow beaks and bright button eyes. They were preening themselves, quacking and dunking their heads in the water now and then. *Ducks are a-dabbling . . .* When they appeared again, silvery droplets pearled over their backs.

The nurse hadn't been exaggerating. It really was quite fun.

Agnes was enjoying the sunshine and the fresh air. She felt light and happy. She'd had worries before. Problems. She didn't remember exactly what sort of problems they had been, but now they were gone, and Agnes could finally start to enjoy her time at Lime Tree Court. It had been hard enough getting in, after all. Barefoot and in her nightie.

Weird.

A bloke with bushy eyebrows, whose wheelchair wasn't parked far from hers, winked at her. Agnes waved. Maybe she should be thinking something, feeling something, but actually, it was far too nice a day for that. The ducks still had sweet yellow beaks and bright button eyes. They were preening themselves, quacking and dunking their heads in the water now and then. When they appeared again, silvery droplets pearled over their backs.

It really was quite fun.

Ducks are a-dabbling, up tails all!

'There!'

Marshall put a new jar of Nutella on the table, and sat down facing his grandson.

'One question, one answer, one spoonful. Okay?'

'Just *one* spoonful?' Nathan protested.

'One spoonful per answer,' Marshall said decisively. 'And if I'm happy with all the answers, you get the whole jar! Agreed?'

Agnes had disappeared two days ago and now Marshall didn't care if his grandson gave himself a tummy ache. Normally he would have perhaps even gone to the police, but after Edwina's latest escapades they were all happy not to set eyes on a member of law enforcement for a few days. No, Marshall had to find out what had happened to Agnes off his own bat, and the key to her disappearance lay in what she had got up to with his grandson in Duck End. He didn't believe the stupid story about the affair for a second. Complete nonsense, wasn't it?

'I'd like to know what you did in the village, you and Agnes,' Marshall said. 'I'd like to know *everything*.'

'She had a scone,' said Nathan. 'And I had Victoria sponge.' He went to grab the spoon, but Marshall held him back.

'That wasn't a proper answer.'

'It wasn't a proper question either.' A stubborn look came over Nathan's face, and Marshall nearly caved, but pulled himself together at the last moment. Nathan wasn't just his grandson any more. He was a witness.

'You went on the bus, didn't you? Did Agnes speak to anybody on the bus?'

'No!' Nathan reached for the spoon, and this time Marshall let him.

'Did she speak with anyone at all?'

'Yes!' Nathan grinned and shovelled.

Marshall realised he was sweating. This interrogation was a race against time. He had to get some sense out of Nathan before he gorged himself on Nutella.

'With whom?'

'First with a woman,' Nathan said. 'A cleaning lady.'

'What about?'

'The hungry animals,' said Nathan. 'We were doing a collection. And then . . .' He thought for a moment, 'about someone else.'

'Mildred?' asked Marshall. 'Olive?'

Nathan shovelled and shook his head. 'Theresa. But the cleaning lady didn't know much because she was new and she only gave us ten pence for the animals. Only ten pence!'

'Then what happened?'

'We went to another door, but nobody answered.'

'And then?'

'Peanuts. At the guy's next door. He said he was engaged.'

'To Agnes?' Marshall asked in alarm.

Nathan shook his head, but he couldn't remember who the

281

man had been engaged to instead.

'He liked animals,' he said. 'He had lots of pictures of dogs on the walls. And he gave us twenty quid. And then we went to the café.' He looked at Marshall triumphantly.

Marshall gave it some thought. Should he take the animal lover with the peanuts to task himself? Agnes had been investigating, no doubt, she had . . . Nathan was shovelling, and suddenly Marshall found it difficult to concentrate. A wave of panic came over him. What if Agnes had got too close to the murderer? What if *that* was the reason for her disappearance?

He shouldn't have let her go off on her own so readily, armed with only the Grandson, but secretly he had been happy to have a little break. With hindsight, Agnes had been acting a bit strangely since their outing to Lime Tree Court. He should have taken better care of her, found out what she . . . If only he hadn't been so stressed.

'It was wrong to steal the photo,' Nathan said suddenly between two spoonfuls, tearing Marshall from his thoughts.

'What photo? She . . . err . . . *borrowed* something?'

'Yeah.'

'At the, err, engaged man's?'

His grandson nodded with his mouth full. He had created a huge pit in the middle of his Nutella now.

'And what was it of?'

'Don't know. But she was secretly looking at it the whole time in the café.' Nathan frowned. 'I don't think she's interested in transformers,' he said with regret.

Agnes was still sitting by the pond watching the ducks do their duck thing, but her inner peace had secretly slipped away. *Ducks are a-dabbling, up tails all?* Why did the ducks keep dunking their heads into the water? There had to be a reason for it. Agnes didn't like it. It unsettled her.

The carer had just left her sitting there, and a light wind was giving her goose bumps on her bare forearms. The bloke with the bushy eyebrows was still there winking like mad, but Agnes was trying not to look at him. She didn't like the way the bloke was winking any more. She didn't like anything there.

She shouldn't be there, of that she was suddenly certain. There was a place where she belonged, and that place wasn't Lime Tree Court. She had to do something – and sharpish! But what?

She stared fixedly at the ducks and tried to concentrate. Not everything there was glittering and smooth and sparkling and sunny. There was more. Somewhere, deep down there was a *bottom*. She just had to stick her head beneath the shimmering surface of the water, just like the ducks. The world would look different from there, complex, murky and shadowy, but also honest and real. Whatever she was looking for, it was to be found beneath the surface.

She made a few attempts to get out of the wheelchair, but it didn't work. Nothing worked. There was a belt, but her hands were playing dumb and couldn't undo it. Agnes sighed. Something had to happen, and fast. The toilet! That was it! She had to go to the toilet! There lay salvation! If she could make it to the toilet somehow, everything would get better.

'Everything alright, Mrs Scott?' The nurse was back and

bent down so close to her that her face went blurry in front of Agnes's eyes.

Agnes made a concerted effort to appear calm and together, but 'toilet' was an awkward word that didn't want to roll off her tongue. She tried 'loo,' but that didn't seem to work properly either, and now she was just confused and agitated.

'Lo. Lololo.'

The nurse smiled patiently, and for a hopeful moment, Agnes really thought she'd got through to her, but then the woman placed a reassuring hand on her forearm.

'It's a bit cold out here, isn't it Mrs Scott? Don't worry, we'll soon be in the day room, it's snuggly and warm in there, there's tea too!'

It was enough to make her cry, but in the moment it took for the nurse to stand up straight, Agnes caught a glimpse of her name tag.

ALICE was written on it. It shocked Agnes, but also spurred her on. Suddenly she knew what her problem was again. The problem's name was Alice!

AliceAliceAlice.

Agnes held onto the word tightly. She would hold her head under the surface, and sooner or later she would get to the bottom of it!

Up tails all!

She had some pretty things. Marshall was searching Agnes's underwear drawer and in doing so felt like part explorer, part criminal. It was unforgivable, just going into her room like that, rummaging about in her things and invading her privacy.

Nerves had already made him drop a little vase, and Nathan had left behind numerous chocolatey fingerprints on cushions and tablecloths. Agnes would be furious – but what else could they do? They had to track down the photo and hopefully find out where Agnes had disappeared to. After all, a furious Agnes was so much better than no Agnes at all.

They looked in desk drawers and wool baskets, beneath crocheted blankets and stacks of books.

In the wardrobe and the bathroom. Under the bed, where Nathan almost got stuck. Nothing! In fact, Agnes's room was downright shockingly devoid of photos.

'Maybe she took it with her?' Marshall sighed and sat on the bed, exhausted. He wouldn't put it past Agnes at all to confront the murderer with evidence – but why hadn't she told them anything? Sure, Edwina caused one cock-up after another, Charlie was new, Bernadette blind and brusque, and Winston was in a wheelchair. But him at least . . . ?

A triumphant scream from the wardrobe pulled him back to the present. Not holding out much hope, Marshall looked up – Nathan had probably just found some ancient box of chocolates. But his grandson was brandishing a solid-looking black crocodile handbag with a bamboo handle.

'She had this with her!'

Marshall tore open the handbag and, next to a crumpled-up bus ticket, a five-pound note and a tin of mints, he found a small Polaroid.

A garden and an umbrella.

There really wasn't much to see, but something about the way the umbrella floated through the landscape, round and ominous, took Marshall's breath away. His heart was beating so loudly he could hardly hear what his grandson was saying. He had seen this umbrella once before! But when? Where?

There was something threatening about the umbrella. Like a dark, dark cloud.

This umbrella was up to no good!

The carer had parked the wheelchair under an indoor palm in the reception area, so she could chat to a man at the desk, while Agnes got annoyed at the palm frond in her face. She wasn't medicated any more, that much was obvious. Presumably that was because Mrs Scott was considerably smaller and more delicate than she was. Wrong dosage. Blessing in disguise. She tried to imagine what it would have been like if she had coincidentally happened upon a fat patient's bracelet. It didn't bear thinking about!

But even like this, the effects of Lime Tree Court were bad enough. Whilst the inside was becoming a bit more Agnes-shaped, the outside was less obliging. She could use her hands more, but her fine motor skills were severely lacking, and the belt buckle stubbornly eluded her grip.

But Agnes finally knew again why she had to go to the loo: there was a bag with her passport in it, her identity, in fact the whole Agnes. If she could show she wasn't Mrs Scott, they had to let her go, didn't they?

She thought about the real Mrs Scott, who was presumably still out and about in her dressing gown, completely unmedicated. For a moment she almost had a guilty conscience, but then she thought better of it. Mrs Scott was free and herself, presumably for the first time in ages. That had to be worth a little discomfort, didn't it?

Lime Tree Court may look like a paradise, but it was no place for people who still had something like an inner life. Nobody there was worried about the inside. The inside was medicated. Without a doubt, Lillith had been right: better a bullet to the head!

The clack of heels on the polished marble floor made Agnes look up. It was an irregular clacking. The clack of someone who had a limp.

Clack-*clack*. Clack-*clack*.

Agnes peered past the palm frond, and what she saw almost made her heart stop.

There stood Isobel, wearing an elegant black fur-trimmed jacket, clutching a walking stick by its silver handle.

She limped slowly past Agnes towards the reception.

Agnes thought, as quickly as she could in her shaken state. It all made sense! Now that Mildred was dead, Isobel didn't want to live in the big house any more. She felt lonely. She wanted a place at Lime Tree Court. Nobody had explained the thing about the outside, the inside and the ducks. Agnes's innards flipped in shock and sympathy. She couldn't allow her old friend to just . . . She had to warn her! And another thought flashed through her mind: if Isobel recognised her, she could get her out of there. If Agnes somehow managed to get her attention, within ten minutes they could both waft away from Lime Tree Court in a dark limousine, doubly saved!

Agnes frantically tried to push the palm frond away, but it was a hair's breadth out of touching distance. The belt wasn't giving. Shout! She had to shout!

Isobel! I'm here!

Isobel!

Let's get out of here!

But, objectively speaking, all that Agnes got out was a gentle gurgle. It was enough to drive her mad. She had to throw something! But there was nothing . . .

Agnes looked on in desperation as Isobel briefly spoke to the receptionist and the nurse, nodded, smiled, signed something, and then, in a cloud of violet scent and fur, limped past her into Lime Tree Court.

'Oh, hello, you two!'

Wide blue eyes and a surprised, but delighted smile, you had to give it to Edwina – when she wanted to be, she was a gifted actress.

The policeman was back, now minus the red hat, but with dark bags under his eyes instead. He looked like someone had crumpled him up and carried him around in their trouser pocket for a few days.

He had the short-haired policewoman with him for back-up.

The remaining residents of Sunset Hall had gathered on the veranda to act innocent. Bernadette and Charlie, Winston and Marshall, Hettie and Brexit. Nathan was in bed with a tummy ache and refusing to have any herbal tea.

Edwina waved and held Hettie out towards the policeman. 'Hello, Constable!'

The policeman flinched. He was still a bit unsteady on his feet and turned imploringly to his colleague. She nodded, partly sceptical, partly encouraging.

'My colleague here has made some serious allegations . . .' She paused, looked doubtfully at the ancient residents of Sunset Hall and tried another tack. 'We'd just like to quickly check something, please – could we perhaps take a quick look in your cellar?'

'That's a bit much!' Bernadette mumbled.

Marshall shrugged his shoulders. 'If you must. But it seems a bit unorthodox to me.'

The short-haired policewoman and her colleague looked at one another furtively. Marshall had hit the nail on the head. This wasn't an official visit. Nobody really believed what the policeman was saying – but the short-haired policewoman had stupidly allowed herself to be persuaded to check out the crazy story. Unofficially. Off the record.

'Down there.' Charlie said, pointing towards the cellar door.

'I know where it is!' the policeman spat.

'Cellars are normally downwards,' Bernadette said drily.

As soon as both police officers had disappeared inside the house, the innocent looks vanished from their faces. This was it!

One after the other they followed the police officers into the cellar.

Lastly, Edwina and Hettie were alone on the veranda. For a moment, Edwina looked into the garden with a smile on her face, then put Hettie down and rushed to join the others.

Agnes was up to her neck in it. Not literally obviously, literally she was sitting with lots of other Lime Tree Court residents in the day room watching the more mobile patients as they sluggishly, but decisively went back and forth between coffee tables and the cake counter.

But figuratively speaking, Agnes was sinking, not into the ground, but into her own rage. A tight, painful feeling sat in her throat, kind of like a cry that was stuck. She had been so close to salvation. If it weren't for that stupid palm frond . . . It was enough to make her weep. And the thought that Isobel might end up at Lime Tree Court was tying her heart up in knots.

It couldn't go on like this! She had to do something!

She tried again, 'Lo. Lo. Looo!'

'Loo!'

That sounded better! All she had to do was get the attention of one of the carers. In the meantime, it couldn't hurt to take advantage of her current position next to the cake counter. There was shortbread, muffins, lemon drizzle cake, and fruit slices, all cut up into senior citizen-friendly little chunks. Better than the slop from before. Agnes took a biscuit, then a muffin. She was suddenly really hungry.

As she fished for the fruit slices, an image suddenly entered her head. A sign:

EVERYONE WELCOME!

A room full of mistrusting faces. Another table with different cakes, amongst them Olive's cream slices. Agnes had never got around to asking the kitchen assistant Rosie where the cream slices came from. And then she suddenly saw Rosie before her eyes, leaning against the wall smoking with Bernadette, her face pale and yellowish like badly chosen make-up, the implausibly red hair, like a wig, the huge sunglasses resting on her nose.

Not like someone who had dressed up for a coffee morning – more like someone going to a costume ball. In fact, they had barely seen any of Rosie's face at all. Could it be that . . . ? Could something so important really have escaped Agnes for so long?

AliceAliceAlice.

Agnes thought. The height was about right. Had she noticed anything else? Voice? Gait? She wasn't sure. It was so very many years ago. But she remembered the care Rosie had taken to tie a scarf round her head after she'd said goodbye – to prevent the wig from being blown off?

Overcome by the thought that she might have just found Alice, Agnes laid the half-eaten fruit slice on her lap.

Suddenly the nurse was standing next to her. Alice.

AliceAliceAlice.

It was a sign.

The nurse took the fruit slice from Agnes.

'Just because we can't eat any more, doesn't mean we have to make such a mess, Mrs Scott.'

Agnes's thoughts returned to the unpleasant present. Lime Tree Court. Right. Now it was more important than ever to get out of there as quickly as possible.

'Loo!' Agnes said with wonderful clarity.

'Loo. Loo. Loo,' she repeated happily. It was working! Salvation was close!

'Do you need to spend a penny Mrs Scott?' the nurse asked.

Agnes nodded eagerly, and the nurse smiled reassuringly.

'Don't worry, I'm taking you to your room soon anyway,

then we'll spend a penny, and after that we'll have a nice little siesta. What do you think of that, Mrs Scott?'

Agnes didn't think much of it at all. If she had still been holding the fruit slice in her hand, she would have thrown it at the nurse in rage and desperation. She didn't want to 'spend a penny' in her room, she wanted to go to the communal toilet in the hall, to get her things, but that obviously wasn't getting through to the carer. Siesta? Ridiculous. Agnes wouldn't get a wink of sleep in the hell hole that was Lime Tree Court!

As the nurse turned the wheelchair in three efficient movements, Agnes suddenly noticed the box of chocolate bars that had been partially hidden by the lemon drizzle cake. A wave of home-sickness hit her. Chocolate bars! Winston!

Sunset Hall!

Before she could think about it, her hand shot forward, got hold of a chocolate bar and disappeared under the blanket with it. Agnes looked surreptitiously up at the nurse, but she was far too busy with her three-point-turn to notice anything.

They rolled out of the day room, through an electronically operated door and then along a labyrinth of corridors. The nurse was humming a pop song.

Agnes clutched the chocolate bar underneath her blanket like it was treasure.

'*That's* the coal cellar?' The short-haired policewoman looked around doubtfully.

'Err, I . . .' The policeman looked around in a panic, from one coral-red wall to the other, from the door to the television, from the wingback chair to the embroidered wall hanging.

'It used to be,' Charlie explained urbanely. 'Now it's our television room. Our *secret* television room. So that the little rascal up there doesn't notice anything.' She winked and conspiratorially put her finger to her lips.

The others nodded. Marshall had boarded up the coal hatch and put the television in front of it. Now they really hoped nobody noticed that the television, for want of a socket, wasn't plugged in.

'It's all very different to how you described it,' the short-haired policewoman said to her colleague in a low voice. 'Are you sure it was here?'

The policeman was still looking around frantically. 'It was here. But it was different. They've changed it . . . You've got to believe me, Mel!'

At that moment something on the short-haired policewoman's face changed. From doubt to a sad certainty.

'I think we should go, Tom.'

'But we *can't* go just like that! We've got to arrest them all! They locked me up, Mel! They drugged me! *They're* behind this killing spree!' The policeman wrung his hands like a washer woman.

'I'm going,' the short-haired policewoman said quietly. 'And if you don't want to be suspended on the spot, you'll come with me.'

'But . . .'

'Not a word!' she threatened. 'I'm risking my career here, for this *nonsense* . . .'

'Was that all to do with the case, Inspector?' Edwina enquired politely.

'I don't think so.' The policewoman sighed. 'I'm sorry to have disturbed you.'

Then the residents of Sunset Hall stood on the veranda again and waved off the police officers. Edwina even followed them a little way so that she could wave more effectively.

Suddenly she was standing facing the policeman. He had stopped and was crouched over Hettie the tortoise. Her perfectly proportioned shell seemed to have grabbed his attention.

Edwina craned her neck out of curiosity. Then she saw it: resplendent in the middle of Hettie's shell was a fleck of thick coral-red paint.

The policeman went to grab Hettie, but Edwina was quicker. She snatched the tortoise and ran back into the house with her.

'Mine! Mine! Mineminemine!'

Someone had their hands around Agnes's neck. Someone was squeezing with an astonishing amount of force.

Was she dreaming?

Agnes remembered her little boxing match with the nurse because she didn't want to spend a penny *together*. Agnes still liked to go to the loo on her own, thank you very much. Then the carer had tried to make her take her pills, then Agnes had laid herself in the bed to pretend to have a nap. And now . . . ?

'Mine!'

Agnes opened her eyes wide and came face to face with the old lady from the park. Mrs Scott. This time she wasn't farting. She was kneeling on Agnes's bed and was in the process of squeezing the life out of her with her bony hands.

What on earth did she want from her? Her band? She was

welcome to it! The band and the whole of Lime Tree Court along with it.

Agnes wheezed.

A sharp pain spread through her lungs.

Strange dots danced before her eyes.

Maybe it was because of the medication, but Agnes observed the whole scene from a certain distance. That was it then. Mrs Scott was trying to strangle her, presumably because she wanted to get back into bed. Ah well, never mind. After her miserable time at Lime Tree Court, it even seemed like a halfway attractive proposition.

There was something in her hand.

A chocolate bar.

Agnes suddenly remembered Sunset Hall, the murders, Alice, the danger her housemates were in. She couldn't just lie back and allow herself to be throttled by Mrs Scott!

She stuck her hand out of the side of the bed and rustled the chocolate bar.

Mrs Scott's head whipped round. She stopped strangling her, and Agnes snatched a few blissful breaths. Mrs Scott reached for the chocolate bar, and Agnes held her hand as far away from her as possible. Then, when the old lady was leaning right over the edge of the bed, Agnes reared up beneath her. Luckily Mrs Scott was light and delicate. She lost her balance and flew off the bed. Agnes heard a crack.

More quickly than she would ever have thought possible, Agnes was out of the bed too, and at the door that luckily was still open.

A furious scream rang out behind her.

Agnes slipped outside and pulled the door shut after her. Then she leant on the wall, gasping for air. The sharp pain receded. The dots in front of her eyes calmed down a bit. Someone was hammering on the door from inside.

As soon as she had caught her breath a bit, Agnes stumbled off to get as much distance between her and Mrs Scott as possible. She ripped the band off her wrist. She didn't want to spend another second as Mrs Scott.

That was it then! Mrs Scott was an aggressive, murderous old woman! That's why she had to be medicated. And thanks to Agnes she had been on the loose for a while! It didn't bear thinking about.

Agnes hobbled through the corridors like she was in a dream. At first, she was walking alone, but then she suddenly went into a room with other Lime Tree Court residents. Tables. Chairs. Board games. A huge television was hanging on the wall, and someone was kneeling in front of the television.

Short hair. Sticky-out ears. Thin beard.

Sparrow!

He had laid out his tools on a blanket next to him and was busy repairing the television. An interested group of Lime Tree Court residents was standing around him. Some were making comments, some were making fun of him, and a few were even trying to take Sparrow's tools.

Sparrow! Agnes was so happy to see him.

She wanted to call his name. Only a gurgle came out. Was it the medication still? Or were her vocal cords maybe just overwhelmed by all the throttling? Whatever. She had to get his attention. Sparrow was her last chance!

She pushed past the other old people and tugged on the electrician's blue overalls. Sparrow looked up briefly and gently brushed her hand off his shoulder.

Then he carried on repairing.

For a moment Agnes stood there as if she had been struck by lightning. Why was Sparrow ignoring her? They were friends, weren't they?

Then she thought about how she had looked when they had last seen one another – freshly done hair, lipstick, funeral finery. And how she must look now – sweaty nightie, tangled hair, probably strangle-induced bloodshot eyes. No wonder he didn't recognise her!

She tried to speak again – in vain – and Sparrow had turned away again and carried on repairing. Agnes balled her fists in rage and desperation, and in doing so, discovered she still had the chocolate bar in her hand.

A chocolate bar.

Just like the one Winston had given to Sparrow for communication purposes. Back then she had scoffed. Today, she took a decisive step forward and held the chocolate bar out in front of Sparrow.

Sparrow froze. He turned around again, and this time he *saw* her. His eyes widened.

Agnes gave him a friendly wave with her chocolate-barred hand and floated away into blissful . . . unconsciousness.

18

COTTAGE PIE

Agnes was digging. With her bare hands. In the middle of the woods.

Her sister, Alice, had never been a practical person. Dropping a hammer from the apple tree was one thing, but getting rid of it afterwards was something completely different. So, it had been Agnes who, with her heart pounding, had dared to venture near the sack of flour that had once been Titus Coldwell, grab the hammer with both hands and drag it into the woods.

Now, years later, she was digging once more. Her heart was pounding again. What if there was nothing there? Or too much? What if Titus Coldwell's blood was still glistening darkly on the wooden handle? Loamy earth forced its way under her fingernails.

The twins watched her with a mixture of fascination and revulsion.

'Are you sure it was here?' Isobel had leant over her, partly to help, partly in horror.

'Yes!' Agnes said, although she wasn't so sure any more. It had been so dark in the woods back then, so strange and big, with flowing shadows and loudly squawking night birds. But she thought she recognised the trunk of the old beech tree, the pattern of the roots, spread wide like arteries, and between them the place where the earth had been soft and yielding, obliging almost.

'She *isn't* sure!' Mildred proclaimed as she leant on the beech's trunk smoking, and although she appeared to be nonchalantly blowing rings of smoke into the air, Agnes had the feeling that Mildred was the one who was the most frightened.

Agnes hadn't been paying attention for a moment, and suddenly her hands touched something hard, something that wasn't a stone or a root. Too cold. She pulled her hand back, as if she'd burnt herself.

Mildred stopped puffing rings of smoke and shone the torch.

'I can't see anything.'

'There!' After the initial shock, Agnes's hands ventured back into the hole, found the cold metal head, then the wooden handle. It was just a hammer after all. Just a hammer. Nothing more. She uncovered the handle and pulled. With a squelching sound, the hammer popped out of the hole, still heavy, but not as heavy as it had been in Agnes's memory.

'And you used that to . . .' Mildred had stepped closer now and gingerly, almost covetously, reached out her hand.

'Alice,' Agnes corrected her.

'Of course.' Mildred rolled her eyes. 'Alice.'

Agnes had stood up and was looking down at the dirty hammer with pride and horror.

This was the truth.

Nobody else knew about it.

It was her gift to the twins.

'And nobody ever . . . ?' Isobel asked.

Agnes shook her head. 'Never!'

When Titus Coldwell had been found under the apple tree with his skull bashed in, they had suspected convicts, tramps and travellers, but not little girls.

'She didn't mean it,' Edwina said soothingly, and turned Hettie the right way up again. 'I think she's dreaming.'

Agnes was back in her bed. That was something! All the Sunset Hall residents were gathered around her, relieved and worried at the same time. Edwina had put Hettie on her chest to cheer her up a bit, but Agnes had just mumbled away, making strange digging motions with her hands and in doing so had accidentally turned Hettie on her back.

Most unpleasant.

Winston, Charlie and Marshall exchanged meaningful looks. Brexit was licking Agnes's fingers – when they stayed still for long enough, that is. There was no denying it, they were worried about their friend.

That afternoon, Sparrow had arrived at theirs in a bit of a state and got Agnes out of the back of his van. Smuggled out of Lime Tree Court. Whatever next! How Agnes even managed to get into Lime Tree Court was a mystery to them. It couldn't have been easy. Even on first glance, you could see that Agnes wasn't exactly in good shape. She was wearing a god-awful nightie, obsessively clutching a chocolate bar and when she spoke, it was with a strange, croaky whisper of a voice.

Charlie, who had apparently once been a nurse (in another life, before her first husband, the rogue), looked into Agnes's eyes and declared that medication was probably involved, but not only that. She seemed hypothermic and dehydrated, and someone had well and truly throttled her. Not exactly a glowing advert for Lime Tree Court.

But what worried them the most was what Agnes was spouting in her delirious state, about Mrs Scott and ducks and flowers and a certain toilet. It didn't make much sense.

Winston had wanted to call a doctor, but it was highly likely that they would immediately take Agnes away again, so her housemates decided to try some bed rest first. They had poured several cups of tea down her throat and put her in bed with a hot water bottle.

Now Agnes was asleep, but it was a restless sleep with incomprehensible mumblings and agitated hand gestures. A sleep that had put Hettie on her back.

'Somebody should stay with her,' Marshall said earnestly.

The others nodded. For, despite her delirious state, Agnes had insisted on one thing over and over again: that someone or something was in mortal danger.

Agnes opened her eyes and saw a face above her, blurry at first, then clearer. In a twinge of panic, she went to push the intruder away, but then she looked more closely.

Round cheeks. Black cherry eyes. Mop head.

The Grandson!

She relaxed. What had she expected? Some kind of killer? Ridiculous!

'I brought you some biscuits.' Nathan said, grinning shyly. 'Save the hungry animals!'

Agnes, who really did feel a bit like a hungry animal, grabbed a biscuit. Shop-bought biscuits, soft and crumbly, not Edwina's rock-hard creations. Thank God.

She chewed and swallowed. Swallowing hurt a little, but the biscuit did her good. Agnes grabbed another.

'Where are the others?' she asked after a third biscuit had also gone the way of all sweet treats. Her voice sounded strangely strained and stretched. Her throat hurt. Tonsillitis? Maybe.

Nathan thought for a moment. 'Grandad's on the internet, but he won't let me. Charlie's cooking some chicken soup. Winston's having a catnap, Hettie's digging, Edwina's doing yoga and Bernadette . . . I don't know what Bernadette's doing.'

Agnes nodded. She felt good after the biscuits. Fresh, almost optimistic. Like she had been born again. She was in her own bed, in her own house. Her friends were pursuing their stupid little everyday projects, Brexit had curled up on the bedside rug, and Nathan had brought her biscuits. She was filled with happiness. It was simply wonderful – she didn't know why exactly, but it was wonderful.

She sighed contentedly and stretched. Everything hurt, perhaps even worse than usual, but that didn't matter. The main thing was . . . what was the main thing? Suddenly a kind of dark cloud popped into her mind. *Everything* wasn't wonderful, was it? They were in mortal danger! She had to tell the others! Straight away! Something important!

A moment later – at least it felt like a moment to Agnes, although it must have actually been longer – her housemates had gathered around her and were eagerly awaiting what she had to tell them.

Charlie, Edwina, Winston and Marshall looked down at her expectantly.

Brexit was wagging his tail and Bernadette was listening intently.

'I . . .' Agnes began. 'We . . . They . . .'

She fell silent, filled with panic. Suddenly she had no idea what it was she so desperately and urgently had to tell them. She fumbled around in her mind, but there was nothing there. No memory. No idea. No clue. Just cotton wool, soft and pleasant, but completely useless.

'Err.'

Her housemates cast nervous glances at one another.

'I really missed you all,' Agnes said finally, although she didn't understand how she could have missed them. Had she been away? She felt like she had, but she didn't know how and where.

She sighed in frustration, but the message was well received by her housemates.

Charlie smiled, Marshall grinned from ear to ear, and a surreptitious tear ventured from beneath Bernadette's sunglasses.

'We missed you too,' Winston said emotionally, and patted her hand.

Aha. So, she *had* been away! Interesting. But where? And why?

Her housemates looked so happy that Agnes decided not to worry about it for now. Everything would work itself out in time – after a few more biscuits and a little nap, maybe.

After all, it couldn't be that urgent, could it?

It was already evening, cool and quiet outside when Bernadette heard a knock at the door. The others were busy pepping up Agnes or taking care of their little chores – weird, when Agnes was well, she had to constantly nag them, but as soon as she was laid up, everything ran like clockwork. Since Bernadette seemed to be the only one who had heard the knock – none of the others made a move – she made her way to the front door, her hand on the wall all the way.

She opened the door and drank in the air. Nothing familiar. A whiff of fabric softener and some kind of food aroma.

'Hello, what can I do for you?' Bernadette listened carefully. Someone was moving in front of her, shifting their weight from one leg to the other.

'Hey, you blindworm!'

She recognised the voice immediately: Rosie, her new friend from the coffee morning. Bernadette realised she was smiling. They had clicked immediately, from the moment Brexit had dragged her into the coffee morning kitchen. That didn't happen often, and never to Bernadette, who most people approached with a strange mix of fear and misplaced sympathy. Blind? The poor thing!

But she wasn't poor, she was just Bernadette. Rosie had understood that straight away, and Bernadette was happy that she had finally taken her up on her invitation.

'Hey!' she said.

'Sorry it's so late,' Rosie said. 'I've got a lot on at the moment.'

'Scrounging?' Bernadette asked.

'Amongst other things,' Rosie said, a smile in her voice. 'But I thought I'd just bring dinner over. For you and the other freaks!'

Bernadette felt something being held out towards her. The smell of food got stronger. She sniffed expectantly.

'What is it?' she asked.

'Cottage pie,' Rosie replied. 'Just needs about twenty minutes in the oven. There's enough for everyone.'

'Was that scrounged too?' Bernadette asked.

Rosie laughed. 'I made it myself!' she said emphatically.

'Come in.' Bernadette pushed the door open farther. 'We'll put it straight in the oven, it's right on cue, you know. There's a lot going on here at the moment, and to be honest, I'm sick of the sight of tinned food.' Bernadette laughed at her blindworm joke, and a moment later Rosie joined in.

Bernadette turned around and felt her way along the wall towards the kitchen. She could hear steps behind her and the door being gently, but firmly shut.

Bernadette found the oven and switched it on. 'Just check it's the right temperature.'

'Yep!' Something was put on the kitchen table, and Bernadette could hear Rosie pulling a chair out for herself.

'What's going on, then?

'Well. The Grandson is here, and Agnes is – ill, and Edwina . . .' she stopped herself before she could tell Rosie the story about the policeman. Maybe Rosie would have understood – but then again, maybe not.

'Ill, huh? Nothing bad, I hope?' Rosie sounded concerned.

'Just a sore throat . . .' Bernadette didn't want to explain the muddled Lime Tree Court story to her. They didn't know each other that well, after all. 'I think the cottage pie can go in the oven. I'll let the others know that dinner will be in half an hour. They'll be amazed!'

'And then we can both have a nice ciggy in the garden, huh?'

Bernadette had to smirk. Rosie was just her kind of guest – and today she really sounded like she was on top form.

Agnes woke with a start. Her room was a dusky blue. That late already! Brexit was still snoring away on her bedside rug, other than that there was nobody in the room. Thank goodness! She could use a few moments of alone time. Meanwhile, she had digested more than just the biscuits and wanted to get her thoughts together in peace.

Lime Tree Court! Hard to believe! So, she'd really made it inside. And – by the skin of her teeth – made it out again. If it hadn't been for that chocolate bar . . .

Agnes shuddered and pulled the bedcovers more tightly around her. Had it been worth it? On the one hand, she now knew that Lime Tree Court one hundred percent wasn't for her. Lillith had been right: better a bullet to the head. It was good to know that her house project was the right path for her, and hopefully for the others too. Agnes couldn't imagine a single one of her housemates being happy in Lime Tree Court.

As far as solving the murder case went . . . She had to admit that she had been wrong with her mistaken-identity theory. The person sitting, or rather lying, in Lime Tree Court under

Theresa's name really was Theresa, and she didn't know very much. Olive, on the other hand, had known the murderer, had tried to blackmail him – her! – and had died because of it.

Those were the facts. It wasn't much. Despite that, Agnes couldn't shake the feeling that she had discovered even more in Lime Tree Court.

The medication had done funny things to her, dampened her thoughts, suppressed her feelings, and somewhere in between, old truths had stirred into motion like prehistoric monsters, they had paddled to the surface and given Agnes their shiny scaly backs. Or something like that.

Agnes looked down at Brexit breathing steadily and tried to remember. Images ran through her head. Ducks on the surface. *Up tails all!* A nurse in a white bonnet, her finger to her lips. A name tag, white plastic against a white cotton blouse, black writing on it in capital letters. Suitable for senior citizens.

Agnes screwed up her eyes as if she was trying to read something in her memory.

ALICE.

That's what had been written on it, and that was what her subconscious had been trying to tell her for quite a while, Alice!

She sat up abruptly. What should she do? If the murders really were what she thought they were – a neglected twin's revenge – she was far from safe.

And something else was unsettling Agnes: the murderer had brought the gun back to them. She had put it in the middle of their table. If she wanted to murder again, she would have to look around for another method.

'Smells good!' Charlie said appreciatively.

She, Edwina, Bernadette, Nathan and Rosie were standing around the dining table looking at the steaming cottage pie.

'It needs to rest for a few more minutes.' Rosie smiled humbly.

'I'll make a salad,' Edwina said helpfully, and the others looked relieved. Salad was basically the only thing Edwina could prepare with any degree of success.

Charlie started to set the table, and Rosie told them that the next coffee morning had been cancelled because they were all scared of the murderer. 'Ridiculous!'

'We should take Agnes some to her room,' Marshall said. 'She's got to get her strength up.'

Nathan jumped up. 'I'll do it!'

Normally they would have been suspicious of a greedy child like Nathan, but he really seemed to enjoy feeding Agnes like a hungry animal, and so they put a steaming spoonful of cottage pie on a plate, put a fork and a napkin with it, and sent Nathan upstairs with a tray.

Edwina was trying to train Hettie with lettuce.

'Stay!' she said. Indeed, Hettie didn't move, and Edwina fed her a lettuce leaf.

Again!

'Stay!' Perfect. Edwina looked around the group triumphantly.

'Can she do anything else?' Rosie asked.

Edwina looked at her resentfully. 'Staying is difficult enough for her.'

'Dinnertime!' Charlie announced, to prevent an argument.

Edwina fed Hettie the Wonder Tortoise another lettuce leaf and hopped over to the table.

'Salad first!'

That was the healthiest way!

Agnes was still sitting upright in bed, ready, but indecisive, when the Grandson came walking in again, this time with a tray.

'Dinner!' Nathan beamed. He really could beam beautifully when he wanted to.

Agnes shook her head reluctantly. She didn't have time for messing around. She had to find Alice and catch her, before she could do any more harm, and she, Agnes, was certain she had found out something about Alice's identity in Lime Tree Court. But what? Every time she tried to remember, she just saw Mrs Scott's furious face in front of her.

She felt shivery. Maybe a hot meal really wasn't such a bad idea. So, she waved Nathan over and signalled for him to put the tray on her bed.

Then she was about to usher Nathan out of the room, but something made her suspicious.

What was steaming there on her plate wasn't sausages or noodles or tinned soup or anything else from their limited repertoire of recipes. It was a *new dish*, a moist golden square. And it smelt really good.

Agnes prodded it curiously with her fork. 'What is it?'

'Cottage pie!' Nathan beamed.

One of her favourite meals! Always had been! Agnes was touched. Her housemates were taking wonderful care of her.

She manoeuvred some onto her fork and blew on it. Still quite hot.

'That's really kind of Charlie!' It must have been her. She must have made it. Nobody else was capable of making a dish like that.

'Charlie didn't make it.'

Agnes lowered her fork again. Who did then? Edwina? No way! And Marshall could grill sausages or boil spaghetti at most.

'From the internet, huh?' You could order everything nowadays. It was the only possible explanation.

Nathan shook his head. 'That woman made it.'

'What woman?' Agnes's fork hovered in mid-air.

'Bernadette's friend. Red hair. Smokes.'

And what before had been a blurry, vaguely threatening inkling, suddenly became awful certainty. Agnes dropped the plate, rolled off the bed with no regard for the consequences, and grabbed Nathan by his collar.

'Have you eaten any of it?'

'No!' Nathan protested, too shocked to be offended.

'The truth!'

'I *am* telling the truth!'

Nathan broke free and ran out of the room, while Agnes ripped her dressing gown from the hook and rushed to the stairlift barefoot.

Only once all the two-legged creatures had disappeared did Brexit get up too. He shook himself and stretched and sniffed the dropped piece of cottage pie with interest.

It smelt delicious!

If it was on the floor, it belonged to him, those were the rules!

Brexit wagged his tail happily, then he woofed down the cottage pie in big bites as only dogs can, and licked the plate clean.

They had all obediently eaten their salad and were just about to start on the appetising cottage pie when Agnes was suddenly standing in the doorway, in her nightie and open dressing gown, her hair wild, her eyes even wilder.

She whacked Marshall's fork out of his hand, gave the cottage pie a shove, launched herself at Rosie like a fury, and grabbed her by her red hair, screaming. The hair moved, slipped and whooshed off Rosie's head like a shocked furry animal. Suddenly their guest was sitting there with a bald head and weird sticky-out ears. Agnes stood next to her brandishing the red hair, shrieking something about poison and revenge and murder.

The light fitting wobbled.

Bernadette asked what was going on, but nobody knew what to say.

Charlie dabbed her mouth with her napkin in shock.

Marshall had jumped up to support Agnes, who had lost balance and was floundering against the table.

Winston was having one of those rare moments where he didn't look dignified for once, just flabbergasted.

Rosie was sitting there with her hand on her bald head, her eyes wide, speechless.

The cottage pie wasn't steaming any more, and Edwina was covering Hettie's eyes.

19

ICE CUBE

'Another ice cube?' Edwina asked helpfully.

Rosie shook her head silently. Her wig was on again, but at a strangely wonky angle, making Rosie look like a has-been rock star. A has-been rock star with a bump on her temple.

'Ice cubes aren't going to help!' Bernadette spat.

Edwina shrugged her shoulders, clamped Hettie under her arm and left, sucking on an ice cube.

'But she's got a wig!' Agnes mumbled from the wingback chair, somewhere between defiant and rueful.

'It's not a crime to have a wig!' Bernadette yelled.

'No,' Agnes admitted. 'Not directly!'

Charlie loudly lamented that she'd wasted her whole hash supply on the policeman when they really could have used it now. Then she went in search of a gin and tonic.

They had bundled a worked-up Agnes into the wingback chair and calmed her down to an extent.

Now they had to find out what was actually going on.

'Well, Agnes?' Winston patted her hand, more accusatorily than calming.

'I thought . . .' Agnes began. 'I *was* . . .' She broke off, distraught. 'I made a mistake!' She fell silent, opened her mouth searching for words – and shut it again. A few minutes ago, everything had been so clear. How could she have been so wrong?

Rosie got up uncertainly. 'I need a cigarette!'

'You can smoke here,' Bernadette said considerately.

'No!' Rosie said with an eye on Agnes. 'I'd rather not.'

Bernadette and Rosie swept past Agnes towards the back door.

Agnes could have wept. Had she not still been happy a few hours ago, glad to be home again, with her friends? And now those friends were looking at her, as if she'd . . . well, as if she'd violently attacked and humiliated a guest, hurled a homemade and unusually appetising cottage pie on the floor and generally acted like a madwoman. Madness. Was that it?

Anything but that!

She had just wanted to save them – but something had gone awry.

'I just wanted . . .' She tried again and noticed her voice was shaking. Her hands were shaking too. In fact, her whole world was shaking.

Marshall stepped towards the wingback chair and offered his arm.

'You belong in bed,' he said sternly, and Agnes didn't dare argue. She let him help her out of the chair and obediently followed Marshall into the hall, to the stairlift and back to her room. It was there she realised that even Brexit had done a runner.

Marshall made sure she was tucked in well, and put a glass of water on her bedside table. Then he switched off the light.

Agnes shuddered. How cold the world had suddenly become – and how strange!

Two circles were endlessly chasing one another through the darkness, never giving up, never touching, one blue, the other green. No idea how long he'd been sitting there for. It was dark outside the window, but also in his room, and even inside Marshall himself.

Nathan and the transformer were lying on his sofa, two little lumps under a duvet. Nathan was breathing gently, the transformer wasn't.

Marshall sighed. At least he had somehow managed to get his grandson to bed before losing himself in front of the screen. The rest hardly mattered – the good thing about the internet was that it was always patiently waiting. You could disappear in the fog for minutes or hours at a time, and when you returned, you could pick straight up where you left off. He had been searching for something, hadn't he? He moved the mouse, and the next moment a gun was peering at him from the screen. Good condition. And not a bad price. Marshall stared spellbound into the blue light. Buying antique firearms on the internet was ridiculously easy because there supposedly wasn't any ammunition for them any more. But he had ammunition, and he had this foreboding feeling that after recent developments he would be needing a gun again very soon.

But you couldn't find everything you needed on the internet.

He had been searching for something else too. Something was missing. Agnes! Agnes was missing! He jumped up in a panic, reached for his dressing gown, hesitated. No, no, she was back, wasn't she? With her nightie and a chocolate bar and strangulation marks on her neck. But even that wasn't completely true. The Agnes who had returned from Lime Tree Court was different to the one who had broken in there two days before. Something wasn't right with her – a part of Agnes was still lost.

Marshall slid into his slippers, tiptoed past Nathan, carefully opened the door and slipped out into the hallway, in search of the lost Agnes.

Agnes was so exhausted she couldn't even summon the energy to reach for the glass of water on her bedside table, even though she was thirsty. Despite that, she couldn't sleep. Thoughts raced through her mind like sharks, baring their teeth, eating one another, being eaten, chewed up and born again.

She was hungry too. The cottage pie had mysteriously disappeared from her room, and obviously nobody had thought to bring her something to eat, after she'd completely ruined supper for everyone like that.

She hadn't found and exposed Alice. Far from it! Instead, she had ripped the wig from an innocent woman's head and made a fool of herself in the process.

How on earth did it happen?

The scene ran through Agnes's mind over and over again, first her panic and the awful certainty that her housemates were just about to be poisoned, then the short, sweet moment of triumph when the red hair did indeed move and a bald head emerged underneath.

Seconds later she had known that the person she was staring at, hairless and horrified, couldn't be her twin sister Alice. Sure, many years had gone by, but still . . . Agnes was sure she would recognise Alice anytime, anywhere. The person who had emerged beneath the wig was a stranger anyway. Her nose was too small, her mouth too wide, her eyes . . . Surely it wasn't possible for your eyes to change colour in the course of your lifetime. Apart from that, something was missing *in* her eyes, a playful, wild, wicked spark.

Agnes realised she was disappointed, not just because she wanted to catch a murderer, but also because she had been looking forward to the reunion with her long-lost twin. Alice might well have become a monster in the meantime, but she was *her* monster!

Rosie on the other hand . . . Rosie was a good egg. After Agnes's attack she had behaved with the utmost decency. What must she think of her? A fresh wave of embarrassment swept over Agnes. She tossed and turned until she had found a position that partially agreed with her mistreated hip. There! That's it!

She started to feel a little bit better. Sure, it was an unpleasant situation, but nothing bad had really happened. Better to ruin one or two cottage pies, than let yourself be poisoned out of sheer politeness!

And the fact that Rosie wasn't Alice didn't necessarily mean that Agnes's theory was completely and utterly wrong. Alice might not have been found, but in Agnes's eyes she was still the main suspect in this case, and soon, one way or another, their paths would cross. It was all just a matter of time.

Just then, Agnes heard a dull thud, not in her room but down on the ground floor, directly below her.

In the sitting room.

Marshall was searching. He had forgotten what it was he was searching for, but that didn't stop him from systematically pulling book after book off the shelf, opening them and closing them again in search of . . . something. A word? A picture? He didn't know, but he knew it was *important*.

Vitally important.

His fingers wandered over the spines of the books and he watched them with a certain fatalism. The fingers knew what they were doing. Marshall didn't. It did him good to sit back for a moment and leave the thinking, worrying and planning to someone else.

A loud crash behind him made him look up. The reading lamp had fallen over. Probably his fault. He hadn't been paying attention for a moment. Dutifully, his fingers abandoned the shelves to set the lamp up straight again, then they were back, determined, relentless.

Marshall realised that he was suddenly holding an old photo album in his hands. Agnes's photo album. He should have put it back on the shelf like a gentleman, but instead he looked on as his hands routinely went to open it at the last page.

No.

Suddenly the fog cleared and Marshall was the master of his hands and thoughts again. He eyed the album curiously.

It seemed like he had seen it before at one time or another.

Agnes's family album. Maybe not such a bad idea. He didn't want to snoop around, really he didn't, but maybe it would help him get to know Agnes better – maybe he'd find the lost part of Agnes again.

He switched the now upright reading lamp on, sat on the sofa and opened the album.

The first page was blank, on the second page someone had written *My family* in a childish scrawl and drawn a misshapen heart. Marshall's equally rather misshapen heart skipped a beat.

On the second page, a wedding photo in faded sepia tones. The bridegroom looked proud and military, the bride was wearing a veil, but a pretty, worried face peered shyly from beneath the cloth. So young.

So long ago.

On the next page the couple were no longer alone. The man had lost some of his poise, the woman was sitting in an armchair with dark circles under her eyes. She was holding two chubby-cheeked babies in her arms. One left. One right.

Two.

Twins.

Mummy. Daddy. Me and Alice.

He hadn't even known that Agnes had siblings!

The next picture was of just the two children, no longer babies. They were sitting up already, a teddy bear between them, and looking into the camera with identical quizzical looks.

Something in the picture seemed familiar to Marshall. The rug? The window in the background? It dawned on him that the photo was taken right there in the sitting room, just a few feet from where he was sitting right now.

So near. Yet so far.

Time and space were funny things.

Marshall tried to remember the time when his daughter, Sabrina, was the same age as these twins, but nothing came to him. Presumably he had been on a tour of duty somewhere and only appeared at home every now and again, at Christmas, Easter, maybe a few days in the summer. He could vaguely remember a Christmas tree, a child in his arms – and that back then he would have preferred to have been holding a glass of whisky.

On the next page the two girls were already standing. The teddy bear was still in on the action, but he looked well-worn. A glass eye was hanging off, one ear was missing. The twins' hair was plaited in thin bunches, their collars starched. One of them was looking to the side, blurred in motion, a vague cloud of a child, the other girl was looking straight at the camera.

For the first time Marshall thought he could see something of Agnes in the child's round face. An insatiable curiosity. A quiet determination. But was it even Agnes? They were like two peas in a pod.

The photos on the next page were so tiny that he couldn't make anything out without his reading glasses, but someone had scrawled in the middle in big round letters again.

Me and Alice and Mummy at the bucks.

Marshall assumed it was about ducks.

A blank page followed, then a second, then the family appeared again, serious and dressed in black, father, mother, child.

Just one child.

The second girl was missing, but someone had drawn a stick figure on the edge, with line plaits and a triangle skirt. A shiver ran down Marshall's spine.

New pages, new pictures. The girl with the pigtails really was starting to look a bit like Agnes. Stubborn mouth. Big eyes. Sceptical frown.

Sometimes she was holding a rabbit in her arms, sometimes a book, sometimes her mother's hand, but she was always looking assertively and quizzically at the camera.

The pigtails got longer. She had to be of school age.

The father had since disappeared from the pictures too.

Marshall flicked on, fascinated.

Another blank page, this time with a rough patch in the middle, as if someone had ripped a picture out.

The next photo was different to the others. More relaxed, more natural, and it showed two girls again, in identical white smocks. *Two.* It took Marshall's breath away. How was it possible? But on closer inspection, it turned out the picture had fooled him. There was just one child. Agnes in front of a mirror. Different from usual, she was looking away from the camera, seemingly into the distance, but the girl in the mirror was staring at him with a sly, strangely knowing look.

Marshall felt an unpleasant tingling in his neck. That look wasn't like Agnes at all. Someone had written something under this picture in round child's writing too.

Me and Alice.

He stood up abruptly and pushed the album back onto the

shelf. He felt rather queasy, as if he had seen something rotten –
like a peek in a grave. He realised there was something lying at
his feet, an oblong, yellowed piece of paper. He picked it up and
looked at it thoughtfully.

Just as he was about to slip the paper back into the album,
he heard a sound behind him and looked up. Agnes was
standing there in the glow of the reading lamp, with drooping
arms and a glazed expression.

Agnes, but also somehow not Agnes. Tired, out of place. *A
stranger.* They stared at one another for a while, far too long
for Marshall's liking, then Agnes raised her hand in greeting.

'It's you.' It seemed to Marshall as if she sounded
disappointed.

'You should get some sleep, Agnes,' he said gently.

'I *can't* sleep.' Agnes slumped onto the sofa and looked
down at her hands. 'I'd like to explain it to somebody,' she
said quietly.

'Explain what?' Marshall cautiously sat down next to her.

'Everything. The thing with Rosie.'

'Ah.' Marshall had other things to worry about now, but
he was still curious.

'You don't have to worry, Agnes,' he said. 'If you don't
like Rosie, she doesn't have to come here again. Bernadette
can meet her somewhere else. It's your house after all.' Agnes
shook her head frantically.

'That wasn't it. I like Rosie. She's really decent. I didn't want
to be mean to her. I just thought that in reality she was somebody
else, because of the wig. I couldn't have known that she lost her
hair because of chemo. I thought she had come to poison us.'

'Rosie?'

'Alice!'

'Alice?' Marshall looked at Agnes strangely, and suddenly everything bubbled out of her, from the beginning, all the bottled-up years, even the thing about Titus Coldwell.

Not a soul knew about the Titus Coldwell thing, except Isobel.

Marshall looked more and more concerned.

'I should have stuck by her, you know,' Agnes whispered. 'She would have done it for me anyway. But what she did . . . was so *awful*.' She shook her head. 'I didn't want to think about it any more, that's the truth. And I wanted to have friends, real friends like Isobel and Mildred. And for some reason . . . I couldn't take her with me.'

Marshall was silent. He looked unhappy. Did he understand what Agnes was trying to tell him? She started again. 'I saw the crime scene photos, you know, at the station. Mildred was . . . "disembowelled" isn't such a bad word. It wasn't a burglary. It was something personal, a very old, long-held resentment. Believe me, it used to be my job.' She smiled wistfully. 'Olive's murder, on the other hand, was practical – she had been trying to blackmail the murderer somehow. But Mildred . . . and the gun on our table . . . It's about us. About *me*. It *must* be Alice! She's here somewhere. She's been hiding and watching us. And I think she wants revenge!'

So, the words were out, in the open, and Agnes felt like a balloon that all the air had finally escaped from. Limp and pliable, and somehow relieved. The high-pitched ringing set in, but at that moment she hardly cared. It was good to have let

Marshall in on it – he was nobody's fool, and together they would somehow manage to prevent the worst from happening. Apart from that, she was happy that he now understood the business with Rosie and didn't think she was a madwoman any more.

Marshall took her hands in his and looked into her eyes. Agnes could see he was worried.

'It'll all be alright, somehow!' she said encouragingly. 'We'll manage.'

Marshall spoke emphatically for a long time and Agnes tried to throw in an 'Ah!' or 'Oh!' or 'Exactly!' every now and then, to make an intelligent impression, but Marshall got more and more worked up. He let go of her hands to gesticulate wildly with his, and finally he laid a yellowed piece of paper in her lap. Agnes squinted and peered down at the pale rectangle. Presumably there was something written on it, but without her reading glasses it was impossible for her to find out what, and definitely not in this light. She sheepishly stuffed the paper into her dressing gown pocket.

Marshall had leapt up and was offering her his arm again. Agnes went red – he was trying to get rid of her!

Then she was hurtling upstairs on the now unusually quick stairlift, waving down at Marshall. He wasn't waving back, instead he just stood there with his hands in his pockets.

It was like a goodbye.

Marshall waited until he heard Agnes's door click, then he went over to the kitchen to track down a drink, gin and tonic at a pinch, but preferably a whisky. He found a bottle and a glass, poured himself a drink and listened to the liquid glugging. He took a first sip and realised his hands were shaking. They never used to shake, not even during operations in the field, but nowadays . . . Maybe it was his age.

He emptied his glass in a few big gulps and would have gladly had a top-up, but decided against it. Better not – he needed a clear head. At least one of them did.

At least him.

Of all people.

For a while he sat there deep in thought, then he stood up, washed up his glass and left it to dry. That's how the old Agnes would have wanted it.

He went over to the dining room, opened the safe and got out the black book. His hands were shaking again.

When you lived in a household like theirs, you had to be ready to make difficult decisions at some point. The black book was there to make decisions like that easier for them. There, before witnesses, each of them had written down when it was time, in their view, to throw in the towel.

When I can't do yoga any more, Edwina had written. *And when I can't look after Hettie any more.* She had drawn Hettie underneath – and a butterfly.

When the pain is too much, Lillith had written. *When I can't work in the garden any more – and when there's no hope left.*

Luckily the decision with Lillith had been easy. She had got the diagnosis, unambiguous, immutable, and informed them all over Chelsea buns that her time had come. They had cried a bit, and Lillith had hugged each of them in turn. 'Do it when I'm distracted,' she had said. 'When I'm doing something nice. Like . . . like a surprise. And I don't want a big fuss. I'm lucky to have friends like you!'

So, they had all drawn lots, and there was an X on Marshall's. The next day he had gone into the shed, where Lillith was busy with her seedlings, and said goodbye to her with a clean shot to the head. It had been difficult, but not too difficult. It was something he wanted for himself too, and he was still convinced that it had been the right thing to do.

This, on the other hand . . .

What if the person in question couldn't decide any more? What if they were becoming a stranger, bit by bit? What if somebody else had to decide for them? He had often asked these questions about himself. What if the fog got too thick? Each time the decision had seemed simple to him. He didn't want to turn into a stranger, a weird, confused, helpless geriatric. He wanted to die as himself – and that's exactly what he had written in the black book. But he had never really imagined suddenly having to make this decision for someone else, especially not for Agnes. Agnes had always been the most sensible of them all, the one with the lists and the rules, the one with both feet firmly on the ground, while other people were doing yoga or stockpiling chocolate bars or aimlessly surfing the internet. But in recent days . . . He was still shocked by what he had just heard. He wasn't sure which of the things Agnes had explained to him about Alice were reality and which she was imagining, but one thing was clear: too much of it was pipe dreams – *must* be pipe dreams. And the way she had nodded and smiled as he had desperately tried to make her see sense – as if she didn't understand a single word.

With a heavy heart he leafed through the black book until he got to Agnes's page.

When I can't speak and think clearly any more, was written there. *And when I'm a danger to others.*

Agnes was back under her bedcovers and felt strangely euphoric. It was so good to have got everything off her chest. She felt like Marshall had taken her seriously. Tomorrow they would convince the rest of the household, even Bernadette, and then they would find Alice and stop her in her tracks!

She was just about to fall asleep when she remembered the slip of paper Marshall had pressed into her hand. What was on it? She was gripped by a strange curiosity.

Eventually, she switched the light back on, awkwardly dragged her reluctant body out of bed and padded over to her dressing gown. She pulled the paper out of the pocket and went to look for one of her many pairs of reading glasses. When you didn't need them, they were in the way all over the place, but once you were really looking for a pair, they were nowhere to be seen. Typical!

After she had spotted a pair on her dressing table, she put them on her nose and padded back to bed to study the secretive paper under the glow of the bedside lamp.

At first, she didn't fully understand what she was looking at. There was a photo of a small girl printed on it, not much older than maybe four years old. Agnes recognised the white frilly dress the girl was wearing, and she recognised the girl herself, Alice. She even thought she could remember the moment the photo was taken, on their father's birthday. The house had been full of important guests, and someone had promised them gateau if they would just keep still for the photo. In those days you had to keep still for photos for quite a while. Agnes looked more closely and realised she was in the photo too, at least her left shoulder was. Back then it had been as good as impossible to get a photo of one of them on their own. The very definition of inseparable.

But somebody had cut her off.

She stared uncomprehendingly at the black border surrounding the photo, and then at the old-fashioned script printed beneath it.

Alice Sharp

I am the resurrection and the life.
He that believeth in me, though he were dead,
yet shall he live.

(John 11: 25)

May she Rest in Peace.

20

CHELSEA BUNS

Outside, a bird was singing, loud and clear and bold, as if nobody had informed it that it was hardly worth it anymore. That it was autumn now.

The morning sun cast a shadow theatre of dancing leaves onto the wall.

Agnes had her eyes open and was watching the shadow leaves in their light show. For a moment, she dared to be optimistic. A new day, a sunny one to boot. Who knew how many days like this you had left? They were to be welcomed, the sun-soaked days, treasured and enjoyed. The hydrangeas with their plump, yellowing flowerheads would look wonderful in the morning light.

Then on the bedside table, the black-bordered picture, caught her eye. It was too late for optimism. Someone was dead.

Alice.

Alice

was

dead.

Agnes tried to understand what that meant, but the whole thing seemed unfathomable, unsettling, a glass-smooth cliff of a thought, with no way up. But there was no way *round* either, so she had to try, step by step.

The picture was real, it was old, and it really was Alice, a little girl of about four years of age with short rat's tail bunches and a broad, happy grin.

Agnes remembered this Alice, blurrily, as if she were spying on her through a sheer cloth, but without a shadow of a doubt.

But she also remembered another Alice. The Alice who crouched in hedges and climbed trees, let snails crawl across her skin, and collected little pale bird skulls in a hollow stone.

Alice with the tangled hair that never saw a comb; Alice who wasn't afraid of storms; Alice who ran through the rain singing.

This Alice didn't exist, had never existed.

Agnes should probably have known.

Her mother would never have ever allowed a daughter of hers to sleep in tree hollows and catch frogs, to dance in puddles and run around unkempt in the world, with ripped clothes and ladders in her stockings. Never ever.

That's why Alice hadn't gone to school.

That's why she hadn't had any friends.

That's why the two of them had always been alone.

The second Alice wasn't real, she was someone Agnes had made up because the true Alice had left her. She was the sister Agnes had wanted, wild and free and fearless, no pigtails and not a care in the world. She didn't allow herself to be bossed around by her mother, and it was good to sit under trees with her and laugh at the world. She was exactly how Agnes wanted to be.

The dreamt-up Alice.

Agnes closed her eyes. The shimmering foliage on the wall was confusing her. She was already high up on the thought cliff, and if she looked down, she would fall. It wasn't that unusual for children to have imaginary friends, especially lonely, confused, sad children, as she had been. Why not also an imaginary sister, when she had lost a real, cheeky, happy one? Inseparable.

What of it?

But one thing didn't make sense. One thing was worrying Agnes, if wild-haired Alice only existed in her head, who exactly had climbed up into the apple tree back then and dropped the hammer on Titus Coldwell?

Agnes looked down, at the sharp, glassy cliff – and fell.

Marshall returned from the garden with one of the last hydrangea flowerheads still in bloom. He carefully removed a few leaves and put the hydrangea in a little vase. Then he put the vase on a tray, which already had buttery toast, orange juice, a pot of yoghurt and little bowls of strawberry jam and orange marmalade, honey and Nutella waiting on it. Soon a cup of very milky coffee was added, just as Agnes liked it.

A fierce discussion was raging behind Marshall.

'Hettie says Agnes didn't mean it!' Edwina explained.

'It doesn't matter what Hettie says!' hissed Bernadette. 'I'm not going to be dictated to by a tortoise. It can't go on like this! She's got to apologise to Rosie.'

'We're never going to get a cottage pie like that again,' Winston moaned.

'It absolutely does matter what Hettie says!' Edwina

retorted, patting the tortoise's shell. 'You should apologise to *her*!'

'Pah!' Bernadette turned her head away demonstratively.

'Where's the Nutella?' Nathan asked, who hadn't learnt a thing from his latest tummy ache.

'An apology would be good,' Charlie mumbled neutrally and fed Brexit a slice of toast underneath the table.

Brexit wagged his shaggy tail in Bernadette's face.

Bernadette grimaced. 'Agnes made a complete spectacle of herself.' Then she turned to Marshall. 'I really don't understand why you're spoiling her.'

Marshall sighed and looked down at the tray. Everything necessary was there. No reason to draw it out any longer.

'We should have a quiet word about Agnes,' he said to nobody in particular. 'Around midday, maybe, over some cake?' With that, he lifted up the tray and gestured with his chin towards the sideboard.

On the bread board next to the sink sat some frozen Chelsea buns, thawing.

Stories. It was what it was all about. Life consisted entirely of stories. She herself, Agnes, was made of stories. There was the story of Sunset Hall. The story of Lillith. The story of Mildred and Isobel. Agnes and Alice. The story of Titus Coldwell.

What if one of those stories was wrong? Warped?

The point was to disentangle your own stories, and Agnes was bravely picking up a particularly obstinate thread.

If . . . then . . .

If . . . then . . .

If her wild, secret sister Alice hadn't existed, there was only one person who could be responsible for the hammer in the apple tree and Titus Coldwell's sudden demise.

Her. Agnes.

Her, Agnes, a murderer? It was inconceivable.

Sure, Titus Coldwell had been a monster, a soul-destroyer, and she a frightened child, maybe ten years old. Nobody would have believed her, especially not her mother. She had every right to look for a way out, any conceivable way out. Either . . . or . . .

The hammer or the lorry.

There was no third option.

Despite that, it had been a dreadful deed, and Agnes wondered if by doing it something had been broken – something that had never been properly put back together?

She had left behind the imaginary Alice at Titus Coldwell's gravestone because she wanted nothing more to do with the part of herself that had swung the hammer.

Ever again.

And Alice had shuffled off and let Agnes live her life. At least that's how it seemed until today . . . But life was rarely so simple, was it? Agnes, who had worked in the police for many years, knew that.

What if, ever since, Alice had been struggling to get to the surface again? What if the dreamt-up Alice had returned?

What if the monster that she couldn't find was lurking inside herself?

There was a knock at her door and Agnes gave a start. She put her hand over her mouth and listened.

After a breath or two, she could hear Marshall's voice outside.

'Agnes? Are you awake? Can I come in? I, err . . . I've got you breakfast.'

All Agnes wanted to do was disappear under the bedcovers forever. Marshall, of all people, who she'd regaled with her murder theories about Alice and Mildred yesterday! And it was Marshall who had pressed the obituary into her hand! He knew too much . . . She had even told him about Titus Coldwell.

'Agnes? Are you in there?'

Agnes racked her brain. The bedcovers wouldn't offer enough protection. She needed a better plan. If she could make it to the bathroom door before Marshall . . .

But it was too late.

A final, impatient knock, almost a bang, then the door handle moved, and Marshall was standing in the room, a tray in his hands. Agnes stared at him in terror over the top of her bedcovers.

'Huh, err . . .' Marshall said looking down at the tray sheepishly. 'So you're awake. Good!'

'Good morning.' Agnes croaked.

'Morning,' Marshall mumbled, but avoided her gaze. He shifted his weight from one foot to the other a few times, then he remembered his mission and held the tray out towards Agnes.

'Breakfast!'

Whilst he deposited the tray on a pillow in front of her, another awful thought occurred to Agnes. What if Titus Coldwell wasn't the only person she had on her conscience?

What if *she* had killed Mildred and Olive? *Her* as *Alice*? Her dark side? Her evil twin?

The thought was so terrible that she involuntarily flinched.

The orange juice sloshed over.

'Careful!' Marshall warned.

You didn't have to tell Agnes twice. Careful, careful! Hold your horses – or in this case, old nag! How on earth had she . . . Mildred . . .

Nothing to it. She would have just had to somehow get hold of Marshall's gun and go over to the Pucks' house with it – just like she had only a few days ago.

And Olive? She'd also just recently made it to her house entirely under her own steam. Everywhere the murderer had been, she had been too! The photo of the umbrella and the pointy shoe – was it maybe actually *her* shoe?

'Not hungry?'

Marshall was still standing next to her smiling, with a somewhat pained expression on his face. She had completely forgotten about him!

'Everything alright, Agnes?'

'Yes,' she said. 'Wonderful!'

But obviously, there was absolutely nothing wonderful about this at all. Suddenly Agnes was her own prime suspect and the world had been turned upside down.

She remembered the last time somebody had brought her something on a tray: Nathan, the blasted cottage pie. Yesterday, when the world had still been relatively alright. When the only thing she had to be worried about was a crazed poisoner out there – not *in here*, in her head.

'No Nathan today then?' she asked, just to say anything at all because Marshall was still standing next to her as if he was waiting for something. Why wasn't he going? Why didn't he leave her in peace?

'No,' Marshall said decisively. 'No Nathan.'

Of course not! Who would send their own grandson into a murderer's lair? At that moment Agnes knew that Marshall had his suspicions and that he knew that she knew that he knew and so on, *ad infinitum*.

'Shame,' she squeaked.

Marshall looked up, surprised and a bit hurt. 'I thought I'd bring it myself. I thought you'd be happy . . .'

'I, err, of course . . .' She *would* have been happy if anything like happiness was currently open to her. As it was, she was floating somewhere between panic and embarrassment, and really wanted the ground to swallow her up. Instead, she tentatively picked up a slice of toast, spread it with honey, shoved it in her mouth and waited until the toast softened a bit. Then she chewed and swallowed. It tasted of nothing.

'Delicious!'

Really, she wanted to throw her arms around Marshall's neck with gratitude, that despite her tirade yesterday he had still thought it necessary to bring her breakfast. But that would have thrown the aforementioned breakfast and tray off balance – and probably more than just the breakfast.

So, she limited herself to smiling and helping herself to a second round of toast.

Spread, soften, carefully chew, swallow. At least that was working! She had a sip of orange juice.

'Err, I . . . about what I said last night . . . err . . .'

She fell silent, searching for words while Marshall looked at her expectantly. Agnes felt herself go red. The inside and the outside, problematic as ever. There might be a cold-blooded murderer sitting somewhere inside her, but what she was spouting from the outside sounded more like a confused five-year-old. Even Hettie would have expressed herself better. Wordlessly and unambiguously.

She grasped the next best thread and went for it.

'I know I was wrong. About a lot of things. I'm sorry.'

Marshall nodded in resignation. 'Everyone's wrong every now and then. It's not such a big deal, Agnes.'

But it *was* a big deal. She had deceived herself, deluded herself, played cat and mouse with herself. Now she was sitting here confused, and nobody else could help her to disentangle herself.

Or maybe they could?

There was somebody, Theresa.

What was it she'd said again? Olive had seen the murderer, had seen her *standing* – weird way of putting it, really. And before someone – Alice? Agnes? – had held a gun in Olive's face, Olive had managed to reveal at least a part of the puzzle to Theresa. The old gossip-monger! If Agnes could hear the truth from Theresa's lips maybe it would then be a bit easier to accept that she was a monster too. Certainty was better than mere suspicion, even if it was a terrible certainty.

Theresa. She had to speak to Theresa again. Now, where had her slippers got to?

She tried to wriggle out from under the breakfast. The coffee sloshed over. Marshall lifted up the tray and looked worried.

'What's the matter?'

'Lime Tree Court,' Agnes puffed in desperation. Would he believe her now? 'I've got to go back! I've got to speak to Theresa again!' Just yesterday she had sworn that wild horses couldn't drag her back to Lime Tree Court again, but a single imaginary Alice had managed it just like that. Agnes needed certainty. Everything else was secondary.

Marshall had a strange look on his face, and Agnes froze. She suddenly had a very bad feeling.

'Theresa is dead, Agnes.'

'Dead?' she croaked. 'But how? She was . . . Since when?'

Marshall shrugged his shoulders. 'Since very recently, I'd say. Bernadette heard about it yesterday from Rosie, before you . . .' He diplomatically fell silent so as not to keep going on about the cottage pie incident.

'Just . . . like that?' Agnes whispered, although she already knew that the response wouldn't be 'just like that.'

Marshall put the tray on the bedside table. 'An accident' is the official version, but Rosie's postman's daughter works in the kitchen there. Strangled, she said. Attacked by another resident and strangled. What a place! I'm glad you're out of there.'

He looked deeply into her eyes, reproachfully as it seemed to her.

Her head was spinning. Theresa? Two days ago, she had been quite perky and was looking forward to aqua aerobics . . . Strangled. How was it possible? *She* was the one who had been strangled! But maybe Mrs Scott had attacked other Lime Tree Court residents after her. And she, Agnes, had helped set her loose, unmedicated, a danger to the public. Theresa's death was her fault!

Or . . . her heart was suddenly pounding so loudly she could hardly hear herself think.

Boom. Boom. Boom.

What if she was even more directly responsible for Theresa's death? What if, with Theresa, the murderer had silenced the final witness? The murderer?

Her.

Agnes Sharp!

Is that why she had been so intent on smuggling herself into Lime Tree Court and finding Theresa? Had she just imagined the wrestling match with Mrs Scott? Was *she* the one who had attacked Theresa?

She remembered it differently, but she had been pumped full of medication after all – and it was looking like lots of things were different to how she remembered them. A murder or two, for example!

Her hand wandered to her neck as if of its own accord, to the sensitive areas, where she had been strangled. But what did that prove? Maybe Theresa had tried to defend herself, and strangled her back.

'Agnes? Everything alright?' Marshall had taken a few steps back from the bed and was eyeing her suspiciously. Why did he keep asking her if everything was alright, when obviously *nothing* was alright?

The murderer had struck again – and once again Agnes had been at the right place at the right time! She had worked in the police for long enough to know what that meant!

'You really should eat something, Agnes.' Marshall looked

sadly over at the lovingly prepared breakfast. The coffee was definitely already cold by now.

Agnes reached for the cup and took a sip.

And then she stopped sipping. Another terrible thought had entered her head, Marshall knew too much as well. She herself had told him about Alice yesterday evening, and even about Titus Coldwell. Marshall knew too much!

He was in danger – and the danger was *her*!

She had to get rid of him, quickly, before Alice could strike again.

Hell-bent on picking a fight, she put the coffee cup back on the tray.

'The coffee's cold.'

'Little wonder,' Marshall mumbled.

'And apart from that, I don't like it with milk.'

'You *always* have it with milk!'

'Not any more.' Damn, how did Marshall know how she liked her coffee? Griping alone wasn't going to shake him off. Agnes decided to change tactics.

'Shouldn't you really be watching your grandson instead of standing around here? The brat's probably up to no good again.'

Marshall retreated a few steps, visibly upset. 'But you said he was welcome.'

'What else could I say?' Agnes caterwauled with gusto. 'After all, you did hold a gun to my head.' A bit of a poorly chosen turn of phrase, but Agnes tore on regardless. 'He's disturbing me though. He's disturbing all of us. We're just too polite to tell you.'

'Until now that is,' Marshall said quietly. How cold his voice could be. 'Well, good. As you will, Agnes.'

Without another word, or looking back, Marshall made his way to the door.

As soon as he was out of the room, Agnes heaved herself out from beneath the bedcovers, hobbled to the door at breakneck speed, locked it and pulled the key out of the lock. There! Now she just had to hide it.

But how did you hide something from yourself? It was impossible. Everything she knew, Alice would know too. There was only one possible option!

Without giving it another thought, Agnes hobbled over to the window and launched the key into the garden. For a moment it glimmered silver in the light like a rollicking fish, then it disappeared amongst the hydrangeas.

Agnes sank back onto the bed, exhausted. There! She'd done it! Marshall was saved, and Alice was trapped!

She felt like weeping.

Hettie was stalking along the gravel path at her fastest tortoise pace. This time it would work.

She'd had enough of her digging being interrupted over and over again by the Lettuce-holding Hands. The Hands undoubtedly had her best interests at heart, but they knew nothing about the art of digging, and the situation was gradually becoming urgent. Hettie had to dig, in light, cool, crumbly luscious earth, dig and dig, until she herself turned to earth, deep down, covered by leaves, one with the ground. Then everything would be perfect, dark, quiet and just the right temperature.

The tortoise had decided to undertake the arduous journey to the outer picket fence, to finally escape the Lettuce-holding Hands. She turned off the gravel path, rushed across the lawn to the place at the fence where the grass was taller and scratched tentatively with her foot. The ground yielded, a black fragrant furrow opened up, and moist earth stuck to her claws. Perfect!

She had already made a decent hole, when suddenly a shadow fell over her.

Hettie raised her head in annoyance and came face to face with two black, pointy, strangely lurking Big Feet.

The Chelsea buns had finished thawing, and Marshall had stuck them in the oven for a few minutes, to give them a bit of colour.

Charlie was making tea, Winston was distributing the forks, and Edwina was ceremoniously folding napkins. Chelsea buns – even misshapen ones – were not something to be taken lightly.

Normally it was Agnes who cut up and shared out the Chelsea buns, but this time her seat at the table was empty, and every time someone asked after her, Marshall mumbled something incomprehensible and checked on the buns in the oven.

Finally, Charlie got up with a sigh, took the buns out of the oven, grabbed the knife and started carving them up as equally as possible.

It was unusually quiet at the table.

'What's the matter with Nathan?' Winston asked with concern.

Marshall grinned guiltily, but also with a quiet sense of

triumph. 'Computer games. I don't think we'll be seeing much of him in a hurry. What I need to discuss with you . . . isn't for him.'

Bernadette chuckled in acknowledgement. Marshall may mislay the odd gun or two, but he was still a strategic genius!

'What's it about then?' Charlie asked cautiously.

'Agnes, of course,' Marshall sighed. 'It's about Agnes, I'm afraid.'

'Not again,' Edwina mumbled and took a bite of her Chelsea bun.

Just then, the light above them flickered a few times and went out. Power cut!

It wasn't a good sign.

A skull grinned, then blood suddenly spurted all over the place.

Boom!

Nathan was tickled pink.

His grandad's computer game was the coolest for miles around – not educational like the rubbish his mother let him play every now and then, with teddy bears and number puzzles. This didn't beat about the bush! Zombies with cold glistening eyes swarmed across the screen, and exploded when he pointed the gun at them, releasing an astonishing amount of blood in the process. Did zombies even have real blood? Here they did.

Nathan wasn't scared. After all, he still had three lives left, and apart from that, he had a transformer sitting next to him. What could possibly go wrong?

It was all just a game anyway.

He was just about to go onto the next level when the zombie on the screen froze mid-explosion. The screen went black.

'Shit!' Nathan said to the transformer. It was a word that you apparently shouldn't use, but since his mother had the *aifair*, his parents weren't exactly setting a good example, and Nathan had managed to accumulate a considerable arsenal of bad words.

'Arse. Shit. Fuck. Wanker,' he murmured and pushed the reset button a few times. The screen was still black. There was nothing for it.

Nathan slid off his grandad's desk chair, grabbed the transformer and trotted out into the hallway. What now?

Maybe he could make it to the garden without crossing the path of his grandad or one of the other residents. The people there were alright, no doubt about it, a whole lot cooler than he had initially feared. He had collected for hungry animals with them, toasted marshmallows and burnt a policeman's clothes in the garden. He had seen a wig ripped from a woman's head, and painted the cellar coral-red with Edwina.

All cool things, but sometimes his grandfather's friends were a bit too clingy for Nathan. It would be good to have a few minutes to himself. He had his eye on a sandpit behind the widest tree, where you could undoubtedly make a wonderful marshy landscape with the help of the garden hose. Then Nathan would go exploring with the transformer.

He crept down the stairs, slipped out into the garden, found the pit and the hose and got cracking.

Soon he had created a considerable lake district and was piling up wet sand to make hills when suddenly a shadow fell over him.

Nathan looked up and saw a lady with an umbrella. 'Hello!' said the lady beneath the umbrella.

'Hello,' said Nathan squinting. 'I'm Nathan!'

'I know,' the lady beneath the umbrella responded, smiling.

'I'm building a zombie landscape,' Nathan explained politely.

'Very nice.' The lady didn't let him out of her sight. 'You look like a very hungry boy, Nathan, and that's a stroke of luck, because I've got a lovely cake waiting at home. Far too much for me on my own, but with the help of a strong boy like you . . .'

She reached out a thin, bony hand towards him, but Nathan hesitated. He knew that you shouldn't just go off with strangers, not even old ladies.

Apart from that, his hand was really muddy.

'What sort of cake?' he asked cautiously.

'Chocolate,' said the lady beneath the umbrella. 'Chocolate and raspberry.'

That clinched it. 'Chocolate and raspberry' sounded marvellous, and the old lady wasn't a complete stranger to him after all.

Her bony fingers closed around Nathan's hand, and then the lady dragged him behind her, into the woods, with an astonishing amount of force.

21

CHOCOLATE LIQUEURS

'So, that's it then?' Charlie asked.

'That's it,' said Winston, exhaling and taking off his apron.

They were all standing round a plate of fried egg, beans and toast.

Nearly all of them.

And that was the problem.

Agnes wasn't with them.

She was above them, in her room, and was refusing to come out. It couldn't go on like this! They couldn't just let her sit there, stubborn, confused and nothing like the old Agnes they knew and loved. Something had to give!

Brexit sniffed the plate hopefully and brusquely turned away.

'I wish there was another way,' Marshall said. 'I wish we could just talk to her.'

'That's what we all wish,' said Winston.

'I tried . . .' Marshall said wringing his hands. 'But . . .'

'This is the best solution,' Bernadette interrupted him and

straightened her sunglasses, although there wasn't actually much straightening up to do. 'We've discussed everything.'

They *had* discussed everything, and they had come to a decision. And yet . . .

Edwina didn't say a word, she was just absent-mindedly playing with the cord on her tracksuit top.

Marshall sighed and transferred the plate onto a tray, on which a spoon, fork and a steaming cup of tea were already waiting.

'Do you think, she'll eat it, just like that?' Charlie asked. 'After the whole cottage pie saga?'

'Of course,' Marshall said defensively. 'She would never sus—' He broke off and stared with hostility down at the beans for a while.

Then he put the tray back on the table.

'I can't do it,' he said flatly. 'I know we discussed everything. I know it's the *right* thing to do. But still . . . I can't do it!'

Winston couldn't either.

Edwina was playing with her cord and good for nothing.

Bernadette was blind and not particularly good at balancing trays. It would look suspicious if she, of all people, took the food.

All eyes turned to Charlie.

'Me . . . err . . . That's not fair!' Charlie looked around searching for a gin and tonic, but to no avail. 'I'm new, and I'm expected to just—'

'Exactly,' said Bernadette. 'You're new. She won't hold it against you.'

'And we're all right behind you.' Winston added.

'Below you!' Edwina corrected, since the kitchen was almost directly under Agnes's room.

Charlie mumbled something about hypocrisy, but picked up the tray anyway.

Brexit whined.

Agnes wouldn't like her pills being administered covertly after she had been secretly shoving them down the sofa and in plant pots for weeks.

She wouldn't like it at all.

She was huddled with her back to the door and had no idea how she was supposed to get out of this position and upright ever again. Maybe if she could somehow pull herself up on the coat stand . . .

Never mind. That wasn't important now. Agnes was there to listen to Charlie, who was whispering through the keyhole and trying to get her to open the door, with lunch and a thousand good reasons.

They were very plausible reasons, for a change, and the smell of fresh toast wafted temptingly through the crack of the door, but it didn't help at all. Agnes had thrown away the key. Full stop!

In the cold light of day, it had been a short-sighted strategy. Agnes had wanted time to somehow outsmart the Alice in her, but up to now she hadn't notionally progressed even an inch – and now she was hungry.

Despite that – it was nice that her housemates were thinking of her, and Charlie really was trying her best out there.

'Agnes? Agnes, can you hear me? Are you in there? Agnes, why don't you open the door?'

Because of Titus Coldwell and Theresa, because of Mildred and

Olive and, above all, because of my murderous dead twin sister, Alice. Because of me. And besides, the key's gone!

It was too complicated to explain through a keyhole, to explain it at all, so Agnes limited herself to nodding mutely and uselessly, and whispering a 'thanks' every now and then.

Eventually, Charlie had had enough.

'I'm going now, Agnes. I'll leave the tray here in front of the door. It's getting cold, Agnes!' She seemed strangely relieved. Agnes listened to her footsteps as they moved away through the hallway, then she peered up at the coat stand. Operation Upright could commence!

Charlie went downstairs almost buoyantly. Agnes hadn't opened the door. She couldn't give her the lunch. The beans would go cold on the plate, the toast soggy, the tomato sauce would form an unappetising dully shining skin. Soon somebody would clear away the plate and scrape the cold food into the bin.

They had been spared the poisoned chalice for now, not just Agnes, but Charlie too.

She was rushing towards the kitchen to treat herself to a somewhat early, but well-deserved gin and tonic, when she heard an awful scream coming from upstairs.

Agnes hadn't managed to pull herself up and was now struggling towards the bed on all fours with sore knees. The bedpost was her last hope.

She grabbed hold and pulled. Her knees didn't like it.

Agnes groaned.

348

She wasn't that heavy! Since when were her arms so powerless?

She caught a glimpse in the mirror and was horrified. She looked like a ghost. A ghost in a nightie, her hair a rat's nest.

Was it really her?

Since when?

How had it come to this?

It couldn't go on like this, Alice or no Alice. She had to somehow get herself together. Up on her own two feet. Then a shower. Her false teeth cleaned and back in place. A nice skirt and a fresh cardigan. Maybe a bit of lipstick. She mustn't let herself go!

And then – only then – could she figure out how to get out of her room, turn herself in to the police . . .

'Gone! He's gone!'

Marshall was standing in the middle of his room, ashen-faced, a frantic look in his eyes. Behind him a dark screen and an empty desk chair.

Edwina understood immediately and looked under the bed and in the wardrobe, where uniforms gleamed. Charlie rushed up the stairs, Winston was transferring himself onto the stairlift to see if everything was alright.

'I don't get it.' Marshall fussed, casting one look after another in the direction of the desk, as if Nathan could spontaneously appear there at any moment. 'He's never voluntarily left a computer screen. Ever! Not even for food!'

'The power cut!' Winston cried as he hurtled up the stairs.

Marshall facepalmed. A loud, dull thud. Charlie, Winston and

Edwina looked at one another. Of course! So simple! So . . . *stupid*! If they hadn't been so busy working out how to best get Agnes's pills into her . . .

'When was it?' Bernadette asked, who had come out of her room, sunglassed-up and worried.

Winston glanced at the clock.

'It was quite a while ago. A couple of hours maybe?'

Marshall groaned. A couple of hours. For an adventurous and greedy grandson like Nathan, that was a small eternity!

'Right,' Charlie said rolling up the sleeves of her kimono, more symbolically than practically. 'Let's look for him. What else can we do? Let's start in the dining room.'

With more luck than judgement, Agnes had somehow managed to heave herself upright. As planned, she'd had a shower and put on something presentable. Her hair was on point. Her false teeth in situ. She had found a packet of chocolate liqueurs in her wardrobe – from her last birthday or perhaps the one before last – and poured herself a glass of water. Now she was sitting at the window sucking chocolate liqueurs watching her housemates searching the garden for Nathan in the rain. She had a bad feeling about it all. Nathan was a clingy little lad actually, and since they'd sourced Nutella, there really was no reason left for him to run off.

No. The more she thought about it, the more likely she thought it was that something had happened to the Grandson. But what could possibly happen to someone in a sleepy village like Duck End?

Ask Mildred! said a voice in her head. *Ask Olive! Ask Theresa!*

But hadn't they all fallen victim to *Alice*? And hadn't she, Agnes, had Alice locked safely in her room for quite a while now?

Edwina, Charlie, Winston, Bernadette and Marshall had already searched the house, then the cellar, then the shed – without success.

Now it was time for the garden.

Charlie and Marshall bent wet hydrangea branches to the side.

Winston shouted loudly for Nathan.

Bernadette hissed at Winston that he should keep his mouth shut so she could listen in peace.

Edwina and Brexit, who had the most experience in searching for and finding things, people and tortoises, quickly and efficiently combed through the flower beds. It was a big garden, and since Lillith's passing, it wasn't quite as neat as it could have been. There were hollyhocks and buddleia, witch hazel and dahlias, wild roses and wisteria. There were a lot of brambles and weeds. There were trees that you could climb up. There were cavernous, cobweb-filled spaces under bushes. There were hollow tree trunks, which even a podgy boy like Nathan would have fitted into.

Only Nathan was nowhere to be seen.

It had started to rain, but nobody really noticed. Water ran down Marshall's cheeks and dripped from his walrus moustache. Winston's thin wisps of hair stuck to his head, damp and flat. Bernadette's dark glasses glistened with hundreds of little water droplets and were disturbingly reminiscent of the multifaceted eyes of a fly. Edwina looked like a walking botanical exhibit with leaves, cobwebs and even a small but active snail on her shoulder.

Of course, it was Brexit who finally got them on the right track. He gave a single short, sharp bark and sniffed the damp sand behind the cypresses with an air of importance. The rain had already ruined Nathan's carefully constructed marshy landscape a bit, but it was obvious that a child had been playing there – and even more obvious that there was no child playing there now.

'He was here.' Charlie patted Brexit's wet head proudly.

'But he's not here any more.' A pale-faced Marshall stared down at the sandcastles, already eroded by the rain. Soon they would all disappear, just like his grandson.

'Hettie's gone too!' Edwina added for the sake of completeness and wiped cobwebs from her face. 'She's nowhere to be seen. Not in any of her places. Hettie's got *places*, you know? Especially when it's raining.'

'My grandson has disappeared, and you're looking for the stupid tortoise?' Marshall snapped at her.

Edwina wouldn't be swayed. 'Hettie is not stupid. Quite the opposite. Maybe . . . maybe the two are connected . . . Maybe they've both been *kidnapped*!' She frowned and ran her fingers through her short hair, deep in thought. Damp leaves flapped to the ground. 'If Hettie's with Nathan, it's not that bad. She can keep an eye him!'

She smiled, spotted the snail on her shoulder and went to find a good place for it, somewhere it couldn't cause too much damage with its snail appetite.

'No offence, Edwina,' Bernadette murmured. 'But nobody kidnaps a damn . . .' She fell silent. 'Quiet! Be quiet! Everyone! There's something there!'

Agnes stood in front of the mirror checking her lipstick. She wanted to look presentable when she was arrested, maybe for the last time in her life. As far as she knew, make-up wasn't exactly a priority in prison, but that didn't mean she couldn't arrive in style.

The open wardrobe caught her eye, in particular her raven-black funeral hat.

Should she . . . ? Why not!

It might not be a funeral, but somehow it wasn't dissimilar. A farewell. Forever.

She took the hat out of the wardrobe, turned it to and fro, and looked at the black feathers glistening. That heartened her. She felt ready. Now she just had to wait.

Agnes sighed, sat at the window again and reached for another chocolate liqueur.

It took a moment for the others to finally keep quiet and listen. Then they heard it too: crunching.

Crunching gravel.

They rushed towards the sound and even from a distance, recognised Hettie the tortoise as she came crawling along the garden path with an air of indignation.

Hettie – but not just Hettie.

Something about her silhouette wasn't quite right. Someone had stuck something to her shell.

A thing.

Agnes limped up and down her room like a geriatric tiger, slightly tipsy on chocolate liqueurs and far too worked up to stay still.

She had seen everything. She had seen *far too much*, and finally she knew who the killer was. Not her!

Not Alice!

No, the true murderess was a great deal more unlikely than she could ever have imagined. It was about time she was stopped in her tracks. She had to get out of there as quickly as possible.

In frustration, Agnes kicked over the footstool she had been sitting on, and for the hundredth time she cursed the stupid idea to just throw the key into the garden.

'Glued!' Edwina repeated for the fourth time and held a defaced Hettie up to anyone who would look. 'Glued! To Hettie! Hettie's not an object.'

Nobody had ever seen her so furious. No wonder. Someone had stuck the transformer to the tortoise's shell, and it didn't suit her one bit.

An icy silence had spread through the other residents of Sunset Hall.

Now it was clear. Nathan wasn't just gone, run off, lost somewhere – he had been kidnapped. Kidnapped . . . or worse.

Whoever had stuck the transformer to the tortoise was taunting them. It was a cold, cruel joke. It was unpleasantly reminiscent of a certain gun that had been put on their dining table not so long ago.

They thought about Mildred who had been shot on her own terrace not far from there, and they thought about the pictures of dead Olive on Sparrow's phone.

They didn't want to think any further than that.

'That's it!' Marshall whispered in a voice that wasn't actually a proper voice any more, but more like the sound of cold air striking a shattered stone. 'Enough. We're going to the police. We're going to the police *right now*!'

With that, he stormed off towards the garden gate. The others followed him as quickly as they could. Charlie tried to call a taxi on her mobile as she went.

Only Edwina, Hettie and the transformer remained on the gravel path. That was a shame, since she would have had a few things to say to the others, not least that going to the police was exactly what the murderer expected of them. Maybe he was trying to lure them away.

Tricks like that might work with Charlie and Marshall, but not with Edwina! She lifted Hettie to eye-level and looked at her briefly but decisively.

'Just us two, then!' she declared to the tortoise. 'Typical! You have to do everything yourself.'

Then she wedged Hettie under her arm and marched out of the garden gate, to stop the unscrupulous tortoise-gluer out there in their tracks.

Agnes watched from the window as her housemates disappeared out of the garden one after the other. She had shouted, screamed and waved her crocheted tablecloth back and forth in the window, but nothing had helped. They were all too far away and too busy with Hettie and the transformer to notice her. She was at her wit's end. She was going cold, then hot, then cold again, and that had absolutely nothing to do with all the chocolate liqueurs she had consumed.

They were going in the wrong direction. It was enough to send her bonkers!

She was just weighing up her chances of managing to climb out of the window down into the garden in one piece – bad, really bad – when the crow hat waiting on her bed caught her eye.

It wasn't her. Now it could carry on waiting!

Then again . . .

A hat like that was made of fabric and thread, feathers and . . . wire!

Wire!

Agnes stepped closer to the bed to give the hat a thorough inspection.

A short while later, the hat looked like a sad, plucked crow and Agnes had a piece of wire in her hand. You didn't need more than one piece of wire to pick an old-fashioned lock like the one on her door, did you? There couldn't be much to it. Edwina could do it in her sleep and probably Bernadette, who had apparently spent part of her career on the wrong side of the law. Agnes, on the other hand, had paid far too little attention to the criminal elements in her vicinity during her time in the police. She should have learnt from them, instead of just locking them up!

But this should do the trick. She turned the stool the right way up again, pulled it in front of the door and started poking around with the wire in the keyhole. She was poking for quite some time, systematically at first, then frantically, then with rage. How hard could it be to pick this bloody . . . ?

Now and then she cast a worried glance towards the garden gate. Time was of the essence. How long would it take for her housemates to get into the village? The walk to school was about thirty minutes, if you had long pigtails and were good on your feet. At least forty-five minutes for a man of advanced years like Marshall, not to mention the others. Unless the bus came – but the bus never came when you needed it. Agnes wasn't very worried on that score.

She absolutely had to get out before the police arrived. The police would not believe her. The police would just make everything even worse!

Eventually Agnes gave up.

She let go of the wire and leant forwards, her forehead against the door.

That's it. Over and out. She really had tried everything, but . . .

Click.

Gentle as a thought, the door yielded under Agnes's forehead and swung open.

Agnes nearly fell off the stool, but then she was up on her feet.

Raincoat!

Good shoes!

Ready!

She would never know whether she had opened the door with her poking onslaught or whether perhaps it hadn't been locked properly anyway, but that didn't matter now. What mattered was the outcome.

Out the door and then . . .

Then she was standing in something soft, squidgy, red. Beans on toast. Yuck. Agnes screwed up her face and lifted her foot out of the tomato sauce. In doing so, she caught sight of the spoon and fork lying on the tray next to the plate. She grabbed both eating implements and shoved them in her skirt pockets, one left, one right.

She was hardly up straight, and she was already rushing to the stairlift and hurtling downstairs at high speed. She grabbed her walking stick and limped determinedly out the door, through the garden and on to a rendezvous with a murderess.

All that she left behind her was a tomato-red trail of footprints, that got lighter and lighter, and disappeared into nothingness somewhere on the bare swept planks of the veranda.

The lady was taking a strangely long time in the loo.

Nathan sat on the sofa swinging his legs, just a bit at first, then more and more wildly, until his heels were bouncing off the upholstery making a dull, satisfying sound. It was a bit naughty, and he was half hoping the lady would appear again and tell him off, just like Charlie or Agnes would have done.

But nobody came.

A little scared, he drank his juice. It was unusual for him to be left alone for so long. Normally adults didn't give him any peace. Out of sheer habit he considered secretly grabbing another piece of cake from the tray, but he decided against it. He had already eaten quite a lot of cake, and he felt a bit sick.

Maybe the lady had had a mishap on the loo. Old people were always having mishaps, and if his mother, Sabrina, was to be believed, lots of those accidents happened on the loo. That's why she didn't want Grandad to live in the house with all the other old fogies, but in a proper old people's home instead. But Nathan liked the house with the old fogies. They may not know anything about transformers, but other than that they were alright. In particular, Agnes, Charlie and Edwina were a lot of fun to be around. Not to mention Hettie. Hettie was almost kind of like a transformer herself, soft and armoured at the same time. Nathan realised he wanted to go back. To start with, this house had seemed like a cabinet of wonder to him, full of glittering and curious things, but now it seemed gloomy. Apart from that, Grandad would be worried. Grandad was always worried. That was kind of his job.

Nathan had a faint suspicion that it had been wrong to just go off to eat cake with a lady who was practically a stranger. Sweet, but wrong. Like an *aifair*.

He would look for the woman, help her off the loo, if necessary, then politely but firmly make his excuses and run home as fast as he could with all of the cake in his tummy.

It was a good plan, and he felt better straight away.

He quickly slid off the sofa and looked around for the door. But there wasn't a door, at least not at first glance. And there were no windows either. Nathan would have liked to look outside, to see if it was still light. To his mind, more time had passed than was good. Far too much time.

Maybe the lady was a ghost.

Maybe she was standing behind him now, half see-through and with a stony expression. That, as far as he knew, was what ghosts did. They stood behind people and sent shivers down their spines. He spun around, but there was nothing there apart from a floral armchair in the half-light. But he felt the shiver, a trickle down his spine like cold, cold water.

Then frantic, harried breathing. Only after a little while did he realise that it was his own breathing.

'Pull yourself together, Nathan,' he said out loud. His voice sounded small and squeaky, but he noticed his breathing calming down bit by bit. It was his mother's favourite game: pulling yourself together, and without trying, he'd picked something up from her. Nathan had a think. It was all nonsense. Ghosts didn't have to go to the loo. Apart from that, he didn't really believe in ghosts. In wizards and zombies, maybe, in transformers definitely, but ghosts . . . that was kids' stuff. The lady had to be somewhere.

He started to do a circuit of the room, always keeping one hand on the wallpapered, strangely cool wall. Once – then a second time.

Only the third time did he discover the door. It wasn't actually a proper door, but a hairline crack in the wall – but there was a little hidden keyhole. A secret door! And it was clearly locked. Normally he would have been delighted with the discovery of a secret door, but now he wondered how secret this door was exactly. What if it was *too* secret? What if only that one lady knew about it? Maybe the lady was forgetful, just like his grandad was forgetful sometimes? Maybe she had gone to the loo and just forgotten about him and the chocolate cake?

Maybe the door would never open again.

Nathan whimpered.

A transformer would know what to do. A transformer would transform into something practical, a digger maybe or a crane, and just bust down the door.

Nathan looked imploringly at the coffee table.

Only as it became clear to him that his transformer was missing too, did he really take fright.

360

The sun was already low in the sky, and the shadows between the trees were confusing Agnes. She couldn't properly judge the unevenness of the ground, roots and vines, and was stumbling far too often. But up to now her walking stick had prevented her from falling each time, and she finally spotted the big house at the edge of the clearing.

As she got closer, she saw a figure on the veranda. A figure in black, an open umbrella over her shoulder. She had her back to Agnes, but that didn't make a difference.

Agnes knew exactly who it was.

If she was honest, a part of her had known for quite some time. The evil twin. Her subconscious had been on the right track. Only it wasn't *her* twin . . .

She must have made a noise, because the figure on the veranda suddenly turned towards her and smiled at her. It was a real smile, and Agnes's heart skipped a beat, out of wistfulness, but also hope.

'Hello, Agnes.' the figure said. 'Finally! I've been waiting for some time.'

Agnes took a deep breath and carefully climbed up the steps onto the veranda.

'Hello, Mildred,' she whispered.

22

SCONES

Agnes had been doing more at her window than just scoffing chocolate liqueurs. She had watched as her housemates had searched the garden, discovered Nathan's sodden marshy landscape and later found Hettie and the transformer.

But from high up at her window she had seen more than the others. Much more.

Even though reading and knitting only worked with the help of glasses now, her long-distance vision was still top notch and so she had seen Isobel Puck, umbrella over her shoulder, as she stood smiling at the garden gate for a moment, then crossed the road and nimble-footedly disappeared between the trees.

Isobel Puck.

But she wasn't limping at all!

Agnes had slowly unwrapped a new chocolate liqueur from the gold foil, put it in her mouth and let it gradually melt on her tongue. Could Isobel suddenly be cured? Unlikely. Had she been putting on the limp from the start? That didn't make any sense . . .

But putting on a limp made a whole lot of sense, if you weren't Isobel at all!

And suddenly she understood . . . understood practically everything. With such certainty that she didn't know how she ever could have taken so many wrong turns.

Who had so much money that it would make a blackmail attempt worthwhile for someone like Olive?

Who went around in a big black limousine just like Olive's paranoid neighbour had photographed on the road on the day of the murder?

Who only needed to stroll across the road to put a gun on their table?

Who had turned up at Lime Tree Court just before Theresa had been found strangled there?

Isobel!

Isobel! Isobel! And once again, Isobel!

And yet Agnes hadn't been even slightly suspicious. For a start, because Isobel was so bad on her feet. Someone who had to prop themselves up on their chauffeur on the way from the car to the house, didn't normally run around the countryside murdering people. Apart from that, she had *known* Isobel, deep down inside, for a lifetime. She had always known that fundamentally Isobel was a gentle soul, who wouldn't hurt a fly.

Mildred, on the other hand . . .

The outside and the inside. You could hardly tell the two sisters apart from the outside. On the inside however – fundamentally different. Mildred was not gentle. Never had been. She was harsh, biting and restless and, lately, bitter too –

exactly the sort of person who you would think capable of a murder or two! Agnes had concocted the craziest theories lately and suspected almost everyone: Olive, Theresa, Rosie, herself, her long-dead sister, Alice, and even Marshall for a while. The only thing she had never questioned was Mildred's murder itself. Because it was so likely. Mildred had been a real pain lately. In the course of her life, she had trodden on the toes of countless people. Mildred being a murder victim was logical! Only one thing was more logical . . . Mildred being a murderer!

Agnes couldn't make out how it had happened, but at some point, the two twins must have switched places again. In any case, the person standing under an umbrella in front of her now was not Isobel.

Mildred was still smiling.

'You look pale,' she said, then folded up the umbrella and leant it against the wall of the house.

'I didn't sleep very well,' Agnes mumbled noncommittally. Mildred could be moody. A lot depended on her setting the right tone now. But which tone was the right one exactly?

'Tea?' Mildred asked. '"A nice cup of tea, and everything will be alright," Isobel liked to say. Isn't always true, of course. Realised that herself in the end. But maybe it's true today.'

Agnes nodded. Mildred liked to talk. Much more than Isobel did. She should have noticed much sooner how talkative the surviving twin was. She decided to give Mildred ample opportunity to talk.

'Why the umbrella?' she asked. She really wanted to know.

'The umbrella really did send poor Marshall round the bend.'

Mildred shrugged her shoulders. 'You don't get wet. And you don't get any colour when you run around outside instead of lying indoors in bed like a vegetable. And if you use it skilfully, nobody sees you properly. Everyone just sees the umbrella.'

'And you used it skilfully,' Agnes ungrudgingly admitted. 'So, the whole time you were . . . I mean, were you never really a . . . vegetable?'

Mildred laughed bitterly. 'Oh, I was. And what a vegetable. The houseplants could move better than me. I watched them. All day. Their teeny tiny plant movements. How they stretch and strain and turn towards the light. Didn't have anything else to do. I'd have liked to have turned towards the light too, you know? Couldn't though. Couldn't do a thing. Swallowing and blinking. That was it. You don't get far with swallowing and blinking.'

'Oh,' Agnes said, taken aback. She hadn't known it had been so bad. Would it have made a difference if she'd known? Would she have popped by to watch her old friend Mildred blinking? She didn't know.

Mildred sighed. 'It wouldn't have happened over at yours, would it? You deal with problems like that *differently*. Don't look so shocked, Agnes. I know it's a big secret, but quite honestly, if you spend enough time watching people, and then put two and two together . . . I had enough time, believe me. Far too much time. What I wouldn't have given for someone to have put me out of my misery with a gun and given me a decent end! On the other hand, the two of us couldn't have tea together now, could we? That would have been a shame.

Come inside, Agnes. I've got scones. And there must be a bit of chocolate cake left too. With raspberries!'

Agnes didn't particularly want to eat cake, raspberries or anything else with Mildred, but she had to find out what had happened to the Grandson, and for that she had to humour Mildred for as long as possible.

Apart from that . . . she was actually curious.

Mildred noticed her hesitancy and laughed softly. She was in such a good mood. How on earth could someone with such terrible things on their conscience be in such a good mood? Then Agnes remembered that she too had something terrible on her conscience, and for an unsettling moment, she just felt sorry for Mildred.

'Don't look so worried now, Agnes. I've never used poison. Nor had Isobel. We had nothing to do with Uncle Norman's death. Cross my heart. Come on now!'

With that she disappeared nimbly and soundlessly into the house like a shadow. She left the umbrella folded up on the veranda, a bit like a snake leaves its skin behind every once in a while. Agnes could only hope that something soft, vulnerable, human emerged from beneath it.

She leant her walking stick against the wall in such a way that it stood peacefully side by side with Isobel's umbrella. In the best case, it was a kind of sign that all wasn't lost, that they could still talk to one another – in the worst case, somebody would hopefully notice the walking stick at some point and know where Agnes had got to.

She looked wistfully towards Sunset Hall one last time, into the glorious sundown, then took a deep breath and hobbled after Mildred, away from the sun, into a shadowy realm heavy with velvet cushions and memories.

Back in the secret service, Edwina had benefitted from quite comprehensive training, and a surprising amount of it still came in handy on a daily basis. For example, surveillance techniques, thanks to which you could establish where Agnes was hiding the real biscuits. Or kung fu moves that you could use to kick the dust out of rugs.

Or . . . tracking.

Today in particular, tracking seemed like an eminently useful skill.

On the other side of the garden gate, she put Hettie down on the grassy verge and gave her strict instructions not to run off or hinder the investigation. Then she got to work on the muddy country lane. Obviously, there was a big muddle of different footprints and wheelchair tracks right in front of the gate. But whilst most of the tracks turned relatively quickly towards Duck End – Charlie's, Winston's and Marshall's – there had to be one or two footprints marching to a different tune. After all, Hettie complete with transformer hadn't floated back to Duck End. Someone had *planted* her there.

What Edwina was looking for were footprints leading away from the house. Guilty, stealthy tracks that didn't just follow the road. Footprints making a secret getaway.

It took a while, but eventually Edwina spotted two promising candidates: one right and one left shoe print that didn't seem to fit in anywhere properly. Small, pointy footprints with distinct rectangular heel prints. These footprints were older than her housemates' and were lost at points in the general hodgepodge. But Edwina was not deterred, and at some point, the suspicious footprints really did break away from all the others, step by step.

They left the road and disappeared up the verge. Damn. It hadn't rained properly for quite a while and unlike the road, the verge wasn't wet. The footprints disappeared, as if their owner had vanished into thin air. Edwina went down on all fours and patted the ground in the hope of discovering a small hole made by a heel somewhere.

Then she saw it, a broken branch at about hip level.

Edwina scrabbled over and dived into the bush. Sure enough, a short, square heel had gouged into the ground there. And then a second. A third . . .

Edwina rushed back to where Hettie had just heartily munched down an undersized dandelion, grabbed the tortoise and plunged into the undergrowth.

She was onto something.

The hunt was on!

'Another scone?'

Agnes nodded sheepishly. She had sat down with Mildred in the drawing room and had developed a surprisingly healthy appetite. And obviously it was sensible to mix the chocolate liqueurs with something a little less alcoholic, wasn't it? After all, she had quite a lot on today. Rescue grandson. Take out a murderer. Somehow get back to Sunset Hall in one piece. She would be needing a calorie or two for that.

A record was turning on an old-fashioned record player.

Mozart's clarinet concerto, if Agnes wasn't mistaken. Round and round. Tea was steaming. Blackberry jam was glistening darkly in a little bowl, golden scones bulged, cream billowed in a dish like a big cloud, and soft butter shimmered like satin. Mildred was an attentive hostess. Agnes could almost have believed she wasn't sitting with a triple murderer and grandson kidnapper, but just an old friend.

However, she was still keeping an eye out for possible allies. Where were all the servants that usually wandered around the house like ghosts? Maybe one of them had seen Nathan?

Mildred noticed her furtive glance and smiled indulgently as she put another half-warm, deliciously crumbly scone on her plate. 'Don't worry,' she said. 'I gave them all the day off.'

'Ah,' Agnes murmured cutting her scone in half with the butter knife. How much damage could you inflict with a butter knife like that? For a moment she was tempted to find out.

But no, Mildred was nimble and far too smart to allow herself to be caught off guard like that. If Agnes lost her nerve now, she would never find out what had happened to Nathan.

She had to play the game.

Mildred's game.

A game of words and memories.

Agnes buttered her scone and spread the jam.

'How on earth did you do it?' she asked jovially. 'The stroke was real, wasn't it? How did you stop being a vegetable?'

'I don't really know properly myself,' Mildred said and

stirred her tea earnestly. 'It was like . . . When you're trapped, in a small, small space . . . To begin with you can't believe it. To begin with you rattle at the door like mad the whole time. I tried and tried and tried. To say something. To move my hand. To nod. To stand up. It was all a waste of time. After a while you give up. Let yourself drift. Let yourself go. Forget that anything like a door even exists. And then, at some point, you touch the doorknob again. And the door swings open . . .'

Agnes, who had only recently experienced something similar herself, smiled sympathetically. Mildred smiled back. 'I can't explain it any other way. I couldn't do *anything*, and then, suddenly, I could. Obviously took a while for my muscles to play ball again, but basically . . .'

Mildred sipped her tea animatedly. 'I've tried to do a bit of research since. Obviously discreetly. A second stroke perhaps. A stroke that reversed the symptoms of the first. But I can hardly ask a doctor about it.'

Agnes nodded and bit into her third scone. She had heard a similar story on the radio. About someone who couldn't speak because of a stroke and then, after a second stroke, suddenly started merrily chatting away and had scared his poor wife half to death. Only Mildred hadn't just scared Isobel, she'd shot her in an especially cruel way.

Agnes realised she was frowning and quickly attempted a more neutral expression. Too late.

'Don't look so critical, Agnes!' Mildred hissed. 'That's the honest truth. Do you think I would have *pretended* to be a vegetable for years? I'm not mad!'

'Of course not,' Agnes said a bit too quickly. 'But, why the secrecy? Why . . . why didn't you just tell Isobel?'

'Yes, that's the crux of it, isn't it? I was lying in bed wriggling my toes, mad with joy. I imagined surprising Isobel. And then I really *imagined* it. And do you know what I saw?'

Agnes shook her head, although she kind of already knew.

Edwina wasn't out of the woods yet – literally, but also figuratively.

She had lost the thread, the tracks, the scent, and even Hettie was stumped. Not that there was a lack of footprints – quite the opposite, there were far too many of them, footprints everywhere. A whole host of footprints, all left behind by the same pointy shoes with square heels, some newer, some older, some half faded so that you could only make out the heel holes. The shoe owner must have been running about all over the woods, back and forth, up and down, for months.

Like a caged tiger.

Edwina sighed.

Whoever had left these tracks behind, was light, nimble and good on their feet. And not just good on their feet, but on their feet *a lot*. He – or probably she – could have come from anywhere.

Edwina was at her wit's end.

So that she could think more clearly, she put Hettie down on the ground for a while, but nothing came to her. She was used to that. Thoughts seldom came to you when you needed them. Sometimes they didn't come at all. She decided to pass the time with a little game.

'I spy with my little eye,' she said. 'Something that is green!'

Hettie bit into a cloverleaf, bored.

'Wrong!' Edwina cried and clapped her hands together in delight.

There in the woods, lots of things were green, and Hettie would never ever guess the right answer.

'Disappointment!' Mildred hissed. '*That*'s what I saw! Oh, Isobel would obviously have quickly got a hold of herself and feigned joy, but initially she would have been disappointed. She's blossomed since I've been a vegetable, that's the truth. *Blossomed!* A lifetime in this bloody house, just to not leave her in the lurch, and then . . . *she blossoms!*

A tear made its way across Mildred's papery cheek and disappeared into the furrow next to her mouth. Against all reason, Agnes felt sorry for her.

'And . . . I couldn't bear it, seeing that disappointment. Better . . . better I carry on playing the vegetable. I only stood up when I was on my own. And I was on my own often enough.'

She laughed an unpleasant laugh.

'It was so wonderful to *walk*. To walk through the woods. The light. The ground beneath my feet. The air. The smell. An absolute miracle. To begin with I was quite content with just secretly walking through the woods.'

'But not for long,' said Agnes.

'I was a bit lonely, I guess,' Mildred admitted. 'So, I started watching Sunset Hall. Watching *all of you*. I know you all quite well by now, you know? Better than you know yourselves, probably. It's a wonderful project, Agnes, honestly.

'When I heard the gunshot, I suddenly understood just *how* wonderful it is. And then Marshall came out of the shed with the gun in his hand and this weird look on his face, as if he wasn't really there at all, and I thought to myself, I'll take a little risk, and I crossed the road towards him. Of course, I made sure he didn't see my face under the umbrella, but he didn't react very much. He just dropped the gun and went back into the house. And I picked it up. It felt warm, like something alive, and at that moment I knew what I wanted: Sunset Hall! The . . . companionship – and the certainty that I'd never end up a vegetable again.'

'Ah,' said Agnes. So, this was the way the wind blew. Three murders and a grandson kidnapping weren't exactly character references, but at least she knew what Mildred wanted now. Despite that, the whole mystery still hadn't been solved.

'But . . . Isobel?' Agnes whispered. 'That's what I don't understand. Why Isobel? I mean, she was your . . . you were so . . . *close*.'

Mildred dabbed scone crumbs from her plate and licked her finger with a pointy, rosy tongue in a not very ladylike way.

'Nice house isn't it?' she mumbled. 'You could put up with it here, you might think. Not me. I've wanted to get away from here for as long as I can remember. Tried to run away. Didn't work, as you know. I could barely wait for my twenty-first birthday. Then I would have had my own money. Bought a ticket to France. Paris! The world! The whole grand adventure!'

Mildred smiled, both longingly and furiously.

'Completely . . . on your own?' Agnes asked a bit offended. They had been friends back then, best friends, but she was hearing about Paris for the first time.

Mildred shrugged her shoulders. 'I wanted to be myself, I guess. Not always just a twin, one of a pair. Myself!'

Agnes realised she was still sitting there with some scone in her mouth and had forgotten to chew. She swallowed. With a furious clatter Mildred put her cup back on the table.

'And then the stupid saga with Uncle Norman happened.'

Agnes jumped, and Mildred shook her head impatiently.

'No, don't worry. We didn't poison him. Why would we have done that? For money, like people thought back then? *Money*? Please. The old fox was actually quite alright.'

'But . . .'

'No buts, Agnes! The cook claimed to have seen one of us in the kitchen. That was all it took, you know. She wasn't quite right in the head, the old cow. She probably did it herself, by mistake, or out of spite. But one word from her was enough. The case was never solved, but everyone thought it was us, at least one of us, and we were stuck, not just in the village, no, here in the house. Isobel had had enough of the world. She was so *disappointed*. She only felt safe here in the house. With me. Nowhere else. And obviously nobody wanted anything to do with us anyway. Everyone ran away. *You* ran away.'

Mildred's scrawny finger pointed accusatorily at Agnes.

'I . . .'

Agnes suddenly had an unpleasant, empty feeling in the pit of her stomach. Mildred was right. She had run away, to start with the police and hunt monsters.

'Only *I* couldn't run away. I couldn't leave Isobel in the lurch after the whole sad story. Of course not! She was my sister. I loved her!'

Mildred spat the word out like a piece of rotten fruit. With the last sentence, Agnes sensed a change in her hostess. The friendly chatty Mildred had disappeared. Instead, Agnes now had the feeling she was sitting opposite an angry spider, in the middle of her web, full of venom and bad feeling. And she suddenly felt like a fly.

Now she had to tread carefully. Mildred had always been prone to abrupt mood swings, and if Agnes didn't manage to quickly change the topic, she would soon sink into angry silence. Agnes couldn't afford for that to happen. Somehow, she had to get the truth about Nathan out of her.

She forced a smile and cautiously sipped her tea. 'Olive.' she said quietly. 'What about Olive? At any rate, you set that up very cleverly, Mildred!'

'Wrong!' Edwina mumbled. 'Wrong. Wrong. And wrong again.'

Hettie had tried ferns, honeysuckle, blackberry leaves and quaking grass, but she hadn't come across the right answer, and since dusk was spreading through the woods, nothing was really green any more anyway, more blue and grey and black.

Edwina gave up. 'It's you, you silly fool!' she cried and picked Hettie up. 'You're not very good at solving puzzles, are you?'

Hettie looked acerbically from out of her shell and didn't say a word.

'Well, it wasn't very easy,' Edwina admitted. 'But you could have got it, if you'd tried harder!'

That was the thing with trying hard. Shouldn't she be trying hard too, to solve the puzzle, to remember something? To *find* something? It felt like it, but she couldn't for the life of her think what.

Well.

Maybe it was about time they went home.

'What was I supposed to do?' Mildred hissed. 'Olive had seen me.'

Agnes nodded. It was exactly as she'd thought. '*Saw her standing*. Strange way of putting it, I'd thought at first, but now I get it. She saw you standing up, didn't she? She knew you weren't a vegetable any more.'

Mildred made a dismissive hand gesture. Rings sparkled. 'Not long ago, she came round to ours collecting for the church. You know what she was like. Any excuse to nose about in other people's business. Isobel would never have even let her in, but Isobel wasn't there and that stupid cow of a maid . . . Olive obviously didn't stay in the drawing room, as is right and proper, but started to open doors and stick her nose in different places, and I had just stood up to treat myself to a sherry . . . Me in my weird nightdress. She knew what she had seen straight away, and disappeared like a rat. After Isobel's death she must have somehow put two and two together, in any case she wrote me this *ridiculous* blackmail letter. What a scream, Agnes. I would really like to show it to you, but obviously I burnt it.'

Agnes looked disappointed. The blackmail letter really would have been valuable evidence. 'I once threw a knife at her, you know?' she said. 'At Olive.'

Mildred sniggered appreciatively, and Agnes bit into her scone, emboldened.

'And the cream slices? Made here?' she asked with a mouth full. Her table manners were quickly going downhill.

Mildred shrugged her shoulders. 'Olive might have thought she was the baking queen of Duck End, but quite honestly, with professional staff . . . I just didn't want her to be found too quickly. I'm no expert, but the vaguer the better, I thought.'

Agnes, who had had similar thoughts not too long ago, nodded.

'So, I took one of her weird cheap little visiting cards off the fridge and then sent Fisher to the coffee morning with the card and the slices. Ridiculously easy. The police don't have the faintest idea! They think I'm just a little old lady with mobility problems that can't even handle her walking stick, let alone a gun. If someone had told me before that murder would be this easy!'

'Theresa.' Agnes said. 'That can't have been easy.'

Mildred's smile sparkled. 'Risky, but not difficult. I heard that she had regained consciousness, and, well, I thought, I'll pay her a visit. I was paying for her after all! Really, I only wanted to threaten her, you know, but then she was hardly responsive, and the nurse was called out of the room, and well, an opportunity like that wasn't going to come along again, I thought. It was quite quick, with my hands and a pillow. The old dear didn't feel a thing, believe me. And afterwards she looked just as peaceful as beforehand. Maybe even more peaceful. Who knows how long it actually took for someone to notice she was dead. Lime Tree Court obviously hushed it up. Lime Tree Court has a reputation to uphold!'

Agnes shuddered and realised that her appetite for scones had vanished. Behind Mildred's familiar face was a stranger, a cold, calculating, callous being. The inside and the outside. Agnes saw that the hand holding her butter knife had started to shake, and tried to pull herself together.

'You probably even did her a favour,' she said as lightly as she possibly could. 'This Lime Tree Court . . . I saw you there, you know? I thought you wanted to move in there. I wanted to *save* you.'

'No,' Mildred corrected her, abruptly putting her cup down. 'You wanted to save Isobel. That's not the same thing, you know?'

Agnes glanced at the window and realised that it had started to get dark already.

Hettie under her arm, Edwina padded through the woods towards Sunset Hall, strangely dissatisfied with herself and the world.

She had wanted something. Something important. It wasn't right to go home empty-handed. But what was she supposed to do when she just couldn't remember what her bloody mission was?

Maybe Lillith would know what to do.

Or Agnes.

Or . . . Hettie.

Edwina took the wriggling tortoise out from under her arm and looked at her critically, but Hettie didn't have anything sensible to say either. And why did she have that silly plastic figure on her . . . ?

And then, suddenly, Edwina knew what it was about again: a missing grandson, three people murdered and – worst of all – a defaced tortoise. And she, Edwina, had to drain this quagmire of crime, because everyone else had run in the wrong direction.

Only it was probably just the wrong moment for it because in front of her, just a few feet away, somebody was standing under a tree staring at her, their eyes glistening.

The record had reached the end and was just making clicking noises now. The situation in the drawing room had escalated drastically.

The tea table had been tipped over, scones were rolling across the floor, the blackberry jam was in the process of leaving behind a nasty stain on the luxurious silk rug (and it looked like it probably wouldn't just be the one stain).

Agnes's chair had fallen over. She was lying on her back, helpless as a tortoise and at least twice as bewildered.

Mildred was standing over her. She had smashed the teapot and was holding the handle with a dangerous-looking shard of porcelain in her hand.

They had just been talking. It had all gone so quickly. Like a bolt from the blue.

Agnes must have said something wrong, even if she didn't have the slightest idea what it had been.

'Mildred,' she croaked. 'I didn't mean it like that!'

Mildred looked down at her with a stony look in her eye. 'That's what Isobel said too. The silly cow! I *saw* what she meant!'

Agnes tried to feign interest. Mildred had flipped, but she was still talkative, and she, Agnes, was just about the only person she could speak to about the messed-up little world of her soul. Still.

'I understand.' Agnes groaned.

Mildred hesitated. 'You don't understand a thing. I didn't want to shoot her, you know? I wouldn't have imagined for a second . . . I only took the gun with me because I wanted to tell Isobel all about it. Sunset Hall. Your pact. What a fantastic thing it is! So that she would believe me. I was excited and had completely forgotten that she had no idea yet . . . that I wasn't a vegetable any more!'

Agnes nodded and stared up into Mildred's face, spellbound. Maybe it wasn't all over yet. Maybe she had a tiny chance.

'She was sitting on the terrace. Completely relaxed. Happy! In her pyjamas. With a latte. And when she saw me coming – you should have seen her, Agnes! She was *horrified*! She wasn't even *a tiny bit* happy!'

Agnes could well imagine how Mildred had burst out of the bushes all of a sudden with a fierce expression on her face, a gun and an umbrella. Like the living dead. Like a ghost. No wonder Isobel was shocked!

'So you shot her,' she said drily.

Mildred shrugged her shoulders. 'Had to be done. Then I went upstairs and got in her bed. And slept until that stupid goose of a maid started screeching.'

She smiled smugly, and suddenly Agnes remembered again who, a long time ago, used to squash innocent firebugs, with the same blasé expression on her face.

Mildred.

Because it was easy.

Just as easy as firing a bullet into Isobel's stomach and then getting into bed. Just as easy as shooting Olive in the face. Just as easy as smothering a sedated Theresa in her bed.

Just as easy as it would be to slit Agnes's throat with the remains of the teapot as she lay on the floor.

Then again . . .

Maybe that last one wouldn't be as easy as it seemed.

Agnes felt around in her skirt pockets, got hold of the fork and immediately felt a bit better. If Mildred really wanted to get to her throat, she would have to come quite close to her, and Agnes would do her best to not be done away with just like that.

She was no firebug after all!

She tried to ignore Mildred's raving babble and come up with a plan instead. She would wait until Mildred was really close and then stab her with the fork anywhere it would hurt. That was the easy bit.

After that she had to get out of there as quickly as possible. Only, how quickly was actually possible? Not particularly quickly, unfortunately. Agnes was under no illusions, under these circumstances she would never ever manage to get back on her feet. And even if she succeeded, she didn't have the slightest chance of giving Mildred the slip, even if she did have a fork stuck in her.

But maybe she could turn over and crawl away while Mildred was distracted? It couldn't be far. She'd only manage a short distance – if at all. But maybe there was a hiding place somewhere?

She cautiously peered in all directions, while Mildred was lost in her tirade. Twinness. Paris. Isobel's unnerving weakness for ABBA.

Agnes tried to concentrate. The sofa – useless. The window – too high. The door – too far away. But there was another, second door, right behind her, smaller, more discreet, ajar. If she could somehow manage to crawl through there, get herself upright, maybe even barricade the door shut behind her . . .

A sudden silence lay over her like a blanket. Initially she was inclined to blame the high-pitched ringing, but no. Above her, Mildred had stopped babbling and was staring fixedly at her with a cold, glazed expression.

'You're not listening to me!' she screeched. 'You're not even listening to me! Just like Isobel!'

Agnes clutched her fork and knew her life hung in the balance. All that Mildred had wanted from her was an ear, the opportunity for somewhere to finally pour out all the absurd thoughts that had been running through her head for months, and if Agnes wasn't any use for that any more . . .

The attack came suddenly like that of a snake, a shimmer of sharp white porcelain, flying towards Agnes's face, but

Mildred didn't follow through, instead she jumped back with a shrill scream, because suddenly there was a fork stuck in her foot, so deeply you couldn't see the prongs any more.

Then, somehow, Agnes was on all fours, crawling.

23

SPOON

The glistening eyes stared fixedly over at Edwina, and she hid the hand holding Hettie protectively behind her back and went into a sort of crouched attack position. Without thinking, pure reflex.

Years of training.

Then movement behind the glistening eyes.

Back and forth.

A . . . *wagging*?

A long tongue appeared, rosy even in the twilight.

Edwina relaxed. 'Brexit!'

Charlie was right, Brexit came – whether you were ready or not! He'd probably got bored in the garden after everyone else had disappeared. He had followed their scent and found them. Edwina patted his shaggy grey head and Brexit benevolently licked her fingers, Hettie's shell and the transformer.

Brexit.

Scent.

Transformer.

That was it!

Brexit had found her in the middle of the woods, just like that, almost incidentally. Whilst she had painstakingly learnt tracking during her secret service training, Brexit was practically a living and breathing tracking machine. A nose on four paws. Born to sniff things out!

With a serious look on her face, Edwina stood up in front of the wolfhound and let him sniff the transformer.

'We have to find Nathan,' she explained to him. 'Get Nathan!'

Brexit started wagging his tail again. His moist, black nose delicately investigated the transformer, then it was suddenly on its way along the forest floor. Brexit sniffed intently through the foliage. Up and down. Up and . . .

And then he was gone, his nose constantly to the ground. Hopefully it was Nathan he was following, and not the first available rabbit. Edwina clamped Hettie firmly under her arm and ran after him as quickly as she could.

Somehow, Agnes had made it through the little door and turned the key. Now she was sitting with her back to the wall breathing heavily in the dark. Her heart was beating like mad.

Mildred was clamouring at the door.

'I really gave you every opportunity, Agnes!' she shrieked. 'Scones! Tea! Intelligent conversation! All I wanted was a bit of company, but no, not from you . . .'

Agnes wondered how much of the rabid creature out there was really still Mildred. Had she always been a bit like that?

Damaged? Out of kilter? Had all that time as an invalid sent her mad? Or had the strokes affected her brain in some way? She would have liked to believe that the monster wasn't her old friend any more, but someone else. A stranger.

But she needed to face facts. And the facts were . . . unpleasant.

'And how do you thank me for it?' Mildred raged at the door. 'With a fork! That's low. I wouldn't have thought you capable. Not even you! You snake!'

Something hard banged against the door, probably a piece of teapot, then Agnes heard a furious scream. Maybe Mildred had cut herself.

Served her right!

Agnes took a deep breath. She had been sitting on her backside for long enough. As soon as her breathing had settled down a bit, she got back on all fours to investigate the extent of her hiding place.

There wasn't much to investigate.

She quickly came up against a bare wall, then a second, then something cool and furry. She almost screamed. A dead animal! But straight away, her trembling fingers came across a straight edge, a seam, something silky. Suddenly Agnes knew exactly where she was. In the cloakroom! It wasn't good news. She had hoped to have ended up in a different room, a room with windows and doors, through which she could have slipped away, whilst Mildred let out her rage on the door. The cloakroom, however, was barely more than a walled cupboard.

Agnes was trapped. There was nothing she could do but lean her head on the old fur coat in the glorified wardrobe and listen to Mildred's tirade.

'I would have moved in with you all! I would have treated you all like friends! I would even have given the brat back! That's why you're here, isn't it, Agnes? You were never really interested in me.'

Agnes moaned in exhaustion. Mission Grandson was going really badly. She should have done things differently, waited for the others or at least left a note behind, instead of just going off on her own like that . . . What had gotten into her?

Strange really, she had started the day behind a locked door and was on the verge of ending it behind a locked door too. The day – and probably her life too. Locked up. Alone with herself. Alone in the dark. That was exactly what her house project was supposed to prevent: a lonely death somewhere behind closed doors, sealed off from humanity. And now this!

Suddenly it was as if Agnes had understood something important, important in life – whatever there may be left of it – but also important for her situation in the cloakroom. Essentially, it was about putting up with yourself, in a confined space, even when everything else had slipped away: family and friends, health, mobility, memory and sense. And that was exactly what was so severely lacking with Mildred. She was trapped, inside herself, just as trapped as Agnes was in the cupboard, on her own, spoon in hand.

Agnes realised she really was holding a spoon in her hand. Her last weapon! Her last chance! She could just sit around and wait for something sufficiently nasty to occur to Mildred out there, or she could stand up, open this door and try to somehow spoon her into submission.

No question.

She grabbed the fur coat and heaved herself up. Luckily it was tight quarters, so she couldn't really fall over. After a few clumsy tries, she was back up on two feet, in pain and a bit unsteady, but determined.

She approached the door and put her hand on the key.

'Hey, Mildred!' she shouted. 'We have to put up with ourselves, you know? Not with one another, I mean, but with our own selves, do you know what I mean? If you can't put up with yourself, you can kill as many people as you like and it won't help one bit.' It was a serious piece of advice, and Agnes listened expectantly for a response, but none came. Had Mildred heard her? Was she even still there? Or was the silence just a trick to lure her out of the cloakroom?

Agnes would have liked to spy through the keyhole, but her back wouldn't allow such a low bend.

'I'm coming out now, Mildred,' she shouted, and was annoyed that her voice sounded so thin and cracked, 'and then you have the chance *not* to kill me. That would be a good start! Trust me, it's basically your only chance!'

Nothing. Silence.

And then a kind of a crackle.

Agnes sighed. She hadn't seriously expected Mildred to understand her cloakroom epiphany, and so the only thing left was the spoon.

She resolutely clutched the eating implement in her right hand, whilst she silently turned the key in the lock with her left, pushed the door open a crack and cautiously peered out.

She stared uncomprehendingly into the fog and listened to her heart make a few unsteady skips. She had by no means been expecting anything good out there, a teapot-wielding Mildred at least, or some other nastiness. But not this!

Snakes!

Snakes everywhere!

Snakes of smoke!

Agnes stepped out of the cloakroom in a panic. Acrid fumes immediately filled her lungs. She started to cough and looked around, her eyes streaming. What was going on? Where had all the smoke come from all of a sudden? And where was Mildred?

The next minute she saw blood at her feet. Not terribly much, just a drop here and there, but continuous. From the fork presumably. Agnes felt a certain sense of satisfaction that her aim had been so good.

The drips led out of the drawing room over to the library. Spoon in hand, Agnes limped after them. She couldn't afford to not know where Mildred was hiding. Not in the least.

In the library all hell had broken loose. The huge rose-red Persian rug was in flames, as were the armchairs and sofas. The fire was climbing the shelves and ripping into the books, book by book by book. So much paper. It was only a matter of time before the whole house went up in flames! The light crackling from before had developed into a full-fledged roar.

Something crunched under Agnes's shoes, and she looked down.

Shards of glass. Broken bottles. A whole home bar of smashed spirits. This is where the fire had started. Mildred had soaked the rug in alcohol, and then . . .

'Mildred? Mil . . . ?' Agnes's voice was lost in a coughing

fit. No matter where Mildred was hiding, there was no getting through now anyway. Agnes took a step back because the heat almost bit her face off, turned around and stumbled back into the smoke-filled drawing room. There was another door somewhere close by, wasn't there? One leading to the gruesome hunting room with the many animal heads, which in turn led to the entrance hall. But where? Agnes made herself take a few shallow, but controlled breaths. She had known this house since her childhood, knew it like the back of her hand – but it was a hand that had changed a lot over the years. She thought about the speed at which the flames had ripped into the books over in the library – this time her memory couldn't play any tricks on her. Not this time.

She shut her eyes for a moment to concentrate, until she could feel her pigtails again, left and right, heavy and disliked and dark-brown. She had spent the majority of her youth there, hadn't she, giggling, eating oranges, drinking tea. She didn't need to be able to see much to find her way. On the right-hand side was the coffee table, that she and Mildred had sat at a short while ago, behind it the display cabinet of porcelain, a few steps on – half-cloaked in smoke – the old grandfather clock.

And behind that – Agnes opened her eyes to narrow, streaming slits – the door leading to the hunting room. It used to always make her feel a bit uneasy, half out of sympathy for the dead animals, half out of fear of the many staring glass eyes. But now she stumbled in without thinking, gasping for air like someone drowning, happy to have escaped the acrid, black fumes in the drawing room. Smoke had already spread in the hunting room too, but there was much less, more like each of the dead deer and boar had secretly smoked one or two cigarettes. Agnes imagined the animal trophies relaxing with cigarettes and whisky in unobserved moments, making fun of their hunters. Then, shaken by a coughing fit, she had to stand still. What kind of nonsense was this? She had to get out of there, out of the house, instead of losing herself in daydreams! Without a second glance she stalked past the animals, out into the hall.

There was somebody standing there, surrounded by smoke, silent as a painting, waiting for her.

Brexit was sniffing like mad, and at some point, Edwina smelt it too.

You didn't have to be a sniffing genius to smell the smoke, which was billowing through the woods in grey, sinister plumes.

When they reached the clearing, they saw it.

Brexit stood still and put his tail between his legs. Edwina patted his shoulder reassuringly. Together they watched as white flames licked out of the windows of the big house leaving black sooty streaks on the façade.

The house gleamed in the twilight like a huge, ill-fated glow worm.

The blaze was fierce.

Brexit sniffed the air and suddenly made a sharp about turn, away from the house, back into the woods.

Edwina didn't blame him.

391

At first, Agnes thought it was Mildred lurking there in the hall, and raised her spoon threateningly, but the figure just shook its head and smiled.

Agnes saw that she was smaller than Mildred, as small as a child, with clear eyes and wild curls with blackberry leaves in her hair, and fingers red with blackberry juice.

Alice!

Agnes's heart leapt. She shyly raised her hand in greeting.

Alice waved back, and Agnes felt light-headed and dizzy.

Of course, she knew Alice wasn't real, at least not in the way the ground beneath her feet was real or the hunting trophies or the fire, but she felt a wave of tenderness towards her twin sister, who had returned from the shadowlands of her subconscious to help her, like she had helped her once before.

Alice smiled. Agnes saw a gap in her sister's teeth, that she had never noticed before, and realised she was smiling back with her false teeth.

Then, quick as a flash, Alice had already turned round and was motioning for Agnes to follow her. Agnes trustingly rushed after her. No doubt Alice wanted to save her, show her the way out. But after just a few moments she realised that couldn't be the case. Every step was leading farther away from the safety of the exit and instead, going deeper into the house.

In front of her, Alice had stopped smiling and looked worried now, her brow more furrowed than Agnes had ever seen it before. She kept stopping to spur Agnes on, but Agnes only progressed at the speed of a particularly lame snail.

From the hall into the reception room.

Into the dining room.

Smoke everywhere.

What was she doing there? Maybe Alice didn't want to help her? Could she really trust her imaginary twin?

In the dining room Agnes tripped on a chair that had emerged from the smoke too suddenly. Her eyes were still streaming like mad, and it was warm, far too warm. She could hear the roaring of the fire again, not close, but there.

A promise. A threat.

Soonyoullburntoo! Soonsoonsoon!

Suddenly she knew what Alice wanted of her: Nathan. He must be somewhere in the house – Mildred had as good as admitted it earlier. If Agnes didn't find him soon, it would forever be too late, for Nathan, but also for her, for Marshall, Edwina, Charlie, Winston, Bernadette, Brexit, Hettie and Sunset Hall. If the Grandson went up in smoke, they would never be able to live together again. She had to find him! But how? The house was huge, and she had at most a few minutes left to find him and get him to safety. If that . . .

Maybe it was already too late.

But a part of Agnes knew exactly where to find Nathan. The part that had never grown up, the part that remembered every game of hide-and-seek: Alice!

Suddenly Agnes understood what Alice was trying to tell her. The secret room! It was so obvious. Why hadn't it all occurred to her much earlier? Probably because Mildred had attacked her with a smashed teapot and she hadn't really had the time to think.

There was a long, narrow room between the wall of the dining room and that of the drawing room, a room without windows, where servants, unseen and unheard, used to wait for someone from the household to ring a bell. Then, nimble as little elves, they had appeared as if from nowhere, to clear away plates, refill wine glasses or serve dessert. The secret room had been Mildred's favourite hiding place. The other two girls had avoided it because inside the door handle had broken off. Since then, it had been more of a trap than a hiding place, if the door inadvertently closed, you were trapped until somebody found you. But that had never worried Mildred – she had just assumed she would be found.

Agnes looked around frantically. Where was the room again? Which wall was it behind? Where was the door? Back there? Her clumsy fingers rushed across the damask wallpaper. There had to be a little bump somewhere, carefully covered with green material, almost invisible.

Somewhere . . . There!

Agnes pulled the lever and a red-faced, tear-streaked Nathan tumbled towards her.

'Red sky at night, shepherd's delight!' mumbled Charlie, but she couldn't raise the spirits of the jam-packed taxi.

They had several frustrating hours at the police station behind them and were now on the way home, practically without having achieved a thing. Nobody had taken the matter of Nathan, Hettie and the transformer seriously – Charlie suspected they didn't even know what a transformer was!

'It's really not that unusual for children of that age to disappear for a few hours,' the short-haired policewoman had explained, 'we don't assume foul play straight away. Most of them turn up of their own accord.'

'Most of them? And the thing with the transformer?'

'A schoolboy prank.'

It had been impossible to make clear to the police that nobody in Sunset Hall would ever have allowed a practical joke involving Hettie. Especially not Nathan.

'Don't get so worked up! It's not good for your health.'

They had been advised to go home and make a nice cup of tea, perhaps take a sleeping tablet or even two, and then very carefully . . .

They would never find out what they were supposed to do very carefully because it was at that moment that Marshall had lost the plot, grabbed the first available police officer by the collar and shaken him whilst yelling, 'I am not senile! I am not imagining things! I want my grandson back this minute!'

In the ensuing little scuffle, the Sunset Hall crew hadn't done so badly, despite Edwina's absence – where even *was* Edwina? – but they were eventually thrown out by some out-of-breath police officers.

'That is no way to behave!' the short-haired police officer had explained to them at the door. 'I understand you're worried, but violence is not the answer either. We will keep our eyes open and if nothing has happened by this evening . . .'

This evening was too late! Lots would have happened by this evening, and nothing good! Charlie ruffled her hair on the back seat of the taxi, as well as she could with Bernadette to her left and Marshall to her right. After his fit of rage at the station, Marshall had fallen into a kind of reptilian trance and was staring fixedly straight ahead at the taxi driver's balding head, as if he could bore a hole in his head just by staring at it.

Bernadette sniffed. 'Smoke!' she said.

'That's not a red sky!' cried Winston, who from the passenger seat had the best view. 'It's fire. Something's burning somewhere!'

It was a day that was hard to top in terms of bad news.

'Bugger me!' the taxi driver shouted, not putting too fine a point on it.

'Sunset Hall!' Bernadette lamented. 'Sunset Hall's on fire!'

But as they got closer, it became clear the smoke and red glow was rising from the other side of the road.

'Bugger me!' the taxi driver shouted a second time looking sideways into the woods, where red embers were lighting up the trees like a rather kitsch shadow theatre. 'It's the big house! The big house . . .'

Just then, there was a dull thud, and something big crashed into the windscreen.

For a moment, nobody said a word.

'Edwina!' Winston cried in shock.

'Brexit!' Charlie screamed.

'Shit!' yelled the taxi driver.

Initially, Edwina had thought Brexit had just been running away from the fire, but after several painstaking sniff stops and a spooky howl it had become clear to her that that wasn't the case.

Brexit was *hunting*.

But what?

Or *whom*?

It wasn't easy for Edwina and Hettie to keep on Brexit's tail in the ever-darkening woods, and they only managed to keep catching up with the wolfhound thanks to the sniff stops. Edwina was panting like she hadn't panted for a long time, and Hettie was visibly green around the gills.

Even the transformer had a strange look on his face, as if he felt sick.

Then Brexit suddenly stood still, and Edwina almost ran into him. His black nose raised up from the ground and searchingly sucked in air.

A protracted, triumphant howl.

Then he tore off.

Edwina heard something breaking through the undergrowth in front of them. The final spurt! She pressed Hettie safely against her body and ran after him.

Then through the trees, light.

Headlights.

A car.

The road.

Edwina saw something dark stumble out of the woods into the road.

Dark and upright.

Not a deer.

Not a dog.

A *person*.

Then the figure disappeared from out of the headlights again, and Edwina heard a dull, unpleasant sound.

The car came to a stop, and Edwina stayed next to Brexit on the verge.

Brexit was wagging his tail.

Winston, Charlie and Marshall were staring at her out of the car, wide-eyed.

Edwina raised her hand and waved at her housemates.

Lying in the middle of the road was a lonely black pointy shoe, and on the other side of the headlight beam you could just about make out a small, dark bundle in the semi-darkness.

They called the fire brigade.

They called an ambulance for Isobel, who contrary to expectation was still breathing a bit after the collision with the taxi.

They made the shocked taxi driver a cup of tea, waited for the police, laid Hettie on her sleep stone and put a rather excited Brexit on his lead.

Then Marshall couldn't take it any more and made his way over to the big house, where the fire brigade was vainly fighting the fire with water cannons.

He had a bad feeling deep in the pit of his stomach. It couldn't be a coincidence that on the very same day his grandson had disappeared, the big house had gone up in flames. The two things were connected in an unpleasant way.

Marshall watched for a little while as, bit by bit, the burning house transformed into a smoking ruin. The fire brigade rolled up their hoses and cordoned off a large area around the sombrely smoking building, while Marshall stood silently on the edge of the woods and grew gradually, but utterly desperate.

It was a dingy night, not only because clouds of smoke

were still billowing through the woods, but also because forgetfulness had reached out its vague, greedy fingers towards Marshall again. This time he was alright with it. This time it was welcome. If anything had happened to Nathan, the forgetting couldn't come soon enough.

What was he doing here? Why was he so sad?

Marshall put his head back and looked through the fingers of the trees at the velvety night sky.

Moon and stars.

Beautiful really – but why did he have such a heavy heart?

Marshall sighed deeply.

When he looked down again, he saw two black figures appear between the trees.

One tall and thin, one short and fat.

Holding hands.

Wide-eyed.

Staggering.

Why was his heart leaping around in his chest like a spring lamb?

Why did he suddenly feel so light?

The taller of the two figures stumbled, stood still and leant on the nearest tree as if it were an old friend.

She spotted Marshall and triumphantly held up a spoon towards him.

24

ANGEL CAKE

'Green!' Edwina demanded.

'Purple!' Winston suggested.

'Blue!' said Agnes. It was Lillith's favourite colour, and it seemed to her, as if her old friend should have a say in the matter, dead or not. Once a member of Sunset Hall, always a member of Sunset Hall.

'So, traditionally, it's white and pink and yellow,' said Charlie.

Bernadette was staying out of it. At least someone was.

It was Nathan's last day with them and they had decided to bake him a farewell cake. His favourite cake.

An angel cake.

Marshall had found a recipe on the internet and ordered the necessary ingredients. Charlie had put on an apron and Edwina was armed with a wooden spoon. Eggs and flour were at the ready. But now they couldn't decide which colours from the food colouring set should be deployed.

'Green!' Edwina insisted. 'Greengreengreen!'

Charlie sighed and fished the green tube out of the packet.

'Blue!' Agnes repeated emphatically. Just because Edwina was screaming the loudest as usual, didn't mean she had to get her way by a long shot.

'Purple?' Winston asked, shyly.

In the end they decided for layers of green, blue *and* purple. The result looked different to any cake they had ever come across. Not particularly angelic, more like part rainbow and part zombie, but they thought Nathan would like it.

Marshall poked his head round the door.

'Ready?' he asked.

'Ready!' said Agnes.

The door opened and Nathan walked in. It was a different Nathan to the one who had arrived with them barely a week ago. Dark circles under his eyes. No mop of curly hair, a military buzz cut instead. No transformer. The transformer had not survived the separation from Hettie, executed with the help of solvent and sheer rage.

They had done their best to put Nathan back together after the kidnapping. Miraculously the Grandson had escaped from Mildred's inferno completely unharmed, and even Agnes had only burnt her hand because she hadn't let go of the burning hot spoon. They had both lost some body hair though. Eyelashes. Eyebrows. Hair.

Singed off.

That wasn't so bad for Agnes. She had started wearing one of Charlie's colourful silk scarves tied around her head and felt sophisticated. Her hair would grow back, white, wispy and useless as ever, and she hadn't had eyelashes and eyebrows to speak of for a long time anyway.

Things were different for the long-lashed, formerly mop-headed Nathan. He was due to be picked up that evening, and if Sabrina found out that they had let the Grandson be kidnapped and singed, maybe she wouldn't bring him again.

They had since all agreed that they wanted the Grandson to come again.

Now and then.

In moderation.

In the holidays.

So, Marshall had shaved his head and Charlie had drawn on some eyebrows with a pencil. If they were lucky and Sabrina was really preoccupied with her affair, they might just get away with it.

Now Nathan was standing in front of the cake wide-eyed, and the residents of Sunset Hall suddenly had the feeling they should sing something.

Agnes started with 'Happy Birthday . . .' but quickly felt silly. After all, it wasn't really Nathan's birthday, more like a 'survival day.'

Edwina fervently belted out 'Oh Christmas Tree!' Winston attempted the national anthem, Marshall hummed a military song, and Brexit howled. Bernadette covered her ears.

Then Winston passed Nathan the knife. 'Come on, boy,' he said. 'Cut the cake!'

'You can't just give the kid a sharp knife . . .' Marshall protested.

'Nonsense!' said Bernadette. 'You can never start too early when it comes to learning how to handle a knife like that.'

Nobody had anything to say to that.

So, Nathan clumsily, but happily, hacked a big piece off the cake. Then another. And another, until every member of Sunset Hall had angel cake on their plate, even Brexit.

'The last piece is for you too, Nathan, if you'd like,' Marshall said generously. The Grandson shook his head silently. Recently a chocolate and raspberry cake had got him into a whole lot of bother. Too many sweet treats were bad for your health – he had experienced that first-hand.

'One's enough,' he said quietly.

Charlie poured coffee and orange juice, Edwina distributed the cake forks, and then they all got stuck into the adventurously coloured, but delicious angel cake.

'Better than the coffee morning!' Charlie said cheerfully.

'Much better!' cried Edwina. 'Hettie thinks so too!'

The truth was that Hettie was dosing rather apathetically on her sleep stone. Come to think of it, she had been dosing quite a lot lately.

Bernadette was the first to finish her cake. 'What about the cream slices?' she asked. 'Who actually brought them?'

Agnes smiled. She had already told her housemates a few times, but it was probably her last case, so it couldn't hurt to drag the thing out a bit. And the story of the cream slices was a universal favourite, presumably because there was food involved.

'For Mildred, it was about Olive not being found too quickly. She wanted to cover her tracks. And she knew people would notice if Olive's bakes were missing from the coffee morning, so she just organised replacements. Olive was a good baker, sure, but Mildred had *staff*. The scones were a dream . . .' Agnes fell silent and thought back to the strange moment when she had sat in the house of memories with Mildred, somewhere between life and death, having tea and scones. Then she shrugged. 'Nobody noticed a thing. Nobody was really interested in Olive. It was all about her baking.'

She put a piece of angel cake in her mouth and chewed appreciatively with her trusty teeth. Her housemates sat in silence, deep in thought. Sad somehow, when the only thing that was missed about a person was a cake.

'It's a miracle that nobody got wise to her sooner.' Charlie finally said.

'No,' responded Marshall. 'The miracle is that Agnes rumbled her in time.' He stood up and held up his cup to her, as if he were proposing a toast. And then suddenly all the members of Sunset Hall stood up, even Bernadette, and raised their cups. To Agnes.

'Bravo!' said Charlie.

'Hear! Hear!' cried Winston.

'Hear! Hear!' the others joined in.

'Save the hungry animals!' Nathan added.

Her cheeks burning, her eyes downcast, Agnes sat there. She felt warm like she hadn't for a long time, a warmth that came from inside and bit by bit spread right to the tips of her singed hair.

She was herself again, and she was home.

Come to think of it, the night of the fire had been a night full of miracles.

The biggest miracle was that Agnes, Nathan and the spoon

had made it out of a fiercely blazing house unscathed. They had Alice to thank for that, she remembered, imaginary Alice, the chimera who, with a steady hand, had led her twin outside through the kitchen and then gone up in a puff of smoke forever.

The medium-sized miracle was that, for a change, the police didn't connect Agnes with the fire – presumably they didn't want to have the truculent members of Sunset Hall at the station again. So, back at home, they had been left undisturbed to wash their sooty faces, free Hettie from the transformer and make plenty of tea. The police proceeded on the assumption that the alleged Isobel had lost it following the death of her sister and set the house on fire – and for once, they weren't too far out.

And then there was a third little miracle that, unnoticed by the members of Sunset Hall, played out in the early hours on the local train platform. Normally, the first train to London met with an empty station, but that day, two passengers were sitting on a bench, not too close to one another, but not that far from one another either, a podgy middle-aged woman in mourning clothes and an ex-policeman with dark circles under his eyes.

The woman had broken a raft of rules at the B&B and been chucked out by the landlady (mainly for the loud TV and eating snacks in her room) and after this defeat had decided to let the death of her mother lie for now, to go home and look after her family again. After all, the police were there for solving murders, and maybe – just maybe – she didn't actually want to know exactly what her mother had got herself wrapped up in.

The ex-policeman, however, had woken up in the middle of the night irrevocably certain that he didn't actually want to be a policeman, but a dog trainer. He had only started with the police because he had assumed there would be dogs involved, well, not a dog in sight, suspension and a load of hassle. For what? Somebody else could solve the stupid case! Or nobody, as usual. He'd had enough of the whole thing. This very morning, he would go to his cousin's, who worked in an animal shelter. One small step for mankind, and one giant leap for him personally.

The train pulled in and they both got up from their seats, Pippa with a lot of luggage, Tom with something almost like a spring in his step.

As the train moved off, they had both disappeared from the platform, and the only thing still stirring there was a cheery roundel of withered leaves.

25

VEGETABLE

Mildred's face looked so small on the pillow, small and white, her eyes shut, mouth and nose surrounded by tubes.

Not a person any more, not really, more like a familiar pattern on a white canvas.

Eyes.

Nose.

Mouth.

That was all that was left of Mildred Puck.

'That's it then, isn't it?' Charlie asked, and the others nodded.

They had come to the hospital in a taxi to visit Mildred, not really out of sympathy, but because they wanted to confirm that the murderer and grandson-kidnapper really was out of action.

But confronted with the silent white pillow landscape and the beeping machines, they felt a sense of unease rather than satisfaction.

What were they doing there? Marshall opened his mouth,

no words came and he shut it again.

Bernadette sniffed, straightened her sunglasses and swallowed.

'We should go,' Winston murmured. He was right.

Edwina stepped forward and pulled Hettie out of a basket. She held the tortoise over the bed to show her that there was no need to be afraid of Mildred any more. Hettie looked indifferent.

Then they really had done everything they needed to, and one after the other the residents of Sunset Hall filed out of the hospital room.

Agnes stayed behind.

She stepped closer to the bed with the beeping machines and examined the serene face, looking for . . . what? Was Mildred still in there somewhere? And if she was, which Mildred? The one who had played hide-and-seek with Agnes all that time ago? Or the one who had three people on her conscience? Or were they perhaps one and the same?

Did Mildred know Agnes was there? Did she expect something from her?

An important-looking tube coming out of one of the machines and disappearing under Mildred's bedcovers caught Agnes's eye, it was within easy reach.

Should she perhaps . . . ?

But did Mildred deserve that? Could anyone ever deserve something like that?

Agnes bent right down to her face, until it became more and more unfamiliar, and eventually went blurry in front of her farsighted eyes.

'You could never have moved in with us, Mildred.' she said quietly. 'Never ever! Edwina would never have forgiven you for sticking the transformer on Hettie!'

She straightened up. Right! Maybe that was all there was left to say. Then again . . . What if Mildred did wake up? She knew far too much about Sunset Hall. Maybe it stood to reason . . . ?

Her hand hovered indecisively over the tube. It was so hard to know what it all meant, life and death and killing, mercy or punishment, selfishness or stupidity, self-preservation or murder.

EPILOGUE

SALAD CRISPER

They laid Hettie in a little wooden box to rest, their nicest box, with squiggly coats of arms etched on the outside. The box had once contained a gift set of posh mustards – fig, truffle and (the overall favourite) green peppercorn. Now the box was filled with dried autumn leaves, and Hettie was resting inside, still and peaceful, her head tilted to one side a bit.

All of the inhabitants of Sunset Hall were gathered around her, more than just a bit emotional. They had even got Lillith out of the flower window so that she could attend the ceremony.

'The time has come.' Marshall said softly.

Edwina nodded bravely and gave Hettie a final, careful kiss in the middle of her shell.

'Bye, Hettie,' she said quietly. 'Sleep well! And when you wake up, there'll be daisies, and I'll tell you all about what's happened in the meantime!'

With that she stepped back, tears in her eyes. Winston sympathetically slipped her a chocolate bar.

Agnes picked up the box containing Hettie and carried it over to the fridge. Bottom drawer.

Salad crisper.

Hettie spent every winter like a vegetable in the fridge, and every spring she emerged feisty and dignified as ever to be spoilt with daisies by Edwina.

It was the cycle of her life. It was how things had to be.

Charlie quickly got a piece of paper out of a drawer. On it she wrote:

Warning! Tortoise!

Not for human consumption!

and put it on the box. You couldn't be too careful. Marshall was getting more and more forgetful, and ravenous Nathan had promised to pay them a visit again at Christmas.

Marshall gently closed the fridge door and let out a deep sigh.

Brexit sniffed the air a bit wistfully.

Bernadette ate three fondant creams in quick succession.

Even Agnes blinked away a tiny tear.

Although Hettie was only going into hibernation, this time the farewell was particularly difficult for them. Winters without a tortoise could be long and cold and dark, even when a cosy fire was crackling in the grate.

And who could say what the world would look like when Hettie poked her head out of the leaves again in the spring?

Nobody.

And that was the way it should be.

NOTE FROM THE AUTHOR

Tortoises are animals with specialised requirements, and as with every pet, research should be undertaken before getting one to find out exactly what is needed for the – very long! – happy life of a tortoise. Depending on the species, it can vary greatly.

It goes without saying that only a minority of tortoises enjoy being handled and carried around as much as Hettie, and hibernation in the crisper drawer is (as is well documented) a rather unusual practice.

The keeping of animals in all its forms is a huge responsibility and shouldn't be approached lightly.

ACKNOWLEDGMENTS

My thanks to my agent Astrid Poppenhusen, my editor Claudia Negele and my publisher Grusche Juncker. The idea for The Sunset Years of Agnes Sharp came into being as the four of us were having lunch together, and if it hadn't been for their instant enthusiasm and encouragement, the hippies of Sunset Hall might still be one of the many ideas relegated to the depths of my little book of ideas.

To Susanne Wallbaum for her wonderful editing. It's thanks to her, that there's now "more Hettie" in the book!

To M for shepherding. To Camilla and Bella, Werner and Susi, Steffi, Conrad and Amelie for their honest feedback. To Steffi and Barbara for allowing me to pick their brains on keeping tortoises. To Rumi for the moral support. To Rob for his support full stop. To Fyo for taking me on our long daily walks to clear my head.

For the English edition thanks go to Amy Bojang for her excellent translation – and the pleasant process of getting there.

To my American editor Rachel Kowal and the team at Soho Press.

To my UK editor Lesley Crooks and the team at Allison & Busby.

LEONIE SWANN's debut novel, *Three Bags Full*, was an instant hit, topping the bestseller charts in her native Germany for months. It has since been translated into 26 languages. She lives in Cambridgeshire.

@_leonieswann